ARIZONA WAR

A COLTON BROTHERS SAGA, No. 3

A Novel

MELODY GROVES

La Frontera Publishing

Arizona War
A Colton Brothers Saga, No. 3
A Novel
Copyright © 2008 Melody Groves

Cover illustration from the original painting by Mort Künstler
"Riders of the Whistling Skull" © Mort Künstler, Inc. www.mkunstler.com
All rights reserved, used with permission

Cover design, book design and typesetting by
Yvonne Vermillion and Magic Graphix

Copy edited by Matti L. Harris

Printed and bound in the United States of America
First edition
First Printing, March 2008

Publisher's Cataloging-in-Publication
(Provided by Quality Books, Inc.)

Groves, Melody, 1952-
    Arizona war : a Colton brothers saga : a novel /
Melody Groves. -- 1st ed.
    p. cm.
    LCCN 2008920822
    ISBN-13: 978-0-9785634-3-1
    ISBN-10: 0-9785634-3-3

    1. Brothers--Arizona--Fiction. 2. Apache Indians--Fiction. 3. Arizona--History--Civil War, 1861-1865--Fiction. 4. Historical fiction. 5. Western stories. I. Title.

PS3607.R6785A75 2008   813'.6
                        QBI08-600007

Published by La Frontera Publishing
(307) 778-4752 • www.lafronterapublishing.com

Dedication

For Birtie Douglas, who has patiently waited ... and waited ...
and waited.

Acknowledgements

It's said that writing is a lonely profession. I find it just the opposite. My fictional characters stay in my head and keep me company. Sometimes they include me in conversation; sometimes they don't. But, human characters are just as interesting and just as helpful. I don't think it's possible to name all the "characters" who've contributed to the making of this book, so a short list will have to suffice.

Thanks to:

Mike Harris, who has faith in me
Johnny Boggs, who is always in my corner
Myke Groves, who patiently listens to the voices in my head—
even when they get too loud
Erin Montoya, who has my back
Haley Crawford, who has my front
Margaret Dean, who is my biggest fan
and
Keith Pyeatt, who knows which words go where
and how to use them correctly

FORWARD

W hen people think of the Civil War, usually the names Gettysburg, Vicksburg, Leesburg, or Bull Run come to mind. Few think Picacho Pass, Glorieta Pass, the Battle of Fort Fillmore (Tortugas), or even the Battle of Albuquerque, but these are very real, very important elements of the Civil War.

At the end of the Mexican-American War in 1848, the Guadalupe Hidalgo Treaty gave the United States possession of nearly half of Mexico. The United States took possession of current-day New Mexico, Arizona, Colorado, California, Nevada, Wyoming and part of Idaho. At the time of the signing, New Mexico and Arizona came under one title: New Mexico.

With the signing of the Gadsden Purchase in 1854, southern New Mexico and Arizona joined the United States, creating the boundaries closely resembling those of today. Arizona later became its own territory, but none of the towns were very large. Therefore, politicians took little heed or notice of this desert population.

It was no wonder that southern Arizona and New Mexico began to associate more with Texas than the rest of the country. Texas was closer geographically, and Texans understood problems associated with living in a desert—Indians, heat, lack of water, remoteness, etc. In February 1861, an Arizona delegation traveled to Mesilla, asking and encouraging New Mexico Territory to join the Confederacy. It made sense. Soon, the Confederate States of America flag flew over Mesilla. The town was important. Mesilla ("Little Tableland" in Spanish) claimed the largest population between San Antonio and San Diego, and was a major player logistically, economically, and commercially in the Civil War.

Fast forward to July. Lt. Col. John R. Baylor, who had been appointed Governor of Arizona by Confederate President Jefferson Davis, marched his regiment of approximately 250 soldiers up from Texas. Their intent was to eventually turn at Mesilla and march west to the coast of California, picking up silver in the Arizona mines along the way. Once the Confederates controlled the coast, victory was almost assured. The one obstacle in the army's way was the Union-held Fort Fillmore, located three miles south of Mesilla.

When Fort Fillmore's commander, Major Isaac Lynde, received word of Baylor's forces on his doorstep, his 400 men are said to have filled their canteens with "medicinal whiskey" and staggered/ marched east. They headed toward the Organ Mountains, through San Augustine Pass (current-day Highway 70 between Las Cruces and Alamogordo) to the sanctuary of Fort Stanton. In fact, Lynde abandoned the fort so quickly, he forgot to take down the flag. It didn't take long for Baylor to scoop up the men strung out along the road. Since Baylor couldn't feed and house 400 prisoners, he offered paroles to everyone. Several joined his forces, and most accepted parole, but 18 men spent time in stocks, refusing to accept Confederate rule.

Colonel Baylor declared Mesilla the capital of Arizona Territory and used a building located where the Fountain Theater is now (half a block from the plaza) as headquarters. In fact, the Confederate brass held big parties in the back room of what is today the Double Eagle Restaurant. One ballroom still contains the original gold-stamped ceiling, only one of two west of the Mississippi.

The Confederates separated Arizona Territory from the United States by drawing a line east/west along the 34th parallel. The southern half was Arizona Territory and sympathetic to Confederate causes (including the legalization of slavery) and the northern half with Santa Fe as the capital had the ear of Washington. They leaned toward the Union, but continued with a "wait and see" attitude.

Union troops marched across the Sonoran Desert to Yuma, where reports state that they met up with Confederate troops. No shots were ever fired, no battles, no skirmishes reported. The men were probably just glad to make it across the desert—who wanted to fight?

However, Union troops, under Colonel James Carleton's leadership, came under attack from a Rebel unit at Picacho Peak, Arizona. Outside of the Yuma Indian village, a Union scouting party led by James Barrett rode through the Picacho Pass on April 15, 1862, and were ambushed by Confederate forces. Although Barrett and two privates were killed, three Rebels were taken prisoner. Considered a Union victory, Carleton continued to push the Confederates back toward Texas. Thus, the Battle of Picacho Pass fought its way into history as the westernmost battle of the Civil War.

Throw into the mix the Apaches. Up until around 1860, they'd allowed Americans (anyone who wasn't Indian) to pass through their land. Often, trade would take place—firewood for food or other commodities. When Cochise's brother was hanged by the US Army in 1860, Cochise, along with Mangas Colorado and Geronimo, declared war on anyone marching across their desert. The First Battle of Apache Pass, Arizona, took place in April, 1860, and the US Army limped away declaring themselves the victors. Cochise, determined to drive out unwanted guests, seized the opportunity to ambush soldiers at the same Apache Pass on July 15, 1862.

Cochise and the other two leaders waited for the army to squeeze through the pass near present-day Bowie, Arizona. When the 128 soldiers started into the pass, Cochise and the warriors rushed down. Much to their despair, the US Army turned their two mountain howitzers on the Apaches, killing a few. Cochise retreated to re-think ambush tactics and to continue his strategy of smaller attacks.

Shortly afterwards, the Confederates with their dwindling supplies, their exhausted soldiers, and their defeat in northern New Mexico at the Battle of Glorieta, along with Indian harassment, withdrew to Texas. By September 1862, the United States flag flew again over Mesilla, New Mexico Territory. On Feb. 24, 1863, Federal law split New Mexico Territory in two, officially creating the Arizona Territory. New Mexico gained statehood on January 6, 1912, followed by Arizona on February 14, 1912.

Even after the Confederate troops pulled out of Mesilla, the Indian problem persisted. Marauding bands intent on stealing livestock and harassing residents intensified. Forts sprung up all over the territory to protect settlers and travelers. Also, many soldiers, once mustered out of the service, stayed in the Southwest and became merchants, lawyers, and businessmen.

If successful, the conquest of New Mexico/Arizona might have led to a Confederacy larger than the Union, a confederacy able to marshal two or three more field armies, a Confederacy with an unblocked Pacific coast, a Confederacy rich in minerals and able to breathe new life into a sagging economy. But it was not meant to be.

Civil War—Southwestern style.

Melody Groves,
January 8, 2008

PART ONE

CHAPTER ONE

July 1861

G*lowing eyes bear down on me. I shrink back, struggle against binding ropes. Those eyes—hundreds, thousands—burn like a million fires. They inch closer. I scream, writhe. Gnarled fingers rip my shirt, my skin, then wind around my neck. A painted face—terror itself—hovers over mine. The fingers tighten, strangling me. I—*

James Colton's eyes flew open.

Tender hands stroked his bare, sweaty back. "Relax, honey, you're just havin' another one of your nightmares." Chubby fingers traced numerous raised lines across James' sweaty skin.

James stared at the woman sitting cross-legged on the bed. The devil? An errant blond curl dangled over her left temple. No. Just Katie. He blinked.

"You're doin' it again, darlin'. Thrashin' around, yellin'. You fightin' those Apaches?" She kissed his forehead while pulling up a camisole strap that had slipped down around her elbow. Her pasty white shoulders shrugged. "Ain't nobody here but us, lover."

Safe for the moment, James rubbed his eyes awake. From this vantage point on his back, he took in the splotchy white paint of the wood-planked ceiling, brown wood showing through parts of it. His gaze trailed down the faded wallpaper less than a foot behind Katie. Little purple flowers lined up and down, floor to ceiling—just like tiny purple soldiers. He stretched back on the mattress, then rolled onto his side, the single sheet bunching under his naked body, and pulled in air.

Dry air. Mesilla's desert air. This little town sat next to the Rio Grande, which flowed only in late spring after the snow runoff from the Rockies wended its way this far south. Mesilla, with its low adobe houses, cottonwood-lined plaza, and surrounding valley full of vineyards and cornfields, teetered on the borders of Mexico and the United States. James pulled in more desert air and looked at Katie. The woman's rounded face, etched with lines of hard living, softened with his second look. He ran his clammy hand across his forehead, through his unruly, shoulder-length brown hair, then across her pale leg. He pushed up a leg of the bloomers, then kissed her bare knee. Her hand drifted down the muscles in his arm.

"For a man who's only twenty, there ain't a place on you not marked, James." Her hand gliding over his hip, Katie traced wide, raised scars. "Your adorable rear end's got 'em."

"Uh huh." James grasped the warm hand then kissed the palm.

"Even got 'em on the bottom of your feet." Speculation lined her forehead and her painted lips sprung into a pout. A soft finger traced the line on his left cheek. "How many of them whip scars you reckon you got?"

"Seventy."

"How you know?"

"Shhhh." James pressed his stubbled face against her leg.

Katie sighed. "Wanna try again? One of these days you might just be able to do it, James, honey."

James closed his eyes while cradling her leg. "I love you, Lila."

"Lila?"

She sat upright and pushed away his hands. "James Frances Michael Colton! How many times I gotta tell you? I'm not Lila, I'm Katie."

James frowned up into her rouged, pockmarked face. Her soft but strong hands pushed his body onto his back. He rolled with the light impact.

"Ever' time you come around that's all you ever call me." She smoothed her hair and ran her hands down over her camisole. "That tramp show you as good a time as me?"

"Tramp?" James clenched his teeth. "Don't ever say that about her! She's not like *you*." He shoved himself upright.

"Like me?" Katie bent her voice to a whisper. "You mean someone who'll touch you?"

"Don't ever say that!" Afraid he'd hit her if she didn't leave, James rolled off the bed and scooped up her clothes. He threw them in her face.

4

"You're nothin' but a two-bit whore!" James yelled as he yanked her off the bed, squeezing her shoulders without regard for pain, and shook her. He shoved her toward the door. "Get outta here!"

"This is my room, *you* get out!" Katie clutched the clothes to her chest.

James rammed his body against the woman, pinning her to the wall. His breath spurted in her face. He raised a fist overhead ready to pound her face, but even under whiskey's influence, he couldn't bring himself to hurt her. Instead, he opened his fist and whacked his palm against the wood, inches from her face. The impact echoed in the tiny room.

Prying her body out from under his, Katie scooted along the rough wall and grabbed the door handle. "I'm gettin' the sheriff."

"You do that. You fetch my brother. See if I care."

Door opened, she turned to face him.

"You're nothin' but a drunken, broken, pathetic excuse for a man." Katie's words took on a hard edge. "No wonder this Lila person ran off with someone better." She spun on her heels and bolted through the doorway.

James balled his fist at her disappearing back, slammed the door, and then pressed his forehead against it. "Lila?"

He waited for the love of his life to answer. For her sweet voice in his ear. Tears pushed against his eyes. A knot formed in his throat. "Lila"

This time, the words bubbled out. No voice. No Lila.

Never will be. Dammit, never again!

He turned and spotted a whiskey bottle on the far side of the bed. Pain killer. He lurched toward it, falling across the lumpy mattress. On his way down, he grabbed the amber liquid that deadened his world.

His numb hands ran up and down the bottle. The curves smooth.... Just like Lila's. He lifted the bottle to his lips. Three long gulps drained it. Head tilted back, he waited for the last drop to trickle into his mouth. His tongue ran around the rim. Dry.

James hurled the bottle against the purple flowered wallpaper and glared at the shattered glass on the floor. He threw himself off the bed, scooped up a jagged piece, then pressed it against his left wrist.

Nothin' but a drunken, broken excuse for a man.

5

Katie's words drove into his head.

Drunken? Yeah. Broken? Cochise tried to break me and Trace when he captured us. I survived your torture, Cochise, but I'm about dead from your memories.

The barbed edge poked his skin. He stared at the knuckles on his right hand turning white.

No more demons. No more pain. No...

Numb, he watched his shaking hand stab the thick shard into the skin.

James twisted the jagged point and dragged the glass toward his elbow. Electrifying pain shot into his arm, past his shoulder.

Blood dripped to the floor and pooled at his feet. He squeezed his eyes shut. White dots turned into red streaks, then faded into black.

* * *

"He's lucky, Sheriff Colton."

The voice swirled around James' head. Noises soared through his ears. One by one, the muffled sounds formed words.

"How's that, Doc?"

James recognized the husky voice of Mesilla's sheriff, his twenty-four year old brother. He nudged one eye open, but daggers of sunlight burst through the window and pierced the dimness. James clamped his eyelid shut.

"Your brother lost a lot of blood, but his...his *companion* returned before he bled to death. Said she heard a bottle shatter and a loud thud like a body hitting the floor. Good thing she went back to check."

"I'm surprised she did. Most sporting girls wouldn't. She was still shook up when I talked to her."

"Katie's got a good heart. You know...underneath all that powder. Deep down she truly cares for him."

James listened to the voices. Must still be alive. Damn. It was time for his life, for *him*, to be over. A hand brushed back the hair on his forehead, a hand whose touch was familiar. Words still floated around his ears, and the bed under him felt harder than the one at Katie's.

"He's coming out of it," his brother said. James detected worry, something close to panic in Trace's voice.

"Sure is. When he comes to completely, he'll need a good meal, plenty of rest. It'll take a few days for him to get back on his feet."

"I'll see to it. Appreciate your help, Doctor Logan."

"Got another patient needs tending, Sheriff. I'll be in the next room if you need me."

James listened to footsteps fade. A chair dragged across the floor and stopped near him. He imagined Trace sitting in it, then heard him breathe out a deep sigh, a breath of defeat, total despair.

Again he forced his eyes open and squinted at his older brother. "Hey," James croaked, his voice deeper and more gravely than usual. James flopped his bandaged left arm toward Trace. His brother's familiar form appeared fuzzy around the edges, but James recognized the anguished slumped shoulders, the droop of Trace's head. He'd seen that posture before, *caused* that posture before.

"Trace?"

No response.

James turned his attention to the familiar smell of a doctor's office, the wood grain alcohol assaulting his nose. Looking around, he eyed a small table to his right holding the necessary tools of a town doctor, the stethoscope coiled like a snake ready to strike. Rolls of white cotton bandages covered the remainder of the small surface. A framed certificate, perhaps a diploma, hung in the middle of the wall at James' feet.

His gaze returned to his brother. Staring. The brown eyes narrowed, lips drew tight, strong hands clenched. No hint of a smile.

James raised the corners of his mouth into a slight curve. What could he say? Small talk would just delay the lecture he knew was coming. Trace had more to worry about than his kid brother's drinking and whoring. If only those terrifying memories would fade—

"It stops now, James." Austerity laced Trace's words. "You're done, this feeling sorry for yourself or whatever it is you're doing. It stops now."

Lifting the light blanket, James peered under it, then covered himself again. "Where're my clothes?" He pushed back a hank of his hair hanging in his face.

Trace Colton relaxed his fists and studied his hands. "Sent them out to get washed. Found them wadded on the floor under you. Not only did you almost bleed to death, apparently you got sick and... well, you were a mess."

7

"Bring me clean ones."

Trace eyed his brother. "No."

James struggled to bring his arm under himself to push up to a sitting position, but strength drained from his body. Eyes closed, he sagged back against the mattress. Bile rose in his throat. Queasy stomach turning over and over, he rolled to the edge and vomited.

Trace scooted his chair back and jumped aside.

Cold sweat beaded on James' forehead. After a final dry heave, he wiped his mouth with the sheet, lay back, and closed his eyes.

"Whiskey," James ordered. "Get me whiskey."

"No."

"What?"

The absurdity of the denial refused to make sense. James frowned at his brother now kneeling on the floor, rag in hand wiping up the mess.

"I need whiskey. Only thing that helps."

Trace glanced up. "I said no. No whiskey, no more whores. No nothing."

James pushed himself up on one elbow. "Dammit. You can't—"

"It ain't up for discussion." Trace threw the rag at a bucket in the corner. "You've been drinking way too much, out cavorting with whores, haven't had a proper bath or hair cut in weeks. Hell, you don't even have a job. It stops now."

Using every ounce of energy he could muster, James propped himself up farther and glared at Trace. "I'll do whatever the hell I please."

The older Colton brother returned the glare. "What'd Ma think about you?" He challenged. "What'd you tell her if she walked in here right now? What'd you tell Pa?" He stood and faced his brother. "You'd tell them you assaulted a woman, a whore at that? Nearly drank yourself to death?"

"I'd tell 'em about Cochise and the months you and me barely survived," James snapped back. "How the torture haunts me day and night. How every time I breathe I see their faces, feel the pain all over again." James squeezed his eyes shut. "How One Wing's whip..." He massaged his forehead. "God, it hurt so bad, I couldn't even scream."

James leaned back, felt Trace sit on the bed and grab his hand. Wrenching loose, James rolled away from the comfort of his brother.

*   *   *

Blood drips off fangs inches away. Faces twist and snarl. Fiery breath scorches my skin. Please, no... not again! No more agony, no—

Hands shook him into consciousness.

"James? Son? You're having one of those nightmares again. Wake up now." The powerful grip on James' shoulders forced his sweat-drenched body against the hard bed.

"You can do it, open those eyes."

James' eyes fluttered open and shut several times before focusing on the face only inches from his. Doctor Ezra Logan. A kerosene lamp on the table threw soft yellow light around the room and bathed the doctor in a halo.

"Dead?" James hoped for the right answer.

"No."

"Damn."

Hands released James' shoulders. The silhouetted figure disappeared. Somewhere nearby, a chair scraped against the floor. A cool hand on his forehead, then the same hand wrapped around his right wrist.

James blinked at the gray-haired man leaning over him.

"Keep having those memories, Doc. Me and Trace driving the stagecoach, the Apaches shooting us off. Then Cochise and One Wing holding us to trade for Cochise's brother." He swallowed anguish. "What am I gonna do? Can't go on like this."

A long silence knotted James' stomach as he waited for an answer. Doctor Logan released James' arm and sat back. Logan's steel gray eyes roved over James' face.

"You've been through a helluva ordeal," the doctor said. "No one knows how you and your brother managed to survive. Just pure nerve, I guess." Logan pulled out a pair of glasses from his vest pocket and put them on.

Trace's encouragement echoed in James' ears.

You can do this, James. We'll survive. You and me. Hold on tight and believe.

James fought back to the present.

The doctor wagged his head as he unwrapped the bandage. "When you and Trace came dragging in three months ago, I'd never seen anyone abused as you. Trace was real bad off, but

9

you—broken bones, deep bruises, multiple concussions. Hell, your blackeyes are just now healing up. Your whole body was flayed from that whip."

James closed his eyes, desperate to shut out memories. "If Trace hadn't got back when he did, I'd have died."

The doctor swabbed James' left wrist with alcohol. "Glad you lived."

"I'm not. I've got nothing. No job, no girl." James eyed Doctor Logan. "Just these nightmares."

The doctor sopped up the liquid running down James' arm. "Trace have nightmares, too?" He glanced up over his spectacles.

"You'll have to ask him, but I'm sure he does. Keeps them buried, doesn't like to think about being a captive. You know, after two months they sent him to get Cochise's brother out of jail. Apaches held me 'til he got back, whipped me every day. Said it'd make Trace ride faster. But, still took him fourteen days."

"They'll fade. Some day you'll forget all about them."

"I'll *never* forget." James searched the man's face. "And it's more than the beatings, the whipping. Know what it feels like to... to..." He looked away and slammed his fist twice against his forehead. "I was forced to marry a captive Pima girl. God, she wasn't more'n fourteen. I... she... we had to—"

"It's all right, James."

"No, it ain't all right!" James pounded his fist against the mattress. "Dammit, they killed her. We loved three times before they took her in the desert and—"

"You keep flailing around like that, you'll rip out the stitches. Stay still now." The doctor gripped James' arm and looped the gauze underneath. He glanced at James. "Can't imagine what it was like."

"Well, I can't stop imagining it. Living it once was too much, but those memories keep repeating." James rubbed his eyes. "Over and over."

"I had no idea."

"No one does. Women hate me 'cause of all these scars." James' right hand ran over his chest. The blood red welts had faded into bright silver-pink ribbons. "The only girls who'll even talk to me are whores."

Anger kept tears from running down his cheeks.

The doctor patted James' arm. "Son, the last three times

you've been brought in here you haven't said a thing. Glad you told me now. But, if you're honestly ready to help yourself, I'll be glad to assist you."

I'm beyond help.

Doctor Logan tied the ends of the bandage. He scooted the chair back, followed by a heavy sigh. "You know, your family would—"

"Get along fine without me." James shot a piercing glare at the doctor. "Life's just a waste of time." Using all the energy in his body, James turned onto his right side, then squeezed his eyes tight. "Just leave."

After several heartbeats, the golden lamp glow faded with the footsteps.

CHAPTER TWO

J ames shivered under the blanket and pulled it up tighter under his chin. Heavy breathing, a snore and snort broke the room's silence. James knew its origins. Trace. His brother had spent half the morning sitting and sleeping in the chair.

A sudden pang of jealousy hit him. Why couldn't he be more like Trace? His brother seemed to have put his captivity behind him. Did he still see Apaches and terrifying images? All Trace did now was put things back together after James drank and fought. How many men carried bruises from James' quick, angry fists? James had lost count.

"Uh... Trace?" Words pushed their way over the knot in James' throat.

Mesilla's sheriff jerked his eyes open. A couple blinks and deep breaths. Trace removed his hat and ran his fingers through his straight brown hair. A yawn. He refitted his hat then pulled his chair up closer to the bed. He placed his hand on James' forehead. A nod.

James searched his brother's face. Trace's brown eyes matched his hair—just like James. He had a broken nose, like James— thanks to the Indians. And scared lips—like James—usually quick to smile that famous "Colton Family smile." In all, a face that looked a lot like his.

"Cold," James mumbled.

"I'll get another blanket." Trace said as he stood, the chair grating back against the floor. "Guess that cut on your arm's giving you fits. Be right back." He turned, threw a quick look over his shoulder, then walked out of the room.

Try as he might, James couldn't keep his teeth from chattering, especially as he watched his brother disappear. Disappear just like Lila.

What's she doin' right now? Where is she?

His stomach tightened.

She's not mine any more. Let her go.

If he couldn't figure out how, the agony alone would kill him.

Trace stepped back into the small room. He tucked in the sides of the second blanket, and then stood at the foot of his brother's bed. "Doc'll be in shortly, says the arm'll heal up. Just need rest and food."

James nodded.

Trace pulled out his pocket watch. "It's dinner time, brother. I'll bring you something good. Ham sandwich all right?" He snapped the case shut.

James shook his head. "Whiskey."

"Sandwich or soup?"

"Whiskey."

"Right. Sandwich it is. Be back in ten minutes."

"Wait." James held up his bandaged arm.

Trace moved closer to the bed.

"You see 'em, don't you?" James asked as he searched his brother's stoic face. "You see those Indians, listen to 'em holler, don't you? You feel the rawhide burning your wrists, the knife jabbed in your throat?" He clutched Trace's pant leg. "The—?"

"Yeah." Trace hung his head, massaged his temples. "All the time." He wagged his head and raised his eyes to meet James'. "But I can't let 'em rule my life. They stole two and a half months from me."

James studied his brother. A sense of defeat, tinged with acceptance, ringed those brown eyes. Trace's lips, scarred from many Apache fists, set a tight line. And his entire body, slimmer but more muscular than before the capture, moved with wound-up tension much like a stagecoach spring—always ready to absorb more abuse.

Trace patted James' shoulder. "I'll be back." He moved toward the door, then stopped and turned back around. "Two months... and that's all they're getting."

He stepped through the door.

* * *

At sunrise the third day, James woke, stretched. The blankets were soaked. His fever must've broken during the night. He pulled off the covers and sat up. His legs swung over the side of the bed

13

and his feet touched the wooden floor. The mud plaster walls of the room spun, and the door tilted at an odd angle, but the urge to pass out evaporated. New strength flooded into his body. Maybe today he'd pull his life together. He nodded. Today would be the day.

A figure appeared in the doorway. James' vision blurred but managed to focus on the smiling face of his brother. The six-foot image walked toward him, pulled up a chair and sat.

"Up early," Trace said as he placed his hand on James' forehead. "Feeling better?"

James nodded. "Could use some water." He massaged his throat. "Feels like I swallowed sand again."

Trace handed him the cup from the bedside table. A sip. Cool liquid slid down James' throat and eased the rawness. A luxury he hadn't had in Cochise's camp. He pushed aside bitterness.

"Trace ..."

"James ..."

Both men grinned.

"You go first, you're older." James sipped once more.

Trace's eyebrows arched. "All right." He paused then rushed his words. "Teresa and I... want you to come live with us. Just for a few weeks. 'Til you can get to feeling good."

James stared at his brother. Trace and Teresa had been married only what, a month now? Why would they want him there? Besides, Trace'd be watching where he went, how long he stayed out. Who he was with. Hell, it'd be like prison.

"I know that look on your face, little brother," Trace said as he leaned back in the chair, one corner of his mouth curved up. "I'm not gonna be Ma if that's what's worrying you. Not gonna follow you around, tell you what and what not to do." He shrugged. "You're a grown-up man. Hell, grown-up more than most, I figure. But I think you'd like staying with us."

James opened his mouth, but when thoughts didn't form into words, he closed it.

Trace leaned forward. "Hell. *I'd* like you staying with us."

James studied his hands. The tightly-bandaged left arm throbbed, the white gauze wrapping elbow to wrist. He shook his head. But hadn't he wanted to straighten his life around? Get back to where he was before... before those Apaches had wrecked his life, destroyed him. They say what doesn't kill you only makes you stronger, but in this case, it didn't seem to hold true.

"Well?"

Trace's voice interrupted his thoughts. James looked up at the shining brown eyes he'd known all his life, the eyes of his best friend.

"What d'you think?"

James' world tilted again, his brother's image growing fuzzy. "Think I need to lie down."

CHAPTER THREE

"Sometimes I think I'm not such a lost cause anymore, Doc," James announced while watching Doctor Logan unwrap the gauze from around his arm. He sat up straighter on the examining table.

"Why's that?" Logan glanced up over his spectacles.

James shrugged and considered. "This past week at Trace's has been great. I feel better than I have in months. Teresa's a good cook, especially her fried chicken." His stomach rumbled at the thought of supper a mere hour or two away. "Maybe even put on a pound or two. My trousers aren't quite so baggy."

"Good." Doctor Logan tossed the gauze wrapping into a nearby trashcan. "You're still drinking, I hear tell." He ran an alcohol-laced wad of cotton across James' healing arm. "But haven't heard of any fights or anything like that."

"I'm trying. I really am." James swallowed hard at the sight of scissors and tweezers the doctor selected from the table. Time for the stitches to come out. He remembered all the other times in the past few months when he'd been sewn up. Getting them out stung more than James cared to admit. At least when they were going in, he was numb or unconscious. Now, he was stone cold sober and awake.

Doctor Logan held up the scissors. "How're the nightmares coming?" He clutched James' arm like he was expecting it to fly off. "Hold still now."

Nightmares? James closed his eyes. The nightmares were just as fearsome as ever. Every night he relived the agonizing sting of the rawhide thongs slicing his bare skin. The wet leather strip around his forehead tightening as it dried. James remembered thinking his head would pop like an overripe melon. The stabbing pain of the knife tip plunging into his neck brought new tears to his eyes. He still felt the blood running down his skin. He smelled his fear. And trembled.

A pat on the shoulder and a voice in his ear jerked him into the present. "You all right? You're shaking. They're just stitches. It's all over."

Over? James opened his eyes and met the doctor's. *It'll never be over.* He wanted to say thanks, but his mouth had gone dry, too dry to speak. Instead, James slid off the examining table and nodded as he headed out the door.

* * *

Supper had passed in quiet conversation. James liked Trace and Teresa's little house. This room in particular was his favorite— the dining room. Most houses didn't have one, but since Trace was sheriff, the town fathers provided him with a bigger house. This one had two bedrooms, a living room, kitchen and dining room. The smells of cooking beans and corn still lingered in the house, even though most of it was now in James' stomach. To top the meal off, Teresa always provided desert, just like Ma.

A final piece of blueberry pie speared on his fork, Trace held it mid-air and cleared his throat. "I was talking to Big Swede who owns the livery stable today, James." He popped the bite into his mouth.

James looked up from his own pie, fork poised over the plate. "Yeah? He say anything interesting?"

"Maybe." Trace hesitated, glancing at Teresa on the opposite side of the table. "Said business is so good, he can't get to all his chores. He's looking for help in the stable and wondering if you'd be interested in working there for a while."

"What'd you tell him?"

"I'd ask you."

James looked into Teresa's brown eyes then his brother's and frowned. "You want me to muck out stalls? Hell, I'm a shotgun guard for the stage line."

"*Were* a guard."

James dropped his fork onto the plate; it clattered against the rim. He scrubbed his face with the cloth napkin and glared at his brother. "Yeah, you're right. I'm not anything any more. I'm nothing."

"I didn't mean—"

"I know exactly what you mean." James leaped to his feet, the table lurching as he pushed against it. "I'm just a pathetic excuse for a man. Isn't that what Katie said?" He wadded his napkin then pitched it onto his plate. He stepped to the door, grabbing his hat from the table beside it.

Trace jumped up and rushed toward him. "Where you going?"

"Out." James jerked the door open, charged through, then slammed it.

The slight evening breeze did nothing to cool his temper. Then a tight grip on his arm slowed James' march. He twisted to wrench his arm free. "Let go!"

Trace's hold tightened. "Not until you've heard me out."

"I've heard all I want to." James pushed Trace back, managing to free himself of the iron grip. "Leave me alone!" His voice rose to a shout, his fist leveled shoulder high.

"You wanna hit me?" Trace's arms flew out to his sides. "Go ahead. If that'll make you feel better, do it!"

James planted his fist in Trace's stomach. A grunt and wheeze. Trace doubled over. James stormed down the street, his long legs carrying him to Katie's. To get a drink. To get away. He punched a cottonwood tree as he marched past. Before he reached the street corner, a strong hand grabbed his arm. He wheeled around.

With the front of James' shirt bunched in his trembling hands, Trace pulled his brother up close. "I don't even know you any more." Trace whispered between clenched teeth.

"Yeah? Well, neither do I." James sucked in air and clawed at his brother's hands. "Let go. I don't wanna hit you again." He knocked his brother's hand from his shirt. Light from the windows of a nearby adobe house lit Trace in shades of gold. James huffed. "Move!" He stormed off toward Katie's.

"Where you going?" Trace ran to catch up.

"Get drunk. Get good an' drunk."

"I won't let you defile yourself any more."

"Defile?" James froze. Then he stepped in close, his face inches from his brother's. "What a big word. A *big* word for a *big* man." He spit the venomous words. "*Sheriff* Colton. Proud of your title, brother? Proud of what you can steal with it?"

"Steal? What're you talking about?"

"The old sheriff stole my girl. You wanna steal the rest? Hell, you're too late. Ain't nothin' left. Lila took it all when she deserted me."

"She thought you were dead, James." Trace lowered his voice. "Everyone thought we were dead."

"She should've waited. We were getting married Saturday." James' arm jerked toward the stately San Albino Church whose steeple jutted up from behind a cottonwood. "Dammit, we were getting married."

"She thought—"

"And you go and take the sheriff's job after he leaves with Lila. Sheriff of the biggest stinkin' town in New Mexico Territory!" James spread his arms up and out. "How come they didn't offer me a job? Why just you? Why?" His words crackled. "I wasn't good enough?"

"You weren't *strong* enough." Trace gripped his arm. "I could work, you weren't ... ready."

A pounding in James' ears spurred his anger into frenzy. "Cause I stayed with Cochise and took that whip." James knew his words would hurt his brother, but they couldn't be contained. "You rode off and left me. Alone. Just left me to die."

"Dammit, you know that's not true. Cochise made me—"

"I know what the hell Cochise did! I know." James' fists balled. One of them smacked his thigh. "Hell, you got a girl and a job. Nothing's left for me! I got stinkin' nothin'!"

James glowered. More light spilled from windows and doorways. A few people stood at the thresholds.

"Let's take this inside. Calm down."

"Calm down? I've just begun!" James drove Trace's shoulders back with opened hands. Both men struggled to stay upright.

"Stop it. I don't wanna have to hurt you." Trace grabbed one of James' wrists and held it away from his face. "But I'll do whatever it takes to stop you."

"Whatever it takes? You said that about ol' Cochise." James snorted and wrested his arm free. "Whatever it takes to survive. I survived. I'm still alive. If you call this living. Look where it got me. Hell, you're the big, bad sheriff and I'm... I'm nothing. Got nothing but these."

James yanked his shirt over his head. Buttons flew as the material ripped from his body, revealing crimson-pink raised scars that glowed in the dim light.

James lifted his arms. "See?" He spun like a crazed ballerina. "Katie says the ones on my back are worse."

Similar ribbons snaked across his back, under his arms, around his sides. He leveled a look at his brother, knowing Trace had seen his scars many times, yet he was determined to remind Trace again just what those two extra weeks in camp had cost him. The horrified look on Trace's face proved James had made his point.

Teresa stood a few yards away in the street. James loped over and pointed at the scars. His finger tracked the deep pink line on his left cheek. After another glance at the shock on Trace's face, James then turned his full attention on Teresa, whose brown eyes opened wider than usual.

"Ugly, ain't they?" James hissed.

His sister-in-law took a step back, her hands covering her mouth.

"Don't James. Don't."

"There's more. Lots more. Look!" James fumbled with the buttons on his pants, his hands shaking so hard he only managed to get two undone before Trace tackled him. Both men hit the ground. Rolling like boys in a schoolyard brawl, Trace at last managed to land on top, pinning James' arms over his head with one hand.

"Stop it!" Trace's command hissed between clenched teeth.

James struggled under Trace's weight. Tears of anger and frustration welled up as he used every ounce of strength to push his brother off. It wasn't enough. "Sonovabitch!"

James sucked in a quick breath and locked his gaze on Trace's fist. It barreled toward his left cheek.

Teeth-jarring whump. All too familiar pain. Another whump. Wet warmth ran down James' face. His body relaxed, the anguish receding before blackness covered him.

CHAPTER FOUR

"What else needs doing, Mr. Bergstrom?" James stood in the livery stable, pitchfork in hand. Sweat rolled down his forehead and into one eye. He swiped at it with his shirtsleeve and then spied the canteen hanging on a nearby stall gate. A drink. A drink would taste good right now.

"Let's see." Bergstrom gazed around the stables. "Pinto that just came in this morning needs shoes." He pointed to the end stall. "File down his hooves while I get the coals heated again." Bergstrom headed outside to the anvil and pile of horseshoes.

James nodded, placed the pitchfork near the front of the open double doors, and snagged the canteen. He uncorked the container and peered around. Bergstrom's Livery Stable. He sized it up while the cool water slid down his throat. Fresh hay—the aroma was reminiscent of his ranch home back in Kansas. He, Trace, and his two younger brothers had spent many happy hours playing in the hay. Forking the mounds of dry grass into the hayloft became a real chore as he grew older. Hay didn't hold the charm it had when he was a youngster, but it still stirred something within him.

Another sip, then a deep breath. The whiff of horses, leather harnesses and saddles mingled with his sweat from hard work.

A grin lifted one corner of his mouth. It felt damn good to be working again. Trace was right—as usual. Why did he always have the answers? Guess that's what big brothers were for. James knew he should've been working as soon as he got back to Mesilla three months ago. Why hadn't he?

James reflected on the answer. With a final sip, he replaced the cork. Since returning from his months' captivity, being tortured and beaten nearly to death time and time again, people thought he was crazy, a madman. Maybe he was. His body had healed enough, but sometimes it felt like Cochise and his second in command, One Wing, still held him, intent on breaking him. They wanted to confuse him, make him believe they would kill him. More than once, he remembered, their torture made him pray they would.

He swallowed hard. Since his time here in the stable, the hay and horses had helped push the nightmares aside. With new things to think on, those demons stayed in the back of his mind more often now. Was he getting better? Really better? He considered. Maybe. There was hope now. A terrible, horrific part of his life was over. Over and done. He had to move on.

He squeezed his eyes shut, but then thought better of it. He focused on Katie, afraid of the images he knew would come if given the chance.

So I am crazy. What sane man couldn't close his eyes, afraid of imaginary Indians? Hell, I don't even have to close my eyes.

James knew those phantom Apaches would attack again. And he'd fight them because he had to. He'd fight them like the crazy madman he was. Folks didn't even bother to talk behind his back—they'd say it to his face. And who wanted a crazy man working for them? A man half-cocked and ready to fire at every opportunity. But he was a survivor.

With a glance down the row of stalls, James realized the owner, Big Swede as Trace called him, was a survivor, too. He'd immigrated from Europe many years before and endured hardships—not enough food, endless seas, theft and sickness on board ship. Dangerous overland travel from New York hadn't kept him from continuing his journey west. He didn't stand around and whine about his tough life. He just got on with living and, as James looked around, got on quite well.

James walked to the end stall, slipped a rope around the pinto's neck, and led him out into the middle of the stable. He tied the reins to the post, picked up a nearby curry comb, and ran his hand along the horse's rump. Hidden under the white hair was unmistakable red paint. A red hand print.

Apache.

The curry comb slipped from James' hand and hit the dirt. He backed away from the horse and slammed into a wooden post. But it wasn't a post. Instead, an Indian warrior wrapped strong arms around him, keeping him from escaping. James' gaze fixed on the pinto. In a heartbeat, One Wing had shoved him onto the horse's back.

"Ride," the Apache growled at him and Trace. "Or I slice you end to end."

James spurred his horse. Down to the settler's ranch. Down to where people scrambled for their lives.

The spirited horse under him pranced through the scene. Slaughter—dying ranchers, children, a woman. Screams of death. Acrid fumes of lives going up in flames.

A hand on his back, someone at his side. James jerked away and shouted, "No! I won't!" Hot tears pressed against his eyes. His balled fist swung at air.

Two strong hands on his shoulders shook him. He struggled to wrench free.

"James? What's wrong?" A voice cut through the agony.

James grabbed the front of the man's shirt and stared into One Wing's snarling face. He gulped air. "Don't make me... Please."

"James? James."

Hands shook him. His knees threatened to buckle.

"You don't have to. It's all right."

Something about that voice. Not One Wing. Not Cochise. Definitely not Trace. James trembled. Little by little, the face came into focus. Swede Bergstrom. Livery owner.

Bergstrom released his grip and tugged on James' arm. "Sit down over here, son. I'll get you some water."

James sank to a wooden crate in the corner of the stable, swept his hand across his face, and then across his mouth. He battled for each breath. Stomach boiling, lunch rose. He fought it down.

Bergstrom perched on another crate across from James and handed him the canteen.

The container shook, but James planted the metal rim against his lower lip and sipped. With a second long gulp, he jammed the cork back into the canteen. From the corner of his eye, he noticed the livery owner staring at him.

"Tell me about it." Bergstrom's soft voice was commanding, yet compassionate.

James studied the man sitting across from him. The lines of concern etched across the forehead set off Bergstrom's thinning blond hair and light blue eyes. Would this livery owner be a man to understand and not judge him for being a coward?

It was time to take a chance. James nodded.

He stared at the canteen in his hands, but saw into the past. "I haven't told anybody what happened, not even Doc. Only Trace knows 'cause he was there."

"Then it stays right here." Bergstrom nodded.

A deep breath. Shaky hands raked his hair. A flick of the eyes to Bergstrom, then back to the canteen. "Cochise made Trace and me go with them to raid a ranch. Those Apaches killed everyone including children and a woman. One Wing forced me down on that rancher woman, ordering me to scalp her. He had us worn down—hard—to the breaking point. He thought he would have more power over us if we'd take the hair of a white person." James shut his eyes and held the canteen against his forehead. "God, she was still alive."

Apaches whooped. Blood swirled around his feet. James forced his attention back to the present. His gaze hit the dirt floor.

"I don't remember too much afterward, but three times I tried to get away, not to scalp her." James spread his fingers wide, then bunched them. "I can still feel that knife in my hand. Her head flopping around while he made me... pull up on her hair. I still hear..." He squeezed the canteen. "God, she moaned..."

"You sure?" Bergstrom leaned closer.

James nodded and covered his eyes with a trembling hand. "I heard her heart beat through her back. God. I was shoved down on top of her." He lowered his hand and glanced up at Bergstrom. "Trace tells me I turned the knife on One Wing after that. Cut him pretty good."

"You don't remember that?"

"No, just that he was gonna kill Trace if I didn't scalp her. They were gonna scalp her anyway. I couldn't change that. But, I wasn't thinking too clear. Went kind of crazy, I guess. After that, Trace knocked me out, and he finished the job." James wagged his head. "One Wing kept her scalp by the door of his lean-to as a reminder he'd broken us. We would do whatever he asked."

James peered out the door into the bright sunlight. "Her hair—just like Lila's—soft and curled. It even smelled good, like lavender." His eyes shifted to meet Bergstrom's. "How could I do that?"

"It wasn't Lila." Bergstrom shook his head. "Would you have taken the woman's hair?"

James wiped his nose on his sleeve. "I'm not proud of it, but like I said, I was starting to. I'd do anything to keep Trace alive. Even that. But, I never got the chance to finish the job." He clenched his trembling hands.

Bergstrom sat back and took a deep breath. "James, what you did is nothing to be ashamed of. You were willing to save your brother and yourself. I hear nothing but bravery in your story."

"But, I..." James stared at but didn't see the man in front of him. *Vicious eyes. Glinting knife. Rivers of blood.* He buried his face in his hands. "It was horrible."

Bergstrom gripped James' shoulder. "But you can't change the past. Put it in its place and move on."

James kicked at a clod of dirt. "Don't know how."

"Just like you did when Cochise held you. Take it day by day, minute by minute. You're safe now." Bergstrom pushed himself to his feet, then held James' arm and nudged him up. "Glad you told me, son. I know it was hard." One solid pat on the back, then Bergstrom turned and stepped through the door.

James hung the canteen on the hook and stared at it as if that metal container held all the solutions to his problems. But it didn't. A drink. Only thing that helped him forget. He needed a drink—and not water. It'd take something a hell of a lot more powerful than water to chase away these demons. He drew in a breath and nodded.

CHAPTER FIVE

James pressed his forehead into the hard table at the Rio Grande Saloon, desperate to shut out the honky tonk music. Couldn't the piano player play something new? Smoke stung his eyes every time he opened them. But from this vantage point back here in the corner, he could listen to people come and go, and he could cringe at the women laughing at men's stupid jokes. Most times, people left him alone to drink himself into a fog and then melt into a blissful stupor. A stupor to forget.

A deep male voice buzzed in his ear. He swatted at the annoying sound. Same voice again. More honky tonk assaulted his ears Another swat. Hands planted themselves on the table. That annoying voice the third time.

"At it again?"

Trace. Did James even want to sit up and talk to his brother? Maybe if he played dead, Trace would leave. He felt a firm shake of his shoulder.

Guess he's not leaving.

James picked his head up and was surprised to find the upper half of his body coming with it.

Trace leaned into James' ear. "Dammit. I thought you'd given this up."

"Apaches won't let me," James mumbled as he reached for his empty glass and the half-full whiskey bottle. Trace grabbed the bottle then plopped it on a nearby table.

A clamp around his upper arm, then a jerk, and James found himself on his feet, his brother at his shoulder. James swayed, his knees turning to rubber. He knocked into the chair, sending it scooting backwards. With that, the grating piano playing stopped.

James yanked out of Trace's grip. "Don't need no help." He reached for the bottle. "Just one more. On me."

"You've had enough. Let's go home." Trace slipped his hand under James' arm and tugged.

"All right, all right." James swatted at the grip. "Let's get the hell outta here." He leaned against Trace and surveyed the saloon. All eyes stared back at him, a titter here and there. Whispered conversations. More stares. James searched the room then turned his back on everyone. "And go find some women. Lots of women."

After a couple of halting steps, he turned back to the table and grabbed his hat. It took both hands to fit it on his head. He jammed it down tight.

With his brother right beside him, James watched the ends of his legs move through space then hit the wooden floor. Someone else's legs and feet. He couldn't feel a thing. The more steps he took, the more ponderous the situation. He stopped, turned to a blurry Trace, and pointed at his feet. "How can I walk when my feet ain't even touchin' the floor?"

"With some help, I think," Trace answered as he guided James through the swinging doors.

Laughter erupted behind James as he stepped into the evening air. The piano burst into a frenzy. James shut it out. All of it.

Each step grew more difficult. His legs—was something holding on like anvils? Maybe he should stop, just for a minute, just to rest, just to close his leaden eyes.

"Wait. Gotta rest." James slowed, but Trace's tug prodded him further. "Tired," James insisted. "Need to sit."

"You're mumbling. Just keep walking."

Walking. One foot in front of the other. One step at a time.

As if coming out of a fog, James realized Trace's grip on his arm had tightened. At the same time, his legs gave out. No longer willing to carry his weight, they just buckled. He crumpled to the ground, bringing his brother down on top of him.

Trace let out a string of oaths and untangled himself.

"Is this the way it ends?" He asked.

"What?" James pushed himself up, then sat on the hard ground. "What're you talkin' about?"

"Your life. A man who's got the world at his fingertips just throwing it away." Trace lowered his voice. "I can't stand to see you like this."

"That's all you ever think about—yourself." James struggled to his knees. As usual, the whiskey's effects wore off way too soon.

"You don't like what *you* see? Well, I don't like what *I* see. Every time I close my eyes, I see... them. Every time." His world tilted. His stomach churned.

"You gotta let them go."

"*They* won't let me go! You think I *want* them around? I invite them to stay in my head so I can't think, can't sleep, can't breathe without them hurting me? You think that's what I *want*?" James used his trembling hands to push his weight off the ground. He stood, all of a sudden sober. Too sober, too soon.

Trace stood, eyes down at the ground. His words turned soft. "Maybe you should go home, back to the folks, for a few months."

"What?"

"I know Ma wants to see you again. In every letter she always begs you to come. Bet Pa's got lots of chores that need doing, too."

"You're sending me away?" James swayed, then caught himself. "Why?"

Trace looked over James' shoulder. "Hell, James. You left work early again today. That makes what... three, four times now? I also found out you're spending time at Katie's again."

"It's my life."

"And you don't need to be wasting it drinking and whoring."

"But, I'm not..." James spread his arms. "Hell, I'm gettin' better."

"A little. But I think going home is best." Trace draped his arm over James' shoulders, nudging him toward the house.

As James shook his head, his world blurred. "But what about my job?" His stomach lurched. He bent over, grabbed his knees. James lost his dinner and his dignity.

* * *

James leaned against the bedroom doorjamb. Should he wake Trace or let him sleep? A quick peek out the window on the opposite wall—still dark outside, although gray lit part of the sky. Snoring from Trace and deep breathing from Teresa. Both still in dreams, where James should be. No. His dreams were nightmares. He dreaded sleeping.

Mind made up, he tiptoed over to the bed.

"Trace?" James tapped his brother's shoulder. "Wake up. Gotta talk to you."

Trace sat up. His dark shape silhouetted against the early

28

dawn of the bedroom. "What's wrong?" Trace whispered.

"Been thinking about what you said last night." James' voice boomed against the mud plaster walls.

"Shhh." Trace glanced at his sleeping wife and then back at his brother. "Let's go in the kitchen."

Minutes later, James studied his hands, once again callused from honest, hard work, and listened to the coffee boiling on the stove. He loved the smell of coffee; it reminded him of home. At least the Apaches hadn't drunk coffee. Maybe Trace was right. Maybe going home was the solution. Hell, he could fight Apaches back home as well as here.

He rubbed his throbbing temples and searched his brother's face for the strength he needed. His shoulders rose and sank with each breath. After a few starts and stops, James pushed the words out. "Hate to say this, but you're right."

"How's that?"

"Thinking on it, a visit with Ma and Pa might help. Luke and Andy need their older brother to tell them how to get their chores done."

Trace poured coffee into two cups. "I'm sure the boys'll be happy to have your help." He handed a cup to James and then stood in front of the window. Trace sipped and peered at the world just now beginning to wake. "Wasn't supposed to be like this," he said softly.

James blew on the steaming liquid, then gazed into his cup. Taunting him, that Apache war leader, One Wing, snarled back, black eyes gleaming. A hand on his shoulder. James flinched.

Trace eased into the chair across from James. "When're you leaving?"

James shook the images of One Wing from his mind. Somehow, he had to get over this. But he couldn't. He couldn't even drink a damn cup of coffee without it all coming back. Would One Wing follow him all the way home?

"Couple weeks," James answered. "I've got pay coming soon and I don't want to go empty handed."

Empty handed. Hell, he knew empty handed. Everything he'd worked for, planned for, everything he loved—gone. Gone in less than the minute it took those Apaches to tie up him and Trace. James brought the coffee cup to his lips. Was that Indian still there? He chanced a peek. One Wing sneered at him from inside his cup. That damn Apache refused to die. James balled his fist and sprung to his feet. The cup clattered against the table.

Trace stared at James. "What?"

"Sonovabitch Apaches!" James turned his back to his brother.

"It'll be all right."

Thumping in his ears. Short breaths. "Dammit, Trace." James whipped around knowing his frustration would send him over the edge again, but he was powerless to reel it in. "When? When will it be 'all right'?" Shaking hands gripped the cup, its contents splashing over the side.

"I don't know." Trace's shoulders shrugged.

Frustration collided with rage. James marched from the table to the work counter, and then back to the table.

"Dammit! It ain't enough to kill One Wing once. That sonovabitch won't die! Dammit, he's still here. Everywhere. Haunting, tormenting... still controlling us. Our lives shot to hell because of him." James' words rose to a shout. "Too bad that sonovabitch is dead. I'd kill him a hundred times. I'd force sand down his throat just like—"

"Quiet down. Teresa's still asleep." Trace glanced toward the bedroom.

James squeezed his half-empty cup and glared at the Apache face glaring back. "Leave me alone!" He hurled the demon against the wall.

Ceramic pieces clattered to the floor. James bolted to the splintered cup. "Sonovabitch! Leave me alone!"

He sank to the floor, then scooped up a jagged shard. He clutched it, knowing that broken piece held the answer. With his back against the wall, he brought the fragment close to his face. Bits of a painted red rose stared back at him.

"Can't take any more," James whispered. "No more."

The solution gripped in hand, his eyes followed its path until it hovered over his scarred left wrist, over the newly-healed wound. The ceramic point pricked his skin, then dug into flesh. Why didn't he feel pain?

Trace knelt in front of him and pried the crockery piece out of his grasp. Tossing the remnant to one side, he slid his arms around James' shoulders and pulled him close. James trembled.

"Just let me die. Let me die." Tears blurred James' vision, but from over Trace's shoulder, he watched the coffee drip down the wall. Just like the blood on his brother's face the first time One Wing sliced him.

James squeezed his eyes tight and gave in to his brother's embrace. Words sputtered through sobs. "Help me, Trace."

James, the frightened little boy inside this shivering grown man, buried his face in his brother's chest. "God. Please help me."

CHAPTER SIX

Again, the aroma of hay and horses pushed one corner of James' mouth up. In less than two weeks, he'd be home. Back home with hay and horses on his parent's ranch. He dug into the haystack, pitchfork in hand, and brought up a mound. Fresh hay smells wafted over his head. His grin widened.

The livery stable door squeaked open. James looked over and spotted his brother stepping in.

"Good news, Trace." James leaned the pitchfork against a rail and waved. . "I just bought a ticket home. I leave next Tuesday." He grinned at the man he'd known his entire life. "Four more days!"

"Great! Wish I was going, too. As much as I love Teresa, I sure miss the folks and those brothers of ours." He patted James on the back. "I can taste Ma's fried chicken and corn bread right now. Suppose it's as good as we remember?"

"Probably better." James rubbed his stomach. "Makes my mouth water just thinking on it." He held up one hand. "I'm not writing, let them know ahead of time. Just want to surprise Ma."

"She'll be surprised all right." Trace grew serious. "But she'll find out about what happened to us. You can't hide those scars."

A knot pressed into James' chest. He breathed in then out over it. "I know. Been thinking on that a lot. But she'll see I'm alive and in one piece." James pushed aside nagging doubts. "Little brother Luke's how old now?"

Trace scratched his chin. "Let's see. You're what? Twenty?"

"Twenty-one come September. You know as well as I do!" He pulled a light punch aimed at his brother's arm.

Trace groaned massaging his arm as if he'd been slugged. Then he laughed and smacked his brother's chest. "Yeah, I do. So, that'd make Luke coming up on nineteen." Eyebrows knitting, he breathed. "Already?"

James nodded. "Makes Andy sixteen."

A shake of his head, Trace looked over his brother's shoulder. "I'm getting old."

Swede Bergstrom joined the two men, leather harness clutched in hand. It dragged on the ground. A broken strap and twisted metal rings. James put a bit of thought on what had caused the twisting, but his attention was focused more on his brother and his future plans than anything else.

Bergstrom nodded to Trace. "Sheriff. Nice to see you again."

"Just thought I'd stop by and see if my little brother really is working or if the dirt and sweat he brings home is from playing all day."

Bergstrom planted a gloved hand on James' shoulder and rocked it back and forth. "He works hard. And he's been staying all day."

"Good." Trace nodded at James.

The livery owner thumped James' back. "I'm glad to have him here, and truly sorry he'll be leaving."

James puffed out his chest. "I'll be back, Mr. Bergstrom, don't worry. Just gotta go see how my folks are doing." He shot a sideways glance at Trace. "They need my help you know."

A nod then Bergstrom shifted the weight of the harness. "I understand. But right now, *I* need your help. Gotta get this fixed, James."

Taking the cue, Trace jerked his head toward the door. "Gotta get going myself. I'll let you get back to work. Good news, James. See you at supper." Trace nodded. "Mr. Bergstrom."

James watched the back of his brother disappear into the bright June sunlight. As he turned, a thought flickered through his mind. Would he really come back? Maybe this was the end of one portion of his life. Maybe the old James Colton was dead and the new one was emerging from a dark hiding place. Either way, he knew going home would be the best solution to his nightmare.

Bergstrom held up the heavy harness. "We'll take this apart then I'll go over to Harry at his leather shop, give him the straps. Should be able to fix them pretty soon. While I'm out, get the coals heated again and start on those rings. It'd be interesting to know what happened to cause wear and tear like this."

James turned the broken rings over and over in his hands and inspected the chewed metal. Chinks and nicks in the rings.

Something traumatic caused that heavy iron to bend and break. The o-connectors were stretched out of shape, one of them looked battle worn. A fleeting tidbit of information invaded James' thoughts. He'd heard somewhere about a battle. What was it?

As he worked the huge bellows and watched the coals glow red, he remembered what he'd heard. Some man named Baylor, a colonel in the Confederate army, was busy marching around the Territory. James sighed as he donned the heavy gloves, grabbed the long iron tongs. Some Arizona congress had already declared Mesilla and the territory to be part of the Confederate States. But that didn't mean much to him. Why should it? He wasn't about to go out and fight other Americans. If the South wanted to become their own country, let them.

The South. Lila was from the South. James reflected on Lila Belle Simmons, the love of his life, the girl who'd saved him from dying then almost killed him by leaving. If he could've died from a broken heart, he would've been buried months ago. He shook his head. Maybe she went back to South Carolina in the middle of the revolution. His thoughts roamed further. That's where she belongs—in another country.

Heating the rings then pounding them against the anvil, he gripped the hammer and thought again of Lila. Where was she, anyway? After he got back from Cochise's, she'd left a note saying she was going away to think. He'd heard a few weeks later, when Sheriff Fuente resigned, Lila and her new husband had moved to Texas. His eyes narrowed as he thought *he* should have been her new husband. Those were the plans they'd made. One more Tucson run with the stagecoach then they'd be husband and wife.

Stop thinking. Desperate to keep his anger under control, he knew he needed to think of more pleasant things. Going home was pleasant. Feeling his heart slow its pounding, he knew he was beginning to get a grip on his emotions. Maybe some day he'd be able to put Cochise and One Wing in their place, way back in the corner of his mind.

"You can put the hammer down now, son."

A voice in his ear spun James around, missing plowing into Bergstrom by inches. He looked up at his arm suspended over his head, heavy hammer still gripped, then James grinned and lowered it. Why did he have to think so much?

"You made quite a picture, young man. Reminds me of the

34

story of Thor with his hammer." Bergstrom paused and furrowed his eyebrows at James. "Thinking again?"

James let out a long sigh and nodded. "Trying to keep Cochise as far away as possible." He needed to change the subject. "Think I might know how this harness got bent."

Bergstrom picked up a thick iron ring and studied it. "How?"

"That old colonel, Baylor, I hear's not too far from Mesilla. Could be this got torn up in some battle. Maybe it's part of a Confederate rig... or Union?"

"Pretty exciting times, eh?" Bergstrom's eyebrows relaxed, but his entire body emitted tension.

James shrugged but a sudden shiver ran down his spine. "Mr. Bergstrom? What's gonna happen if that army fella really takes over Mesilla? Are we gonna be at war, too?"

The livery owner gripped the ring until his knuckles turned white. "Let's hope not, son. War's an ugly thing. No one wins. Our valley's too pretty to let ugly in."

James filled his lungs with sweet desert air and nodded.

CHAPTER SEVEN

James whistled as he worked alone in the livery stable. Days had melted into each other while he planned for the trip home. Tomorrow. Stage pulls out of Mesilla first thing in the morning, James thought. Again, Trace had been right. Going home was what he needed to do. Home, where his parents and two brothers would help him put his past in place and move on. They would make him whole again. He hadn't seen them for more than a year, and being a close family, he honestly, unashamedly missed them.

In the past few days, he'd picked up small gifts for his brothers—a dime Western novel for Andy who liked to read, a small silver flask for Luke.

For his parents he'd had a hard time deciding on just the perfect present. He and Trace at long last chose a beautiful Mexican silver picture frame. The part he knew his folks would like most was the picture inside. A man had just opened what he called a photography studio in Mesilla and took a picture of Trace and James. The process took a few hours, but James was proud of it.

The brown images in the picture, an ambrotype the man had called it, did resemble Trace and him. What James saw in the mirror every day when he shaved was no longer good looking, but the face was still his. A broken nose never looks the same after it's healed, his scarred lips and the pink ribbon running across his left cheek added to the old image. But there in the picture was his face, smiling back. Smiling at being alive.

The livery stable door creaked. James spun, surprised someone could ride up and open the door without his noticing.

Must be a bit preoccupied.

He hadn't been this happy in months.

James located the source of the creak and froze. He was staring at a demon from the past. Alberto Fuente, former sheriff of Mesilla

36

and current husband of Lila Belle Simmons, stared back. Those big round eyes set off his ruddy cheeks. James sized him up. Last time he'd seen Fuente was at least a month before he and Trace had been captured. Fuente was still old. His gray-streaked brown hair still hit his collar. His shirt still strained at the seams. Fact was, he may have gotten a little more stoop shouldered. James smirked.

Old age does that to you.

Both men stood, feet apart, eyeing each other. Seconds dragged. At long last, Fuente grabbed a deep breath, the corners of his mouth rising into something close to a smile. He exhaled through his nose, looked at his own hand as if for the first time, then extended it. "James... Colton. Surprised, but glad to see you. You're looking... fit."

James glared first at the man and then at the hand. Bile rose in his throat, and his stomach caught fire. He spoke through a clenched jaw. "You mean for someone who's dead? That's what you wanted, wasn't it? You told Lila I was dead." James planted a foot closer to the devil.

"No, I didn't." Fuente dropped his hand. "Reports came in from all over saying the same thing—nobody survived. They found your stage, blood on the seat. We put two and two together. Figured it was best for Lila to move on."

"She wasn't supposed to move on to *you!*" With fists clenched and eyes narrowed, James focused on the man now within arms' reach. Hell, close enough to punch. The stalls, horses, gear inside the stable blurred. "You wanted me dead, out of her life so you could move in. Marry the girl I love!" James swung.

Fuente jerked back, but stood his ground and held up his hands to protect his face. "Son, no," he said. "It wasn't like that at all. We prayed you and Trace had lived, but the odds were against you. Nobody survives capture by Cochise."

"I did." James moved in closer.

"After you got back, I even stopped by the doctor's several times to check on you, but you were unconscious. And your brother wasn't in any shape to talk." His eyes scanned James from boots to hat. "Doc never told you?"

"You stole my girl!" James took another swing. Fuente ducked it.

He grabbed the front of James' shirt. "Listen to me," Fuente said.

James pulled out of the sheriff's clutches and stared at Fuente's eyes. Age lines jutted out from the corners. How in hell could Lila love somebody that old? It'd be like marrying her own pa.

Fuente's soft but firm voice grabbed James' attention. "I gave Lila the chance to back out of our marriage. You need to understand that. I know what you meant to her. I'm not a blind fool."

"No!"

"Yes. She chose to stay with me, James. You have to face that fact and accept it. She chose *me*." Fuente stuck out a hand again. "No hard feelings."

Curled fingers balled into a fist, James planted it in the old man's face. A sickening whack. "Sonovabitch!" James yelled. He struck again, this time his knuckles slid across the bloody cheek. The next blow sunk into Fuente's stomach. A wheeze.

The former sheriff righted himself and connected with a sharp hook to James' left cheek. James staggered back, crashing against a wooden stall.

Fuente swiped at his bloody lip. "I don't want to fight you, boy. Don't wanna hurt you." He shook his head. "I'm truly sorry for your misery. Must've been terrifying, the months you spent with Cochise. I didn't want that for you or your brother."

"Liar! You've never wanted me around. From the time you tried to get me hanged, you've wanted me dead." James glanced to his right, where he spotted the pitchfork leaning near his clenched hand.

"That's not true and you know it," Fuente said as he stepped toward James, arms spread out at his sides.

James grabbed the spiked farm tool, then pointed it at the former sheriff. "You son of a..."

"Put that down. Let's talk. Lila's over at the hotel right now."

"Lila's a fool for marrying you. You're not half the man I am, *Fuente*." He jabbed the weapon at the former sheriff. "Now get outta here."

"Fine. I'll leave." Fuente shuffled his feet, looked at the ground, inched backward, then glanced up at James. "Might not be the best time to tell you." He met James' gaze. "But guess you'll find out soon enough." He leaned closer. "Lila's with child."

James lunged. Sharp tines embedded the arm and side of

Alberto Fuente. Fuente clutched his side, his face twisting. A moan, a gasp. James focused on the devil reincarnate.

"That hurt? Good," James said as he tucked the pitchfork under his arm like a battering ram. Then there was a sound, a shout, somewhere behind him. He pushed the noise aside and strengthened his grip on the pitchfork.

Another shout.

James raised the pitchfork shoulder high. "You sonuva—"

The back of James' head ignited. The pitchfork clattered to the ground. His knees dug into dirt. James' world spiraled into blackness.

CHAPTER EIGHT

"**R**oll over."

Can't. Body... won't move.

"Open those eyes."

Head... on fire... gonna burst.

"You're all right."

Insides roiling. A hand on his shoulder—pushing him further face down into the dirt?

"Wake up now."

James drew in air and coughed. Dirt tickled his nose. He sneezed—twice. His head exploded. He screamed and grabbed at the pain.

A hand rolled him onto his back. A groan. Was that his?

"James."

When his pounding head had eased to throbbing, James chanced another breath and rubbed his temples. The hand shook him again.

"Wake up."

It was a familiar voice.

Bergstrom?

James pried one eye open. A face stared back. A strand of blond hair hanging over one blue eye.

Definitely Bergstrom.

"Welcome back. Sit up."

Sitting was the last thing James wanted to do, but a muscled hand gripped the front of his shirt and tugged. His body came with it.

"Take a sip."

A warm hand supporting his sagging body, a metal canteen rim pressing against his bottom lip. Cool water ran down his throat, soothing the rawness.

Bergstrom released the canteen to James' hands and gripped his shoulder. "You were talking in Apache, son. Don't know what you were saying, though."

Blurred images pulled themselves together with each sip James took. An inch at a time, James moved his eyes, then his head, to take in the rest of the stable. The horses stood in their stalls, ears pitched forward. Harnesses hung against the wooden uprights. The anvil, hammer, and mound of horseshoes remained piled in one corner. The pitchfork was on the ground nearby. Icy waves swept through James' body.

"Oh, God." James wrenched his stare away from the weapon. His eyes locked on the man kneeling beside him. "Fuente. Mr. Bergstrom, what—"

"You stabbed him good." The livery owner wagged his head.

"God." James dropped the canteen and rubbed his eyes. He'd killed a man. A lawman. Lila's husband.

"Your brother's got him over at Doctor Logan's right now."

James prayed he'd heard right. His head snapped up, despite the pain. "Doc, not undertaker? He's still alive?"

"Yeah. Bleeding real bad, but Doc's a good man. He'll do his best." Bergstrom touched the top of James' head. "Sorry to hit you so hard with those tongs, but I was afraid you'd stab him again."

The knot on the back of his head throbbed. James ran his fingers over the growing lump and winced. "Suppose I should thank you."

Bergstrom picked up the canteen and finished off what little was left after James had dropped it uncorked.

The throbbing in James' head receded to a roar. "Why'd he come back?" James asked. "Why now?"

A hand on his shoulder. A tight grip. Not friendly, more like a clamp. Like One Wing's. Only this time it was Bergstrom's. James turned to his boss.

"I'm going to jail, aren't I?"

Bergstrom nodded. "Afraid so. Your brother wants you here when he gets back."

"He thinks I'm gonna run?"

"I'm not sure what he thinks. Just don't try anything foolish." He released the death grip. "I'd hate to have to chase you down myself."

The door behind James creaked. Bergstrom looked up and

nodded. James couldn't see who had just come into the livery stable, but he guessed it was his brother.

Please God, don't let Fuente be dead.

Bergstrom extended his hand and pulled James to his feet.

James hung his head when he recognized his brother's distinctive footfall heading toward him. The sound circled in front, then stopped inches away. Trace's boots filled James' view.

His brother's low voice rang in James' ears and echoed off the livery stable walls. "You all right?"

James nodded.

A deep breath, then air rushing out. "I gotta arrest you. Hold out your arms."

Cold metal tightened and clicked around his wrists. James tasted the terror of captivity. *Again.* A glance into his brother's eyes revealed nothing but agonizing sorrow and defeat.

Neither brother spoke. Each looked at the horses, Bergstrom, the stable rafters, anything but each other.

Strength gathered, James dared to ask, "Fuente still alive?"

Trace nodded, gripped James' arm, and tugged it toward the door. "Let's go."

James turned back to Bergstrom. What words would make things right? To explain? Nothing formed in his brain. Another tug and James watched his own feet scuff across the stable dirt then out into the sunlight. He let his brother guide him toward the dreaded jail. He deserved to be locked up. What he'd done was wrong, undeniably wrong. But, he'd been provoked. Fuente had no right to waltz in and say the things he'd said. He had no right to ruin his life. Again.

Trudging down the street and across the plaza, James thought about the consequences of stabbing Fuente. If he died, it was obvious what would happen—James would swing. They'd stretch his neck tighter than a wire fence. No doubt. But, if the former sheriff lived, it would be up to the judge and jury to decide his fate.

Questions paraded through his mind as he watched his feet push his body closer to jail. Would Lila come visit? Did he want her to? Did she really choose Fuente over him? Why? How much did Lila really know about his captivity?

* * *

Lila rushed into the doctor's office, her stomach knotting as she remembered the smell of alcohol, of hurting, pain, and suffering. It'd been over three months since visiting James here when he'd come back from Cochise's camp. Memories threatened to overwhelm her. She pushed them aside and realized an important part of her life was behind her. Her future lay in another room—wounded, perhaps dying.

Stepping into the small room on one side of the front office, she watched her unconscious husband being bandaged. The doctor turned at her footsteps, nodding for her to step closer. She tiptoed across the room and ran her hand over Alberto's head, smoothing the errant gray and black strands of hair.

"He's still out, Mrs. Fuente." Doctor Logan's voice was soothing. "I think he'll be fine. The tines of the pitchfork missed anything vital. He's gonna be out of commission for a time, but unless these puncture wounds get infected, he'll recover."

"Thank you, Doctor."

Logan finished tying the last of the white gauze, stood, and turned his gaze to Lila. "He needs to rest. Take my chair. I'm done here. Holler if you need me." He patted her arm, then walked out of the room.

Lila eased into the chair, leaned over her man, brushed the hair off his forehead, and then kissed it. She reaffirmed how much she loved him, admired this man who'd been sheriff of Mesilla, a man who'd been a rock when she was so desperate about James. She shook her head.

James.

The first love of her life. He'd been the kid she saved after his vicious beating in Santa Rita, the kid who promised her a life he'd never be able to provide. Looking again at her husband, she decided James would always be just a kid. Alberto was a man.

Alberto Fuente opened his eyes. They traveled to Lila, sitting at his side. With a sigh, he flopped his arm toward her. She patted the trembling hand that had once been like iron, but now was soft as a child's.

"Doctor says you'll be fine, Alberto. Water?"

Fuente nodded. A few dribbles, a big swallow. He licked the corner of his mouth, capturing a drop. "Won't make it to Santa Fe in time."

"Shhh. Rest now. Don't worry about that silly trial. It's not important. They'll find somebody else to testify."

The former sheriff nodded, closed his eyes, and then coaxed them open. "You seen James?"

Lila's throat tightened, her hands grew clammy. Images, emotions raced across her heart. "No. You're my husband. I belong at your side, not his."

She watched her man stare back at her and wondered what he was thinking. The laudanum, she knew, clouded his thoughts, made his judgment fuzzy at best. There would be plenty of time to heal old wounds if she decided to visit James. He'd be in jail for a while, more than likely go to prison for what he did. Would she want that to happen? Would her husband press those kinds of charges? Gazing back down at Alberto, she noticed his eyes close, his breathing become rhythmic.

Lila Belle Simmons Fuente pulled the light blanket up around Alberto's chest and kissed his forehead.

* * *

Teresa eased the thick wooden door shut and stood in her husband's office. Trace sat behind his desk, head in hands, eyes closed. He didn't look up as she walked in, didn't seem to even know she was there. He was so still that she wondered if he was asleep. With her heart breaking, she stood watching him for half a minute.

My wonderful husband.

A few steps over to him, then a hand on his shoulder. The familiar warmth of his muscled body still radiated strength. Lifting his head, he gazed up into her eyes, then clutched her around the waist, his face buried in the folds of her skirt.

Teresa knew he wouldn't cry, but she also knew he wanted to. She thought about the many times she'd wake in the middle of the night listening to his sobs. He almost never spoke of his time with Cochise, but she knew it took all his strength to keep it in perspective. And this thing with his little brother taxed the rest of her husband's energy. How he managed to be a respected sheriff and an attentive husband was a mystery.

Trace's body trembled against hers. She'd have to be the strong one right now. Sliding her arms around his shoulders, she let her lips brush the top of his head.

A full minute passed before Trace pulled back and spoke through his agony. "Doesn't he understand? Can't he see? He has more outside scars, but mine are deep... inside. Can't he see the pain, the guilt I carry?"

Teresa stroked her husband's shoulder-length brown hair.

Words edged with true sorrow tumbled from Trace's lips. "I couldn't get him out, stop his torture. Guilt eats at me all the time."

She hugged him tighter and fought tears.

"Doesn't he realize what those Apaches did to *me*?" Trace asked. "I was beaten, too, had my share of torture. But every time... *every* time they hurt him, they'd force me to watch and listen to his screams, his... his pleas for mercy." Trace bit his lower lip and clenched a fist.

"They'd drag him off and he'd stare back at me with that look. I watched his eyes, saw his terror. Each time they beat... God, they sliced his throat. He almost bled..." Trace massaged his temples. "They did things to him he still won't talk about—even to *me*.

"They'd laugh and point when he cried." He drew a ragged breath. "Nothing I could do." Trace looked up at the window. "A couple times, though... they let me hold his hand 'til he passed out."

Teresa stroked his hair. Tears stained her blouse.

"Blood. Mine... his." Trace shook his head. "God, it was everywhere and nothing I could do about it. Dammit! *Nothing* I could do, no way to help. I was tied too tight, knives in my own throat, Apaches all around... no chance to save him."

Teresa knelt by his side. A single tear trickled down Trace's cheek. He swiped at it.

"All I could do was listen and pray he'd die," He said as he turned his eyes to Teresa. "Have any idea how that feels? To beg Almighty God for your little brother to *die*?"

What could she say to this man to ease his pain? How could she help him? Teresa cradled his chin in her hands.

"No one knows—except James," she said, hoping her words would help. "He's got too much pain himself. He can't see anything right now, but trust me, some day he will."

Again, Teresa prayed this nightmare would end. She pleaded for her husband and his brother to become the same men who rode off one day full of hope and excitement for the future, only to return months later as shattered strangers. How could she help put the pieces back together?

Trace blinked, then looked at Teresa. "I'm sorry to have told you all that. You didn't need to know."

"I'm glad you did." Teresa swiped at a tear threatening to slide down her cheek. Trace drew in a long breath, gripped her hands and kissed two fingers.

"Have you seen Lila?" He asked.

"I'd like to." Teresa looked out the window. "Even though she was my best friend, I just don't know what to say to her."

One corner of Trace's mouth lifted. "I've never known a woman who had nothing to say. Don't know what you females talk about, but you do it all the time."

Teresa ruffled his hair. "We talk about men mostly. Ours and everyone else's."

Turning serious again, Trace stood and guided Teresa to her feet. "Go to Lila. She needs you." A tender kiss. "I love you, Teresa Sherman Colton."

* * *

Hell. I certainly hung the horse this time.

James glanced up at his jail cell window, then pushed his tired body off the cot. On tiptoes, he gripped the window bars and peered out. Long strands of white clouds hung against a jubilant summer sky. People passed through the alley, jabbering about whatever was important in their lives.

The inner door creaked open. Without bothering to turn around, James spoke over his shoulder. "Hey, Trace? Heard anything about Fuente? Still alive?"

"Thank God he is."

James spun around at the feminine voice answering him. He took in the blond hair swept up off the neck, the lips set in a tight line, Lila's wide, blue eyes sparkling from the light streaming through the window.

He wanted to run to her, hold her in his arms, caress her beautiful hair. His chest muscles constricted. Frozen, he couldn't think, his world shrinking into black and white images.

She studied the floor, the empty cell next to his, the clouds through the window. James stared at the thin gold band around her finger. Just like the one he'd bought for her in Tucson. The one still wrapped in a handkerchief in his dresser drawer.

He shoved colliding emotions to one side. "I... I'm sorry about your, your… Fuente. It's just that I get crazy sometimes and—"

"I've been worried about you."

Anger surfacing all at once, James crossed the cell in four long steps and grabbed the bars. "Then why the hell'd you desert me? Just when I needed you most, you left!"

"James, I—"

"The only thing that got me through was knowing you'd wait." James pressed against the iron bars. "The *only* thing."

"Let me—"

"You'll never know how hard it was, how bad it hurt. But I got through it because of you. You, Lila. I held on to our hopes, our dreams, knowing you'd be holding on, too." Bitterness accentuated each word. "I never thought you'd be holding on to another man."

"I know you—"

"You don't know nothin'. How can you come waltzin' back into my life and expect me to understand?" He grabbed a deep breath and glared into Lila's stunned face. "You know, One Wing's whip, knife, and fists hurt more'n I knew was possible… more'n a man could take." His words turned icy. "But your leaving hurt worse than all the torture put together. One Wing couldn't kill me—but, you did."

CHAPTER NINE

Low whispers and muted conversations from behind James irritated him. He turned around and gazed at the men and few women crowded into the courtroom. Three or four were jammed into the doorway; several stood against the back wall. James counted close to fifty people shoved into this two-bit law office that the town liked to call a courthouse. It was nothing more than a big room with kerosene lights hung around, a well-worn desk in front and a few chairs lined up to serve as a jury box. Nothing special.

James turned back around at a tug on his arm from Trace, then leaned over to the defense attorney sitting at his elbow. "What d'ya think, Mr. Bershum?"

"Hard to tell." The lawyer shrugged. "Your testimony was about as sincere and heartfelt as any I've heard. If the jury buys it, you may get off with a light sentence. Maybe even a slap on the wrist."

"And if they don't?"

"Like I said before… prison… for a long time."

James slumped back against the hard chair.

Damn that Fuente.

He thought again.

Maybe it wasn't all Fuente's fault. Should've kept my head and just walked away.

A low sigh from his brother seated on his right interrupted his thoughts. James rolled his eyes toward Trace.

"How long you think the jury's gonna be out?" James asked. "It's already been fifteen minutes."

"Hard to tell." Trace clicked the lid on his silver watch shut and shoved it in his pocket.

"Why is everything so damned hard to tell?" James' voice rose above the murmur in the room. "Either they find me guilty or not. Shouldn't take this long."

James stood, pushing the chair back along the rough wooden floor. The legs screeched as they slid. He twisted his torso, his back aching from the hours spent sitting in that hard chair. Vertebrae popped.

"Sit down." Trace grabbed his brother's forearm and pulled.

"Take your hands off me. I'm not going anywhere. Hell, seems the only place I've ever gone to is jail. Either behind bars or snared by Indians. Wouldn't know what to do with myself if I was *free!*"

He felt his brother's body against his. James flinched. There was comfort in Trace's presence, yet there was an ominous feel as well. Trace leaned in closer and spoke in his ear. "You're out of control again. Let's go outside."

The pressure on his arm as Trace pulled him into the hot July air reminded James of One Wing leading him to another round of torture. There was something definite, controlling about the grip.

Once outside on the wooden boardwalk, James paced back and forth.

Keep it together Colton. Reel in your crazy thoughts. Don't do anything stupid.

Trace dug into his pocket and pulled out his watch. With a glance at the hands, he snapped the lid shut and turned to James. "Gotta meet the stage, brother. Walk with me. Fresh air'll do you good."

"Meet the stage? Since when's that a sheriff's job?"

"Since all this talk of war. I like to see who's coming into my town. Things are getting a little tense. Just like to make sure nobody gets off the stage who shouldn't."

Trace pulled out the handcuff key and tapped it against James' chest. "If I take those bracelets off, will you promise, on Grandpa's grave, you won't run?"

James stared down the street. "Yeah," he said. "Already done too much to hurt you... seems everything I do just adds to my list of bad decisions. You always end up paying the price." His gaze swung to his brother. "Trust me. I won't run."

He held out his wrists. Trace removed the handcuffs.

As James walked the long three blocks around the plaza, he glared back at each person who stopped to gawk at him. Several people stepped off the boardwalk, allowing him extra room.

As if I have something contagious.

While he walked shoulder to shoulder with his brother, he wondered what each passersby saw in his eyes. Did they see him

49

become an animal just to survive Apache captivity? Did they see the pain and anguish from the torture or the destruction left by Lila's treason?

Do I still have the shattered look? Isn't that what Teresa called it? Shattered.

The stage station loomed ahead in the southwest corner of Mesilla's plaza. James reflected on his shotgun riding days with Trace. That had been for the Butterfield Overland Stage, which had gone out of business while Cochise had held him and his brother. Before their capture, those had been good months, riding with his brother, seeing the country from Mesilla to Tucson. Taking passengers across breathtaking terrain. Good days.

They stopped and positioned themselves on the edge of the crowd. Trace stood next to him, still clutching his arm. James figured the tight grip was more for Trace's benefit, his own nervousness showing.

Guilt punched James' knotted stomach. All of a sudden he realized this must be damn difficult for Trace. Here's Mesilla's sheriff having to arrest and parade his own little brother.

A few people stood on the boardwalk, either staring at James or desperately trying not to. He met the stare of a few, then disregarded them.

Shaking Trace's arm to get his attention, James waited until his brother's eyes met his.

"Been meaning to ask you," James said. "How come you took the job as sheriff instead of driving for this stage company?" He jerked his head toward the adobe building behind him. The big, black letters, "San Diego & San Antonio Stage Lines" announced the building's business.

"Didn't they offer you a job after we got back..." James swallowed the lump in his throat. "...From Cochise's camp?"

Trace shook his head and shrugged. "They offered me a job about two weeks ago, but before then I was too hurt to drive. That's what they said."

The oldest Colton brother glanced up at the mid-summer sky, swiped at a bead of sweat perched on his eyebrow. "They said I've healed up enough just now that they'd consider me. But, I don't want to work for them what with Teresa and you here. I took the sheriff's job at the mayor's request, knowing I could watch after you and stay home with Teresa."

"I didn't realize you were hurt as bad as that," James said, his eyes on Trace.

"There's a lot of things..." Trace met his brother's gaze.

A deep breath. James pulled his hat further down his forehead, then massaged the bright pink rope scars around his wrists. "Tell me truthfully. Am I going to prison?"

Mesilla's sheriff exhaled a long stream of air and stared off in the distance. "Dammit, probably. Fuente's a well-liked man. Real popular sheriff. Folks won't take kindly to youngsters stabbing him, especially with pitchforks."

James' stomach soured. Bile rose in his throat. A search of his brother's face disclosed only sorrow.

Trace continued. "Look at it from a jury's point of view. In this town, people talk. Everybody knows you were tried and convicted of murdering that Pinos Altos sheriff a year ago. True, new evidence proved you shot in self-defense and you were acquitted of all charges, but I think the jury'll hear only that you've already killed one sheriff, and last month tried to make it two."

James stared at his feet and twisted his clenched hands. "Will you come visit me?" He asked quietly. Before Trace could answer, the clatter of stagecoach wheels, the screeching of the brake, and the shouts of the driver over thundering hooves drowned out any further conversation.

Despite his gloom, one corner of James' mouth curled up at the sight of the arriving stagecoach. There was always something exhilarating when he and Trace pulled into a stage stop, especially here in Mesilla, but in any place where people were waiting. It always made him catch his breath and puff out his chest just a little more. It was exciting then, and it was exciting now.

Trace released James' arm and stepped off the boardwalk as soon as the horses stopped. Turning back to his brother, he held up two fingers and motioned. "Come on."

"I'm not running away. I'll wait right here."

Trace reached back and yanked James' arm, forcing him off the sidewalk. "Next to me, brother."

James shook his head as he followed Trace behind the stage. Trace opened the door and helped two women and a man off. At once, all three were surrounded by smiling, crying friends and family. Hugs and kisses were exchanged. James smiled at the love

51

and excitement he saw. His emotions turned upside down. Regret, sadness, and anger mixed and burned.

Next trip I make's gonna be to prison.

A quick nudge on his arm brought his attention back to Mesilla. James glanced at his brother, then followed his gaze to a man stepping down from the coach. Although shadowed, something about him was familiar. Was it the clothes, or the way he carried himself?

Trace grabbed the passenger, threw his arms around him, squeezed tight. The man returned the hug and then spun around to face James, those brown eyes glowing just like Trace's.

"Andy!" James exclaimed as he gripped his kid brother with a rib-shattering bear hug.

"James!" Andy's muscled arms returned the embrace.

"My God, boy, look at you!" Trace wrestled him from James and held the youngest Colton brother by his wide shoulders. "Grown half a foot and got twice as ugly, too."

"Ma says I'm the tallest in the family now." Andy's grin covered his entire face.

James stood shoulder to shoulder with Andy. Yep, at least an inch taller. A closer look. That boy was now shaving! And at sixteen, his shoulders had broadened. Andy occupied the body of a grown man. Muscular from hard farm work, he wore a tan like some men wore leather coats. It looked good on him and fit well. His light brown hair, lighter than James', hit above his ears but had a tendency to hang in his eyes. Straight hair ran in the family. And all of it brown. Those brown eyes glowed and that family trait of a turned up nose set off his grin. That wide contagious grin, courtesy of their Pa, blossomed on his dusty face.

Trace looked from James to Andy and back again. "I'll be damned if you two don't look enough alike to be brothers!" He pushed James shoulder to shoulder with Andy. "Yep, taller."

"Ma says God always saves the best for last." Andy patted Trace on the upper arm and tossed a quick wink at James. "Never said anything 'bout the first, big brother."

"What're you doing here?" James tapped his brother's chest. His question was answered with a wide grin. Trace pushed his two brothers out of the dusty street while nodding to the driver who was tossing luggage off the top rack.

James turned to Trace. "You knew he was coming? Why didn't you tell me he was coming?" He grabbed Andy's sleeve. "How long you gonna stay?"

"Gotta get back, James." Trace said as he picked up Andy's well-worn canvas bag and wrapped an arm around his teenaged brother's shoulders. James fell into place on the other side, and the three men marched down the boardwalk.

Conversation ran fast and furious until they stopped in front of the courthouse.

The seriousness of his situation had been forgotten for the moment, but now it all crashed down around James. His throat closed. Words forced themselves out. "This is it, Andy." He shielded his eyes from the glaring mid-afternoon sun and peered up at the front of the building.

James' attorney stepped outside. "There you are. Good. Jury just came back."

Panic burned through James. Trace's hand gripped his arm again, but all James wanted was to run. Or die. He couldn't decide which would be better.

Trace pulled the handcuffs from his gunbelt and held them in front of his brother. "Sorry. It's the law."

Die. I choose dying. Wouldn't hurt as much as this.

James stared at the wooden sidewalk and held out his arms. The metal covered half the width of the old rope burns around his wrists. A click.

Captured again.

His heart pressed against his ribs, as breathing became impossible.

"Let's go." Trace said. He tugged James' arm, then glanced at Andy's somber face. "Wanna come on inside?"

"All right."

James forced his legs to move forward.

CHAPTER TEN

Andy found a seat near the front while Trace escorted James to his chair behind a small table in front of the judge's bench.

James eyed the twelve men who sat in judgment, men who had already decided his future. Bile gnawing at his throat, James watched the twelve images blur into twelve crazed Apaches riding down on him. Red and blue striped faces sneered. He sneered back.

"Can't kill me!" James suddenly shouted, as his handcuffed arms covered his face. He scooted the wooden chair back and screamed at the terrorizing Indians. He crashed to the sandy desert that felt like wooden floorboards, rolled to his left, and pushed up to his feet. A hand grabbed at his arm, but rage tore the grip loose.

Twelve sets of Apache eyes glowered with lustful hatred. Their faces blurred, but James knew he had mere seconds before they attacked.

"No!" He rushed the Apache hordes and leaped into the crowd. Punching, biting, and kicking, he screamed. "Kill you first!"

Fists pummeled his body, but James fought with every ounce of strength and courage dredged up from the depths of his soul. Breaths snorted. His teeth clamped onto an Apache arm. He tasted blood.

Strong arms wrapped around his legs and tugged, while his bound hands formed a club and plowed into a soft face. Although his head was rocked back by a blow to his cheek, the impact only strengthened his wrath. As arms and legs swirled before him, he lashed out at indistinguishable faces and bodies.

Multiple arms snaring him, James thrashed against the entrapment. Faces of snarling, blood-thirsty Apaches circled within inches. Sky, cactus, and Indians spun around him as he hit

54

the ground and struggled to free himself. Rocks poked his back as he screamed insults at his captors. Like a tormented snake, James twisted under the Indian now perched on top of him.

Beads of sweat bathed James' face. Terror convulsed his entire body.

His shoulders were ground into the dirt by the Indian's weight, and James felt the overpowering strength of the Apache. Again. He stopped struggling. Squeezing his eyes tight, he waited for the final blow. It was over. The Apaches won. A final lungful of air, he steeled himself for an agonizing death.

"James?" A voice in his ear startled him. "Take it easy. You'll be all right. No one's gonna hurt you."

Another pathetic Indian trick. Want me to think it's Trace, then you'll stab me, and while I'm dying, parade my scalp on your lance. Parade it around for all to see and laugh at. Not me. Can't fool me.

Strong arms gripped his shoulders, shook them. "Snap out of it. Look at me!"

Nope, not this time. Been fooled before.

"Look at me!"

James felt his head and shoulders yanked off the ground. The same voice in his ear begging, pleading for him to open his eyes.

Go ahead. Kill me. I won't watch you do it.

A deafening silence pierced his soul.

What're those Indians doing? Figuring out the most agonizing way to kill me? One Wing's ready to slash my throat.

Muscles taut, James jumped at a familiar voice in his ear, the touch on his shoulder comforting. "James. It's me, Andy. Your brother. You're all right now. Indians're gone." The voice strengthened. "See for yourself. I'm right here beside you." The voice swallowed air. "I wouldn't lie to you."

James knew he shouldn't, but something about the voice encouraged his eyes to flutter open. Instead of crazed Apaches ready to kill him, James recognized the faces of his brothers. The worry and panic etched on both knotted his stomach. He squirmed under Trace's weight.

"Indians?" James asked.

"Gone." Trace cocked his head to one side.

James studied his brother's face and watched beads of sweat cascade over the growing knot on Trace's right cheek.

"Never were Indians, were there?"

Trace shook his head and shifted his weight.

"Damn."

Andy scraped strands of hair out of James' eyes. "Never seen anyone fight like that. If those had been real Indians, he would've won."

Trace glanced at his youngest brother. "If those had been real Indians, he would've been dead."

"Get him to his feet, Sheriff."

James looked up at the judge towering over him. Other faces gathering around peered down. Many sported red cheeks, rising welts, and fist marks. Angry mumbling and grumbling assaulted his senses.

"Crazy kid."

"Nothin' but a white Injun."

Trace glared at the mumbling men. "Sorry 'bout that gentlemen," he said as he glanced over his shoulder. "Stand back and give me some room."

With the help of Trace and Andy, James regained his feet. Judge Falls regarded James, then spoke to the crowd.

"We'll take a thirty minute recess. Give you jurors time to collect yourselves." He turned to Trace. "Keep your prisoner under control."

Trace nodded and pulled James closer. Andy and the attorney stepped in close as grumbling people filed out of the courtroom. One man held a neckerchief to a bleeding arm. Several women rushed to their men while pointing and glaring at James.

More mumblings, this time feminine voices.

"Oughta be locked away."

James clenched his fists.

"Menace to society."

His gaze hit the floor.

"Imagine. Letting him roam free, out in society, after... Lord knows what he'll do next."

James thudded into his chair, dropped his head to the table, and closed his eyes. His brother and attorney on either side of him, their chairs screeched on the wooden floor. What words would they use on him this time? Same ones more 'n likely. Another long lecture. But instead of chastising him, they spoke to each other as if he was invisible. He listened to their words floating over his head.

"What d'you think, Mr. Bershum?" Trace asked.

"Trace, your brother's got more of a problem than I knew. Why'd he do that?"

"Seems like whenever he's nervous or surprised, something triggers memories and he just reacts to them."

"Why didn't he attack Fuente again? He was just sitting right over there."

James clenched his cuffed hands, as muscles constricted around his chest.

"Who knows?" Trace replied. "I'm guessing James saw a whole band of Indians instead of just one."

"Why don't you act like that, Trace? You were Cochise's captive, too."

James heard his brother take a deep breath. A trembling hand, Trace's, rested on his upper back.

"Truth is, I see 'em often, too. But having Teresa around helps. He doesn't have anyone like that. He's got just me, and that's not enough."

James swallowed the knot in his throat.

Trace's voice grew hard. "He also spent two more weeks in camp than I did, and all along his torture was worse than what I got. A lot worse. I'd get kicked once. He'd get beat unconscious. Things happened that he won't talk about. I can't count the times he got dragged off only to come back hours later looking like... looking... shattered. Destroyed. Don't know what they did."

Trace's hand slid to James' shoulder and drew him close. His brother's sympathetic touch brought guilt to the surface.

Should've been stronger, like Trace.

James shoved memories into the dark corners of his mind.

Trace sighed deeply. "One Wing hated James and took out his anger on him. Hell, you've seen those whip marks. That Indian did everything in his power to break him."

Andy spoke for the first time. "Guess it worked."

Silence stretched into minutes. James drifted into a world free from pain and torment. His beautiful Lila waltzed in her stunning green dress. He caressed her soft skin and breathed in whiffs of her intoxicating lavender-scented hair. Savoring the surrender of her body into his, sudden grotesque images of the dead ranch woman's face danced before his eyes. The head flopped back and forth.

Blood splattered his body.

James' manacled hands covered his head. Shaking, he dug his face into the desk and tried not to scream.

* * *

"James Francis Michael Colton, please rise."

The judge's voice rang in James' ear as he pushed himself to his feet. His attorney's presence on his left and his brother's on his right brought little solace.

Unfolding a piece of paper, Judge Falls read it, then peered at James. There it was. James knew. Guilty. That verdict was written all over Falls' face.

The judge sighed and squared his shoulders. A glance at Trace, then at the twelve men.

"Jury? What say you?"

The foreman stood. "Guilty, your honor. Guilty of attempted murder of former sheriff Alberto Fuente."

James' breath stuck in his lungs as bells rang in his head. Why was he surprised? He knew he was guilty. Everybody knew.

"Mr. Colton." The judge crooked one finger. "Approach the bench."

James, Trace, and attorney Bershum made their way to the judge's desk. Murmurs from jurors and people in the courtroom grew to a crescendo, but a glare from the judge silenced the crowd. He fixed his eyes on James.

"Mr. Colton, this isn't the first time you've been before me. I remember you last year as a frightened young man who followed his heart instead of his head and nearly got hanged for it." The judge took a deep breath. "However, this is different."

James stared at a spot on the wall behind the judge.

Wish I was still that boy.

The judge leaned over the wide desk. "Mr. Colton. When you first returned from Cochise's camp three months ago, everyone in this town felt sorry for you. Both you and your brother. Went out of our way to try best to understand you, help you. We all sympathize, more than you'll ever know. But, our patience is done. You cannot continue hurting others whether you're aware of what you're doing or not."

More crowd murmurs. One man stood and shouted, "Damn right, Judge. I say lock 'im up!"

"Throw away the key!"

"Maybe we ought ta just hang him!"

Cheers and agreement flew across the courtroom. Judge Falls banged the gavel and glared until his courtroom grew silent. At long last, he returned his attention to James. "As I was saying, I cannot, in good conscience, leave you free to roam the streets. Therefore, I am handing down a choice of sentences."

A collective gasp from the courtroom.

James glanced at Trace then over at his attorney. Both shrugged.

Judge Falls pointed his wire-rimmed spectacles at James. "Prison may be the place for you, Mister Colton. You'd be away from society for ten years, unable to hurt innocent people. Therefore, that is option number one. Number two is the army. Join either one, I don't really care which, Union or Confederate. But," he lowered his voice and pointed his chin toward the men in the crowded courtroom, "the Confederates are coming close to Mesilla and if I were you, I'd want to get as far away as possible."

The judge leaned back and took two deep breaths. "Therefore, due to the unique circumstances of this case, it is the judgment of this court to allow your choice of corrective punishments. You and your attorney have one hour to make the decision. Meet me in my chambers at that time."

The jurors and crowd exploded. Falls pounded his gavel. People jumped to their feet. Threats and curses bounced off the courtroom walls while insults flew toward James.

"You're crazier'n Cochise!"

Trace gripped James' arm.

"Oughta string ya up!"

Trace wedged James between the judge's desk and himself.

Four furious men rushed forward. "Send 'im back to them Indians. He ain't a white man no more!"

Whipping out his gun, Trace aimed it at the stampeding men. "Another step, one of you die." Trace cocked the revolver.

All four men slid to a halt, grumbling but not moving any closer.

"That's it. Now turn around and walk away. Go home. Trial's over and done. Judge made his decision and we'll all have to abide by it. Now git."

James held his breath until they turned and headed for the

door. A tall male figure walked toward him. James' hands shook harder when he recognized who it was.

What in the hell does Fuente want now? Hasn't he already done enough damage?

James stared at the approaching former lawman, then glanced to his right and located Trace just a couple feet behind James, speaking with the judge and Mr. Bershum.

Fuente's going to apologize, to say how very sorry he is for stealing my girl, for causing so much aggravation, for ruining my life.

Fuente stopped in front of James. "Again, I'm sorry about your Apache capture." Fuente offered his hand. "Hope you get better."

Better?

James turned his back on Fuente.

Expecting footsteps to fade away, he instead heard breathing. The old sheriff was still there.

James spun around and glared at Fuente. "Son of a bitch! Done to *you*? I—"

"Lila almost lost that baby 'cause of you! She was so worried she's been in bed for a month!" Fuente grabbed the front of James' shirt, twisting the material into a knot.

The lawman's eyes narrowed, and his angry lips drew up into a tight line. Fuente leaned within inches of James' face and dropped his voice to a low snarl. "You've put me and mine through enough, James Colton. Grow up, little boy. You lost her. Take it like a man."

"I'm more man than you'll ever be," James snapped.

"You sniveling bastard. I oughta kill you right where you stand." Fuente's balled fist exploded in James' stomach. It sank deep into flesh and muscle.

James gasped, then slumped to his knees.

"Damn you!" Trace yelled as he grabbed the back of Fuente's shirt and flung him across the floor. The former sheriff spun and skidded to a stop against a chair.

Rushing the attacker, Trace hoisted Fuente to his feet and hissed through clenched teeth. "Ever touch my little brother again, I'll personally hand you over to Cochise. See how you like living with him." Trace retrieved Fuente's hat from the floor and slammed it into his chest. "Now git."

James shook his head trying to clear the bells ringing in his ears and fought to keep breakfast down. With Andy's arm around his shoulders, James struggled to his feet and glanced at his brother. He made a feeble attempt at smiling. "Be all right."

"Let's get you some place safe," Trace said as he stepped over to James. "Andy, you keep him up on that side, Mister Bershum, the other and I'll walk in front. Let's get him down to the jail."

James groaned and mumbled. "I'm fine, really." Glad to have Andy's support, however, he took halting steps down the courtroom aisle and out the front door.

Once inside the jail cell, James lay on the hard bunk, one uncuffed hand rubbing his sore stomach. Closing his eyes and listening to the conversation around him, he thought about the magical nights back home when his folks would sit around the fireplace talking while his younger brothers curled up on Ma's and Pa's laps and fought sleep. He loved hearing Pa's wild tales of growing up in Ohio.

I'll never hear those stories again, never tell mine to my own kids. Hell, at this rate, I'll never even have kids.

"Sorry you had to see that, Andy." Trace's voice echoed defeat. "He's had a helluva time trying to get his head put back together."

Andy's voice softened against the adobe walls. "You both have. Glad I came when I did."

James heard a long pause, both brothers breathing. He heard creaking bunk springs, someone standing. James opened his eyes and sat up on the edge of his cot, waiting for his stomach to quit spinning. He focused on Andy perched on the other bunk. Trace was leaning against the iron bars, and the cell door was standing wide open. He met their stares.

"Got so many questions to ask you, Andy, it'll take days to get 'em all answered." James ran his hand through his hair. "How come you're here?"

Andy glanced at Trace, then back to his other brother. "I come soon as we got Trace's message. Said you couldn't come home any time soon and it would be a good idea if one of us came here."

"Why isn't Luke with you?" Trace asked as he reset his black hat.

Andy's grin stretched across his tanned face. "Number three brother got himself tied down with a girl." He paused and looked from brother to brother. "And a baby."

61

James pushed to his feet. "What? Little Luke? A daddy?"

Andy nodded and continued to grin. "It's a boy. Born a couple months ago."

James spread his arms wide. "Why didn't anybody let us know? How come Ma didn't write?" He noted the same question on Trace's face.

Andy lowered his head. "She did." He turned toward Trace. "You and James were... gone and a letter came back saying you two had moved."

"What?" Trace stood up straight.

"Yeah. Got a note from Sheriff Fuente saying he would forward Ma's letter as soon as he knew where you two were."

"Fuente!" James growled. "Should've known."

Andy nodded. "Then Fuente wrote less 'n two months ago and said you two were back." His voice dropped to a whisper. "Didn't say anything about your being kidnapped by Cochise."

"At least Fuente did one thing right," Trace said. "He didn't tell Ma and Pa. We haven't told them 'cause we don't know how. Damn, Ma'd worry herself sick." Trace looked at Andy, who nodded.

James' anger twisted in his stomach as he marched to the cell window. Blue-black clouds formed in the west.

If Fuente hadn't stolen Lila, if Cochise hadn't stolen Trace and me...

He squeezed his eyes shut, desperate to block those recurring nightmares and visions. A hand gripped his shoulder.

"Bershum's brought some supper, and we've only got forty-five minutes to figure out what to do." Trace's calm voice in James' ear brought his focus back to the present.

James' attorney had entered the room and closed the door while balancing four small plates of food. As they ate, the men discussed James' options, weighing each choice. Finally, James pushed aside his untouched meal, took a sip from his cup. "I appreciate your help, gentlemen. I've made up my mind."

The three men put down their forks, stared at James.

"I wouldn't last ten days in prison, much less ten years." James' shoulders sagged. "And with Baylor and his Confederates so close to Mesilla, I'd be stuck here with the really angry people of this town. I'd probably find myself back in this jail or worse before too long."

Trace nodded, dropped his voice. "So, you're going Union, over to Arizona, join the California Column. Right?"

Trace's melancholy stare, those sad eyes. James swallowed hard. What could he say to this brother who'd been through so much with him, at his side in the worst conditions possible, his best friend, his protector all these years? His whole life. How could he say thank you and goodbye in the same breath?

PART TWO

CHAPTER ELEVEN

James reined his horse to a full stop at the crest of the west mesa. Turning in the saddle, he studied the expansive Mesilla Valley stretching below. Bands of green fields pointed toward the ever-changing ribbon called the Rio Grande. It was truly beautiful in the summer.

Hell, the only time it isn't pretty is during those damn windstorms. Then the entire world's blotted out with sand and dirt. But, for the most part, it's close to perfect. Am I ever going to see this again? I had so many hopes and dreams.

James glanced at his younger brother. What was he thinking?

Andy returned his gaze. "It's gonna be all right."

"Yeah." James straightened his shoulders and sat up taller. "Don't need a nursemaid, though."

"I didn't come along to tend you, brother. You heard what Trace said. I was to ride along with you, make sure you don't get your durn fool head shot off. That's all. And, I sure as hell ain't gonna wash your clothes and cook for you!" Andy's smile spread across his tanned, open face.

James stared back, envious of the innocence there. He forced a grin. "Let's go then."

* * *

Five days of hard riding brought the brothers into the thriving village of Tucson, part of the newly-formed Arizona Territory. Every street corner displayed signs encouraging army enlistment, windows exhibiting weapons, or advertising supplies for a stint in the military. James had been ordered to report to a Captain Greene out of California, and he'd been told that men, Union supporters, were joining the officer in Tucson, where they would make final preparations for an assault on Baylor's forces.

Following their first good, hot meal in a week, James, with Andy in tow, stepped out of the restaurant and shielded his face from the heat blast. Now mid-summer, the sun beat down on him until he knew they'd melt into a puddle on the street. After a quick glance at Andy's sweaty face, now pinking under the tan, James handed his neckerchief to his brother.

They headed for the army headquarters on the other side of the plaza.

Stepping into the adobe room, James wiped a bead of sweat running down his cheek and nodded at the temperature that was easily twenty degrees cooler than outside. The shade brought a welcome relief, and the mud walls breathed a refreshing cool. James approached the beefy soldier sitting behind the solitary desk and waited for him to acknowledge his presence. He grinned to himself thinking that the sergeant and the desk were the same size.

The man looked up, startled to find anyone staring at him. "Yeah?"

James fished into his shirt and brought out a limp, folded piece of paper. He smoothed it, then handed it to the sergeant. Glancing at Andy as the soldier read it, James nodded.

Maybe it's going to be all right after all. Maybe.

The soldier studied the paper, peered up at James, over at Andy, then reread the words.

"Which one of you is Mr. Colton?"

"I am," both brothers answered in unison.

A sigh, wag of head, slump of shoulders. The sergeant monotoned from the paper.

"James Francis Michael Colton."

James leaned closer to the desk. "That's me, sir. I'm James. This here's my brother, Andy. Andrew Jackson Colton."

The sergeant thumped the limp paper with a tree-trunk finger, then tossed the court order to the desk. "Says here you're in trouble with the law. And your punishment is to join the Union army?"

"Yes, sir."

James breathed in the musty smell of freshly drying earth and straw of the adobe walls. The faint odor of liquor assaulted his nose. Could the whiskey smell have come from the sergeant? The need for a drink took control. Where could he get a bottle? Soon as he was done here, he'd go find the nearest saloon.

Thoughts turned to the matter at hand. What would happen if the army didn't take him? He had to admit that joining the army was a strange jail sentence. James glanced at the soldier, his brother, and then an open inner door leading into somewhere dark. His gaze returned to the man in front of him, staring.

"Join the army. Yes, sir. It's a long story, but the judge thought this'd be best."

The wide-shouldered sergeant planted both hands on the desk and grunted as he pushed himself to his feet. He picked up the paper, refolded it.

"Gotta talk to my commander. Wait here."

The bear-like man lumbered through the door, ducking as he disappeared into the dark room. Measuring himself against the man, James knew that at six foot one he was tall, and Andy measured an inch or so more, but this sergeant towered inches above Andy. He had at least a hundred and thirty pounds on them, too. James stared at the receding end of the man.

Andy leaned close, whispering out of one side of his mouth. "Big."

James nodded and studied each wall of the room. A few maps, documents and one picture of President Lincoln adorned the otherwise bare room. The sergeant's desk, chair and another chair in the corner were the only furniture. Cheery place.

Andy moved in close to James and shrugged. "Pretty bare. Bet Ma could really decorate it up." He pointed to a bare window. "Women just naturally seem to know how to do that."

Lila would make it beautiful. In fact anything she touches turns beautiful.

If he married some day, maybe he'd marry someone with blue eyes. What color eyes would their children have? Images of Lila popped into view. She had blue eyes. The brightest, bluest, liveliest eyes he'd ever seen. In fact, she was the most gorgeous woman in the world. All of her, each and every inch, defined beauty.

One corner of James' mouth tilted upward as his Lila danced across the room's floor, her green dress puffing out around her ankles. He gaped at her blond hair bouncing around her face as she laughed.

An angel. She's my angel.

Fuente's figure elbowed his way into the scene. The Enemy

escorted Lila out the door. Snorting like an enraged bull, James threw his hat to the dirt floor, clenched his fists, and ran toward the opening. "Come back here, coward! Lila's my woman!"

Two strong hands grabbed James' shoulders, spun him around just as he rushed into daylight. The afternoon sun blinding him, he swung at Fuente. His fist found a target.

"Dammit, James, it's me!" Andy clutched his brother's shirt front and slammed his body against the outside adobe wall. He lowered his voice as he glanced left then right. "The army don't take crazy people. Court order or not. If you don't act normal, they're gonna lock you up for sure." He leaned into James' ear. "You wanna spend the next ten years in prison?"

James shook his head, the images of Fuente gone.

"Didn't think so." Andy released James' shirt and took a breath. "You all right now?"

Lila and Fuente had vanished—again. Together.

Dammit, he had to pull himself together, James thought. Andy was right. The army didn't take crazy people. He'd have to push out the demons if he didn't want to spend the next ten years in jail.

James spotted the growing welt on Andy's left cheek, the eye already swelling. He reached a trembling hand out to touch it.

"Sorry."

Andy stepped back, smoothed his shirt, tucked in the fabric that had been pulled out of his pants. Massaging his face, he turned his back on his brother, and stepped into the dim adobe building.

James scowled at the world. "Dammit! Damn it all!" The clenched weapons at the end of his arms plowed into the mud walls. Knuckles oozing red and brown liquid, he sagged against the battered wall, chest heaving, forehead pressed into the crumbling adobe.

Need a drink.

Before James could head toward a saloon, Andy reached out from the doorway and tugged on James' arm.

"It's time, brother." Andy drew in a deep breath and whispered. "We're gonna be soldiers."

Captain Homer Greene was as small as the sergeant was big. His slender body was muscled; not an ounce of fat jiggled as he folded the judge's decree and laid it on the desk. The man's hawk-like nose divided sharp green eyes that took in the world at once.

For some unexplained reason, James trusted this man. He knew his life was changing, and Captain Greene would be the man to help him.

Greene extended his hand to James and then Andy. James winced at the grip, but felt strength in the small hand and knew it could do the work of ten men.

"Mister Colton." Greene stared into James' eyes. "What kind of trouble are you in?"

James took a deep breath, then glanced at his brother. "Guess I should give you the whole story so my punishment'll make sense. Captain Greene, what I'm going to tell you may be hard, if impossible, to believe. Sometimes, I can't believe it myself. But, I swear every word is true."

The captain spoke to the over-sized sergeant. "Get a couple chairs and water for these men."

With the four men seated around the desk, James began his recitation of events. He started with his capture by Cochise, including the horrendous torture, in agonizing detail. He related stories he knew would make Andy sick. Hell, they made *him* sick— and he'd been the one to live through them. Despite upsetting his brother, James knew to be open and up front with this officer.

Once in a while, James glanced at Andy whose tanned face continued to lose color, the glowing red knot on his cheek standing out against the ashen tones of his skin. James finished his story by taking a long drink of cool water.

Greene and the sergeant remained silent while Andy held his stomach and sipped his water. The captain studied the ceiling, the walls, and whatever activity was going on outside. James wondered what he was thinking, if he believed even the first word of his story.

The captain raised one eyebrow and picked up a pencil. He tapped it against the wooden tabletop. "Helluva story, Mister Colton. I have no doubt it's all true. No one, not even our own Mister Lincoln, could spin a yarn like that. Certainly not as heartfelt nor painful."

James nodded as the sergeant poured more water into his glass.

Whiskey will make all this go away.

The captain leaned back and turned to Andy. "What's your part in all this? You weren't the brother captured."

71

"No, sir, I wasn't." Andy shook his head. "My oldest brother, Trace, was taken prisoner with James. I was home in Kansas when all this happened."

"And why're you here now? Your name's not mentioned in these court papers."

"I come out to help James and make sure he..." Andy touched his puffy eye. "Well, to make sure he stays outta trouble." Andy tossed a sideways grin at his brother.

Greene's thin lips curled on one end. He cocked his head and eyed Andy. "You old enough to join the great Union army, son?"

"How old you gotta be?"

"Old enough to carry a rifle."

"Then I'm old enough, Captain."

"Good. Welcome to the army, men. Conditions are terrible, food inedible, but at least the pay's rotten. Sign on the dotted line."

CHAPTER TWELVE

Lieutenant Colonel John Baylor stood in front of his assembled troops, a mishmash group at best. However, they were the best fighting men around, the best of what had been sent to this God-forsaken desert outpost called the Southwest. With his help and leadership, they'd be whipped into the best company in all of New Mexico Territory. Then they'd continue doing what they did so well—take over.

And this was a perfect day to start an integral part of his plan. While the men were lined up watching him, he watched the Rio Grande gurgling behind them. Fortunately, it hadn't flooded this year, which meant fording wasn't difficult. He glanced up at the sun. Hot. It was going to be damn hot today. But not as hot as his men were going to make it for those damn Yankees—those Northern sympathizers.

The Confederacy was at war and, dammit, he loved his South. Secession was the only way to keep slavery and the agricultural way of life alive, and he vowed again to fight until either he died, or those damn Blue Bellies gave up.

His own troops would never give up, so when would he tell them the rest of his plans? They'd already taken half of Texas. It was under Confederate rule now. The rest they'd have a pretty easy time controlling, he'd heard. New Mexico Territory was noncommittal. Divided by the size of the area, it was ripe for the picking, ready to be governed by his troops. Ready to be Arizona Territory.

Surveying the men at attention, he thought how he would change history. He would be the one to ride into Mesilla, the booming town of three thousand souls, and conquer them, bring them to their knees. Just like Napoleon. Except he would remain victorious.

Baylor eyed the front row of troops, then allowed his eyes to roam over the rest. He massaged the hilt of his sword hanging at his left side.

"Men," he said, allowing his proud Texas drawl to be evident, "today is only the beginning of a short march to victory. Soon, very soon, we will occupy the most important city between San Diego and San Antonio. Mesilla."

He turned his piercing look on his second-in-command, Captain Rudolfo Garcia. Baylor's stare, steady and commanding, always stopped people in their tracks. That and his erect shoulders. But right now he wanted to be sure Garcia was right behind him. Right where he should be.

Baylor, hands behind his back, strutted in front of the three hundred men he would lead into victory. He enjoyed feeling the strain of his chest against the gray uniform, always the same sensation when he was about to voice his intent.

"Our mission is to force the pathetic Union soldiers out of Fort Fillmore, then swoop down and occupy Mesilla. That city will be at our mercy. The mercy of the Confederate States of America."

Baylor grinned at the shining faces of his young troops. Although tired from days of marching and fighting at Fort Bliss, Texas, they appeared to be ready and willing to continue their quest.

* * *

James had always thought that soldiers did nothing but fight and clean their weapons. Maybe they played cards and gambled on days off, but he wasn't prepared for what they really did. Up early, always before sunrise, he and Andy attended combat practice for a few hours. The rest of the day was spent helping the village residents build adobe houses or putting up corrals for the ever-increasing herds of horses, pigs, and goats. James was the first to admit this routine kept him tired, but content. The visions didn't come as often, and whiskey continued to dull the pain.

James lay on his cot under one of the hundreds of white canvas tents dotting the outskirts of Tucson. It was the end of another hard day spent building fences. He listened to brother Andy sink into his own cot, the groan of wood and canvas. Andy rattled paper in his hand. James peered over at the several pieces of folded paper in Andy's grasp.

"Here's another letter from Trace," Andy said. "Got it at mail call this morning."

James stretched his arms over his back, waiting to hear the familiar pop pop pop of vertebrae realigning themselves. "Makes what, three since we left?"

"Uh huh." Silence hung over the brothers while Andy read the letter.

Paper crinkled, folded, then unfolded. James waited. And waited. Unable to stand the suspense, he sat up, swung his legs over the side of his cot, and ran his callused hand through the hair hanging in his eyes. "And?"

Taking a deep breath, glancing at James, then into the darkening sky, Andy folded the letter again and held it up. "Says he and Teresa are fine, she sends her love, and both miss us."

Something about Andy's expression, those brown eyes narrowing under what? Worry?

"And?" James held out a hand.

"Bad news. Seems a couple weeks after we left Mesilla, a Rebel colonel by the name of John Baylor and his men rode out of Fort Bliss and is heading right for them. Trace says they're expecting the army to come into town, maybe even stay for a while, in a week or two."

James' outstretched hand grabbed the letter. He scanned Trace's scrawling handwriting. Whistling, James tapped the letter against his thigh, then looked at Andy's frowning face. The eyes had narrowed further.

"Trace's sure got his hands full," James said. "Wish we could be there to help."

Andy balled his fists. "Why'd we have to leave before the war starts? We're gonna miss it. All we're gonna get to do is make mud houses—"

"This sound like a game to you?" James waved the letter at Andy. "People die!"

"I *know* people die. But I'm in the army. To protect innocent people and fight the enemy." Andy jumped to his feet. "I'm just sick of making fences and chasing pigs. Wish I saw some *real* action."

James tossed the paper onto his cot. "Dammit, Andy. Our job is also helping folks stay alive." He glared at his brother then pulled in air. "We ain't gonna miss the war." James spoke over gritted teeth. "You're gonna get your action."

* * *

Although energized by the imminent victory—the siege of Mesilla—Baylor was surprised to see smoke rising from the vicinity of Fort Fillmore, named after the President and just a few miles south of his quarry. Built along the east side of the Rio Grande, it was originally intended to be a resting place for tired soldiers rather than a defensible outpost of regular fighting men. This was where he'd also planned to rest his men. However, was it now in flames? The odor of burning wood floated his way, tickling his nose and enflaming his desire for Confederate supremacy.

A glance over his shoulder at his men marching behind him. They'd do well on this quest. He had the fullest confidence in them. Even Baylor's horse seemed to prance with confidence.

Baylor's point guard reined up in front and saluted.

"Sir. We have a situation."

Baylor returned the salute. "Which is?"

"Fort Fillmore, sir. It's on fire."

This was an unexpected, but not unwelcomed, turn of events. "Where are the troops, soldier? What about the officers? The fort itself?" Baylor tried not to stammer with surprise.

"Gone, sir. I know it sounds strange. I checked myself." The soldier pointed back over his shoulder. "It's deserted. In fact, they left so fast, they left the flag."

"Cowards."

Baylor allowed the smile to crease his face. Looked like those boot-licking army jackasses were on the run. That idiotic Major Lynde was not a leader, and his leaving the fort in flames was proof the Union had no intelligence in the command. Baylor suddenly remembered the soldier standing in front of him.

"Carry on, soldier. We'll head on to the fort and see what's left. Pass the word."

The soldier snapped a salute. "Yes, sir." He leaped on his horse like his feet were jackrabbits, and galloped off.

Two more hours of marching found the Confederate soldiers scooping sand over the small flames still burning at Fort Fillmore. Baylor and Garcia inspected the adobe building that obviously had been the army stores. Supplies were overturned as if starving marauding hordes had come through and wiped out everything. Not much was left, just broken crockery, a few upturned whiskey bottles, nothing of consequence.

"Odd, wouldn't you say, Captain?" Baylor held a handkerchief over his nose, the smoke still too thick to allow easy breathing.

"No sir. Just typical Union behavior." Garcia's east Tennessee accent was thick; he often had to repeat himself around Baylor.

Baylor gazed around at the wreckage. "Tell the troops to help themselves to whatever they find. Tell them to get a good night's sleep. Tomorrow, it's Mesilla."

* * *

Ordered to muster at the camp doctor's door, James waited in a long line of soldiers. Mumblings, grumblings, and whispered questions sailed up and down the queue. Nervous laughter, an off-color joke or two hit James' ears, but nothing substantial, no real bit of information answered the questions on everyone's mind.

James turned to Andy, who was behind him, and dropped his voice near Andy's ear. "Wonder what's going on?"

"Soldier back there said they're doing some kind of medical experiment." Andy glanced behind him, then pointed his chin toward the closed door. "They're saying that whoever survives the experiment's gonna get written up in some kind of medical journal. Be real famous." His eyes grew wide, but only concern tinged with fear showed on his face. "You think that's true?"

"You can't be—" James jumped as the door flew open and a pale soldier, eyes wider than Andy's, stumbled into the daylight. The soldier gripped his upper arm.

James watched each step the man took as he staggered away from the adobe office. Once the man was out of sight, James swung his attention back to his brother. Andy's cheeks were whiter than before. "What d'you think?" Andy riveted his gaze on the next soldier who stepped into the doctor's office. He cringed when the door banged shut.

James pushed aside doubt and squared his shoulders. *Have to be strong for Andy. If I panic, he will, too. Just gotta be strong.*

One by one, men stepped into the dark building, and then a short time later, they emerged holding their arms, color drained from their faces. Could there be some truth to the rumors?

His name called, James tossed an it's-going-to-be-all-right nod to his little brother, then took a big step into the medical abyss.

77

The door banged behind him. He jumped.

James took in the features of the dim room and noted that except for an official-looking diploma, the mud walls were bare. Sunlight beamed through one narrow window on the east side, illuminating two chairs and one table that took up the center of the room. A man with a stethoscope draped around his neck held a short needle in one hand and a small bowl in the other. Another soldier standing nearby with pencil and paper was busy scribbling something. Off to James' left stood a long operating table, with two leather straps hanging off each side.

Focusing on those rawhide strips, James heard movement, footfalls, nearby. He spotted Apaches strutting toward him, torture instruments hanging from each hand.

Wet rawhide straps. Drying. Strangling. James rubbed his eyes then stepped back, desperate to make sense of his situation.

"No," James said, backing towards the door. "Andy?"

Walls melted. The two Indians glanced at each other then rushed him. He bolted.

Tight grips on his arm jerked him to a stop.

"Trace?" James cried as he strained against the grip and yelled over his shoulder. "Don't let 'em get you! Run!"

The desert heat was unbearable. James gasped for air as the drying leather tightened around his head, around his neck. He clawed at the strangling hold on his throat, then coughed at the constricting band cutting off his air.

From out of nowhere, Trace appeared, that perpetual worried look clouding his face. Wrenching his arm from the tight grip, James stumbled toward his brother.

"Don't let 'em take me again! It hurts!"

More Indians crowded around.

James threw himself into Trace's arms and clutched the front of his brother's shirt. He sank to his knees. "God, no more."

Hundreds of muscular arms tossed him to the ground. Pinned, rocks poked his back. Tremors made his body quiver. A strong hand clamped around his chin and pried his mouth open. Liquid ran down his throat. He tried not to swallow, to spit it out, but fingers pinched his nose. He swallowed. And coughed.

"It's just laudanum, James."

Trace's face, but not his voice. Andy? No, couldn't be.

James thrashed against his restraints until he was exhausted.

CHAPTER THIRTEEN

Colonel Baylor reflected on the last five miles he'd marched from Fort Fillmore to Mesilla. Uneventful. Along the way, his soldiers, with their chests puffed out around the women, had talked to the ranchers and farmers. Those pathetic people welcomed the army with open arms. They didn't need to know the Confederacy's plans, hell, *his* plans. They'd find out soon enough.

Baylor dismounted three blocks south of the plaza and waited for his men to form into their companies. He caught the eye of his second-in-command. "Captain."

"Sir?" Garcia snapped to attention.

"This siege needs only two companies. Bring A and D to the plaza. And the cannon. Surround this miserable town with the other units. Be sure the men have plenty of ammunition just in case. We want to show these villagers we mean business."

"Sir." Captain Rudolfo Garcia saluted, then barked orders to the men. Soldiers scattered to their offensive positions.

Within an hour, soldiers and weapons sat strategically placed around the small square. His troops took their positions on top of roofs and behind the low adobe buildings. Baylor surveyed the hundred or so residents gathered around the plaza. The townspeople stood in plain sight, out in the open. Prime targets.

By the time the July sun stood directly overhead, with no shadows cooling the men, Baylor knew he and his soldiers were ready. The only thing left to do now was take over the plaza. Laying siege to the rest of the weak New Mexico Territory would be easy. It was so large. He knew the northern half and the southern half were at odds. The north with Santa Fe as the capital was in contact with Washington and served their interests. But the remote southern half was a barren wasteland of desert, no good to anyone. There'd been talk of silver mines complete with large silver strikes, but the area was too desolate and too far from Washington to make any significant contribution to the U.S. treasury.

He'd only agreed to take over this southern portion of the territory because it was a direct path to California. Once that section belonged to the Confederates, a new country would be born. The Colonel grinned at the thought. Given enough time, a few months perhaps, he'd be standing on the shore of the Pacific Ocean, watching a new country, *his* country, form.

"What's going on here, Colonel?" A deep voice shook Baylor out of his reverie.

Baylor spun, glaring at the man sporting a shiny sheriff's badge. "A siege, sir. And you are...?"

"Sheriff Trace Colton." The sheriff's eyes traveled up and down Baylor. "A siege? What d'you mean a—"

"The Confederates are about to take control of Mesilla, sir. Better get these fine citizens off the street before anyone gets hurt." Baylor waved at the people standing on the wooden boardwalks, speaking in hushed tones and pointing at the soldiers and the cannon.

Trace eased his hand down toward his holster and caressed the wooden butt of his Colt .38. "I don't know how you think you can come waltzing in here and just take over my town," he said. "You're sadly mistaken, Colonel. Mesilla's not interested in the war. We want no part of it. I'll give you exactly five minutes to get your men out of here, or I'll remove you myself."

Baylor took a deep breath, brought himself up to his full six foot height. "Is that a threat, Sheriff Colton?"

"No sir, it isn't. It's a warning. I'm in charge here and I want you and your men outta town now." Trace stepped closer to Baylor, then pointed his gun at the colonel. "Now."

Baylor sneered, eying the man in front of him. "Look around you." He swept his arm to include most of the plaza. "There's over three hundred soldiers surrounding you and your dirty, dusty town. You shoot me, you'll be so full of holes your Ma won't recognize your worthless body."

"I don't intimidate easy, Colonel."

"No intimidation intended. It's a guarantee." Baylor moved within inches of the man with the intense brown eyes. "Now put that toy away and I won't have you arrested to spend the next thirty years in jail."

Trace raised his revolver chest high. "Last warning, sir. Leave."

Baylor's eyes flicked to his second-in-command, who moved behind the sheriff. Garcia planted his revolver's barrel against Trace's temple. Baylor raised one eyebrow.

"Good timing, Captain."

"Thank you, sir."

"Arrest this man. Use handcuffs and leg irons if necessary. Toss him in his own jail."

A grin lifted one corner of Baylor's mouth while he made a show of prying the gun out of a tight grip. He chuckled at the stricken look on the young lawdog's face. One down, the rest should be easy.

"You son-of-a-bitch!" Trace screamed at Baylor, then lowered his voice to a hoarse whisper. "Who the hell do you think you are?"

Baylor cocked his head. Without a word, Garcia slammed the butt of his revolver against the back of Trace's skull. Trace's eyes opened wide then slammed shut. Trace Colton crumpled to the ground.

"I'll tell you who I am, Sheriff. I am Colonel John Baylor. And *I'm* in charge now."

* * *

Voices swirled around James' head.

"Got everyone vaccinated, Captain Greene. That makes over a hundred taken care of in the last three months."

First one eye opened, then the other.

"Good to know, Doctor. If smallpox ever breaks out, our soldiers should be protected. Right?"

Images blurred. Kerosene lanterns threw golden light into the middle of an otherwise dim room. It was too dark to identify specific people. James was sure, however, that no one was Apache. The words were in perfect English.

"Yes, sir. That's the way it's supposed to work."

"Worked in Europe, Doc, but hope we never need to find out around here."

The voice floating around James' head chuckled. "Some of the men thought I was conducting experiments on them, Captain. More than one was pretty shook up when I grabbed his arm."

A hand on his shoulder. A deep sigh. A voice nearby.

"I think he's coming to."

81

James focused on the face. The eyes were a dead giveaway. A Colton family brown.

Andy.

Lines of worry cascaded across his young forehead, the eyes reflecting James' own confusion and apprehension, the lips attempting a feeble grin.

Andy squeezed James' shoulder. "Hey, brother," he said. "Thought you'd sleep all night."

James strained against the leather straps. Heart pounding, breaths rasping, he knew he'd pass out again. The rawhide held his body to the table.

"Get those leg straps off, Doc."

James swung his attention to the man on his left, opposite Andy.

Captain Greene.

"Gave us quite a scare, young man. Where are you?"

James swallowed over a raw throat. He licked dry lips. "Tucson."

"Get some water so this man can talk," Captain Greene ordered as he waved to someone on the other side of the room. Within a minute, Andy was holding James' head while James drank the cool water. It soothed the sore spots.

James studied what appeared to be panic on his younger brother's face.

Damn Apaches. No, damn me for letting my guard down, for reacting like I did. For scaring Andy.

He moved his legs, enjoying the freedom. His smile was replaced with a frown as he jerked his arms.

"Relax, no one's gonna hurt you. We'll let you up in a few minutes." Captain Greene touched James' arm. "Just need to make sure you're all right."

Words wouldn't come. But memories did. Lying on the hard sand, rocks poking his back, powerless to get away. One Wing's knife in his throat while he lay prostrate on the ground. Leather strips securing his hands and body to wooden stakes. He thrashed, twisted and kicked.

Trace, or was it Andy, forced his shoulders against the bed. "Calm down. It's all right."

James forced the images, memories, nightmares to one side. He peered up at Andy. Who was shaking harder? Andy or him?

A cup appeared in his brother's hand, the other hand slid under James' head. With Andy's comforting words in his ear, James gulped the liquid. He closed his eyes. Maybe when he opened them again, he'd be normal.

CHAPTER FOURTEEN

A volley of gunfire startled Trace. His eyes snapped open, and he grabbed for his throbbing head. His hands jerked back hard against metal bars. Fully awake now, Trace swung his gaze from side to side and yanked his tethered hands. The handcuffs kept his arms pinned over his head as he lay prone on the floor. Moving his legs, he fought against the chains keeping his ankles shackled together.

Head still thumping, Trace sucked in spurts of breath as he attempted to make sense of his world.

Calm down! Can't be as bad as I think it is.

A glance around the cell. Legs of the cot, the window high above it, hard-packed dirt under him. He squirmed on the floor. With his head tilted as far back as possible, he studied the iron bars above him.

Handcuffed to my own jail cell.

Thrashing like a fish on a hook, he fought against his captivity.

Unwelcome memories flooded into his mind. Cochise and One Wing's snarling faces. Ebony eyes smirking at his pain. His and James'. He tugged at the horsehair rope ensnaring his body, but each pull only served to tighten the noose, ratchet him into the thorny cactus. Wet leather strip tied around his brother's head shrunk with each passing minute.

The agony, the constant terror on his little brother's face, the panic each time the Apaches dragged him away. Feelings of inadequacy, helplessness, his inability to save his best friend overwhelmed him. Visions of his tortured brother reeled in his head. Trace wrenched against the iron handcuffs until exhaustion drove him down—down to a dark place, safe from the horrors.

* * *

Colonel John Baylor looked up from the sheriff's desk as Captain Garcia opened the door and stuck in his head.

"What?" Baylor glared over the top of his papers.

Garcia entered, shutting the door behind him. "Sir. Thought you should know." He saluted, waited for the return salute. "Those two civilians who were accidentally shot?"

"What about them?"

"They're dead."

Baylor took a deep breath, tossed the papers to the desktop, exhaled as he stood. Hands planted behind his back, he stared out the window then spoke over his shoulder.

"Unfortunate causalities of war, Captain."

"Yes, sir."

"Shouldn't have been standing on the plaza."

"No, sir."

"Should've been home minding their own business."

"Yes, sir."

"What'd we tell their families?" Baylor turned around and glanced at Garcia.

"We're sorry."

A nod. "That should do it," the colonel said as he marched back to his desk, sat, and picked up a pile of papers. Silence. Garcia's breathing. Baylor lifted his eyes to his second-in-command.

"Something else on your mind?" Baylor asked.

"Sir. Colton's wife's outside demanding to see her husband. What do I tell her?"

Baylor's mouth twitched. He loved these games.

"Tell her he's tied up at the moment. She'll be allowed to see him when he's free."

Garcia returned a slight grin and saluted. "Thank you, sir." He stepped outside and pulled the door shut.

Baylor leaned back, cradled his head with his entwined fingers. He closed his eyes.

Everything's going perfectly, just as I planned. The reports are true. Mesilla's ripe for the picking and I'm the one to harvest the crop. Today Mesilla, tomorrow California.

* * *

Spiraling lights slowed with each minute that dragged by. Every new breath brought the jail cell into clearer focus. Dirt floor. Cot legs. Window high above. Hot July air flooding into the cell.

Trace's arms ached.

All right, don't panic. Take a slow breath. Yeah, like that. I'll be fine. Now, another breath. That's it.

"Baylor? Baylor." Trace's voice squeaked as he tugged at the handcuffs. Swallowing what bit of moisture was in his mouth, Trace's throat screamed pain. Raw words tumbled from his lips.

"Baylor, you Sonovabitch!"

Eyes shut tight, Trace gulped several more deep breaths.

Calm down. Panic won't help. Didn't help with Cochise, won't help with Baylor. Think, Trace. How can I get through this?

Advice from four months previous sprang to mind: 'Whatever it takes, James. Whatever it takes.'

I was right then and I'm right now. Do whatever's necessary to stay alive. Baylor probably won't kill me, but I'll bet I'm not sheriff any more.

Trace opened his eyes and wagged his head, straightening the thoughts in his brain.

Trace slid around on the floor until the full length of his body pressed against the bars. Handcuffs cutting into his wrists, he again felt the rawhide strips binding him. Blood trickled from his wrists, then dripped down his arm as he tugged and pulled at the restraints. The stout saguaro cactus tether refused to budge. Trace yanked harder.

Where the hell am I?

The cactus melted into iron bars.

My own jail in Mesilla. No Cochise, no One Wing.

Trace's heart pressed against his chest. He stared into his empty jail cell, again aware of his surroundings. He bit his lower lip.

Must be just what James sees. Can't tell the past from the present.

The wooden inner door creaked open. Baylor and his captain stood on the other side of the cell bars. Trace glared at them.

"Now there's a sorry sight, Captain Garcia." Cochise's voice echoed off the rock walls.

One Wing squatted down nearby. A hand gripped his shoulder. "Colton."

Trace exploded. Screaming obscenities at his captors, he rolled back and forth, kicked at the bars, yanked and jerked at the handcuffs. Blood again poured down both arms.

After an eternity and energy spent, Trace sagged on the ground, panting. Cochise and One Wing stood back, those contemptuous faces mocking his pain. Raspy words tumbled from Trace's lips.

"You'll never break us, Cochise."

"What the hell'd he say?" Cochise turned to One Wing.

A shrug. "Sounded like 'Cochise', sir." One Wing's eyes met Trace's. "Didn't make sense."

Too much. Confusion. Pain. Trace squeezed his eyes shut and tried to block out the attacker's voices. They came through anyway.

"When he becomes rational, Captain, let me know. Have one of the privates guard him around the clock. Don't want him trying to break out of his own jail." The voice, laced with sarcasm, chuckled. "Pathetic."

CHAPTER FIFTEEN

Teresa stood outside almost nose to nose with the soldier guarding her husband's office. It just wasn't right that someone else could come into town, arrest her husband, and then toss him in jail. It had been a couple of hours now. Was Trace all right? Had they hurt him? She thought she'd heard screams coming from inside earlier. Were they torturing him, like Cochise had done? She stepped closer.

"I'll say this again, Captain. I demand to see my husband." Teresa pointed over the soldier's shoulder. "At least let me see him. Know he's not hurt."

Captain Rudolfo Garcia gripped his rifle and pushed against her, determined to keep her from getting past. "No one goes in. No visitors, no doctor, no nobody." His dark eyes trailed from her eyes down to her bodice. "Unless," Garcia lowered his voice and glanced sideways, "unless you have something special in mind to give me. Then maybe you can see him."

"What?" The absurdity of the bribe was unthinkable. Had he really just suggested what she thought?

Garcia lowered his weapon to one side then eased closer. Teresa smelled a slight odor of alcohol on his breath. His free hand inched toward her hip brushing against her skirt.

Teresa backed away, outraged at the audacity. "You can't keep me from seeing my husband. I demand to see him." The sharpness and volume of her words brought a few bystanders to a stop. Her pointed finger waggled near his face. "You can't arrest the sheriff. He hasn't done anything to you!"

Garcia whipped around at the forming crowd. "Break this up. Nothing for you to see here. Go on about your business." He aimed the rifle at the people. "Now!" Mumbles, murmurs, whispered conjectures then the residents ambled away, several looking over their shoulders as they moved down the boardwalks.

Once again alone with Teresa, the Captain straightened his shoulders and lowered the weapon. He held her arm pulling her closer. "You're very beautiful. I'm sure you make the sheriff very happy." The eyes roamed up and down her body.

Teresa squirmed at the scrutiny. This wasn't getting anywhere. She sure wasn't going to give him what he wanted, and he wasn't going to let her in without it. Unless ...

She relaxed and moved within inches of him. As tall as she was, they were close to eye to eye, Garcia being shorter than many men. Teresa took a breath. "Captain." Her words were soft, breathy. "I'll make you a deal. A trade."

"A trade?" Garcia slid his hand up and down her arm.

"Uh huh." Teresa prayed she was strong enough to do this.

"I like trading. You give me one night of affection ... no, make that two nights." Garcia's chest heaved with the carnal thoughts. "No, two *weeks*, every night, and you can see your husband." His hand brushed against her breast. "A deal?"

"Better yet, Captain." Would he buy into her idea? Teresa had no way of knowing. "Instead of making love, how about making money? It'll last a lot longer." Her heart thundered in her chest, but she struggled to remain calm.

"Hum." Garcia leaned back and cocked his head. "How much money?"

As much as she loved Trace, Teresa sure hated to part with the gold ring and locket her grandma had given her. But it was the only thing of value she had, except her virtue, and that she wasn't selling at any price.

She slid a seductive smile up one side of her face then reached behind her neck and unclasped the necklace. "I have a gold chain, locket, and ring that you can have. It's worth at least a year of a captain's pay." Teresa held the locket with a dainty gold ring on the chain. She caressed it in her hand. "It's yours, Captain, if you'll let me see Trace whenever I need to."

Garcia's Tennessee accent mushed his words. "How about one week of love *and* the necklace and ring?" He raised both eyebrows. "I'm very good at making love."

"How about my necklace and ring and I don't report you to Colonel Baylor?" Teresa prayed she had him. Prayed that her prized possession would open the door to Trace.

A long pause, breaths from Garcia. Another gaze at her body.

"I'll go speak with my commander." He scooped the gold bounty from her hand and shoved it in his uniform shirt pocket. "Wait here." With that, Garcia turned on his heels and slipped through the door.

Teresa waited while two women she knew passed by. She couldn't even speak to them right now, her heart hammering in her throat. After what felt like hours, the door opened and Garcia waved her in. She stopped in front of Baylor's desk, the desk that until yesterday was her husband's.

Baylor looked up from his paperwork. "Missus Colton. I understand Captain Garcia here suggests I allow you to visit your husband."

Teresa stared at Garcia, that sneer pushing up one side of his pockmarked cheek. "Yes, sir. Thank you." She started back to the cells.

"I agreed to let you see him only for a minute." Baylor waved a pen at Teresa. "And it better be a damn short minute. We're busy here." He returned to his paperwork.

Feet on fire, Teresa rushed through the inner door and slid to a stop in front of the second jail cell. There lay Trace, her proud, solid husband, just lying on the hard floor shackled to an iron bar.

"Trace? Oh God. What've they done to you? Trace?" Teresa knelt down and reached through the bars and smoothed his hair. She wiped beads of sweat from his forehead. "Trace?"

Trace's eyes fluttered open then gradually rested on Teresa. He frowned. "Teresa? Where are we?"

"We're in Mesilla. In your jail." Teresa glanced up behind her at Garcia. "Would you leave us alone?"

"One minute." Garcia backed away. "You got one minute."

Teresa wanted to kiss Trace's face, take away the hurt and pain she saw there. Instead, she had to settle on knowing that he was still alive and she should be able to return and visit. To make sure he was all right. To make sure he was treated well. To make sure he lived.

"I love you, Trace. We'll get you free. Don't worry." Teresa held his hand and forced a smile.

"I love you, too." Trace's voice was stronger. "Just be safe. I'll be all right." A wide smile lit up his eyes. "You just gotta have faith."

Both Teresa and Trace looked up at Garcia standing in the doorway. "Time's up, Missus Colton."

A final squeeze of the hands then Teresa stood. "I'll be back, Trace. Don't give up. I'll be here every day." Determined not to cry, she turned her back on Trace and marched through the door and into the office.

Garcia slammed the inner door. "Gave you two minutes." He opened the outer door and held it wide. As she squeezed by, he whispered, "You owe me. I'll come collect some time."

Teresa squinted against the bright summer sun. "Don't try it, Captain. I've paid you all I'm going to." She started away then stopped and turned back. "I'll see you tomorrow. And the day after. And the day after."

* * *

Trace perked up at the voices in the outer office. Teresa's and Garcia's. Trace smiled. Those two always argued every time Teresa came to visit. Every time. Garcia would deny her access; Teresa would then threaten him with mayhem if he didn't let her in. Once, she even told Garcia that she'd written Presidents Davis *and* Lincoln about Baylor and his antics.

Trace smiled wider. That was one of the things he loved about his wife. She was so full of "tough," she'd almost grown horns. Not much got past her. Yet, she was still as pretty as the day they'd met and just as desirable. Every day, he loved her more and more.

It was only because of her that he'd been able to fight back to the present. Her constant visits kept him grounded in reality. He no longer watched Cochise and One Wing strut into the cell. Now it was just Baylor and his boot-licker Garcia, a slimy creature if there ever was one. Trace couldn't decide who was more treacherous, Garcia or One Wing.

Teresa's voice rose above Garcia's, then silence. Trace waited. Footsteps then the inner door opened. Garcia pointed, waited for Teresa to scoot past, then he slammed it. Another victory for Teresa.

"You're not going to believe what just happened." Teresa Colton said, her brown eyes locking on Trace's as she handed him his usual tray of food. When her face took on that surprised look, those wide eyes, that mouth that set a tight line, Trace knew something big, something important was going on outside. Outside. Not in this stinking jail.

Trace peered through the bars, happy as always to see his wife—taller than most women, stronger than other women, definitely smarter than most, too. But she was worried. Those frown lines across her forehead marred her pretty face. He pulled her hand through the bars and held it. Was she trembling?

"What?" He asked.

She shook her head. "Baylor just made himself Governor of the Confederate State of Arizona."

"What?" Trace squeezed her hand, and then realized he was probably hurting her. "He what?"

Teresa held up a newspaper, *The Mesilla Times*.

"Says here," she folded it until just the headlines and lead article filled the page. "Baylor's issued a 'Proclamation to the People of the Territory of Arizona'."

"Which is...?" Trace knew he wasn't going to like whatever it said. In fact, he didn't like anything about becoming Arizona Territory. What the hell were people thinking?

She read. "The social and political condition of Arizona being little short of general anarchy, and the people being literally destitute of law, order and protection...."

Teresa looked up at Trace, then continued, "the said Territory, from the date hereof, is hereby declared temporarily organized as a military government until such time as Congress may otherwise provide."

Trace pounded on the bars. "He can't do that! Who the hell does he think he is? We were doing just fine without him."

He wanted to continue ranting, but noticed Teresa waiting. There was more.

"Says here," Teresa read, "I, John R. Baylor, lieutenant-colonel, commanding the Confederate Army in the Territory of Arizona, hereby take possession of said Territory in the name and behalf of the Confederate States of America."

"Hell and damnation!" Trace whipped around and marched across the cell to the windowed wall. "Damnation!"

Both hands fisted, he beat against the adobe. With a deep breath, and rage wrestled down to a controlled level, he turned around and looked at his wife, still standing there, newspaper in hand.

"I'm sorry for the language," he apologized.

"I understand." Teresa's eyes lit up. "I would've said it if you hadn't."

* * *

Lt. Colonel John R. Baylor sat at his desk, the desk of that former Sheriff Colton, and thought about how he could protect the population from Indian attacks. Many of his men he'd had to send north up to Fort Craig to help turn back those Union troops.

Here it was now October, late October, and already he was spread thin. And President Davis hadn't sent reinforcements, much less supplies and money.

Hell, he hasn't even answered my twenty letters.

Baylor tapped his pencil against his newest letter to Davis. What could he say that would make a difference this time? Nothing. He'd tried everything.

Before Baylor had written a word, Captain Garcia rushed into the office, saluted, and then stood at attention in front of the desk.

"What is it Captain?" Baylor was irritated at the intrusion and let his tone reflect it.

"Sorry, sir. But thought you'd want to know." Garcia took a deep breath. "Apaches just raided a ranch about fifteen miles from here. The Corralitos Ranch. Killed everyone. They're getting bold as brass, sir. What d'you think we should do?"

Apaches. Apaches. All his life he'd hated the heathen Red Man. Those savages needed to be stopped.

Garcia caught his breath. "They've already raided Tubac and Pinos Altos as well. They've got sand, that's for sure."

Baylor snapped back. "Wrong. What they've got is *me* to contend with." He stood so suddenly the chair scooted out from behind him. "I'll kill every last one of them. It'll be a war of extermination."

Garcia took a step back. "Do we have the troops to do it, sir?"

"We don't need troops, Captain. We need intelligence."

Baylor paced across the room and stared out the door, a cool autumn wind ruffling his beard. He watched people go about their everyday business, women with parcels in their arms, children chasing dogs, men driving their wagons. Baylor spun around to Garcia.

"Didn't you tell me that Colton back there," Baylor cocked his head toward the jail cells, "didn't he spend some time with Cochise?"

"Yes, sir, he did." Garcia nodded. "If I remember the story right, earlier this year, in fact, him and his brother were held for over two months. Cochise's captives."

Baylor placed his hands behind his back, a habit when he was deep in thought. "Sounds unlikely, Captain. Nobody escapes or survives Apache captivity."

"I'm sure of it, Colonel. In fact, both Coltons were rescued by Colonel Bascom and his men. I remember reading about it in a report. Pretty heroic action."

"Uh huh." Baylor's thoughts turned to the prisoner still held behind bars. Maybe they could cut a deal. Maybe. Baylor marched around Garcia, then pushed open the inner door to the two cells. He felt more than saw Garcia right behind him.

Baylor stopped in front of Trace's cell. It had been over three months that this man had sat rotting in jail—his own jail. Baylor chuckled at the irony of it all.

"Colton." He waited for his prisoner to sit up. "You want out of here?"

Trace eased to his feet. "What're you trying to pull now, Baylor?"

Ignoring his question, Baylor charged ahead. "You've been my prisoner for what, three months now?" Without waiting for a response, he moved in closer to the iron bars. "About as long as ol' Cochise held you, wouldn't you say?"

"What does that have to do with anything?" Trace's long strides brought him almost nose to nose with Baylor. He gripped the bars, his knuckles turning white.

Baylor loved being in this position. He knew he was born to lead and this was just another example of the fine leadership skills he possessed. Baylor lowered his voice.

"That poor wife of yours. Pretty thing, too." He glanced at Garcia at his elbow. "Well, she's been missing you these long, lonely days."

"Leave her out of this." Trace tugged against the bar. "What do you want?"

Time to get down to business. Baylor straightened his already-straight shoulders.

"Just this. I'll let you out of here in exchange for all you know about Cochise. I want details. I want to know everything about those God-less Apaches. Everything."

Trace stepped back. "Why?"

"Just tell me. Yes or no. Which side of the bars do you want to spend Christmas on? Your little wife will have to serve you dinner slipped under the door here. How d'you think she'd like that?"

Baylor knew by the look on Trace's face what the answer was. He turned to Garcia.

"Get the key."

* * *

"It's Christmas time, James," Andy said. "And it ain't even cold. Just don't feel right."

"Yeah, it's a lot warmer here in Tucson than back home. Remember all the snowmen we used to make?" James picked up a washrag and held up his arm. He scrubbed his elbow while water dripped onto the bathhouse floor.

"And the ice forts stockpiled with snowballs? Each battle got bigger and better." Andy formed suds into a ball and tossed it toward James. 'Member me and Luke used to make you and Trace surrender all the time? We whooped you damn good."

"Like hell you did! Gimme one time you beat us. One time." James splashed warm, sudsy water at his teenage brother.

"You gettin' forgetful in your old age? We wiped out your pathetic army every time. Our snowballs were harder and bigger than yours." Andy stood up in the wooden soaking tub and tossed a bar of soap at his brother. "And, we threw farther than our poor, much older brothers."

James launched himself out of the tub next to Andy's, grabbed him around the chest and dunked his head in the soapy water. His brother thrashed until his slippery body slid out of James' hands. Andy gulped air.

Grin covering his face, Andy returned the favor and splashed James. Soap suds flying, Andy stopped and rubbed his eyes.

"Got soap in my eyes. Can't see," he said as he waved a frothy arm. "Get me a towel."

James snatched a towel off a chair and planted it in his brother's face. He rubbed Andy's entire head. "Anything else, your majesty?"

Andy lowered the towel, his red eyes dancing with excitement. "Ah ha. So you admit I'm king. Me and Luke reign! Told you!"

James grabbed the towel and twisted it into one long whip.

He stretched the towel between his hands and took aim at Andy's rear end. He stopped and stared at the taut material. Shaking his head, he looked up at his brother and lowered the weapon. "No. It hurts too bad. Too much like the real thing."

Andy plucked another towel from a nearby chair, wrapped it around his waist, and stepped out of the tub. "It's all right, James. This isn't a whip, just a towel." His soft words melted into the wooden walls of the bathhouse.

"I know." Unrolling the beige material, James covered his lower body then eased down to the chair. "I'm all right."

His fingers ran across multiple whip marks on his chest, then traced a raised zigzag scar across his side. His eyebrows knitted. "I could never do this to any one." His finger found another raised scar on his cheek. "No matter how much I hated them."

"Guess that's why they call the Indians savages."

James looked up into his brother's face. "Savages? Maybe. But it's more. They just live different, have different ideas about things."

"You're defending them? After they treated you like that?"

James stared into memories. "Sometimes, more times than I like to remember, the women had to feed me. I was too weak and hurt to help myself. They'd give me stew. And bread. One warrior even sneaked Trace extra food one night."

"But I still have nightmares about your other stories." Andy pulled on his trousers, and then buttoned his shirt.

James threaded his arms through his shirtsleeves. "I've been doing a lot of thinking on it, a lot of thinking. In many ways they're like us, Andy. They love their children, they're protecting land they feel's theirs, they want to survive." He picked up his folded pants. "Don't we all?"

"'Course we do. Guess I never thought about them as people."

"Cochise was a true leader, an honorable man. His tribe knew when he gave his word, that was it. Never went back on it. He respected honesty."

Andy smoothed his damp hair. "But—"

"Cochise stepped in at least three times when he thought ol' One Wing was gonna kill me." James fought a growing tightness in his chest. "And that crazy damn Indian just about did."

Andy shot a sideways glance at his brother. "Been wanting to ask. Guess maybe now's the right time."

James turned his full attention to his brother.

Andy cocked his head to one side. "Why'd Cochise keep you alive even when One Wing hated you so much, always tried to kill you? I mean, wouldn't it still have proved their point with just Trace alive?"

James swallowed hard. "No. Cochise needed me alive. Right off he figured out that Trace would do anything to keep me that way—he's the stronger of the two of us. Cochise planned to trade me for his brother."

"But his brother was hanged."

"Yeah."

Andy toweled the back of his neck. "What d'ya say we grab something to eat? I'm starved." He produced a wide Colton smile.

James picked up his trousers, held them in steady hands. "Must be my stomach grumbling. Thought it was thunder." He stepped into his pants and buttoned the top fastener.

I'm getting better. I can talk about Cochise and the rest and not get crazy.

James suppressed a grin.

Andy tugged on his boots, then adjusted the brown felt hat on his head.

"It's been what, seven, eight months since you got away?" He asked.

"Bout that." James stuffed his shirttail into his pants while stomping his boot to settle his foot just right. "Guess the judge knew what he was doing. I did need a change of address."

The Colton boys stepped into the cool afternoon sunshine. James stopped and peered down at his feet. His words were soft. "Just want to thank you for helping me through this. I know it hasn't been easy for you."

"You got that right." Andy slid an arm around his older brother's shoulders and nudged James toward the cafe. "But, you're welcome."

CHAPTER SIXTEEN

Captain Greene squared his shoulders and stood straight. "Gentlemen, the news is not good. In fact, it's not good at all. As you know, Baylor's been in Mesilla for several months, but now he's preparing to advance on California. He's leaving Mesilla with a skeleton crew. But, we're still caught right in the middle."

The knot in James' stomach launched itself toward his throat. He looked down his row of soldiers and spotted his brother. Andy was still in one piece, but how was Trace? Especially now that Baylor was deserting Mesilla. Did that mean his brother would be sheriff again? Or jailed again? And how had Trace handled more months of captivity? Thank goodness Teresa had been sending letters. But now that James and his company were heading out across the desert, it would take forever for the mule trains to catch up with letters from home. He'd just have to hope for the best.

Another harder look at Andy and James detected a gleam in his brother's eye.

Crazy kid. All he wants to do is go fight—Rebs or Indians. Hope he never finds out how terrifying it really is.

"Fact is…" The captain glanced at his sergeant then back at his men. "We don't have enough troops to fight it out here. There's not enough of us to make a stand and keep this town under Union control. Today's the twenty-eighth of December. By January first we've gotta be out of here."

Catching his brother's eye, James nodded, but he felt his stomach flip-flop as Andy flashed a wide grin.

Captain Greene marched in front of the men standing at attention. "Pack whatever you can carry in your backpacks, write a letter home if you need to, and kiss as many *señoritas* as you can before the first. We're heading west to Fort Yuma where we'll meet up with Carleton's men."

Following dismissal, James, with Andy beside him, made his

way to their tent a few blocks away. James noticed the bounce in his brother's step, the whistling, his enthusiasm for this next adventure.

Andy stopped in front of the tent. "Too bad we gotta run from old Baylor, but once we join up with Carleton's boys, we're gonna make those Rebs wish they'd never been born."

Andy sighted an imaginary rifle along its barrel. He pushed aside the tent flaps and stepped in.

James shook his head and followed. "You're just not gonna be happy 'til you get your head blown off, are you?"

"I'll be fine." Andy sighted his rifle again. "It's Johnny Reb that oughta be scared."

"You just don't get it, do you?" James grabbed a shirt off his cot and spun around to face his brother. "We've had this conversation before, but guess you weren't listening. People die. They quit breathing. No more plans for the future. No more tomorrows. No nothing."

"No, you don't get it, brother. And *you* weren't listening." Andy drilled a finger into his own chest. "I'm a soldier. It's my job to stop the enemy, kill 'em if I have to. This is war. Yeah, people die. What d'you expect?"

Good question. James' eyes roved up and down his brother. Andy sure tossed it back, didn't he? A sigh.

"I guess I expect too much," James said. "I'd like people to come to their senses and stop killing. Murder's not an answer." He peered outside.

"You killed several Indians. And..." Andy's words softened. "You're always trying to kill One Wing again. What's the difference?"

Another damn good question. Rebs and Indians. *Is* there a difference?

"James?"

"You're right. I don't get it." James wadded up the shirt in his hand. "I just know killing's wrong. Why can't we just let each other be?"

Silence. Andy smoothed a pair of pants on his cot and folded the sleeves inward. His voice dropped to a whisper.

"Why? Cause it ain't in our nature just to let things be."

With his back turned to his brother, James shook his head again. How could he convince Andy that hurting people didn't solve problems, only made things worse? More importantly, how could he keep Andy out of battle?

A sudden chill ran down his spine.

This must have been how Trace felt every time I did something without thinking. No wonder he always worried about me.

James chewed on the end of the pencil. The blank paper in front of him stared back, taunting his jumbled thoughts. The paper was as empty and scary as the journey ahead. He'd made it so far, but would he survive the rest of his sentence? In fact, would any of these men ever come back to Tucson and Mesilla one day? What would they come home to? His pencil wrote words in rhythm to his pounding heart.

Dear Trace,

Tomorrow we're headed west over to Ft. Yuma, meeting up with Carleton's men. Before we leave, I wanted to get a letter off to you. I'm doing much better now. I haven't punched Andy in several weeks. And I'm hoping the healed bruise on his cheek is the last he'll ever have from me. What a year we've had!

As 1862 looms in front of us, I pray it is a much better year. I'm sure it'll be full of excitement and surprises. Hopefully, they'll be good. I'll write again when the express mule train finds us as we walk across the Sonoran Desert.

Until then, give beautiful Teresa a kiss for us.

-James and Andy

James reread his printing, folded it, and then tucked the letter into an envelope. As he addressed it, a voice outside his tent called his name. Captain Greene's Texas accent.

"Sir?" James answered as he held the flap open, and before he could step out, Greene stepped in. James wasn't sure whether to salute or not. Out here in Arizona, the army wasn't very demanding about proper protocol. Captain Homer Greene stopped in the middle of the tent, its fabric brushing the top of his head.

Aware of the whiskey bottle tucked under his own bunk, James pointed to Andy's cot.

"Please sit, Captain."

Would the captain find the whiskey. Could he smell the latest sip on his breath?

"This is a surprise," James said. "Figured you'd be busy

getting ready for the move tomorrow."

Greene nodded and grunted while glancing around the tiny tent.

"Yeah, lots to do."

James followed his commander's gaze, a knot growing in the pit of his stomach. While Greene sat, he placed his feet in front of his stash. If the purpose of this visit wasn't to bust him for drinking, then what did the captain want? Was it bad news? Had to be. Had something happened to someone in his family? That was the only reason a commanding officer would personally visit an enlisted man. A crazy one at that.

"I got a letter from..."

Here it comes. Maybe it's younger brother Luke!

"...The judge in Mesilla. The one who sentenced you to the war." Greene's thin lips curled at one end. "He wanted to know how you've fared. If the army has helped your 'condition' or if I thought you should go to jail."

James closed his eyes and sent a quick thanks heavenward that this wasn't about his family. He glanced at the Captain.

Greene's eyes met James'. "Well, what do you think, Mr. Colton?"

James thought about the past few months. He'd definitely gotten better. "This was a good choice, sir. You saw me the first few weeks. Everyone ran when I got close." He wagged his head. "They still stay at arm's length, but they're getting closer."

"My thoughts exactly, son. I don't think jail's the place for you. Hell, this is jail enough." Greene stood, bumping his head on the soft, cotton canvas. "See you early tomorrow."

Before Greene threw the tent flaps back, James rushed his words.

"Sir, I'm curious. Wonder if I can ask you about something."

Greene turned back to James, then nodded.

James caught his commander's quizzical stare. "Well, sir, it's like this. Everyone around me, except my brothers, keep me at a distance. Guess they don't like getting bit, punched or kicked." He paused, his gaze falling to the ground. "Hell, even the girls won't... you know."

The captain nodded.

"Well, sir, you've always been so understanding, so patient with me. Even when I punched you in the stomach 'cause I thought you were One Wing. You didn't court martial me." James cringed at the memory. "Why?"

The captain stared into the tent flaps, then into his trembling hands.

Speculation crept into James' mind. Something terrible had happened. Maybe the captain would say and maybe he wouldn't. But the clenched hands gave him away.

Several blinks. A few stops and starts. Greene looked away as he spoke.

"Ten years ago, my kid sister was stolen by the Comanches. She was just twelve."

"I'm sorry, sir. I had no idea."

Greene held up a hand.

"We got her back. Took two years, but we got her back. She'd changed, of course. You can't spend two years with Indians as a captive and stay the same. I don't have to tell you." A wag of the head, a huge sigh.

"It's eight years she's been back, Captain. How's she doing now?"

Greene turned his back to James. "She was much younger than you when she was captured. She didn't understand."

"Sir?"

Greene spun around. His fiery eyes and balled fists made James take a step backwards. Although this officer was easily three inches shorter than James, his anger made up for any lack of stature. James waited while Greene controlled his rage, his pain, his anguish. Little by little the captain's breathing slowed, and he looked into James' eyes.

"She killed herself and her half-breed son last year. Couldn't put it behind her."

James detected a tear in the man's eye. He wouldn't blame him if he cried. There were certain things to cry about, and this was one of them.

Greene's shoulders slumped. "Since I couldn't help Elizabeth, I thought maybe I could do something for you. I've watched you go through the same things she did." He put a firm hand on James' shoulder. "Don't want you to end up like her."

James grasped the commander's hand and shook it.

"Thank you, sir. I know it's been hard."

Greene pulled out of James' grip, turned, and pushed aside

the tent flaps. He held one out, then turned back to James.

"Better watch that drinking. It'll get you in trouble."

The canvas flaps swung back in place. The sides of the tent breathed in and out, whooshing in rhythm to the winter breeze. James turned around, blinked twice, and stared at the Indian chief sitting on the floor. The deerskin wickiup pulsated. A sudden gust of cold wind sent goosebumps over James' skin.

A drink. Whiskey'll fix everything.

James lunged for the bottle under his bed. Eager to fight off demons, he polished off half of the bottle. It went down smooth. Armed with liquid courage, James knew that old nightmare was gone. He turned around, rubbed his eyes shut, then peered through his fingers. Cochise remained on his rabbit fur blanket.

James eased back, his gaze frozen on the image.

"No." Another step. "You're not real."

He forced his legs to move. Shivers shook his body. One more step back, he groped behind him for the wickiup's covering. His hand slid along the hide. He fumbled for the opening. A way out. Escape.

Where the hell was it?

"Here you are." Apache words boomed behind him.

James spun.

It was One Wing.

Cornered like a caged rabbit, James knew there was no escape. The snare had been sprung and those Indians would kill him as soon as they finished the torment. He sidled away from One Wing. But Cochise sat mere inches away, too. Could he run? Somehow dodge the Apaches? Somehow escape?

One Wing held up a black stick. "Look what I got for our trip tomorrow."

The whip. Stolen from Trace's stagecoach.

James stared at the rod One Wing held in his hand. A quick glance over his shoulder proved Cochise hadn't moved—yet. How soon would that Apache leader wrap his strong arms around James, pinning his arms, allowing One Wing to once again bind his wrists, then sink a fist into his stomach or knee his groin?

Cochise's hot breath on his neck. James balled his fists.

One Wing moved closer and waved the whip. "Here. Touch it," he said. "It's a carved walking stick I bought from an old Mexican farmer. Said it brings good luck." He shoved it in front of James' face. "Touch it."

Cochise's arms smothered James.

Kicking out then wriggling free from his captor's grip, James head-butted One Wing. The surprised Indian flew back out the wickiup door and crashed to the ground. James followed and pounced on top of One Wing. "No more. No... more. Kill you."

Both men rolled over and over, like men in a prison yard brawl. James punched his enemy and entwined his free hand in the Indian's brown hair. Perching on the back of the Apache whose face smashed into the dirt, James yanked the head up and searched his own pants for a knife. Finding none, he grabbed a second handful of hair and slammed One Wing's forehead into the ground.

Encouraged by the sickening smack, James lifted the Indian's head, then whacked it again and again into the dirt. Red liquid spread across the sand. James pulled up on the hair, then slammed down the face. One Wing tried to roll over, but James ground his knee into his assailant's right shoulder, smashing it further into the dirt.

"Good God, James!"

The voice rang in his ears as hands grabbed his shoulders. He sailed off of One Wing, rolled several feet across the sand, and stopped under a mesquite bush. Pushing branches off his face, he glanced at the wad of brown hair tangled in his fingers. He shook it off.

James struggled to clear his head. Men yelled with excited voices ordering people here and there. He rolled onto his side and spotted his commanding officer kneeling next to a man lying on the ground. Greene looked over his shoulder. Their eyes locked.

Before James could get to his knees, two soldiers positioned themselves on either side of him, grabbed his arms, and hoisted him up. He recognized them. They were men from Mesilla who'd joined the Union army when the Confederates got too close. One was Albert Fountain and the other was a business owner, last name Reynolds.

"Get the doctor!"

James heard the Captain shout the order at least three times.

Reynolds cocked his head toward James.

"Good thing Captain Greene was close by, Colton. You'd of killed your brother. His head's bashed in pretty good from where I stand."

As if struck by lightning, James realized what he'd done.

"God, no! Andy!"

Spotting the blood soaking into the dirt, James jerked out of the soldiers' firm grasp.

"I killed him. God, I killed him," James cried. He rushed to Andy and slid to a stop. He shoved aside Greene.

"Andy? Andy? God, no!" James pushed the hair away from his brother's forehead and wiped blood off Andy's closed eyes. He cradled his brother, rocking him, muttering apologies.

Vice-like hands grabbed his arms, again hauling him to his feet. Struggling against them, he twisted and turned to wrench free of the restraints. The hands held him out of reach of his unconscious brother.

He looked down at Andy. Blood poured from Andy's mashed nose and trickled from scrapes and gashes on his forehead. James held up his blood-coated hands. Searching the face of his commander, he saw anger mixed with concern lining Greene's forehead.

The camp doctor loped toward him. Struggling against firm hands clamping down, James pulled and twisted, frantic to loosen their grip. Unable to wrestle free, he knew the only thing he could do was stand by as the doctor worked on his brother.

"Doc? Captain?" James peered at the back of both men. "Andy?"

The knot in James' stomach along with whiskey rose in his throat, and the words were difficult to speak over the lump. He jerked against the iron grip.

"Let me go."

Greene glanced over his shoulder, then nodded at Reynolds and Fountain.

James wrenched his right arm out of Reynold's grip and felt his captain's gaze pierce his heart. Released, James knelt at his brother's side. The doctor placed a stethoscope on Andy's chest. James swiped at the blood covering his brother's mouth.

"God, I'm sorry." His words gurgled in his throat.

Another soldier holding several towels knelt beside the doctor. After pulling the stethoscope's earpieces out of his ears, Doctor Meyers looked at James.

"Heartbeat's strong," Meyers said.

James dropped his head and gazed at Andy. "Thank you, God." Then it hit him. His eyes snapped to Captain Greene. "What if I'd had my knife?"

Out of the corner of his eye, James could see the doctor's towel pat Andy's forehead until the scrapes and cuts showed through the blood. With great care, the doctor wiped the sticky liquid from around Andy's nose. The torrent of blood slowed.

"Wake up, Andy. Andy?" James shook his brother. Guilt replaced panic. Why'd he still do these crazy things? When would they stop? And where was Trace at a time like this? He needed him now. Right now. To tell him what to do, tell him how to quit hurting people. He needed help through this. Whiskey would do the trick.

A strong grip on his shoulder jerked James out of his thoughts. "Let's go, son."

James stared up into the face of Captain Greene, flanked by Fountain and Reynolds. One of them produced a revolver.

"Can't leave Andy. He needs me." James tugged against the powerful hold.

"They'll take care of him over at the infirmary until he regains consciousness," Captain Greene said as he pulled James' arm.

"I'm staying. Hell, I'm the one who did this to him. Should be me taking care of him." James wriggled against the tightening clamps on his arms.

"He'll be seen to. Nothing you can do here. Let's go." Greene stared into James' eyes. "You have no choice, son."

The doctor and two men carried his limp brother away.

CHAPTER SEVENTEEN

James stared into the inky blackness and watched the stars twinkle as 1861 came to a close. Guitar music wafted from a popular cantina a few blocks away, shrill laughter from *señoritas,* and then sudden bursts of gunfire penetrated the usually still night. Heightened giggles and a few more shots added to the revelry.

Must be the new year.

He slumped against the adobe jail wall.

Won't be a new year for me. Be just like the old one, only worse.

A muffled voice behind him spoke out of the darkness. "Helluva way to start a new year."

James spun around. The silhouette of a man leaned against the cell bars. Light pouring from a kerosene lantern bathed Andy in a soft amber glow. James took three hesitant steps toward his brother and then stood on the other side of the bars. He hung his head.

"Don't spur yourself, James. I'm all right." Andy mumbled his slow words, as if he held rocks in his mouth.

"Let me look at you," James said. His trembling hands reached through the bars and cradled his brother's battered face, turning it side to side. White bandages covered Andy's forehead, but the red, black and purple marks ringing his left eye and running down to his chin glowed like hot embers.

Andy grabbed his brother's hands, held them away from his face. "I said I'm fine. Don't baby me. Can't do much damage to this face anyway."

"Looks terrible. Hurt?"

Andy grinned, then winced. "Only when I'm awake." He shrugged. "Look, we're leaving tomorrow. Already kissed all the girls. Who needs a pretty face just to march across that old desert?"

James peered out the barred window again. "Thought I'd killed you. What kind of monster tries to kill his own brother?"

"You're not a monster." Andy grabbed the metal bars. "You're a man trying to get *rid* of monsters, fighting demons only you can see."

James' chest constricted, the words hard to say. "I've made a decision. Hope you can understand."

"Better not be what I think you're thinking. I won't let you do it."

"I have to. It's the only way I can protect you and other innocent people. At least this way, the only men I beat up will be low-life criminals. Not my kid brother." He met Andy's stare, then glanced away.

"No! You're not going to spend the next ten years in prison, James. That's not the answer!" Andy reached through the bars and grabbed his brother's sleeve.

Pulled against the cold bars, James jammed against the metal and his brother's arm.

Andy dropped his voice to a whisper. "It's not the answer."

"Then what is? Wait around 'til I beat you so bad you die? You were lucky this time."

Lucky I didn't have my knife.

"Next time it might be worse," James said. He paused and studied his brother's bruised face. "Just what is the answer, Andy?"

Andrew Colton wagged his head. "Don't know for sure, but jail ain't it. This beating was my fault. I should've known what was going on." He touched his lips and nose. "I needed a bigger nose, anyway. The old one was too small."

For the first time in hours, James smiled. The image of his brother lying on the ground, blood spreading around his battered face was replaced with the vision of a red, bulbous nose planted between two tiny, brown eyes. A clown nose dwarfed Andy's face.

James and Andy laughed.

* * *

January 1, 1862, dawned a steel gray sky, cold with a light drizzle of rain, sprinkled with snow. James pulled the thin wool blanket tighter around his shivering body, then rolled over on the jail bunk. With his face to the adobe wall, he thought about what he would say to his brother. Goodbye didn't express his thoughts, but what else could he say? He wished he was going on the march with his company, but there was no way Captain Greene would allow it. He'd be crazy to let James anywhere near sane people. Guess he'd just have to wait here in the Tucson jail until... until what? Until he got better or ended up like Greene's sister?

"On your feet, soldier." The gravely voice bounced off the mud and straw walls.

James jerked his eyes open and rolled toward the cell door. Focusing on the sergeant, he sat up, the blanket falling to the floor.

"Out of the rack, Colton. Got a long walk ahead of you." Sergeant Williams produced a wad of jangling keys, selected one, and then inserted it into the lock. The opening door creaked as James found his feet.

Running his hand through his hair, James studied the large man in front of him. "I'm going?" He stepped into cold boots. "Thought Greene said I'd stay here until 'hell freezes over', or something like that."

"'Bout froze over now. Look. All I know is it's damn cold outside and Greene told me to fetch you to his office. On the double." The sergeant swung the door back and cocked his head to the right. "Don't give me no trouble and we'll get along great."

James thought about the powerful man standing by his side. The rest of his life would probably be spent with people just like this sergeant pulling him and ordering him about.

All right. If that's what it takes for me not to hurt anybody again, then that's what I'll have to do. Might as well get used to it.

Standing at attention in front of Greene's desk, James watched his captain stuff a few folded maps into his backpack. James had stood for close to ten minutes, and with each passing minute wondered if Greene even knew he was there. Maybe he was invisible. Maybe he was still asleep and this was just a dream. No, his legs were telling him he'd been standing for a while.

Greene glanced around the room, ran his hand through his hair, then removed Lincoln's picture from the wall. The captain took four long steps to the desk and slammed the picture on the wooden top.

"Dammit, James," Greene said. "What the hell am I gonna do with you?"

109

"Sir?"

"How in the good Lord's name am I supposed to let you march with the men? How can I protect them from Johnny Reb, Cochise, and you?" Greene pulled Lincoln's picture from the frame, stuffed it into the backpack. He huffed into his chest and grew silent.

"Sir?" James gathered enough courage to speak. "Thought I was staying here. I can still do that if you don't want me to go."

Greene huffed twice more and brought his voice down. "I can't let you stay. Rebs are on the outskirts of town. My orders are to give all the army's stores to the citizens and burn everything else." He stared at James. "We're in full retreat, son."

James' back muscles tingled. Well, Andy wanted war. Now it looked like he was about to get it.

"If I leave you in jail, James, those Confederates will slice you seventeen different ways from Sunday. Won't be anything left of you. I just can't leave you sitting here, completely unprotected." Greene shook the contents of his backpack, tied it while surveying the stark, dim room. "You gotta come with us."

James watched the Captain hoist his pack and head toward the door.

"Sir?"

Greene reached the door, turned around.

James met the captain's stare. "I promise I'll behave. I'll do everything I can to keep from hurting people." He joined the captain at the door.

Greene planted a hand on James' shoulder. "Just hurt people who are truly trying to kill you. All right?"

James nodded and followed his commander into the cold day.

CHAPTER EIGHTEEN

Trace plunged the last fiery horseshoe into cold water. Vapors spurted into air. Metal hissed. Steam clouds clung to Trace's face and shirt. He pulled out the horseshoe and examined the metal. Nodding, he pushed the shoe back into the fire, then wiped his face with his free forearm. Last one for today. Then, home for a quick meal, an hour or so holding the most beautiful woman in the world, then off to bed. Maybe he'd sleep tonight.

Sleep. He shook his head. Although it'd been close to a year since his release from Cochise last February, he still woke screaming most every night. The sleep and rest he needed, deserved, wouldn't come even with his wife's tender embrace. And now, Teresa wasn't feeling well. She didn't sleep any better than he did. Hoping she was just tired from all the work she'd been doing—keeping a house, cooking, cleaning—Trace decided that when he got home, he'd insist she see a doctor first thing tomorrow. Just in case.

"Horseshoe's about to melt, Trace."

Trace lost his grip of the tongs and dropped the shoe into the dirt. He whipped around coming within inches of whacking Judge Falls with the hot tongs.

The man in the black frock coat jumped back and frowned at Trace. "Whoa. Easy. Didn't mean to frighten you." He held up both hands.

"Sorry, Judge. Didn't hear you come in." Trace apologized as he lifted the dirt-encrusted shoe with the tongs, then set both on a wooden table. Pulling off a glove, he shook hands with the man in front of him.

Judge Albert Falls' gaze swept the inside of the livery stable. "Is there a place where we can talk? It'll only take a minute. I know you're busy."

Trace's stomach knotted, and every muscle in his body tensed.

"What's wrong, Judge?"

"Just need to talk, Trace. No one's died or anything."

Mouth dry, Trace cocked his head to his left. "Over there, closer to the door's more light. Want some water?"

Shaking his head, Judge Falls followed Trace to the door, then eased his body onto a nail keg.

What was the judge going to say? Had to be about James. Why was there a permanent knot in his throat regarding that little brother of his?

Wiping his chin, Trace rolled a nail keg across two stalls, settling it in front of the judge. He sat and swiped a dirty hand across his mouth. The water he'd downed had no effect on his dry throat.

"What's going on?" Trace asked.

Falls dug into his coat pocket and pulled out a folded piece of paper. "Got a letter from your brother's commanding officer, Captain Greene. Some of the news is good."

The judge stuck the note back in his pocket without offering it.

Trace studied the judge's face for a hint of upcoming news. Nothing. "Glad to hear it, sir. Seems this past year, all the news was bad."

Falls nodded. "Greene reports that James is becoming more rational, even made a few friends, and has had only a few 'episodes' recently."

A grin lifted one corner of Trace's mouth. "That's great. I knew he'd be getting better."

Silence.

"Judge?"

More silence. Something was wrong, definitely wrong.

Falls peered around the dim stable, then back at Trace. He took a deep breath. "Son, there's been trouble. Seems on New Year's Eve, James nearly killed your other brother. Mistook him for... One Wing?"

Clenching his fists, Trace focused his gaze on the judge's face. "Andy? How's Andy?"

"Broken nose, cuts and scrapes on his face. Unconscious for about an hour. Apparently he had one helluva shiner." Judge Falls glanced outside. "Greene says that James tried to slice Andy's throat but, thankfully, had no knife."

"Good God!" Trace jumped to his feet, then turned his back to Judge Falls. "Didn't bring Andy out here to get killed. Especially by his own kin." Running a hand through his hair, he leaned against a pole. Eyes closed, jumbled images swirled through his head, thoughts bumping into each other, colliding with feelings.

A hand on his shoulder and a voice in his ear shook Trace out of his reverie.

"Just thought you'd want to know about your brothers. A while back I wrote Captain Greene and asked if James belonged in jail, if it'd be better for him. He said no, and despite this latest setback, I agree." Judge Falls shook his head. "I remember when James exploded in the courtroom. I'd never seen anything like it."

Trace's gaze hit the dirt floor.

"I felt so sorry for that young man," the judge continued. "The demons that must taunt him day and night... well, I just can't imagine what he's going through. Wanted to cry, I did. Later when I told my wife all about him, it took her ten minutes to dry up."

Trace clenched his fists.

"I'll never forget the agony on his face, the pain he must've gone through. Still going through." Judge Falls dropped his voice. "You, too, for that matter." He shifted his weight and patted Trace on the back.

Trace turned his attention to the judge. "Sir?"

Falls wrinkled his forehead. "Said I know you both had a hard time getting through that."

"It hasn't been easy, Judge." Trace shoved bitter memories aside.

"I'm glad your brother chose the army. It's what he needed." Falls buttoned his coat. "So, for now, James'll stay in the army and out of jail."

Managing only a nod, Trace shook hands with the judge as he stepped into the fading sunlight. Watching the officer of the court walk down the street, Trace knew he had to find James and help him. Nothing else mattered but helping his brother.

* * *

Trace sat on the sofa, one leg resting on the other, and ran his finger along the edge of his boot. Smells of supper still hung in the air. He sighed and listened to Teresa finishing the dishes. Eyes on his boot, he studied where the leather upper met the sole.

How can I tell her I've got to go? And should I do it now or wait until after she sees the doctor tomorrow? Either way is going to be hard.

"You're unusually quiet tonight," Teresa said as she wiped her hands on her apron, then draped it over a chair as she walked into the living room. She bent over and kissed his cheek. "What's wrong?"

"Come sit by me," Trace replied and patted the cushion next to his. "You've been on your feet all day. Rest."

"I'm fine, really." Teresa sat down and leaned back, her eyes closing. "Feel like I could sleep for a month, or maybe clean through the rest of winter. Wouldn't that be nice?"

"Sure would. But winter's almost gone. It's already February."

Growing silent, Trace's thoughts turned again to his brother. February. This time last year, he and James were struggling to survive Cochise and One Wing's torture. At that time, life with Teresa was a dream, an illusion, something that would never be real.

How lucky he was now to be living that dream.

Trace looked over at his wife and smiled. She meant everything to him and here he was ready to ride off into the unknown to help his brothers.

I need to be two people. Question is—how?

Teresa's breath came in steady rhythm. Trace rose from the sofa, cradled her in his arms, and carried her to bed.

* * *

Lost in thought, Trace pounded yet another glowing horseshoe in rhythm to the beating of his heart.

James and me. We're never gonna recover. We'll always have demons, always cringe at certain sounds, always cry out in the night. How can I help my brother when I'm barely hanging on myself?

Swede Bergstrom wheeled a small cart overflowing with horseshoes over to the pile near Trace and dumped more on top. Wiping his face with a sweaty forearm, he spoke over his shoulder.

"How many horses can one army have, Trace? Those Confederates must replace shoes every three miles!" He nodded. "Good for business though."

Bergstrom waited for a response and turned around when he didn't get one. His blue eyes narrowed.

"What's wrong?" He asked as he pulled off both gloves. "James again?"

Trace peered past his boss and into the dim stable. "Almost killed Andy. I gotta find a way to get rid of those memories before he succeeds. Trace pulled in air, but his shoulders slumped as if they were deflated. "But Teresa needs me here."

"Andy all right now?" Bergstrom stepped in closer, placing a hand on Trace's shoulder. The grip firm, yet comforting.

Trace nodded. Gripping the metal tongs and hammer, he dropped his arms to his sides. "Don't know how to get through this. Don't know how to help myself much less James." His gaze met Bergstrom's. "Tell me what to do."

The livery owner shook his head. "Can't. Wish I could. No, every man's got to figure out his own problems. No one can solve them for you."

Trace shook his head, stepped toward the door, then gulped water from the dipper. "I feel so damn useless. James needs me and there's nothing I can do."

Bergstrom took the dipper from Trace's hand, and sipped the remaining liquid. "Is it he needs you... or you need him?"

Trace stared at the Big Swede. Being hit in the face with a board wouldn't have startled him as much as Bergstrom's question. Did he even have an answer?

* * *

"Supper smells great, Teresa. Fried chicken?" Trace removed his hat and hung it by the front door. Tantalizing aromas of cooking chicken sailed around his nose. He sniffed his way into the kitchen.

Teresa placed the last piece of meat on a plate, then turned to Trace.

Tears were streaming down her flour-speckled cheeks. Trace grabbed her, enveloping her trembling body with his arms. He rocked her back and forth.

"It'll be all right," he soothed. "Whatever it is, we'll get through this together."

Teresa gazed up into his eyes. Her brown eyes reflected Trace's confusion, his apprehension. Her mouth opened and closed. Small sounds escaped, but nothing intelligible came out. No real words passed her lips.

His heart in his throat, Trace ran through a mental list of possible disasters. The doctor gave her two months to live? His folks were hurt, dead? James? Luke? Andy? Her relatives in Santa Fe? The war?

"Teresa. Tell me." Trace cradled her chin in his hand.

Swiping at a tear trickling into her mouth, she met his stare. "You're going to be a pa."

CHAPTER NINETEEN

James pulled off his boot, turned it upside down, and shook out the rocks and dirt. A small sand dune grew by his foot. Removing the other boot, he repeated the exercise then tossed it next to the first one. Both socks yanked off, he wiggled his toes. Cool February air circulated around his bare skin. He didn't fight the grin climbing up his face.

First he plunged his right foot and then his left into the wide Colorado River. His fiery toes sizzled, the water swirling around aching feet. Closing his eyes, James sighed as the circulation returned to his lower extremities. Swaddled in serenity, he knew life couldn't get better than this.

He remembered moments earlier, just when he'd figured his poor feet couldn't carry him an inch farther, the Colorado River had appeared over the hill. At first he thought it a mirage—or a miracle. Splayed out in front of him, the ribbon of water beckoned like an enchanting, seductive mistress. It tantalized his senses until he found himself running into her welcoming arms, throwing himself at her charms, her mercy.

James lay stretched out on the shore, his face warmed with the sunshine. The cool water on his feet brought a sigh up from his soul. Despite his efforts to resist, sleep overtook him.

Face burning, he rubbed his eyes, then opened them. The sun danced and sparkled on the water. The river, running fast this time of year, produced small waves as the water hit the rocks. It gurgled, creating a rhythm all its own. Was that a song James heard?

I must be tired.

Judging by the shadows, it was well after noon, much later than when he'd laid back on the shoulders of that beautiful shore. A glance to his left disclosed an extended line of at least forty soldiers sitting or lying next to the river, their feet also dangling in the water.

117

A few men lay in the river, soaking up the welcome relief.

He shielded his eyes from the bright sunshine and turned to the man closest to him.

"Feels good, eh, Fountain?" James asked.

Albert Fountain didn't bother to open his eyes, but a grin flickered across his face.

"Just what this weary traveler needed, Colton."

James regarded Fountain. If he were to claim a friend, it would have to be the man resting next to him, this man also from Mesilla. Even as a friend, Fountain kept his distance. James didn't blame him. Everyone stayed at least three feet away. A safety zone.

"Glad Fort Yuma's just downstream." Fountain opened one eye, shielded it, and glanced over at James. "Couldn't walk another mile on these stumps."

"Hope we stay here for months. I'm not ready to march anywhere for a long time." James rubbed his wet feet, grinning at the wrinkled skin. "At least they're clean."

"Where's that brother of yours? Aren't his feet on fire, too?" Fountain sat up, opened both eyes, and ran his hand through his black hair.

James' gaze swept up and down the river, then stopped on a nearby figure resembling Andy. He squinted. "Looks like Andy's way up there, headed this way." He pointed north. "He heard a few Indians were selling food and went to buy something to eat."

"Hope he brings us back something." Fountain brushed dirt off his foot and pulled on a sock.

"Yeah. Something good." Arching his back, readjusting his hat, James wagged his head. "That kid. Andy's always been kinda like a big pup. Always sticking his nose in places, smelling everything, and curious as hell about the world."

Fountain let out a laugh. "Know what you mean. I watched him on the way over here. I'll bet there isn't a rock he didn't look under or a mesquite bush he didn't inspect. Clear across that Sonoran Desert. Took four steps for our every one." He brought his feet out of the water and shook them.

James shielded his eyes and looked up at Andy standing over him.

"Look what I bought, James." Andy plopped on the sand between the two men. Holding out his hand, he opened his fist to reveal a small, deep yellow ball.

James picked it up, turned it over and around. "What is it?"

"The Indian lady up stream said it's an orange from California. They put them in straw to keep 'em fresh and eat 'em throughout the year."

Fountain picked it out of James' palm, held it up, and sniffed the rind. "This isn't orange, it's yellow." He turned it over. "They grow in the ground?"

Andy shook his head. "Trees. Big ones, she said. Way over on the other side of the river."

"How 'bout that? I've heard of 'em, but never seen one up close." James turned to his brother. "What's it taste like?"

Andy shrugged. "Don't know. She said they were full of juice and really good." He glanced from his brother to Fountain. A sly grin crinkled the skin around his dancing eyes. "Wanna try it?"

"'Course. I didn't walk all the way across the desert just to eat the same old food from back home." Fountain handed it back to Andy. "Here, show us how it's done."

Andy squared his shoulders and took a small bite of the skin. Lips puckering, he chewed until he could swallow. "Not bad. Not bad at all." He handed it to James.

James studied the yellow ball with the bite taken out, looked at Fountain, and then eyed his brother. Andy seemed to have survived this new food, and liked it. Not to be outdone by his littlest brother, he, too, would try it. A trickle of liquid ran down his hand. James sniffed at it and glanced up. He opened his mouth and plunged his teeth into half of the fruit.

Juice squirted all over his face and ran down his chin. Mouth full of pulp, rind, and juice, James nodded. Wordlessly handing it to Fountain, he munched on the orange and swallowed the tangy meat.

Fountain joined in the experiment, a smile coming to his lips as the tasty fruit hung part way out of his mouth like a roadrunner with a lizard. Juice dribbled down his chin and dropped onto his shirt. Andy popped the remainder of the treat into his mouth and grinned as juice inched down his face.

James swallowed the pulp. "Damn good. If the rest of California's this fine, I'm glad we came." He slapped his younger brother on the back. "Thanks, Andy. That Indian got any more?"

"Yeah, but *you* gotta buy the next one." Andy grinned back at his brother and swiped at the sticky liquid on his chin. He squatted by the river's edge, scooped up a handful of water, then splashed it on his face.

James and Fountain joined Andy and splashed water on their sticky faces. James eyed his brother on his right, then his friend on his left, who was much closer than he usually stood. Without uttering a sound, James grabbed Fountain around the waist, pulling him toward the river. He scooped up Andy with his right arm. The momentum took the three men into the middle of the river. They hit the water.

The men dunked each other, splashing cool river water onto their sweaty faces. James tossed his brother into the deepest part of the wide Colorado, then watched Andy gain his footing and stalk him like a wild bear. Fountain hooted when Andy in turn threw James into the same deep water. A grinning, nearly drowned James stood chest-deep in swirling river water and yelled friendly threats to Andy and Fountain.

Half an hour later, breathing hard and worn out from their fun, the three men dragged themselves out of the water, and sprawled on the ground soaking up the sun's warmth. James lay face down on the bank, head cradled in his arm. When was the last time he'd laughed that hard? He couldn't remember. Seemed like years and years. Yeah, it'd been a lifetime—a helluva lifetime.

Lying on his back next to James, Andy wiped the last drops of water from his face. "Next time you need a bath, big brother, don't include me." He flicked the remaining moisture at James.

Fountain raised his head and glanced at the teenager sprawled next to him. "You needed a bath, too, Andy. Don't go giving your big brother a hard time." He sat up and wrung out his shirtsleeve over Andy's stomach.

Andy bolted upright, grabbed Fountain around the chest, and wrestled him back down to the ground. Both men took turns pinning each other.

"Uncle, uncle. I give, Andy." Fountain rolled out from under the teenager. He sat up and stared at James' brother. "Damn, boy. Where'd you get all your muscles? You're strong as an ox."

"Ugly as one, too." James buried his head in his arms.

Andy jumped to his feet, hoisted his brother up by the back of his shirt. "Ugly? I'll show you ugly." Grabbing him around the chest and shoulders, Andy pulled James toward the river.

Both men hit the water like a cannon ball. Waves exploded

overhead as the brothers thrashed. Within minutes, the Colton boys had dunked each other twice and splashed their friend watching from the safety of the shore.

A voice boomed from the water's edge. "All right, men. Time's up. Gotta get a move on."

James glanced up at the sergeant standing next to Fountain. Energy escaping through his fingertips, James used the last bit of strength to haul his brother up by his shirtsleeve. The two men stood like drowned tom cats, water dripping down their faces, clothes clinging to their heaving bodies. James couldn't help but grin.

Andy scooped up a handful of water and tossed it in his brother's face.

Walking backwards, James splashed handfuls back at Andy. "Good thing the sergeant stopped us. I was just about to win." James stumbled over a slick rock, then plopped back into the water.

"Not hardly." Andy extended a hand and pulled his brother to his feet.

CHAPTER TWENTY

James yawned, stretched, then regarded the warm early morning sun filtering through the canvas tent. Time for reveille already?

Andy was up, tucking in his shirt and smoothing his unruly hair. "What d'ya say we go find some more oranges, James? That one's been on my mind ever since the first day we got here."

James yawned again. Fatigue, brought on by the previous day's skirmish drills and adobe wall building, faded with sleep. "That mean I gotta get up?"

"Well, that old Indian woman sure as hell's not coming here, inside this tent." Andy kicked the bottom of his brother's foot. "Come on. Got half the day off today and the sun's already up."

Another stretch and yawn. "All right, all right. I'm up."

Scratching his bare chest, James ran his hand over the fading pink lash marks. Although he'd become used to them, at moments like this, he recoiled from the ugliness, the memories. He fought the urge to run. Where could he go? No where. There's no where to run, no sanctuary from the memories.

No place to hide.

"James, you all right?"

James glanced at his brother. "Sure. Let's go rouse Fountain and get breakfast."

Half an hour later, the three men headed up river away from Fort Yuma, away from Louis Jaeger's General Store, and followed a wide foot path other soldiers, trappers, and Indians used.

Andy loped ahead of Fountain and James, then turned back, waiting for them to catch up.

"Can't get over how many tents are out here," Andy said. "What d'ya think? A hundred maybe?"

James peered over the sea of white canvas scattered behind every rock and mesquite bush. "At least."

122

"That's why they call it a city." Andy squinted at the encampment. "Arizona City. I like the sound of that."

"Me, too," Fountain said. "There's probably closer to two hundred, though." Fountain spread his arms wide. "All this room and the people jam together like sheep. Guess they think that'll protect them from the Indians."

Andy marched in time with the others. "Why'd anybody be scared of these old Indian women selling things? They seem perfectly harmless to me."

Nerves tense, James peered into the desert. "It's not the old women, Andy. It's their sons. They're still killing the settlers around here."

"So keep your peepers open." Fountain pointed to his eyes. "Don't want to have to scrape up what's left of you." He shook his head and looked over at James. "Sorry. I didn't mean it."

James heard cackling, Indian voices above him as moccasined feet dragged him toward the dreaded saguaro cactus. He flinched at a hand on his shoulder.

James covered his face, hoping to protect it from another whipping. A voice in his ear. "You all right?"

He nodded at the voice, angry with himself for letting memories take control, James lowered his hands, then pulled in a couple deep breaths.

No place to hide.

"It's just right around this next bend in the river." Andy pointed northeast. "Hope she's got more of those oranges. I can taste 'em already."

"If she doesn't, maybe we'll just march over to this California and pick us some ourselves." Fountain said, but his grin had faded. He put his hand on James' arm. "I'm sorry 'bout what I said earlier. Didn't mean to... you know."

James patted his new friend on the back.

"It's all right. It wasn't you. It's me." James paused, squared his shoulders, and cocked his head toward the trail. "If we're gonna get those oranges, we better hurry. Race you!" Taking off at a fast trot, James concentrated on running.

Bluffs rose ten feet overhead. Sand and pebbles crunched under their racing feet. The only other sound—men wheezing. As Andy sprinted out in front, James slowed and wiped the sweat pouring down his face. He sucked in air. Fountain trotted next to him, sweat glistening on his face also. Their trot reduced to a walk.

Fountain peered into the desert. "Where's that kid brother of yours? I swear he's part race horse." His chest heaved with each breath.

Glancing around at the yuccas dotting the sand, the cloudless sky dancing overhead, James shook his head. "Think he left us behind after the first three steps." He held his throbbing ribs.

It's been a year since the torture ended. Why in the hell do I still hurt so bad?

"No tents this far away from Arizona City." Fountain stopped next to James and shrugged. "Ain't much around here, except some old cottonwoods down by the river. Probably rattlesnakes. Hell, I don't even see people."

"Remind me to ask Andy how he found this old woman anyway." James said as he studied the barren desert to his right. "Nothing out here."

Fountain nodded. "Kinda spooky."

James' chest tightened. "Andy? Andy!" His voice echoed off the boulders to his left.

"He's all right." Fountain shielded his eyes from the morning sun. "That pup brother of yours just wandered off again is all. He's probably right up around this bend."

James and Fountain rounded a sharp bend, then slid to a halt. Not more than ten feet in front of them stood Andy, his arms held high overhead, with three soldiers aiming rifles at his chest. James' world froze, but every muscle in his body screamed *run*.

The tallest of the men turned his rifle on James and Fountain.

"Hands up. Over here." He ordered as he wagged the weapon in Andy's direction. The man's gray pants were a dead giveaway. They had to be Confederates.

James eyed all three. Confederates this far west? He raised his arms, then sidestepped toward Andy.

"You all right?" James asked.

A slow nod.

"Shut up, Yank." Another soldier, his bright red hair and freckles set off the sneer on his face which revealed yellowed teeth. He pointed toward a tree. "Over there." He sighted down the barrel of his rifle. "Nice and easy now."

"But we're not Yankees," James said.

Would a lie save their lives? James prayed it would. None of them had been issued uniforms. Maybe this soldier would let them go. Maybe.

"Like hell you're not." The yellow-toothed soldier shoved the rifle barrel into James' chest, the man's rotting breath turning James' stomach. He cocked his red head toward Fountain. "He is. And that makes all of you the enemy."

James glanced over at Fountain's blue wool pants. Yep. Army issue. He'd forgotten about them.

James cut his eyes over to Andy and watched fear and panic wash over his brother's face. Andy's wide eyes and beads of sweat mirrored Fountain's.

A third Rebel soldier, his stringy, black hair hanging to his shoulders, plucked James' gun from his waistband, then shoved it into his own pants' pocket. He turned his attention to Fountain and stuck out his hand. "Give it over."

"Didn't bring it." Fountain shrugged.

Without another sound, the soldier swung his rifle. *Thwack.* The butt met Fountain's head. He spun, ricocheted off James, then crumpled to the ground. Blood streamed down the right side of his face.

James lunged. A rifle barrel pressed itself into his breastbone. He peered down at the indentation in his shirt, then remembered the pain of a bullet wound. He froze, sucked in air, and raised his hands again.

"You. Hero." The tall soldier jammed the rifle barrel harder against James' chest. Tobacco spit dribbled out from one corner of the soldier's mouth. "What company you with?"

A shake of the head was all James could muster.

"What're we gonna do with 'em, Luther?" The red-haired soldier waved his rifle at the three prisoners.

James eyed the carrot top Confederate *That kid's gotta be younger than Andy—fifteen, sixteen at most.*

The tall soldier named Luther lowered the rifle barrel from James' chest. "We'll take you to Captain Lueras." He leaned in close to James. "He'll make you talk."

"And then can we shoot 'em?" The black-haired soldier asked as he stuck his rifle barrel up under Andy's chin, forcing it upward.

Even without looking at his brother, James figured that Andy

125

was terrified. Hell, *he* was terrified and there wasn't a rifle under his chin.

And he couldn't miss from there. The steel barrel dug into the soft spot under Andy's chin and shoved his head back further.

Silence. What felt like years dragged by.

Finally, Luther let out a soft chuckle. "Put your rifle down, Anderson. Let's take 'em back to camp. They'll talk."

"Yeah," the red-haired kid snickered. "Squeal like little girls bein' chased with a snake."

"More like she-dog traitors." Anderson lowered the barrel, then shifted his black-eyed stare to James. "Yeah, you, she-dog traitor. You'll spill your guts then we spill your blood." He lifted his chin at Andy. "We'll make it nice 'n slow. You, hero, you'll watch while we cut him first."

James gave his brother a quick shake of the head. Encouragement, he hoped. He turned his attention to the red-haired, freckle-faced kid. The blood lust in that boy's eyes glowed. The kid licked his lips as he stepped back. He brought the rifle shoulder high.

As if enveloped in a bad dream, James watched the young soldier squeeze the trigger. He cringed at the retort of the rifle, saw the cloud of smoke explode from the barrel, and heard his brother scream.

James whipped around. Andy lay sprawled in the dirt, eyes fluttering open and closed, body rolling back and forth, clutching his side.

"You sonuva—" James ripped the rifle from the Confederate kid's hands then swung it like a baseball bat. *Thwack.* It slammed into the boy's shoulder, spinning him around like a child's top. The Confederate's freckled face plowed into the dirt.

Before James could take a breath, a rifle stock slammed into his back, right between the shoulder blades. The rifle sailed out of his hands and skidded across the sand. James crashed into Luther, knocking both men to the ground. James landed on top punching, pounding, and clawing until Luther stopped moving. Strong hands gripped James' shirt and tugged him off of Luther. Every muscle on fire, every fiber in his body in attack mode, James twisted against the powerful arms, then swung with his balled right hand. A *whump* and Anderson released his grip. In that moment, James head-butted his assailant. Both men thudded to the ground and somersaulted over and over.

Once they stopped, James mashed Anderson's shoulder with his knee as he gripped his black hair. Face-first in the dirt, the soldier twisted under James' weight.

A fistful of hair in his hand, James yanked up on the head, then slammed Anderson's face into the ground again and again. Blood spread across the dirt. He pulled the limp head up one more time, then let it flop into the dirt.

James glanced behind him just as the red-haired Rebel struggled to his knees and grabbed the rifle laying two feet away. He shouldered it and fired.

Another pop. The acrid sulfur of gunpowder assaulted James' nose.

"Sonovabitch!" James yelled while he scrambled toward the soldier whose freckles glowed against his paling face.

Undaunted, the red-haired soldier struggled from his knees to his feet and brought the rifle shoulder-high again, but before he could pull the trigger, James hurled his furious body at the man. They both plowed into the ground. Now perched atop him, James clutched the throat and squeezed.

Months of pent-up anger and frustration exploding, James bore down and moved in time with each jerk of the man underneath him. Eyes closed, James smiled as the man's body twitched, then as the muscles relaxed. Life oozed out.

"Good God, James! You're killing him!" He heard a voice shout.

Strange gurgling sounds escaped the victim's throat.

"Please don't kill him." Andy tugged on James' arm.

Andy's low voice brought chills racing up and down James' spine. Reality twisting into focus, James looked over at his brother kneeling next to him. Anguish clouded his brother's young face. James stared back down at the Confederate, then focused on his trembling hands still clutching the kid's neck.

Andy's words muffled. "Killing's not the answer."

As if on fire, James jerked his hands from the soldier. He swung his leg off the man, then grabbed his brother's shoulders.

"Andy? You all right?"

Andy sagged back off his knees, then sat into the dirt. Blood coated his left side and arm.

"Let me see," James said. He held up his brother's arm, ripped away part of the shirt, then poked at the wound.

Andy flinched.

"Damn lucky, boy." James wiped off some of the blood. "Can't tell for sure, but looks like it just tore off a bit of hide. That's all."

Andy grasped James' shirt sleeve, his voice dropped to a whisper. "Am I gonna die?"

"You'll be fine." James untied his bandana, then pressed it against the wound. "Hold it tight now." He waited for Andy to clutch the red-stained neckerchief, and then he held Andy's shoulder. A gentle squeeze.

Andy stared at his blood-soaked fingers. "I had my hands up. He shot me with my hands up."

"Welcome to war. Hush now, you'll be all right."

Andy's eyes met James'. "I got shot."

"I know." James looked over his shoulder at Fountain who was sitting up, rubbing his head.

Andy held his stomach. "Don't feel so good." Before he could crawl away, he leaned over and vomited. Violent spasms hit one right after another.

Cradling Andy in his arms, James rocked him and wiped the spittle with his shirtsleeve. Three minutes passed, four, before the spasms slowed, then stopped. Andy breathed at a normal rate again. James felt someone kneel at his side, then recognized Fountain.

"You all right?" James asked.

"Soon as these church bells quit ringing." Fountain swiped at the drying blood on the side of his face. "What're we going to do? Tie 'em up?"

As if the Rebels were sneaking up on them, James whipped his head from side to side.

"Jesus! I forgot all about 'em. Grab their weapons, Al."

The three Confederates lay still, breathing, but each one out cold. James held his shaking brother while Fountain gathered three rifles and plucked revolvers from each soldier's grasp. James shook his head. Familiar. Too damn familiar. He'd been in too many fights in his twenty-one years. Too many scrapes with Indians, stage robbers, and now men who wore gray uniforms. When would he live a normal life? He stared down at his brother, watched him grimace with the pain in his gut. Too young, too innocent. Then as if hit with ice water, James shuddered.

Not innocent any more.

Fountain dropped the weapons next to James. "I don't have anything to tie 'em with. Do you?"

James shook his head. "If they were awake, we'd march 'em back to camp. But I sure as hell ain't dragging 'em." Muscles tensing, chiding himself for not thinking sooner, he lowered his voice. "Think there's any more around?"

Fountain sank down on one knee next to Andy. "They would've been here by now." He cocked his head toward Andy. "His getting shot would've brought 'em running."

James turned Andy's ashen face to his and waited for the light brown eyes to focus on him. "We've got to get out of here. Think you can walk?"

Andy's chest rose with each breath. He nodded. James caught him under the arms while Fountain picked up the collection of weapons.

* * *

The trek back to camp proved difficult. Every hundred yards, the men stopped and rested, waiting for Fountain to be able to focus and quiet the pounding in his head. Andy struggled to stay upright.

The sun hung overhead by the time the bedraggled threesome limped into camp. A group of soldiers followed James to the doctor's tent, one grabbing Fountain's arm, another catching Andy as his legs gave out again.

Grateful for the help, James walked beside the man carrying Andy. He didn't think he'd be able to haul his brother one step further. During the long trip back, James had picked him up every time he'd staggered and fallen. Andy was heavy.

Doctor Meyers rushed into the large tent. He ordered, "Everyone out. No room in here."

The soldiers grumbled as they filed out into the bright sunshine. James grabbed the arm of the man who'd toted Andy. "Thanks, Reynolds. 'Preciate it."

The man took a quick step back, nodded, and with one more glance at Andy, followed the other soldiers into the daylight.

"What happened, Colton?" The doctor glanced at Fountain, who was holding his head and slumped on the side of a cot, then over at Andy, stretched out on the other bed.

James related the story while the doctor removed Andy's shirt and wiped the blood from his side.

"Confederates, you say?" The doctor glanced up at James, wrinkles furrowing his forehead. "Ain't seen hide nor hair of 'em around here. You *sure?*"

"Yeah, I'm not color blind, Doc. They had gray uniforms. Ask Fountain." James turned his back on the doctor, balled his hands into a tight fist, and clenched his jaw.

"You don't believe me," James said. "You think I'm crazy, just because—"

"James." Fountain struggled to his feet. "Let's go outside and find Captain Greene. I need some fresh air." He pushed James toward the tent flaps. "Besides, I want to thank you for saving my life. I owe you, partner."

Partner.

That felt good. James smiled.

Suddenly, Fountain sagged against James.

"Better get you back inside," James said as they returned to the tent. He helped his friend ease down to a cot.

Captain Greene stepped into the tent and stood next to Doctor Meyers. "Heard what happened. How are they?"

"Both'll live to fight again, Captain." The doctor finished tying white gauze strips around Andy's chest.

"Good to hear."

The doctor pulled a sheet over Andy's chest. "You were damn lucky, son. If your arm'd been down, well... you wouldn't have an arm now. And an inch more to the right, well... this sheet would be over your face instead of tucked under your chin."

Andy shut his eyes. James stood on the other side of the cot, placed his hand on his brother's shoulder, and squeezed. What would happen now? Would this change the way the men gathered around outside thought of him? Would they still run when he got close? Maybe the Army'd send Andy home. Would he go, too?

Captain Greene moved close to James. "I've sent a squad to find those Confederates. I didn't know they were this far west. I'll need you to fill me in right away so I can get a message to Lincoln."

A sudden shiver raced up James' spine. Not just practice drills, not a game any more. This was war.

CHAPTER TWENTY-ONE

Trace leaned back in his chair, unfolded the letter clutched in his hands. Another note from his brothers. They were sure good about writing. Ma had taught her boys that it was truly important to stay in touch with the family. Family. She'd said that is what matters in life. He nodded at her wisdom.

Icy cold shivers raced up and down his spine as Trace read the words. Gripping the pages, he knew what he had to do. But what about Teresa? Maybe she could go to her relatives in Santa Fe for a while. Trace jumped at the touch of a soft hand on his shoulder.

"What's wrong, Sweetheart? You're as pale as a faded picture." Teresa leaned down and planted a kiss on his cheek. "You're trembling!"

Patting her hand, he gripped it, then brought her around in front of him. He pulled her down onto his lap, stroked her hair, and gazed into her eyes. This wasn't going to be easy, but it had to be done. Several deep breaths. He opened his mouth, but no words formed.

Teresa touched the letter. "It's your brothers, isn't it?"

Trace nodded.

"Who's hurt?"

"Andy." Trace studied his wife's worried face. How did this wonderful woman read his thoughts? The letter shook as he held it up. "Shot by Rebs near Fort Yuma."

Teresa hugged her husband. "How bad?"

"James says he's all right. Lost some meat on the left side, but he's expected to recover." Trace gripped the paper, crumpling it. "Probably a lot worse than he reported. "

"Don't blame yourself. You couldn't have stopped a bullet." Teresa paused. "How long ago did this happen?"

Trace smoothed the letter and glanced at the heading. "Six weeks. He's either pretty much mended or dead by now." Balling his fist, the tightness in his gut sent shock waves throughout his body. "Damn. He's just a kid, my baby brother. He could get himself killed."

"Anyone can." Teresa straightened Trace's vest. "You just gotta believe... and have faith. Just like before."

Trace wrapped his arms around her and rocked back and forth. "I love you," he said.

"Go. Go to your brothers. They need you as much as you need them."

Trace stopped swaying and stared at her. "How'd you know?"

A faint smile lit up her brown eyes. Teresa put her hands on her hips and sighed. "Trace Joseph Colton. I know you better than you think. You've been wanting to go for a while, but with the baby coming, you didn't know what to do." She placed her hand in his. "Well, now you do. You need to go."

"But—"

"I'll be fine. There's plenty of women having babies and I won't be alone. *She's* not due to arrive for a few months, anyway. You'll be back by then."

"She? Don't you mean *he*?"

Teresa swatted his arm and cuddled into his chest.

Trace drew several deep breaths, smelling his wife's hair, feeling her soft body. "I'll leave first thing day after tomorrow."

* * *

James sat cross-legged near Andy; both brothers perched on a wide ledge several feet above the Colorado River. They sat in silence while the sun inched westward. All of a sudden, Andy sat bolt upright and patted his shirt pocket.

"Can't believe I forgot." He said as he pulled out a letter and held it up. "It's from Trace."

"When'd you get that?" James tugged it out of Andy's grasp.

"This morning at mail call."

Opening the crumpled paper, James mouthed each word as he read Trace's scrawling handwriting. Andy peered over his shoulder. Second page finished, James handed the entire letter to Andy, who reread it.

When his brother finished, James grinned. "How about that? Damn, we're gonna be uncles again! First Luke, now Trace. That lucky son of a gun!"

"Wonder what Ma thinks of all this?" Andy's smile lit up his eyes. "Hope it's not another boy. Ma'd like a girl some time. She'd spoil her, dress her all fancy, pink bows and such."

"Sure would." James nodded at his brother. "She'd really like that."

"I'm gonna teach her how to ride a horse." Andy pointed his thumb at his chest. "Better 'n me."

"Don't you mean him? Teach *him* how to ride?" James chuckled at his youngest brother.

Six weeks ago, Andy's future looked uncertain after that bullet. Now, regaining most of his strength and good nature, his brother appeared to be nearing full recovery. Andy seemed to have survived the army so far.

Thoughts turning, James reflected on his own plight. He'd added a few names to his tenuous list of friends, and while he hadn't seen any more Rebels in person, his dreams filled in for any of the missing enemies. The flask of whiskey stashed in his shirt reminded him of his thirst.

Instead of drinking, James looked at Andy and recalled a time when this brother, four years old, chased the yard full of chickens and then gathered the eggs. With meticulous care only a child could manage, Andy placed the dozen or so eggs in a circle, then leapfrogged between each one. James remembered the scowl on his Ma's face when she found only two whole eggs and the youngest Colton brother splattered with yolk and shell. While Ma fumed, James had scrubbed Andy head to toe.

"What are you smiling at, big brother? That's an awful goofy look on your face." Andy's eyes met his brother's. "Thinking about women again?"

James thumped Andy on the chest and shook his head. "Just remembering. I get in trouble every time I think about women."

He sighed at visions of Lila. Only a few days had passed since he was able to smile at her image without tearing up.

A drink. Time for a drink.

He extracted the silver container, unscrewed the top, and sipped. The liquid stung his throat. Guilt taking control, James held it out to his brother. "Want some?"

Andy shook his head and frowned. He drew in the dirt. "Women. Drinking." Stick poised in hand, he studied his pictures. "Only cause trouble."

133

"Nothing wrong with drinking. But whatd'you know about women, baby brother? You holding out, not telling me something I should know?" James eyed this teenager sitting next to him. "You're not gonna pull a Luke on me, are you?" Another swig went down smoother than the first. "You know... get married in a hurry?"

"Nah, not me. Figure I'm pretty safe just thinking about 'em." Gazing over the blue ribbon of water beneath him and the vast stretch of desert on the horizon, Andy dropped his voice. "You ever... you know, *loved* a woman?"

"What?"

"You know. *Lay* with one?" Andy's eyes shot sideways at his brother.

James froze. *Dark Cloud. Lila. The Mesilla whores.* Only one he could claim. And she was dead. James let out a long stream of air.

"Uh huh."

James' head bobbed up and down. He drained the flask. Warmth flooded his body.

"Was it—"

"Nothing to talk about, Andy. Let's just say Cochise changed everything about my life. Everything."

James envisioned that captive Pima girl who became his Indian wife, his first and only times of intimacy. He felt his arms envelop her shivering body, their flesh melding into each other. He remembered how with Katie, that whore in Mesilla, he couldn't... his frustration, his angry fist almost plowing into her back.

Why in hell didn't I bring another bottle?

The brothers sat in silence, watching hawks soar on the warm currents and listening to the wind rustle leaves on the nearby scrub oak. Billowy spring clouds muted the sunshine, then drifted aside to reveal a bright world at the edge of the Sonoran Desert. "Beautiful out here, isn't it?" Andy spread his arms, taking in the scenery.

Pushing down demons, James turned his attention to Andy. What was his brother thinking? Usually a talkative, bubbly teenager, Andy now would spend long hours in pensive silence.

Andy lowered his arms. "I almost missed this. Almost missed the rest of my life." He turned to James. "What d'you supposed happened to those Rebels? When Captain Greene went to get 'em, he said they were gone. Think Indians took 'em? Or did they just get up and walk off?" He swung his head right then left. "Suppose they're still around, watching me, waiting to kill me for sure?"

James shook his head, hoping to be reassuring. He'd told Andy at least a hundred times since the shooting that he was safe, that the Rebels had retreated.

"Nah. They're gone. Probably ran back to Tucson like the cowards they are. Don't worry. They're not about to try something again." He patted his brother's back. "You'll be fine. You got the Union Army protecting you."

Crows cawed over head as the wind rustled a nearby creosote bush. Andy's words started, then stopped. At last he turned his somber brown eyes on James. "Tell me true. Do you still hurt from Cochise? Still see those Indians?"

It was James' turn to study his hands. He could only nod.

"I still see those Rebs," Andy said. "Everywhere. One was in my coffee yesterday. That ugly face just stared back at me. I even saw one...." His voice dropped. "When'll they finally go away?"

James' grip around his brother tightened. "Wish I knew."

Now three of us are seeing ghosts.

CHAPTER TWENTY-TWO

James glanced down the long row of soldiers. He heard others line up behind him, whispering. Andy stood at his shoulder while Captain Greene and this new commander Carleton strutted toward them. From the look on their faces, James knew the news wasn't going to be good.

"Attention!"

Two hundred men of the California Column threw out their chests and riveted their eyes on General James H. Carleton.

The General, Captain Greene on his heels, surveyed the army.

"Men," the General said, "tomorrow's an important day in history. Tomorrow, we begin our march east—east toward victory. We're heading back to Tucson, back to take the territory that should have been ours in the first place."

Carleton huffed into his handlebar mustache. James regarded this man—a legend in some people's eyes. He wondered if what they said was true about his unquestioned leadership skills, or if in combat, events had been blown out of proportion.

James caught Andy's eye. That sparkle for battle had been replaced with a dull cataract of experience. Chest muscles tightening, he ached for his brother's loss of innocence.

"Dismissed." Greene's voice.

What had they just said? James frowned. Daydreaming again. He let out his chest and air at the same time. Sharp commanding words by that same voice hit his ears.

"Except the Colton brothers."

Greene marched toward him. Standing in place while the Captain and Andy joined him, James caught Greene's stare.

Greene glanced to his side, then lowered his voice.

"Look, I'll be completely honest. My army career's on the line here. One questionable incident with my men and that's it for me.

I've got a wife and kids to think of." Greene leaned in closer. "Get my meaning?"

James nodded.

Greene shifted his gaze to Andy, who nodded as well.

"The General doesn't know your past. And we'll keep it that way for now. But, you two will be in front at all times so Sergeant Williams and myself can keep an eye on you." The corners of his mouth spiked upward then returned to their usual thin line. He spun, then marched away.

Fountain stepped up to the brothers and glanced over his shoulder at the receding figure of his commander. "What'd he want?"

"We're gonna be marching in a special place," Andy said, wagging his head as the three men walked toward the camp's sea of tents. "Out in front."

"Quite an honor, young man. They don't let just anyone lead the parade." Fountain grabbed James' arm. "How can I help?"

James regarded the furrowed forehead, the dark brown eyes of this man who'd taken the chance of getting to know him. "Be my friend."

Fountain lowered his voice. "Look. I know it's not much, but tomorrow when we take off, I'll carry your gear."

James shook his head.

"It's the least I can do. Hell, James, you saved my life. All right?"

James studied his feet, then his hands, and then his friend's face. He attempted a grin and stuck out his hand.

* * *

The Colorado River far behind, mesas green with new grass loomed ahead in the distance. Mesquite and juniper covered the desert floor, waiting for the spring rains to bring new life to the region. Proud granite rocks stood on both sides of the road like sentinels, watching the world. Standing guard. The sun filtered through a cloud-blessed sky muting the usually harsh shadows.

Today, not only was the sun's ray diffused by clouds, but sand, carried by Nature's wind, blotted out the world, turning everything a gritty brown.

James stopped marching and looked behind him. Where his foot had just been was now covered over with sand. Just that fast. Strung out as far as he could see in back of him was the rest of his company, his fellow soldiers all battling this damn wind. James turned back and plowed into a mesquite bush, its branches grappling at his legs. He leaped through it, cursing as he went. He pulled a sticker from his pants and cursed louder.

Andy stopped next to him. "It's been three long days of nothing but sand and wind, James. Can't believe Carleton's making us march in this storm," he said as he tucked his chin into his chest and pulled his neckerchief up higher around the back of his neck. "Think he's trying to kill us!"

Andy spit muddy sand, then tugged the cloth over his mouth.

James yelled, "Keep Fountain in sight and I'll watch Reynolds. Don't want them wandering off."

Small rocks pelted James' back, and winds whipped around his body as he struggled to put one foot in front of the other. A gust drove James forward, and he struggled to stay upright.

As if his prayers were answered, Captain Greene marched alongside James and yelled over the gale. "Up ahead about a mile! An outcropping... Gonna stop there for today... Don't wanna lose any of you!"

James nodded. "I'll pass the word back, Captain!"

Within a half-hour, James, Andy, Fountain, and Reynolds spotted a couple of boulders stacked together, creating a slight windbreak. Grateful for the shelter and just like the other soldiers, the four friends hunkered down shoulder to shoulder, closed their gritty eyes, and breathed through bandanas tied over their faces.

* * *

Near nightfall, Reynolds crawled out of the shelter. He stood, brushed encrusted sand off his shirt and pants, pants that were always too short for his long legs, then stomped his feet. The breeze whipped strands of his light brown hair into his face. James handed Reynolds his hat then wriggled out from between Andy and Fountain, careful not to elbow them. He twisted his body, enjoying the tension-releasing contortion.

Reynolds shielded his hazel eyes. Eyes too small for his face, James thought. With a nose that big he'd need eyes the size of dinner plates. James struggled not to snicker out loud. He liked Reynolds, even though he was hard to get to know. Seemed to keep everything to himself.

James gazed across the desert. "Damn. I hate spring. April's the worst month of the whole year!"

"Is it always like this?" Reynolds spit out dirt.

James chuckled. "Nope. Sometimes it's worse."

Fountain and Andy emerged, wiping their eyes. Andy sneezed and drew his sandy sleeve across his nose.

James let his eyes roam over the vast expanse of soldiers, most of whom appeared to be sleeping. Rolled up in blankets or huddled together, the men reminded James of paintings he'd seen in a book back home of soldiers during the Revolutionary War. Soldiers too tired to go on. Too worn out to fight. Too wind beaten to take another step.

A gust of wind whipped Andy's hat off his head. He grabbed for it.

"Fountain's gonna build a fire soon's the wind dies down some more," Andy said. "Think there's a chance Greene'll give us time to go hunting tomorrow? I've seen plenty of quail and rabbit around here." Andy licked his lips. "I can taste 'em now."

Visions of roasting rabbit and quail rushed James' mind. The remembered tantalizing aroma of fresh meat crackling over a campfire whetted his appetite. His stomach growled. He'd eaten almost nothing these last three days, but now his gut was sending messages that three days had been way too long without food.

"Not just quail, James, but doves, too." Andy patted his stomach. "Umm... dove 'n' rabbit stew."

"I'll see what I can do," James said as he peered over the bodies and rocks searching for the captain. He spotted him on the far side of the encampment.

James stepped over sleeping men, around mesquite bushes and snake holes. Mulling over what he should say, he knew he couldn't ask for favors—he wasn't special. Just a common soldier, a lowly private at that. But he and Greene had a connection that army protocol couldn't dissuade.

Stopping next to the captain, James listened to the conversation with Sergeant Williams.

"General Carleton and I figure we've made good time across this damned desert. Don't know how with this blasted wind. But, tomorrow, the troops can take the morning to replenish their supplies, go hunting if they need to. Or they can try to scrape some of the sand off." Greene pointed northeast. "There's a stream 'bout half a mile from here."

"I'm sure they'll appreciate it, sir." Williams saluted the commanding officer. He glanced at James and nodded.

James returned the nod.

Captain Greene pivoted to his right. "Still on your feet, I see."

"Yes, sir. We're all fine."

Shoulders straightening, Greene snapped into his military mode. "What can I do for you, Private?"

"Nothing, now, sir. Andy and I were just wondering if we could go hunting tomorrow. Seen plenty of fresh game around." The aromas assaulted his memory again. His stomach gurgled.

"Get it done before noon. We're heading out then."

"Thank you, Captain." James saluted the officer. He spun, then stopped and turned back. "Thanks for everything."

* * *

Rays of the rising sun cast golden pink glows across the Sonoran Desert. James gripped his rifle and eased around a scraggly mesquite bush. He signaled to Andy on his left. A covey of Gambel's quail several yards ahead skittered from bush to bush, then stopped. The lead bird cocked its head, listening for sounds of predators.

You're doing the same thing we are, bird. Listening for Indians and Rebs who want to kill us.

James sighted his rifle, gripped the trigger.

Survive. Stay alive.

James wiped the sweat dripping into his eyes, then resighted his Hawkens.

Eat or be eaten.

He squeezed his eyes shut.

Why is this so damn hard? Pull the trigger, and let's have breakfast.

Images of One Wing's snarling mouth and vicious eyes exploded in James' mind. Hot breath in his face, James stared into pure evil. A roar from a shotgun jerked James back to reality. The covey of quail scattered, but one of them lay fluttering on the ground. Andy jumped up from behind a mesquite bush.

"Got one, James. Got one!" Andy exclaimed.

Chiding himself for his weakness, James stood and walked over to Andy squatting on the ground. The bird convulsed at his feet.

"Ain't she a beaut? Gonna make good eating this morning!" Andy's smile reflected the luminous sun.

James nodded. Scolding himself again, he pulled in air and kneeled by Andy. "Nice shot. She's a big one all right."

"Sure is." Andy looked around. "The rest took off, but if we're real quiet, maybe they'll come back."

"Why don't you go clean this one and I'll bring in some more? Get Reynolds to start a fire and I'll be back directly."

Andy held up his kill and grinned. "Yep, a real beaut. Don't take long, brother. I'm liable to eat it all before you get back." He stood and trotted off toward camp.

By the time the sun erased all its pink shadows, James walked back into camp, three quails and one duck slung over his shoulder. He grinned at the smell of boiling coffee and roasting bird. Mouth watering, James set his quarry next to his brother.

"We got us a feast now!" Andy rocked on his heels and poked the fire. Flames shot up over the quail.

Fountain pried the stick from Andy's grasp.

"You're gonna fry that bird on the outside, and it'll be raw inside," Fountain said. "Clean those others, and I'll make sure breakfast is ready soon."

A quick grab for the stick, but Andy succeeded only in bumping Fountain's arm. Andy glared at the man now cooking his quail. He stood.

"Just because you're older doesn't mean you know everything, Fountain." Andy grabbed the string of limp birds and headed away from camp.

"What's wrong with him?" Fountain asked. He glanced toward Andy's receding figure and then turned to James.

"You stole his thunder, Al. He's real proud of himself for shooting that quail and now you're telling him he doesn't know how to cook it." James looked at Andy kneeling several yards away. Flashes of morning sun glinted off of Andy's skinning knife.

"Ah, hell. I didn't mean anything by it." Fountain laid the stick by the fire. "Guess I'm just hungry for fresh meat."

James cocked his head to one side and stared at his friend.

"I'll go apologize." Fountain pushed to his feet, then ambled toward the angry teenager.

James turned his attention to the fire and roasting bird. The crackling of fat as it hit the flames brought back fond memories. Images of Ma cooking that big chicken dinner every Sunday flashed into his mind. Happy times. He grinned, picturing himself, his three brothers and folks sitting around that big oak table, laughing, talking, joking, enjoying each other's company. Suddenly, memories of days in Cochise's camp crowded in. Those Apaches spent most evenings around a small central fire discussing the day's killings. Plots for the next raid sailed around the campfire. Although ravenous, James found it hard to swallow his food, knowing that at any minute, One Wing or Standing Pony would—

Those memories get you in trouble. Watch out.

Standing, he forced his attention back to the present. His brother and Fountain shook hands, and then his new friend slapped Andy on the back. Andy produced that wide, contagious Colton family smile.

Noon came much too soon. James hoisted the pack on his back, settling it square between his shoulders.

Fountain thumped James' chest, stepped in front, and headed off for the next leg of the journey. James marched forward.

I've got a friend. I can push those nightmares aside. And I'm still on my own two feet. Normal. I'm finally getting back to normal.

CHAPTER TWENTY-THREE

Tired from five days of riding from Mesilla, Trace rode past the outskirts of Tucson, Arizona Territory. The ranches he spotted appeared to be in fine shape. No signs of death, destruction, no streams of refugees pouring out of town. He'd been told the Confederates had taken control of Tucson, but it looked to him like not much had changed. Despite the pockets of army tents, the landscape was peaceful—almost too peaceful.

The late afternoon sun blinded him as he rode into town and reined up in front of a hotel "The Continental." It appeared to be a well-kept, two-story adobe building. The outside, plastered in whitewash, sported blue paint around the windows. The purpose of the blue paint was to ward off evil spirits entering through the door and windows. Trace raised one eyebrow and secretly hoped the blue would work for him

Its hinges in need of oil, the hotel door grated open with his shove. Trace stepped through and took particular note of the lobby and adjoining room. His eyes adjusted to the sudden dimness. Though narrow, the lobby sported the usual counter for registration and one perfunctory chair parked in the corner. Off to his left in a side room, a conversation was taking place, some of it rather heated. During these times of war, men's talk was often angry.

Trace signed the register. The raven-haired Mexican woman behind the counter frowned at his signature. "I can't read your writing, señor."

"Trace Colton, ma'am." He tipped his hat and placed a dollar in her hand.

"Room *quince*, fifteen, Mister Colton." She nodded toward the stairs and handed him the key.

"*Gracias*, señora." Trace touched the brim of his hat again, picked up his saddlebag and started up the stairs. He stopped. Voices from the downstairs room rose then settled into a murmur.

His curiosity getting the best of him, Trace strained to hear the gist of the conversation.

He eased into the room. Soldiers! Straightening to his six-foot height, he froze. The conversation stopped mid-sentence. All eyes glared at Trace. He counted six Confederate officers gathered around a table.

Desperate for a quick explanation, his words shot out. "Sorry. I'm lost." He held up a hand. "Just looking for my room."

He took two steps backwards. Spinning around, Trace hurried up the stairs.

Trace tossed his bag on the bed and struggled to recall the man at the far side of the table who had stared at him. Familiar. Where had he seen him before? Trace sat on the bed, the lumpy mattress poking his rear. He lay back, that face tormenting his memory.

Trace sat bolt upright. Ice water poured down his spine. Captain Rudolfo Garcia! Baylor's right hand man. Here?

What was he doing here? And where was Colonel Baylor? Still in Mesilla? What kind of trouble would Garcia cause? Would the captain leave him alone long enough to let him get out of town? Trace rubbed his forehead.

I should leave now, but my horse is tired and I'm exhausted. Besides, I've already told them everything I know.

He hated himself for telling Baylor about Cochise and his tribe. How they operated. When they raided and who; when they chose to stay in camp instead of going out killing. Secrets only an insider would know. Somehow it just didn't feel right. Trace didn't want to see the Indians wiped out just because they were Indian. Baylor had no right to go on a manhunt like that. But, Trace also knew that Cochise was a wise and crafty man, who wouldn't get caught unless he wanted to. And that was something he didn't want.

Trace set his jaw. He'd avoid trouble and go straight to a restaurant tonight, then head out of town well before sun up tomorrow. Shouldn't get into any trouble that way. He vowed to stay out of cantinas.

* * *

Enchiladas and *tamales* sat heavy on his stomach as Trace walked out of the restaurant.

Wary of the hundreds of Rebels around town, he stepped into the warm evening air, studied the stars blinking overhead, and listened to music wafting from the cantina two blocks away. A slight breeze picked up the strains of a Spanish song and sent it down the street.

Trace breathed in aromas of cooking fires, horses, adobe, and mesquite. They mixed together in a blend of smells to create what he labeled The Southwest. He smiled at the comforting familiarity. Mesilla smelled exactly the same.

Walking south toward his hotel, Trace turned the corner onto the main street. A muffled cry for help. A woman's voice. He stopped and peered into the darkness.

A few small burning piles of brush placed up and down the dirt street lit patches of the area. More screams and cries for help before he could make out exactly what was happening.

Half a block away, several men stood on the sidewalk watching two people scuffling near the plaza. Trace joined the crowd and frowned at the figures rolling back and forth in the dirt.

Then it hit him. Those weren't two men, but a Rebel soldier and a young woman. He was on top of her, pinning her arms and kissing her. Another cry for help. He tore her blouse. Trace looked around. Why didn't these people come to her rescue? Her anguished cries hit Trace in the stomach. How could they simply stand there watching? Could *he*?

The soldier planted his face in the frantic girl's chest. She screamed louder.

"Enough! Stop it!" Trace demanded.

Knowing he shouldn't, but also knowing he must, Trace lunged for the soldier and pulled him off.

Staggering to his feet, the soldier swung at Trace. The blow went wide. Trace ducked and brought his fist up under the man's jaw. A second punch planted in the stomach sent the soldier reeling backwards. Dirt flew as he thudded to the ground.

Trace stepped back, wiped the sweat pouring into his eyes, then turned to help the girl. She scrambled to her feet then scurried off, sobbing.

Two strong hands grabbed his arms, wrenching them behind his back.

"You're under arrest, Trace Colton."

Trace whipped his head and upper body around to meet the gaze of Captain Rudolfo Garcia.

"Arrest? For what?" Trace asked.

"Interference of a soldier performing his duty, and attempted murder of that same soldier." Garcia snapped Trace's hands upward toward his shoulder blades, then slapped iron handcuffs around the wrists. "Let's go."

The captain shoved Trace onto the wooden sidewalk.

"He was attacking that girl!" Feet planted against Garcia's powerful forward thrust, Trace searched the faces of the people on the street. "Hey! You saw what that soldier was gonna do! I tried to help her! Tell this moron!"

Men shrugged their shoulders, dropped their heads, and then turned their backs to Trace. They sauntered on down the street.

Trace screamed at the backs of the men. "Cowards! You're all cowards! Every one of you! What if that was your daughter?"

Garcia laughed. "They didn't see anything, Colton. Just a soldier keeping the town nice and quiet." He grabbed Trace's arm and tugged. "Jail time."

"Jail?" Trace jerked against the vice-like hold. "What the hell?" He stumbled down the walk a block or so. A yank on his arm, he stopped outside the sheriff's office.

Garcia opened the door and muscled Trace inside. He snapped at the sergeant behind the desk. "Keys. We're throwing this *pendejo* in jail."

"I didn't do anything wrong, Garcia." Trace lurched forward. Two strong hands pushed him through the inner jail door, then past two cells. A Herculean shove. He flew into the dark cell at the end.

Garcia's words echoed off the adobe walls. "Face the wall."

"I wanna see the sheriff! Get me the sheriff!"

Garcia hissed in Trace's ear. "*I'm* the law in these parts, Colton. *I'm* your sheriff."

There was no choice but to do as ordered. Trace's face pressed against rough adobe, the cold iron around his wrists released. Blood rushed back into his hands, and his arms swung down to his side. He flexed his tingling fingers.

The clang of the door, the click of the key. Trace spun. His steps were quick across the cell. "What the hell're you doin'?" He gripped the bars. "You won't get away with this, Garcia!"

"Can and will, Colton." Garcia's icy words punctured the stillness of the jail. "Keep quiet now. You'll have a long time in here to think about what you did."

With a quick snort, the captain nodded to the sergeant, then marched through the door. The wooden door slammed. Laughter filtered from the other room.

Trace pressed his forehead against the bars and squeezed his eyes shut. His grip on the bars relaxed.

Let's think this through. No need to panic. Yet.

CHAPTER TWENTY-FOUR

James' eyes shot open at the firm hand shaking his shoulder.

"Up and at 'em, brother. Nap time's over." Another quick shake. "Gotta get another ten miles under our feet before dark."

Hands shading his eyes, James peered up into the desert sun. "What's going on?"

The silhouette of Andy knelt next to him. James rubbed his eyes, then sat up.

"Sergeant Williams says we gotta get closer to Tucson if we're ever going to take it over," Andy replied. "We're a week away, he says, and that's if we run." He handed James a canteen, and then he stood, wiping sweat beaded on his forehead. One drop remained perched on his eyebrow.

Canteen against his lips, James swigged cool water, the wet sliding down his dry throat. Another sip. He studied the canteen in hand.

There were times at Cochise's camp— Stop it, James! Stop thinking.

James handed the canteen back to Andy, then pushed his tired body to his feet. "All right, Tucson, here we come." James glanced right then left. "Where's Fountain?"

"Over talking to that General Carleton, again." Andy jerked his thumb over his shoulder.

"Don't suppose he's bucking for a promotion, do you?" James picked up his gear.

Andy wagged his head. "Al's just friendly is all." He slung his backpack over one shoulder. "He oughta be a politician or a lawyer the way he gets to know people."

James chuckled and readjusted the pack. "He does get around doesn't he? I'll bet Al's met everyone here and knows something about each one." James shook his head. "Don't know how he does it."

"Some people are just born naturally friendly." Andy patted his brother on the shoulder. "Let's go."

* * *

Which hurt worse? Ankles or feet? James considered. Toes. Had to be toes. The flat boulder under his tired rear end glowed from the setting sun. James rubbed his bare foot. "We've come a long way and still got miles ahead of us." He took a deep breath and massaged his big toe. "When we get to Tucson, I'm buying you new boots. You deserve 'em." He stopped mid-massage.

No wonder people think I'm crazy. I'm sitting here talking to my feet.

There was a tap on the shoulder, then someone plopped down next to him.

"Feet were not meant to be walked on as much as ours." Albert Fountain stretched out his legs. "Think they know they gotta walk three more miles tonight?"

A man James now considered a new friend eased down next to Fountain. Joshua Reynolds peered around Fountain. "Where's that kid brother of yours, James?" Reynolds asked. "Don't tell me he's found another rock to inspect."

"He's off talking to a couple friends, I think. Should be back directly." James tugged the sock on and noted three new holes forming. "Gonna buy new boots and socks in Tucson. Can't wait."

"From what I hear Carleton saying, it won't be much longer. We're just outside of Picacho Peak and then fifty miles southeast is Tucson." Fountain pointed toward the east. "Can almost see that crazy town from here!"

Other boot and sock in hand, James wiggled his toes. "What d'you suppose is left of Tucson? I hear it's not a very nice place right now with the Confederate troops controlling everything."

Fountain pulled off a boot, then a sock. "Guess we're going in and making it a nice place again. Gotta show those Rebs who's really in charge." He inspected a blister on his big toe. "Kill a few of 'em if need be."

James stopped wriggling his foot and stared at his friend. "I'm so damn sick of killing. Seen... done way too much of it, Al. Gotta be another way. Killing's not the answer. Nobody should have to die."

"Yeah? Well, tell that to John Baylor and Sherod Hunter,

hell, even your boy Lincoln. Tell them to play nice and nobody'll get hurt."

Sensing the anger building in his friend, James brought his own rising temper under control. After a deep breath, James pulled on his sock and boot. He brought his voice down. "Don't mean to get you riled, Al, but it just don't make sense. I've seen too much killing, too many lives wiped out. Innocent people destroyed." He turned to his friend. "Can't find a good reason for them to die."

"But, you've killed—"

"Yeah, I have." That perpetual knot grew in James' chest. "But what I did was wrong. Dammit, death is so... so damn permanent."

Fountain slid his sock onto his foot and settled it in his boot. "Better be careful, James. You're thinking again." He glanced at the gray-blue sky, then over to James. Their eyes met. Reynolds stood and extended his hand to James. "You two quit being so philosophical. Makes me sleepy." He pulled James to his feet. "Let's go find Andy."

* * *

Staring out the window, Trace lay on his bunk and watched the early morning clouds perch on still winds. Hands under his head, he turned his thoughts to Teresa, the baby she carried, his folks and brothers. He wondered what James and Andy were doing right now. Probably already practicing more of those bayonet drills Andy wrote about. The way he described it, the exercise was hours of stabbing big bales of cotton or hay. He'd reported that it was harder than it looked.

Apprehension, then frustration, swelled in his chest. By this time this morning, he had planned to be miles closer to Fort Yuma, surprising those brothers. Riding hard, it would take another week to get there, but the effort would be worth it. He couldn't wait to see James and Andy.

His little brother was growing up too fast. He wondered if Andy would be content to go home to farm life now that he'd had a taste of freedom. Would he settle down on a little farm, raise a family, or wander the territory looking for more adventure?

Adventure. Trace frowned. Driving stagecoaches was an adventure and look where it got him. Him and James. Robbed, shot, captured, tortured, unemployed, and now arrested. Damn!

If it wasn't Cochise, it was Baylor. And now Trace's current plans were waylaid by that crazy Captain Garcia.

Quit thinking.

He rubbed his aching head.

It's not getting me anywhere. Gotta worry about now, plan how to get out.

He sat up.

The thick wooden door squeaked open, and a tall soldier stepped in carrying a metal tray.

"Breakfast, Colton. Stand back against the wall."

Trace stood with his back to the cold adobe wall while the private placed the tray and the coffee mug on the cell floor.

Door relocked, the soldier stood back. "Better enjoy this meal."

The private jangled the jail keys in his skinny fingers.

Trace picked up the cup. "Why's that?" He asked as he sipped the lukewarm coffee.

"The way I hear it, you won't live much longer." The private stepped toward the door, then turned around. "We're headin' out of this hellhole tomorrow. Gonna meet up with Captain Sherod Hunter's men and move west toward Fort Yuma. Gonna take California."

His words turned cold, hard.

"Garcia says you're to stay here and rot."

CHAPTER TWENTY-FIVE

"That Picacho Peak over there, James?" Andy pointed northeast to a jagged ridge of mountains looming in the blue distance.

James squinted against the midday sun and shielded his eyes. "Could be. Nothing else out here."

"Plenty of snakes and scorpions." Andy kicked over a rock. "Seen lots of those."

James nodded, stepped around a spreading mesquite bush, and then skirted two large boulders. He tugged on Andy's knapsack, and both men stopped. He slipped the canteen off his brother's shoulder and drank with long, satisfying gulps. He offered it to Andy.

"Almost back to civilization. Next week at this time, we'll be in a cantina throwing back tequila," James said.

"Not me." Andy's eyebrows shot up into his creased forehead. "Can't stand that oily stuff." He spoke around gulps. "I prefer good old beer. None of that cactus whiskey rot gut, that *pulque,* for me. No sir. Just give me good old American beer."

James stared at his brother. "Quite a speech. I take it you're ready to be back in civilization, too."

Andy swigged again, then replaced the canteen's cap. Wiping his mouth, he pointed behind him at the pack. "Stick that empty canteen in there and let's go. The sooner we get to town, the sooner we get outta this dirt, sand, and wind. I, for one, am ready to do something else besides wander around this hot ol' desert."

James walked in time with his youngest brother. What *was* waiting for them in Tucson? Would there be more death and destruction? How many more people would have to die? He glanced over his shoulder and caught Reynold's eye. James' newest friend trotted double-time and soon caught up.

"Thought you're the trail blazer, James. You're slowing down a mite. Not getting old are you?" Reynolds' dark blue eyes danced in the sun.

"Me? Old?" James returned the smile. "Never. Just slowed down so you grandpas can catch up. Don't wanna make you feel too ancient."

"Three years older than you does not make me ancient, boy!" Reynolds smoothed his wide handlebar mustache. "Makes me... mature, wise, more... worldly."

"Uh, huh." James couldn't suppress a grin; it felt too good to have a friend again. "Older is older, Reynolds."

"Older is—"

"Look out!" James yelled while he grabbed Reynolds by his shirt and slung him several feet across the sand. Reynolds hit the ground and careened into a yucca.

James' revolver cleared leather. He shot. Time froze.

James gripped his gun and peered through smoke and sand. A headless rattlesnake quivered and twitched in its death throes. White flashes. Incessant drumming. Acrid gunpowder.

More death. More dying.

A strong grip on his shoulder shook him back to reality.

"What happened? You all right?" Andy followed James' gaze to the snake. "Holy Hannah, James! It's gotta be ten feet long!" Andy knelt and ran his hand over the body. Soldiers clustered around the brothers, elbowing each other for a better look.

Hands shaking, heart thundering, James sucked in air.

Pull yourself together, Colton. It's just a snake.

James holstered his revolver as he stepped over to Reynolds. "You all right?" He extended an arm.

"Yeah, just a little surprised." Reynolds accepted the help, then dusted himself off and replaced his hat. He yanked a stiff, saw-toothed yucca leaf from his shirt.

Andy stood and held the snake at arms' length, the tail dragging in the dirt. He grinned at James. "Helluva shot, big brother." He lifted the snake up higher. "Can I have the rattles?"

Reynolds and James moved in closer.

Andy, surrounded by several of the men, studied the snake. He held it out for Reynold's inspection. "This thing 'bout bit you. Would've hurt, too."

"Got that right." Reynolds held the tail, stretching the snake out its full length. He whistled. "Five, six feet. They grow 'em big in Arizona."

Captain Greene elbowed his way into the crowd. "What's going on?"

Reynolds held up the snake. "Almost got me. Would have too, if James hadn't shoved me out of the way." He glanced at James. "Guess you saved my life, or at least a chunk of it."

Greene nodded to James. "Nice shot. Guess your shotgun days with Butterfield paid off." He spoke over the murmur. "Keep your eyes peeled. This isn't the first we've seen and I'm sure it won't be the last. Now, let's get going."

The men muttered protests about the march, but congratulated James on his save of Joshua Reynolds. James shook the offered hands and grinned at the pats on the back.

Yep. Normal.

* * *

Trace paced wall to bars to window. Back to the iron bars. Captain Rudolfo Garcia had been the last of the many soldiers to stop by his cell and sneer. A few even spit at him. Garcia's final words echoed in Trace's ears.

"Rot in hell, Colton. Nobody's gonna remember you're even in here. Nobody."

With that, Garcia slammed the door. The click of the key reverberated throughout the jail.

That had been what... eight, ten hours ago? The sun had set two hours after Garcia turned his back and walked away. And now Trace had been waiting in the dark. Even the footsteps of the few people walking through the alley had ended hours earlier and no one had answered his pleas for help. No one had even stopped to ask what his problem was or if he was all right. No one.

Trace stood in the ebony stillness and thought about his life. Except for his current predicament, all in all, he was a pretty lucky man. He'd grown up with a good family, been given a proper education, he could cipher numbers and read. And now, he was married to a wonderful woman about to have a child. *His* child. Things would be fine if he could just get out of jail. And keep his brother from being shot again. And kill the demons haunting James. And bury the guilt eating him. And... and... and. Trace pounded his fists against the cell bars.

Trace slumped to the cot then lay back on the lumpy tick mattress. He hated to think of the fleas, lice, other vermin that he was sure lived in there. They would have a feast on him, he knew. He shut his eyes.

Footsteps under the window jerked his eyes open. There was a shuffle of tired feet. He glanced around the grayed cell. There. Again. No, not tired feet. Someone dragging something.

Standing on tiptoes, Trace couldn't catch sight of who was doing what. Even though he stood six foot in bare feet, the window was too high and at such an angle he couldn't see into the alley.

"Hey, you!" Trace poked an arm through the window bars. His hand wriggled in air.

The dragging stopped.

"Hey! Help me!" Trace reached further into the early morning sunrise. "Over here!" He waited, straining to hear anything. A voice, a shuffle, a sound—something.

Nothing.

Pulling his arm in, Trace jumped twice, straining to catch a glimpse of who or what was outside. All he managed to do was note that the building on the other side of the alley had no windows.

Trace sunk to the cot, then held his head. What the hell was he going to do? A lump in the mattress poked him. He adjusted his weight. The cot. He pushed it. It moved a few inches. Relief mixed with hope swirled in his head. The bed wasn't bolted to the wall. Trace shoved the heavy wooden frame across the dirt-packed floor until it rested under the window.

He jumped on the frame and peered into the morning sun. On his toes, he managed to take in the entire alley. His gaze swept up and down the dusty, narrow passageway and rested on a crumpled lump against the wall across the alley. He squinted then froze.

The lump was a man. A dead man.

Good lord, now what?

Trace shook his head and lowered himself to the cot. With his head back in his hands, he examined his situation.

All right. Someone will come by today and inspect the body. Somebody's gotta walk past and stop.

He would just have to wait... and wait. His stomach rumbled. *Fine. Something else to worry about.*

155

CHAPTER TWENTY-SIX

"Colton."

James jerked his head up, stared into Captain Greene's face, then sprung to his feet. The tin coffee cup that James held sloshed its contents. He stared across the campfire at his commander.

"Sir?"

"Did I startle you?"

"Just thinking, Captain." A grin lifted one corner of his lips. He wiped his wet hand on his pants. "Just plain thinking."

"Good." Greene pointed to the rock James had been sitting on. "At ease."

James sat back down while the captain planted himself on a nearby rock.

"This morning we're sending an advance scouting party through Picacho Pass and on into Tucson. General Carleton and I both feel that you and your brother, as well as privates Reynolds, Fountain, and a few others, should be the ones to go."

"Sir?"

"You up to it?"

Shoulders straightened as he drew in breath. "Yes, sir."

"Good. I knew you'd say that." Captain Greene cocked his head toward the center of camp as he stood. "Lieutenant Barrett's gonna be in charge. Five minutes. My tent."

James fought the grin threatening to break out.

* * *

Late afternoon sun warmed James' back as he rode next to Fountain. He studied the four men ahead. Reynolds and a young soldier, Alvarez, rode side by side, and way up ahead rode Andy and Lieutenant James Barrett. It was their job now to scout the area for Confederates and report back. He vowed to do the absolute best he could, even if it killed him. His friends and fellow soldiers relied on him. The responsibility felt good.

White clouds dotted the turquoise sky. Even though it was April, the temperature bordered on hot, and the gusty wind swirled around his horse's forelocks. Adjusting his weight in the saddle, James noted how stiff and sore he'd become. One day on a horse and it felt as if he'd never ridden before. Of course, he'd been afoot for several months; the mounts were reserved for the officers.

"That pile of rocks up ahead, James." Fountain pointed east. "That's what the Indians call Picacho Peak. It's a real sacred place to them."

"We gonna go around it, right?" James asked when he noted the worry in his friend's eyes.

"Nope. Carleton said we need to go through that pass, make sure the Rebs aren't hiding."

"There's a pass?"

Fountain nodded. "Don't you remember from your stage driving days? There's an old stage road through that pass. Hasn't been used in a few years, but it'd make a great ambush point."

James' chest muscles tightened. "Now that you mention it, I do remember. My turnaround point was Tucson, so I never went through here." He squinted at the rocks ahead. "What makes Carleton think those Rebs'd be there? They're barely able to hang on to Tucson. Why'd they be all the way up here? Fifty miles away."

Fountain shrugged. "Don't really know." He peered over at James. "Better keep our eyes open and guns ready just in case."

"Got mine ready to go, Fountain." Alvarez patted his side arm. "Just let 'em come now."

Fountain pointed to his own eyes. "Just keep these open and your head down."

The call of hawks overhead did nothing to put James at ease. He whistled. The two lead riders and Andy reined up. James, with Fountain at his side, rode close to the others.

"Fountain thinks that would be a good ambush point." James struggled to keep his words calm. "Gotta be careful."

Fountain swiped at sweat on his forehead. "Keep your eyes peeled and take it slow. I wouldn't put it past those devils to try to kill us." He cocked his head toward Andy. "I'll take your place as point."

Lieutenant Barrett surveyed the five men. "Stay on your toes. Once we make it through, we're heading for that Pima village ten miles south." He spurred his mount into a slow trot.

James studied the small mountain perched alone in the middle of the desert, its spiked peaks jutting into the sky. Huge boulders lay nearby, many piled on top of each other. They reminded him of the glass marbles he and his brothers would try to stack into pyramids. They had rolled off into the dirt just like these boulders.

His youngest brother rode a horse length behind Barrett, with Fountain next to the lieutenant. All three men disappeared around a boulder deep in shadow. James struggled to breathe.

What if Andy gets hurt again, or God forbid, killed?

James forced air into his lungs.

Don't even think that. This isn't like that time down by the river. He'll be fine. Those Rebs aren't anywhere close around here.

He sat up straight.

That's what we thought that time, too.

A shot. Rifle fire crackled across the desert. Booms echoed from the boulders. James twisted in his saddle. Gray uniformed men rushed from the pass, shouting and firing. Bullets slammed into rocks a few feet away.

James leaped from his horse and ran for the nearest boulder. Hunkering behind it, he readied his revolver and aimed at the enemy.

Yells. Hooves galloping. Shotgun fire. It mixed together and assaulted his ears. Soldiers scrambled for cover. Brown rocks melted into the sand. Orange and gold fire erupted from pistols. James blinked.

A bullet sheared off a chunk of rock near his face, but James thought only of his brother. Andy? Where was he?

"Andy!" James called as he stood and peered around the boulder. He flinched as a bullet sheared off another piece of granite. "Andy?"

Fountain yelled back. "Up ahead. Still in one piece!"

Thank you, God.

James swiped at the sweat pouring in his eyes. He raised his shaking revolver, then aimed it toward the gunfire.

Kill or be killed.

Both hands clutched the gun. It refused to stay still.

158

Shoot. Dammit, James, shoot!

He swallowed hard.

These're men. Not quail or snakes.

Could he take a man's life? Even if the man was the enemy? Could he kill again? James squeezed his eyes tight. He pushed off from behind the rock, then zigzagged closer to Fountain. He slid to a halt and asked, "How many you figure?"

"Ten, twelve. No more than that."

"Got us pinned down good." James studied the rocks around him. "If I can get up in there," he pointed over his shoulder, "I might get a few shots off. At least see what's goin' on."

Fountain followed his gaze and nodded. "It's worth a try. Watch yourself."

James gripped his gun and sprinted from boulder to boulder. The climb left him exposed at times, but his brother's life, as well as that of the rest of his company, was on the line. He had to go.

From his new vantage point, James spotted soldiers in gray hidden among rocks on each side of the pass. On his right, he spotted Alvarez, gun in hand, behind a boulder. Off to his left, his brother was wedged between a mesquite bush and a boulder. James tensed. A Reb soldier hid no more than twenty feet from his unsuspecting brother. The Rebel sighted his rifle.

Directly at Andy.

James aimed and prayed his bullet would stop that man. James waited for the soldier to clear the rocks. Thirty seconds... forty-five... sixty. At last, the Rebel stood and stepped to his right.

James pulled the trigger. His wrist took the recoil.

Andy whipped his head up. The soldier stumbled out of hiding and collapsed face-first onto the ground.

James planted his forehead against a boulder. His shoulders heaved.

Kill or be killed.

A deep breath. James rubbed his eyes. He caught Andy's surprised gaze. James waved. Andy returned the wave with an index finger in the air, then added a strong nod.

Winding his way back down to the base of the rocks, James wondered if Andy would be able to take this skirmish in stride. Would he realize that if the Reb soldier hadn't died, it very well could have been him?

Lodged behind a craggy sandstone boulder close to Fountain, James signaled that Andy was all right. His friend returned the sign and nodded.

Gunshots, ricocheting bullets, men's screams. Reality blurred. A breeze delivered acrid odors of gunpowder. It spiraled around James' head and mixed with the feral odor of fear. He pushed down panic.

Boulder to bush to man. James' gaze stopped on Reynolds to his right crouched behind a rock. He fought so easily that James knew battle skill was second nature to him. Reynolds exuded confidence.

"Gotta get closer, men." The voice in James' ear spun him around.

James caught his breath. "You scared me half to death, Lieutenant."

"Glad I'm one of the good guys, then." Barrett gripped James' shoulder. "You and Fountain circle behind me and head north. I think there's a pocket of Rebels hiding out."

Without another word, James and Fountain clambered over boulders and around bushes before sliding to a stop behind huge chunks of granite. The two men again checked their weapons. Fountain patted the hunting knife at his belt.

"See anything?" Fountain wiped the sweat from his upper lip and stood against a rock. He peeked over the top.

Beads of water crawled down James' back. He wiped first one hand then the other on his pants. He scrambled through a small mesquite bush and leaned against the rock next to Fountain.

"Some of them Rebs must be in the shadows. Can't see a damn thing." James said, squinting.

A rock rolled near James. He whipped around. A gray-uniformed man tackled him. Both men hit the ground and tumbled over the rocks. A fist to his face. James yanked on the Rebel's hair. Another blow to his face. James tasted blood. More punches. Unrelenting punches.

A few Indian tricks from his months in Cochise's camp popped into James' fuzzy mind. He brought his feet under the soldier on top of him, kicked up, and somersaulted the enemy. The Rebel sailed over his head and hit the ground. He groaned.

Groggy from the blows and unable to find his feet, James pushed up to all fours. There was movement on his right. Blurred images cleared. Fountain pulled his knife out of the man's chest. Blood covered Fountain's hand and the soldier's shirt. The Rebel's eyes flared as his body spasmed.

James stared at the man, then wrenched his gaze toward Fountain. His friend knelt transfixed with the bloody knife in one hand, the man's shirt gripped in the other.

Locating his gun stuck barrel-down in the sand, James yanked it out and knelt next to Fountain.

"Damn, Al." James pried the dead man's shirt out of Fountain's hand. James frowned. "Damn close. Thanks." He swiped at his mouth and found blood on his hand.

Fountain let out a long stream of air.

Staccato gunfire. James sprung to his feet. He glanced left then right. Icy shivers raced through his body.

"Andy!" James pointed to his right. "This way."

Zigzagging from rock to rock, both men rushed toward Andy. Shots louder now. James spotted his brother crouched next to Barrett. Both men were hidden behind a boulder, side by side, aiming, shooting, reloading, shooting. They didn't seem to stop and think about the shooting, the killing of people. They just aimed and fired.

Now wedged between two sheared-off boulders, James nodded to Fountain who had taken cover on his left. The return nod assured James that his friend was thinking again.

Without warning, Lieutenant Barrett stepped out from behind the rock, knelt, and fired. A bang. A second bang. Barrett flew backwards and hit the ground. Puffs of dust danced around him. Red liquid stained his shirt.

Before James could shout a warning at Andy, his brother jumped from his hiding place and knelt by the lieutenant.

Andy grabbed Barrett's shirt with both hands and dragged him across the ground toward safety. Even from a few yards, James watched agony and grief assault his brother's face. Andy lowered Barrett.

As if in slow motion, James looked to his right just in time to see a gray-uniformed soldier step into plain sight, sneer at Andy, then finish reloading his gun. James fired toward the Rebel. Slivers of rocks pinged to the ground.

Unscathed and undeterred, the Confederate aimed his weapon at Andy's chest. Staring up into the barrel, Andy mouthed *NO.*

James lunged. Boulders, bushes, sky, and people blurred into swirls of color. A roaring in his ears blocked out any ambient noise except the shot aimed at Andy.

Fountain leaped at Andy, shoving him to the ground. Both men rolled, then slammed against a boulder. Fountain crouched with Andy behind him, leveled his revolver, and fired. The enemy soldier clutched his stomach, sailed backwards, and thudded to the ground.

* * *

"Help! Help me!" Trace shoved his arms through the barred window into the hot, late afternoon air. Again on tiptoes, he spotted two men yanking clothes off the dead man in the alley.

They glanced up, then froze. When they realized Trace was locked inside, they resumed their work. Their rapid-fire Spanish matched the pace of their scavenging. In no time, they stripped the body bare and left it exposed to the scorching sun. The men stood, arms full of clothes and boots.

"Hey! Over here!" Trace yelled again.

The younger looking of the two stepped over and squinted into the jail window. "*Que?*"

"Get me outta here! I'm locked in."

"*Que?*"

"Help me! Find somebody and get me out!"

The man shrugged. "*No se. Todo la jente se van.*"

"What? What about the people?"

"*Se van.*"

Confusion pressed into Trace's thoughts. "They're gone? All of 'em? *Todo? Porque?*"

"*Los soldados.*"

"What about the soldiers?" Remembering his Spanish, Trace repeated the question.

"*Donde esta los soldados?*"

"*Se van, tambien.*" The man glanced down the alley.

"They're completely gone, too?" Trace leaned into the window as far as his body allowed. "*Todo?*"

"*Si.*"

"Everybody." Trace nodded. "Then you come in and unlock this door. *Abre la puerta! Por favor!*"

The man glanced over his shoulder at his partner who shook his head and muttered, "*Vamanos.*"

"Wait! Wait!" Trace glanced around the empty cell. Something they would want—trade for his freedom. He had nothing except what he wore. "Wait." He tugged off a boot and held it out the window. "My boots. You can have my boots. Just get me outta here."

Both men turned at Trace's words. A glance at the stolen possessions clutched against their chests, the men shrugged, then trotted down the alley.

Trace waved his arms. "Wait! Don't go! *Alto!*" He screamed until their backs disappeared around the corner. "At least get me a damn spoon so I can dig out!"

He waited and stared into silence.

Don't panic. Maybe they'll break into the jail and unlock the door.

Trace thudded to the cot, held his head in his hands.

Right. They'll unlock this door and bring me dinner. Right.

* * *

On one knee, Andy, shoulders heaving with each deep breath, bowed his head as he bent over Lieutenant Barrett.

James slid to a quick stop and jerked Andy to his feet. "Dammit, Andy! What the hell were you thinking? You almost got shot, too!"

"He's my friend!" Andy yanked his arm from his brother's grip and again knelt by the fallen man. "I wanted to help. But, dammit, I was too slow."

Fountain moved in closer to James, but spoke to Andy. "He was already dead. You did your best. No one could've saved him."

"I know that!" Andy turned his back to Fountain and James and launched a rock across the desert.

James felt Andy's grief and wished he could somehow spare him any more heartache of war. Concern, cloaked as anger, subsided. James knelt next to his brother by Barrett's body and let out a stream of air. He slid an arm around his shoulders and lowered his voice.

"I know it hurts, Andy." James ran his hand down the lieutenant's face, closing the eyes. "Barrett was a good soldier."

Shrugging off his brother's arm, Andy spoke into the dirt.

163

"Why him? He was good to ride with." He turned back to James. "Had a wife and kids."

"Damn shame." James glanced up at Fountain kneeling on the other side of the body.

Andy stared at Barrett. "It just ain't right." He sniffled.

Pain and sorrow etched Fountain's face, too. After another glance at his distraught brother, James patted him on the back and stood.

"Awful quiet." James said. His gaze swept across rocks and boulders. A sudden chill defied the April heat. "Too quiet. Stay here, I'm gonna take a look."

James turned, then froze at footsteps picking their way over gravel. They echoed against the boulder. Signaling to Andy and Fountain, James jumped behind a rock and whipped out his revolver.

The steps grew closer. They stopped directly in front of James. Someone sucked in air.

"Lieutenant Barrett?"

James peeked around the rock's edge and recognized the other soldier from Mesilla. "Reynolds?"

Reynolds aimed his revolver at James, then lowered it. A relieved grin spread across his face. "Damn, James."

"You 'bout scared me to death." James holstered his gun. He stepped from behind the rock while Andy and Fountain did the same thing. "Where's Alvarez?" James asked.

"He took a bullet in his arm. Be all right, though. I already sent him back to the medic." Reynolds pointed behind him then looked down at the body. "Barrett?" He turned to James. "What happened?"

Andy walked up to the men. "Fountain saved my life. He pushed me out of the way or that soldier would've shot me for sure."

Reynolds nodded at Andy. "Guess it's your lucky day."

Andy lowered his head and looked at Barrett. "Sure as hell wasn't his."

PART THREE

CHAPTER TWENTY-SEVEN

"Congratulations, Fountain." James patted the ebony-eyed man on the shoulder as they shook hands. "You deserve it." Fountain's grip was firm, definitive. Just right for a man in charge. Andy puffed out his chest. "Just think, James. We're friends with a *sergeant*, now." He glanced at James, then shook hands with Fountain. "Suppose you'll still talk to us mere privates?"

Fountain returned the smile. "If it hadn't been for your fool head thinking bullets wouldn't kill you, I'd never been promoted."

Joshua Reynolds elbowed James. "Course it looked really good when our *compadre* marched those three Rebels back into camp." Reynolds slapped Fountain on the back. "What're you gonna do next? Save the entire Union Army and be promoted to General?" He saluted.

With great ceremony, Andy placed his hand over his heart. "Or President?"

"Come on. You know me. " Fountain shrugged. "Not president. I'm humble. I don't expect much. I'd settle for something simple, like... Emperor!" Everyone chuckled. Then Fountain grew serious and turned to Andy. "Saving you was the best thing that happened to both of us."

Andy nodded and ducked his head. "Sure was, Al, sure was."

Fatigue punched James in the stomach. He was tired of trudging across the desert. The lure of Tucson and the ending it might bring, called to him. Maybe they'd spend several months resting up in that dusty town before marching off someplace else. Using the brim of his army hat, James smacked his brother's chest. "Hate to see this party end, but Greene says we're moving out early tomorrow—before sunrise."

Reynolds leaned over to Andy and raised his eyebrows. "Looks like you'll have to break some of those Indian ladies' hearts, my young friend. Notice you've been over at that Pima village quite a bit. You got some sorta *novia* you ain't told us about?"

Andy's face pinked as he glared at Reynolds. "No sir! I'm not sweet on anybody. It's just that, well, we've been here almost a week now and they're real nice to me—the old women and the young ones." He searched all three faces watching him. "Just trying to be neighborly."

"You got that down to an art, partner." Fountain raised one eyebrow and punched him in the arm.

Remembering images of his dead Pima wife, James drew in a sharp breath.

"Kinda hate to leave all this paradise." Reynolds spread his arms as wide as his smile. "Sand, scorpions, snakes, and sun. What could be better?"

James stepped back from his friends. "Better pack. At least we'll travel in the cool of the day." He nodded at Fountain and Reynolds, turned, then trotted off.

Andy caught up and then trotted alongside. "What's wrong?"

James halted, gazed into the sky, and glanced back over his shoulder at his friends still gathered near General Carleton's tent. "Nothing."

"James?" Andy leaned in close and raised an eyebrow. "I know that look."

"Hell, Andy. I'm happy for Fountain, I really am, but..."

"But what?"

"I should've got a promotion, too. I got off a tricky shot from those rocks and saved you that day also. Remember?" James took a deep breath and jerked his thumb back toward the soldiers. "And what about the time a few days ago when I shot that rattler? Would've bit Reynolds, maybe even killed him. Good for Al, but when's it my turn?"

Andy's mouth opened, then closed. No words came out.

A glance into his brother's brown eyes, James read the face he knew so well. "I know I sound childish, but..." Fists clenched, he whipped around. "Ah, hell. Forget it."

James marched across the entire encampment and stopped before Andy managed to catch up.

Now in front of the tent he'd shared with his brother for months, James stared over the canvas sea and watched women in the nearby Pima village go about their evening chores.

Maybe I didn't get a field promotion because people think I'm crazy. Maybe they think that just because I sometimes see imaginary Indians means I can't be a hero. Maybe they didn't promote me because of the bruises I've given almost everyone in the company.

He wagged his head.

Yeah, that would definitely do it.

Andy at his elbow, James glanced to his right and bit his lower lip. The brothers stood side by side watching purple shadows flood the Indian village. The happy chit-chat of women and children preparing the evening meals wafted across the desert. When the wind shifted direction, he caught the tantalizing aroma of mutton stew and piñon campfires. His stomach rumbled at the thought of women's cooking.

Tasting chunks of mutton, which had simmered in broth most of the day and had been spiced with certain herbs the Indian women found growing wild, James' stomach gurgled with memories. One corner of his mouth lifted into a half smile. He thought back to the many evenings he and Trace had sat around Cochise's fire, spooning the tasty stew into their bruised mouths. It had been one of the few comforts, rare pleasant times of his captivity.

Despite his best efforts, memories took control. One Wing hovered over him at the campfire. James jerked his head up and gazed up into that Apache's cruel eyes. Without provocation, One Wing jammed his bowl of mutton stew into James' face, pieces of hot meat gouging his eye. Slammed backwards against the ground, James struggled to breathe, the bowl engulfing his mouth and nose.

Squashed with One Wing perched on top of his chest, and powerless to push the bowl off, James gasped for air. Stew blocked his nose, filled his mouth. James bucked, twisted and turned, but his captor rode him like a wild horse. Lungs screaming, he kicked out but the Indian pressed down. A warm, protective blanket of blackness threatened to cover James. One Wing let go.

"James, you're shaking."

An arm slid around his shoulder.

"You all right?"

His terrifying memories retreating, James sucked in lungfuls of desert air. He wiped mutton stew off his face and tasted the gravy lumps in his throat. He swallowed.

"James? James? Look at me."

Hands on his shoulder, gripping, not hurting him. James stared at the man in front of him and struggled to place the face. Eyes, inches from his, took on an oval shape, the color a worried brown. The nose, smallish yet a bit upturned, perched above open lips. Finally the entire face crystallized into someone he recognized. Andy.

James waited for the memories to slide back where they belonged.

Enough. Let it go. That was months ago.

He regarded Andy and noticed the eyes wide, forehead furrowed. He nodded, then let his gaze hit the ground. The constricting band around his heart eased.

Andy strengthened his grip on James' shoulders.

"I don't care what anyone thinks," Andy said. "Hell, with all you've been through... and survived... hell, James, you're my hero."

James brought his eyes up to Andy's. "I ain't anybody's hero. I'm broken."

"What the hell're you talking about? Broken?"

James stared into the dusky-hued desert.

Just what One Wing wanted.

"Only thing broken on you now's your self confidence." Andy paused, then continued. I'll agree you should've got a promotion, too." He released his grip. "But, truthfully, James, Al spent a lot of time getting to know General Carleton."

"So?" James swung his full attention to his brother.

Andy shrugged. "Face it. Al likes people and they like him. He'll get the promotions. You're only gonna keep getting a pat on the back unless you change your way of thinking." Andy licked his lips and wiped the sweat trickling down his face. "Look. This is hard to say, but—"

"But what?"

"You've been out of Cochise's camp just about a year now, but he's had you by your..." Andy balled his fist. "Well, he's been in control ever since." He glanced at James, then at the sky.

"What?"

Andy drew in a deep breath. "I'm sorry for what you went through. I truly am. Every time I see those rope burns around your wrists, the whip scars... hell, you still got bruises that haven't gone away... I feel sorry all over again. The pain, the terror you went through must've been—"

"It was."

"I'd gladly trade you places if I could, give anything to take away the nightmares. But, dammit, James, those Indians've controlled you too long. I know you can't put it behind you, but you gotta shove the past to one side." Andy touched James' shoulder. "Stop feeling sorry for yourself and move on."

* * *

'Stop feeling sorry for yourself. Move on.' Stop feeling sorry—
The more James marched to Andy's advice, the madder he got.
Feeling sorry for myself? Who does Andy think he is? I'm not feeling...

But what was he feeling? James stepped around a mesquite bush and looked over at his brother marching with Fountain.

Maybe what Andy says is true. But to move on? How?

They'd been marching since sun up, and the day sure wasn't getting any cooler. The sand soaked up heat and sent it right back up through James' boots. About the time he knew his feet were cooked like a well-done steak, Greene called a halt.

James crawled into the shade of a boulder and leaned back.

"How'd you manage to find the one square foot of shade?" Andy asked as he uncorked the canteen and squatted by James. "Captain Greene says we should be in Tucson by dark."

Heat waves shimmered off the desert. A light breeze rattled the mesquite bush by James' shoulder. He glanced at the sky. Clouds threatened to hide the sun. Would it rain? Andy tapped him on the shoulder using the side of the container.

"Want some?" Andy asked.

James squinted against the glistening sand. "I hated you for what you said last night."

"You did?" Andy sat down next to James. "Why?"

James pulled in air. "I'm sorry. I had no cause to be mad at you. It's hard hearing the truth. Maybe I have been feeling sorry for myself. Maybe I haven't tried hard enough to move on. To get past the... the memories."

Muted sunlight filled the desert, while a slight breeze cooled James' skin. He closed his eyes. "I just don't know how, Andy. I just don't know how."

Andy sipped from the canteen, then corked it. "What did Trace do?"

171

James frowned. "Trace? You think he's 'moved on'? Gotten 'over it'?" He shook his head while studying his fingers. "He's still lost. Haven't you seen his hands shake sometimes? Or jump at a sudden noise?"

"One time I touched him when he wasn't looking," Andy lowered his voice. "I thought he was gonna kill me."

"Uh huh." James raised both eyebrows. "So, don't think for one minute that Trace is all right. He's not."

"Maybe you should meet your fear head on." Andy picked up a stick and drew lines in the dirt. "You know. Maybe talk to an Apache. Then maybe you'll see where those memories fit."

James reached for the canteen. "How in the hell'd you get so smart?"

Andy offered the canteen. "Drink."

* * *

The last vestiges of gold and orange painted the adobe village of Tucson, largest town in the newly formed Arizona Territory. James planted one foot in front of the other. He moved forward, more out of habit than out of thinking about it. Watching the low buildings take shape and come into clear view, his energy increased.

Elbowing Andy who plodded alongside, James pointed to the town. "Somewhere, over there, is a cantina with our names on it. Yep. Just ready with a nice beer and friendly conversation."

"I don't believe it. Must be... what'd they call it?" Andy snapped his fingers. "A mirage. Yeah, that's what it is. A mirage. Thought I'd never see this place again." He pried off his hat and swabbed his forehead with his arm. "Tell me it's real."

"It's real all right and looking good." James' smile spread across his dirt-encrusted face. "After we set up camp, maybe Greene'll let us go into town. We could do some scouting. You know... check out the village and make sure it's safe for everyone."

"And while we're doing that, we could be checking out the beer to be sure it's fit to drink." Andy's grin faded. "But what if we run into some Rebs? What then?"

James shrugged. "Guess we take 'em prisoner. I sure don't want to kill again."

Andy shook his head. "You were right 'bout killing and dying. It's terrible. I'll never forget—"

"No, you won't. So let's hope we never have to do it again." James took a couple of halting steps, let out his breath, and placed one foot in front of the other. "Let's go."

* * *

Setting up the tent in the dark proved to be easy. The brothers had done it so often they had it completely erected within minutes of stopping.

Fountain stepped between James and Andy and draped his arms around both of them. "Well, well, the Colton brothers. Looks like tonight's your lucky night. Captain Greene says those cowards in gray uniforms pulled out of Tucson a few days ago and the heroes—that's us— are now in charge."

"Great news, Al. Great news!" James produced his wide grin. "We're going home?"

"Not quite yet. In the meantime, Carleton wants the two of you, Reynolds, and me to take those prisoners into town, lock 'em in jail."

Andy smacked Fountain on the back. "All right! I was hoping to go. Carlos' Cantina, here I come!"

Reynolds joined the threesome, then spoke in a stage whisper. "Think the kid's a bit excited about going to town?"

The men nodded in unison.

"But, question is," Fountain cocked his head. "Can he hold his liquor? Don't want him drunk tonight and have to bring him back draped over his horse. Just ain't fitting for a soldier wearing blue." He glanced from face to face.

"I can drink any of you under the table." Andy puffed out his chest and pointed a thumb at it. "Just try me."

"After we get these Rebs put away, we just might take you up on that challenge, Baby Brother Colton." Fountain turned his back just in time to deflect a hat flipped in his face.

* * *

Riding into town under a half moon, James peered into the various yards and houses on the outskirts of the small town. Although the hour wasn't much past nine, many of the houses showed no signs of life, no lamps burning in the windows, no indication that people still lived there.

The men rode down Congress Street, each one, except Andy,

leading a bound prisoner. A small bonfire off to the side illuminated people who sat near it, bottles in hand.

Andy swung his gaze side to side. "Kinda spooky, ain't it?"

Reynolds turned around in his saddle. "Probably all in bed. Leaves more whiskey for us."

The men reined up in front of the Sheriff's office. James yanked his prisoner from his saddle, then checked the bindings. He knew this Reb wasn't going to cause any trouble tonight. The ropes were tight.

James grasped his captive's hands and ran his own trembling fingers under the coarse rope.

Not too tight, no marks.

With a quick nod, he stared into the man's eyes and saw fear, apprehension, and contempt. James knew those feelings well.

Standing on the plank boards in front of the jail, Andy turned the doorknob. It held fast. Pushing, pulling, he rattled the knob then knocked.

"Sheriff? Sheriff," Andy yelled through the thick wooden door. "It's the *Union* army. We got some prisoners for you."

James banged on the door and tried the handle. "Nobody's home." He peered down the darkened street searching both ways. "Wonder where he's at?"

Andy shielded his eyes and looked through the window. "No lights or anything. Looks like nobody's in there all right." He turned back to the men. "What now?"

Fountain led his prisoner down the steps to the horses. "Go back to camp, return in the morning. Sheriff should be back by then." He pushed his Rebel onto the horse, then mounted his own. "Let's go."

James glanced at Andy. "Guess that drink'll just have to wait." He took the steps easily. "Tomorrow's soon enough."

Andy sniffed the air. "Hey, James. You smell something? Dead?"

James pointed his nose in the same direction, pulled in air. Nothing that smelled "dead" assaulted his nose. "Probably somebody cooking dinner." Helping his prisoner on his horse, he turned to Andy. "Like Fountain said. Let's go."

CHAPTER TWENTY-EIGHT

"Andy. It's broad daylight." James kicked the bottom of his brother's foot. "Time to get up."

"Why?" Andy pulled the light blanket around his shoulders and turned his back to his brother.

James grabbed the cover and rolled him over. "Captain Greene wants us on the double."

Andy groaned then rubbed his eyes. "Ten more minutes."

"Better get a move on." James tugged the arm until Andy's body stretched across the tent's dirt floor. "You want that big old Sergeant Williams coming in here?"

Andy opened one eye and glared at James.

"Didn't think so." James pulled his brother's wadded-up trousers out from under boots discarded in the tent corner. He draped the pants across Andy's face. "Find your feet, soldier."

Less than five minutes later, the brothers stood in front of Greene and waited for instructions. The Captain paced back and forth. Eyes on James, then Andy. Back to James. He stopped to smooth his fledgling mustache.

"I have something special for you two," he said. His gaze roamed James' face. Greene squared his shoulders. "'Bout ten miles east of here's a mining camp, Parkersville. Recently been attacked by Cochise and another Apache leader, Mangas Colorado."

James' heart somehow managed to beat inside his knotted chest. Sucking in air, he discovered his mouth hanging open.

Captain Greene stared at Andy. "You're awful young, son, but I know you can do this." He swung his attention back to James. "Go to that camp, find out about Cochise. See if he's raiding elsewhere, what he's up to."

James shook his head. "I'm not the one you want for this."

"Listen, James, I wouldn't ask if it wasn't important. You know how Cochise thinks better than anyone." Greene paused.

"No one's more qualified than you. You'll be doing your country a great service."

"But—"

"Just find out what's going on and report back by dark." Captain Greene patted James on the shoulder. "You'll be all right."

A lance through the chest couldn't hurt this bad.

James eyed his brother, then turned back to Greene. "But—"

"I know you can do this." Greene lowered his voice, dropped the words to something close to a whisper. "I know how you felt about Fountain's promotion. You think you should've got one, too." He slid an arm around James' shoulders. "There could be a promotion in this for you."

"Promotion?"

James couldn't believe Greene knew his true feelings. But right now a promotion wouldn't keep him and Andy alive. Wouldn't do anybody any good if he was dead.

"But—" James protested.

"The United States army is counting on you." Greene nodded. "Hell, James, *I'm* counting on you."

* * *

Shortly before dark, Fountain, with Reynolds at his side, picketed his horse at the camp remuda, and then both men headed toward the commander's tent. Captain Greene pushed aside the flaps and stepped out into the warm evening air.

Fountain saluted Greene. "Those prisoners are finally locked up, sir."

"Good. Any trouble?"

"Not with those Rebs, Captain. No, they were real quiet." Fountain wagged his head. "Darnedest thing, though. Sheriff's office was still locked."

Reynolds stepped closer. "We looked all around for the sheriff, even the deputy, then we managed to break into the jail, and find the cell keys. We left Ramirez to guard the prisoners."

Greene nodded.

"Captain," Fountain removed his hat, wiped the sweat pouring into his eyes.

Damn this desert heat.

"Ramirez and O'Connor found a prisoner all but dead locked back in a cell."

176

"What?"

Reynolds turned one palm up. "Appeared to have been there six, seven days, maybe longer. Don't know how he survived."

Fountain cocked his head back toward town. "They hauled him down to the doc's. But, of course, just like the sheriff, he wasn't there."

"They just left the prisoner?" Captain Greene frowned.

"Not alone. The doctor's daughter was there. Said she'd see to him until her pa came back."

Greene's eyebrows drew together. "Who was it? Did he say?"

Fountain and Reynolds shook their heads.

"From what Ramirez and O'Connor said, he was unconscious. But, Fountain and me didn't actually see him, sir. We were talking to the hotel manager." He nudged Fountain. "Show Captain Greene what she gave us."

Fountain held out a well-worn, leather saddlebag.

"Explain, gentlemen." Greene said as he took the offered pack and examined it.

"We were busy breaking into the sheriff's office when this woman, the hotel's manager, rushed up to us with this saddlebag. Said we were the closest thing to law she'd seen recently." Fountain pointed to the leather. "We haven't had a chance to look inside."

Reynolds nodded. "She said one of her guests had left it in his room. It'd been there maybe two days when her next guest found it jammed under a table near the bed. She looked through it but couldn't tell who it belonged to."

"What about the hotel registry?" Greene unbuckled the tanned flaps.

"Couldn't read the name. She wasn't the one on duty at the desk when he came in and the other clerk's off visiting her sister in Tubac." Reynolds shrugged. "Mystery man."

Captain Greene tucked the bundle under his arm. "All right. Thank you men. I'll look into it." He turned around.

"One more thing, Captain." Unsure of the level of familiarity his new rank afforded, Sergeant Fountain nevertheless placed a hand on Greene's arm and waited for him to turn around. "We found a body out behind the jail. Sure was stinking up the place."

"And?" Greene readjusted the saddlebag under his arm.

"Just thought you'd want to know. It'd been there a week maybe. Somebody'd stripped it." Fountain wrinkled his nose at the memory.

"Identity?"

Fountain and Reynolds shook their heads. Fountain shrugged. "All I can tell you is he was young, around twenty-five maybe, 'bout six foot, brown hair. Another mystery man." He glanced at Reynolds then back at his commander. "Took him down to the undertaker's."

Greene sighed, scratched his face. "All right. Thank you gentlemen. Busy day. Dismissed."

He returned the soldiers' salutes and marched toward his tent.

* * *

The closer he rode to where the mining camp was reported to be, the tighter James' chest constricted. By the time he got there, he was sure he wouldn't be able to breathe. As it was, he could barely speak. Which was fine. There was nothing to say. Nothing that was new and that Andy didn't already know. If Apaches were still there, could he talk to them, like Andy suggested? Would he be able to put his fears aside and do what the army requested of him? Could he?

A long look at his brother riding next to him. Was his face a bit paler than usual? His lips were sure set in a tight line, and he gripped those reins like he was about to fall off his horse.

Tall Ponderosa pines clustered together, making it hard to see more than twenty feet on either side of this narrow wagon path. Something fluttered in a bush up ahead. James squinted harder, then pointed. He kept his voice low.

"Andy. You see that?"

"Yeah." Andy rode up closer, then leaned over and pulled a pair of man's long johns from a bush. He looked around. "This can't be good."

Chills brushed James' body. Could he go on? What would they find? The closer they got, the more he wanted to turn around and report a lie to Greene. 'Sure, we were there, Captain. Nope. No survivors. Looks like the Indians are gone, sir.' That would be it. Simple. Easy. But was he conquering his fear? Moving on?

Andy pointed to a wall of granite up ahead. "Isn't that where the camp's supposed to be? And there's the stream." Both men reined up.

Doubts. Memories. New resolutions. Panic. They all fluttered and collided like demonic butterflies in James' stomach. He knew he'd throw up.

"Can't. Can't do this." James shook.

Andy leaned over and gripped James' shoulder. "Yes, you can. I'm right here. We'll do this together." Their eyes met. "You'll see. It'll be all right."

James drew in a long, slow breath.

Andy's right. Time to move on.

He nodded. "Let's do it then." He gigged his horse, gently.

Strewn garments, cooking utensils, wagon wheels, and a couple dead mules littered the path. James reined up and tied his horse to a tree. Andy tied his farther down.

Beige canvas tents hung from trees; tin plates and utensils were spread out like a wild picnic gone bad. Then James spotted him. A man lying face down in the mud.

A closer look around and James noticed more. Two lay side by side like they were sleeping. Another man, totally naked, clutched a hunk of black hair as he lay sprawled across a bush. James swallowed hard. Were the Indians still around?

"James!" Andy's voice called out from behind a stand of trees. "Over here!"

James bolted for his brother, afraid for Andy's life. Instead he found him kneeling by a man, propped up against his knee.

The man's hand shook as he swiped at dried blood around his mouth.

"We gotta get him back to camp." Andy peered up at James. "You think he'll make it that far?"

Before James could answer, the man clutched Andy's shirtsleeve. "Apaches," he groaned. "Apaches did this."

"Which ones?" James frowned at his stupid question. What did it matter which ones? He rethought. It mattered a lot.

"Don't know." The man's gravelly voice faded. "Couldn't stop 'em." His clouded eyes trailed up to Andy. "How's Stevens? He all right?"

Andy looked up at James, who shrugged.

The miner coughed, his whole body shuddering. "Stevens? My partner. How is he?" Blood oozed from his mouth.

"I'm sure he's fine, sir." Andy hugged the man tighter. "I'm sure he's fine."

Eyes closing, the miner nodded, then took a final breath.

179

James had to turn away. The tears in Andy's eyes were too much to handle right now. Instead he rubbed his own eyes, fighting the pressure building up behind them.

* * *

The Colton brothers rode into camp well after dark. As much as they'd wanted to stay and bury the dead, that would have to wait. They had to get back to camp. Tomorrow a team could go back and do the digging, the burying, the praying.

After leading their mounts to the remuda, James and Andy removed the saddles, the leather shiny from years of use. Andy slipped the blanket off his horse's back.

"What're we supposed to tell Captain Greene? That Cochise wiped out an entire mining camp? That he's declared war on everyone?" Andy lowered his voice and eyed his brother. "That he's taking no prisoners?"

Hands at once cold and clammy, James forced down rising bile. "Probably for the best. Nobody should be a captive. Nobody." The scars across his back throbbed. He closed his eyes.

"James?" Andy leaned in close. "James. We gotta go tell Captain Greene what we learned." He grabbed James' arm. "You all right?"

The shaking subsided. James nodded. "Yeah."

Captain Greene stood in front of his tent and returned their salutes. "What'd you find out?"

Knowing he should report, as requested, James opened his mouth but words escaped him. He turned to Andy.

"Sir." Andy glanced at his brother. "Cochise is running wild. Apparently after the Army killed his brother last year, he's just gone crazy. Killing everybody he can find."

Greene's eyebrows knotted above his worried eyes. The hazel-green eyes narrowed as if memories raced across a finish line. He straightened his shoulders.

"Too bad. Many of the other Indian leaders are willing to go to reservations, take their people somewhere safe," Greene said. He shook his head. "I was afraid he'd hold out. Guess we're in for a fight."

James nodded, every muscle in his body tightening.

Captain Greene drew a breath and with it, a new voice.

"There's something you two need to see. Could be bad news,

180

boys. Might not be anything at all. Just don't know exactly what to make of it."

That familiar knot of concern forced its way into James' throat. What could Greene possibly want them to see?

Greene returned with the saddlebag clutched in his hands. "This look familiar?"

The brothers glanced at each other as James took the pack. Greene continued, "The hotel manager in Tucson says this was left behind last week. I'm not quite sure what to make of it, but thought you ought to see what's inside."

Greene stepped to his left, allowing the glow of the nearest campfire to shine on the bag. Frowning, James moved in closer to the light, opened the flap and peered inside. Andy looked over his shoulder. Extracting several letters, James held them up and studied the address.

"They're from you, James!" Andy grabbed a letter. "Here's one from me. Addressed to Trace!"

Riffling through the rest of the leather bag, James discovered cash, a few clothes and a note from Teresa. He examined it by the fire. Each new discovery was more confusing than the last.

"Says she loves him, can't wait to see him again." James glanced at Andy. "And she knows that once he finds us, he'll feel better."

"Do you know what that means?" Captain Greene studied the note. "Has he been sick?"

"No, Trace's fit." Andy replaced the money and clothes.

"What then?" Greene handed the paper back to Andy.

"Means he was trying to find us." James lowered his voice, stared into the dark desert. "I know him, Captain." James hugged the saddlebag to his chest. "Finally caught up with him. The past he's been hiding from found him."

"You have my permission to go into town, if you think you're up for it." Captain Greene pointed to the remuda. "Get fresh horses."

"Yes, sir. Thank you." James saluted as Greene walked away.

"*We* gotta find him now." Andy looked around the firelight-dotted camp. "Question is— where do we start?"

The Colton brothers marched back to the remuda and saddled fresh horses. Working in silence, James fought the knot tightening in his stomach. What if Trace had been murdered along the way and they took his saddlebag? What if he was captured by the Confederates? What if those cowards took him prisoner as they retreated? How would the family ever know what happened to him? James glanced at his brother and noted the same questions on his face.

Swinging up into the saddle, adjusting his weight, James gripped the leather reins. The brothers spurred their mounts into a full gallop. Nothing but blurred cacti and one startled coyote greeted them along the way. They raced into town, reining up in front of the hotel. James jumped off his horse, joining Andy already at the door.

Knob in hand, Andy looked at James. "What if he's dead? What if somebody killed him along the way? What if—"

"Keep your head. We'll find out what we can." James studied Andy's glistening eyes, angst creasing the young face. "It'll be all right."

The lady behind the desk couldn't tell them anything new. James studied the registry from the week before and recognized his older brother's scrawled handwriting. He glanced up at the clerk and pointed.

"That's him, ma'am. Our brother."

Andy slapped the counter, his hand landing next to Trace's name. "He *was* here." He turned to James. "Now what?"

"Can we go see the room he rented, ma'am? Maybe we can find a clue or something." James gazed up the stairs.

"Won't do you no good, Mister Colton. Two more guests have stayed there since your brother." She eyed the Colton boys and sighed. "But I guess it won't do no harm either." She presented Andy the key.

A few minutes later, Andy handed the iron key back to the manager. "Thanks, ma'am. Sorry to trouble you."

"Find anything?" She hung the key on the hook behind her.

Both brothers shook their heads. With a hand to his hat brim, James stepped into the night. Andy shut the door behind him. Warm April wind shoved waves of smothering bonfire smoke into James' face. He stood on the wide veranda and stared into the inky night. Were these smoke-induced tears?

A sliver of moon peaked over the Rincon Mountains far to the east. Devilish strands of panic clamped around his throat threatening to extinguish his sanity.

He kicked the wooden post holding up the porch. James spewed oaths, then clenched his hands.

"Dammit! Damn everything!" James cursed. His fists, then his forehead banged against the post. He squeezed his eyes tight. "What the hell'm I supposed to do now?"

CHAPTER TWENTY-NINE

A cool compress slid across Trace's face. He forced one eye open. Golden sunlight filtered through white curtains. He blinked at the glare. Fuzzy images cleared. A lantern, doctor tools, and rolled white gauze lay on the bedside table. An antiseptic odor sailed into his lungs. Coughing would feel good right now. A low bark rattled his chest.

Feeling better, he let his gaze rest on a young woman sitting across the room. Her shiny, black hair was swept up behind her head, and her eyes looked down, focusing on something in her lap.

"Teresa?"

"Don't try to talk, son." A deep masculine voice. Trace flinched. Head easing toward the voice, he squeezed his eyes shut. Every part of his body ached. Another cough.

A hand brushed his hair back from his forehead, then it rested there.

Just like Ma when I was sick.

He let out a stream of air. Someone would take care of him, help him feel better, get him on his feet again.

Just like Ma.

He let darkness take him down.

* * *

James glanced up from his dish of breakfast stew as his brother squatted on the ground next to him. James spoke over a mouthful of venison.

"And?"

Andy shook his head, then poured himself a steaming cup of coffee.

"Greene hasn't heard anything else," Andy replied. "Said intelligence reports still say that Rebel coward, Captain Hunter, took no prisoners last week when he and his army ran away." He blew on the black liquid before sipping.

James stared into the campfire. Months had marched by since he'd felt this depressed. Dammit! Just as life was returning to some form of normal, another boulder blocked his path.

Andy hurled a twig into the orange, spire-like flames, and voiced what James already knew. "We're never gonna find him. And if we do, he'll be dead."

"Quit thinking like that."

"Why? It might be true." Andy snapped a stick and flung half into the fire. "Why'd he have to come? Why couldn't he just stay in Mesilla and look after things? Huh?"

"Could be he's just worried about you and your getting shot."

But James knew better. Trace was fighting his own demons. James set his plate on the ground. Had he just eaten? Plate was empty, so he must have.

Andy touched James' sleeve and lowered his voice. "What're we gonna tell Ma?"

Good question.

James hung his head. Ma had never been told that he and Trace were once Cochise's captives. So how could they tell her that her oldest son died trying to rescue his brother from demons only two of them could see? Part of her would die with Trace.

James patted Andy's knee. "It'll be all right. We'll find him." James' words echoed hollow and meaningless. He didn't believe them any more than Andy did.

"Knew I'd find you feeding your face, James." Fountain squatted between the brothers. "Andy, if you don't hurry, that big brother of yours is gonna eat everything." His smile plummeted. "What's wrong?"

James swung his gaze to his friend. "Remember that saddlebag the hotel manager found?" He waited for Fountain to nod. "It belongs to our brother Trace. Apparently, he registered at the hotel and never came back to his room. Nobody knows what's happened to him."

"We think he's been killed, Al." Andy attempted a sip from his trembling cup.

Fountain knelt, frowned at Andy then James. "Good Lord! Your brother? Why'd he come here?"

"Not really sure." James picked up a stick and fed the fire.

185

"You have any leads, any idea where he might be?"

Both brothers shook their heads, their gaze riveted on the fire.

Fountain's words were full of concern. "What's your brother look like? You know I've been in town a lot. Maybe I've seen him and just didn't know who he was."

"Six foot, just turned twenty-five last month, brown hair like mine, brown eyes more like Andy's. Scars on both wrists—just like mine." James cringed.

Silence. A deep breath. James eyed Fountain. "What is it? What'd you know?"

Fountain removed his hat, then raked his fingers through his black hair. "Should go check it out before I say anything. Don't want you two getting worked up over something that might not be."

James gripped his friend's arm, his knuckles turning white. "What do you know? Tell me!"

"Don't want to alarm you."

James shook him. "Tell us!"

Avoiding James' piercing eyes, Fountain hung his head.

"All right. Me and Reynolds found a body yesterday morning out behind the jail. Been dead for probably a week."

Andy knelt in front of Fountain. "Who was it?"

Fountain glanced at Andy then James. He shrugged. "Don't know for sure." More silence.

"Al?" James' eyes met Fountain's.

"He was around twenty-five, 'bout six foot, brown hair."

* * *

Trace squinted at the bright afternoon light. A soft hand planted itself on his hot forehead, its coolness bringing a thread of a smile to his dry lips. He tried to speak, but only rasped.

"Hush now, don't try to talk." The young woman he'd spotted earlier removed her hand from his forehead and smiled. "Just a little fever. You'll be fine in a few days." She straightened up and reached for a glass of water next to Trace's bed.

"Where...?" Trace managed one squeak. After sipping the water, he sank back on the hard bed. His merry-go-round world slowing, he fought to keep the woman in focus, fought to understand what had happened.

The woman cradled his head and shoved another pillow under it. "You're at Doctor Martelli's office. In Tucson. I'm his daughter, Morningstar."

Trace grabbed for the woman's arm. His mouth opened twice before words would form. "James? James." Confusion and concern swirled in his mind.

Morningstar patted Trace's arm, a comforting smile lighting up her face. "All right, James. Now we know who you are." She stood. "I'll go fetch some broth. You'll feel much better." She swept out of the room and disappeared.

Eyes closed, images of Captain Rudolfo Garcia popped into Trace's mind. He watched the Confederate soldier sneer as he waved goodbye, remembered the slam then distinctive click of the key in the lock.

Then his whole world waited.

Questions whirled. How did he get here? And how long had it been since Garcia left? Most importantly, where were his brothers? Had they left Fort Yuma yet? He'd planned to meet them in the desert, maybe clear over to California. He imagined James' face as he recognized him.

His thoughts drifted. Then his eyes jerked open. What if he'd missed his brothers? What if the army had bypassed Tucson, or went through while he was in jail? What if James and Andy were in Mesilla by now? God! Teresa would be panicked.

Gathering all his strength, Trace pushed himself up, pulled off the light blanket. He gripped the edge of his bed and swung his legs over the side. His world spun. Several deep breaths brought the small room into focus. Feet on the floor, Trace struggled to stand.

"James! What on earth are you doing? You're not ready to be up." Morningstar said as she set the cup of broth on the bedside table. She eased Trace back down to the bed. He leaned against the pillows, and she pulled up the cover around his chest.

"You'll get your strength back soon, James. Patience and time." She picked up the bowl, then spooned a little broth into Trace's mouth.

* * *

James, Andy, and Fountain stepped into the noon sunlight. James lifted his chin and ran his hand over stubbled cheeks.

187

"Thank God it wasn't Trace." James said, glancing over his shoulder at the undertaker's office.

"Sorry to have worried you so much." Fountain wiped beads of sweat on his upper lip. "But that body fit your description."

Andy nodded to James. "You're both kinda lucky. Those scars 'round your wrists and Trace's wrists make identifying you two real easy."

James glared at Andy. "Yeah—lucky us."

"Now what?" Fountain stepped between the Coltons.

Another good question.

James gazed down the dusty main street. He studied the wooden buildings lining both sides and thought about Mesilla. The plaza there was the center of activity. No main street separated the businesses like here in Tucson.

Andy patted his stomach. "Don't know about you two, but I could use a meal."

Gaze resting on his brother, James shook his head. "Ain't close to hungry yet. I don't think a bite would even go down right now."

"How 'bout we humor your brother and go over to the restaurant with him? I could use something to drink." Fountain patted James on the back and lowered his voice.

"It's hard, I know. We'll find him."

* * *

Andy scooped up a warm tortilla and talked over a mouthful of *posole*. The spicy hominy stew, laced with chunks of mutton, swam in thick broth.

"Think we'll ever find Trace, Al?"

Fountain sipped lemonade and nodded. "Don't see why not. That brother of yours can't be too far." He paused. "Suppose he went out prospecting? Lots of men do."

A quick shake of his head. Andy tore off another piece of tortilla. "Not Trace. He believes in hard work that's more of a sure bet, like driving stages and law enforcement. Nah, he wouldn't be out scratching in the dirt."

Spinning a glass on the wooden table, James glanced around the wallpapered dining room. He tapped his foot and squirmed in his chair, then pushed it back. He stood.

"Sorry. I just can't sit still," James said. "Gonna take a walk down Congress Street and see what's going on. Meet you back here."

Before either Andy or Fountain could respond, James opened the door and marched into the warm afternoon.

Another mouthful of *posole*, Andy watched a raven-haired young woman step into the restaurant. She swept past their table. A subtle hint of antiseptic wafted past Andy's nose. It mixed with the aroma of his food. She approached the friendly waitress. Curiosity piqued, Andy listened to their conversation.

"Hi, Pauline." The woman's words were gentle. "May I get another quart of that broth?"

The waitress wiped her hands on her apron. "Of course, Star. Your patient doing better?"

"Your good cooking is doing the trick. He just might live."

"Glad to hear it." Pauline disappeared into the kitchen.

Andy raised his eyebrows at Fountain and dropped his voice to a low whisper. "Must be a nurse, or at least doc's helper. Too bad I'm not sick."

"She's a looker all right." Fountain nodded. "But I've got my Marianna back home. Soon's this war's over, we're getting married."

"What d'ya think? Should I go over and get acquainted?" Andy placed his tortilla on the table, wiped his mouth, and then glanced at Fountain. "She sure is pretty."

"Give you a dollar if you do." Fountain produced a silver coin.

Two deep breaths and another swipe at his mouth, Andy pushed his body to his feet and eased over to the young woman.

"Excuse me, ma'am?" He waited for the woman to turn around. Her eyes glowed like black diamonds.

She met his gaze but did not smile. "Yes?"

"Excuse me, again, ma'am, but I overheard you say you had a patient. You a nurse? Maybe even a doctor?" He whipped off his hat and clutched it with trembling fingers.

"No, my father is. Why? Are you sick?" This time a faint smile appeared.

The waitress, metal container in hand, appeared from the kitchen. The aroma wafted through the air and spiraled around Andy's nose.

Andy cast his eyes downward and sucked in air. "Well, ma'am. Not exactly sick. See, I'm a private in the Union Army and took a bullet in combat a few weeks ago." Andy held his side. "It's been paining me some. Thought maybe a doc should take a look." He hoped his hangdog stance was effective.

Setting the container on a nearby table, the woman touched Andy's arm. "Poor thing. You're so young to be a soldier... and to be shot, too." She wagged her head. "Of course my pa'd be happy to take a look. The office's just down the street."

Andy smiled a woeful smile. "Thank you ma'am. I'll be over directly."

Picking up the tin pail, she nodded, walked through the door, and disappeared into the street.

Turning back to Fountain, Andy grinned. He held out his hand.

"Looks like I've got a date." He flipped the coin.

CHAPTER THIRTY

All right. Now what?

Andy pushed on the doctor's door. Memories of the time when he was shot by that Confederate made his heart race. He held his breath. That moment of terror, the searing pain, the feelings, hadn't gone away. Then it hit him. If he remembered being shot so clearly, what must James go through with his memories? Andy shook his head. No wonder his brother had such a tough time.

Morningstar greeted Andy and Fountain at the door and motioned to the chairs in front of the desk. While they sat, she picked up a pen and took a seat behind the narrow oak desk. She raised her dark eyes to Andy.

"Now, I'm going to need some information first, sir. Your name?"

"Andrew Colton, ma'am."

She scribbled on the paper. "Age?"

"Seven—" Andy shot a warning glance at Fountain, then coughed and deepened his voice. "Twenty."

"And how long ago were you shot, Mister Colton?"

"Please call me Andy. All my friends do." He flashed a grin. Then remembering the seriousness of the attack, his smile melted. "Three months ago. Wasn't it, Al?" He looked at Fountain for confirmation.

"'Bout that." Fountain adjusted his weight in his chair.

"Matter of fact, ma'am, my friend here, *Sergeant* Albert Fountain, also got hurt. Reb cracked him on the head."

Staring up from her paperwork, the nurse fixed a concerned gaze on Fountain. "Are you all right?"

"Fine, ma'am. Just fine." The newly-promoted sergeant touched the old wound.

Andy sat up straight.

All right, here goes nothing.

"Ma'am, now that you know our names, may we know yours?" Andy asked.

The black-haired beauty put down the paper and pen, then stared at the two men. "Morningstar Martelli." She stood and pointed to an open door. "This way, Mister Colton."

Fountain stood and jerked his thumb over his shoulder. "Andy, I'll find go James and tell him where you are."

"James?" Morningstar stopped and looked at Al.

Andy walked toward Morningstar. "James is my brother. He's out wandering around town somewhere."

Morningstar cocked her head. "Isn't that a coincidence? We have a patient here named James. It's not often you get two names like that so close together."

"Well, it is common, ma'am." Fountain said as he swung his gaze to a paling Andy.

A cold chill knotted Andy's chest. "What's this patient look like?" He moved in closer. "See, my oldest brother's missing and he and James are real close. Might be he was mumbling my brother's name. It would be a miracle if he was here."

"I'm not—"

"Ma'am, we're truly worried. Won't take long." Andy gestured to his face. "My brothers. We all look alike."

Morningstar studied Andy's face. "Hmm."

Andy held out both arms. "He's got scars around his wrists. Apache ropes."

"This way." She signaled to Andy.

He trotted down the hall, Fountain on his heels. The threesome stopped in front of an open door. Morningstar peeked in.

"He's asleep," she whispered. "Don't wake him. He needs to regain his strength."

Andy and Fountain stepped into the small room. Sunlight filtered through a window and lit the man whose back was turned to them.

Andy tiptoed around the bed, then gazed down. His head jerked up, his mouth opening and closing like a surprised fish. He waved to Fountain.

"It's him. It's Trace!"

Dropping to one knee, Andy shook Trace's shoulders. "Trace? Trace. It's me, Andy."

Fountain stood next to Andy, peering into Trace's fluttering eyes. "What d'you suppose happened?"

Andy shrugged and patted his brother's cheeks.

Morningstar smoothed the sheet over Trace. "They found him locked in a jail cell here in Tucson. Appears to have been there maybe as long as a week."

Fountain touched Andy's shoulder. "I'll find James."

* * *

James perched on the edge of his brother's bed; Fountain stood in the doorway. James' gaze started at Trace's covered feet, then worked its way up to the face. He smiled at the open eyes.

"How you feeling?" Not waiting for a response, James looked up at Andy for an answer.

Andy squatted down beside his brother.

Trace's bandaged hands patted James' leg.

"All right... day or two..." Trace's words were soft.

"What happened to your hands?" James frowned.

"No spoon." Trace closed his eyes.

Morningstar interrupted the family reunion. "Gentlemen, Mr. Colton needs to get some of this broth down. He can't regain his strength if he doesn't eat."

"His hands?"

Morningstar's eyes snapped down to James at his sharp question. "He tried to dig his way out of jail, Mister Colton. Adobe's too thick." She pulled up a chair on the other side of the bed. Andy plumped extra pillows behind Trace.

Fountain stepped into the room. "James, I'll ride back to camp and tell Captain Greene about your brother."

James looked up at Fountain as if he'd just materialized. "Good Lord, Al, I'm sorry. Let me introduce you to my brother."

Fountain walked around the bed and took Trace's white-gauzed hand. "I've heard a lot about you, sir. Pleased to finally meet you."

"You..." Trace closed his eyes, took a deep breath.

Fountain grinned at James as he released Trace's hand. "Things just have a way of working out, don't they?" He nodded at Andy. "Glad you found him."

The back of James' friend disappeared out the door. The outer door squeaked open then closed. James knew he was truly lucky to

193

have a friend like him. Maybe someday, he'd have more friends.

Morningstar spooned broth into Trace's mouth and spoke to James and Andy. "He's quite dehydrated." She looked at James. "He's not had enough water."

"Yes, ma'am. I know what that means." James studied the twinkling black eyes of the woman across from him. She was pretty. No, not pretty. Beautiful. Stunningly beautiful. Her dark hair and black eyes set off the creaminess of her smooth skin. High cheekbones gave her face a wide, innocent appeal. His heart beat faster and his mouth went dry. He glanced behind him at Andy, who returned the look with raised eyebrows.

"Miss Martelli," Andy said as he placed a hand on James' shoulder. "I haven't officially introduced you to my much *older* brother, James. James, meet Miss Morningstar Martelli, the doctor's daughter."

Morningstar nodded while James tipped his hat, then remembered to remove it.

"Pleased to meet you, Miss Martelli. Thank you for... our brother. He wasn't supposed to be here... like this." James worried his mouth would run away with his thoughts before his brain could figure something more intelligent to say.

"He was lucky they found him when they did, Mister Colton. Another day, and my Pa says he would've died." Morningstar's eyes glowed with compassion. She cast a sideways glance at James.

Andy pulled up the wooden straight-back chair near the bed and sat. "How long you think 'til he's up and running again?"

"You'll need to ask the doctor, but I'd say in a few days he'll be on his feet." A smile inched across Morningstar's face as her eyes met James'. "Now that you're here, I'm sure he'll feel much better."

Morningstar looked from brother to brother and nodded. "Andy, you're right. You three *do* look alike. I'd know you were brothers anywhere." She stared at the second Colton brother.

James' cheeks burned and the knot in the pit of his stomach twisted.

Is she flirting with me? Whoa. I'm only in town just a few more days and I'll need to spend them taking care of Trace. But I'll be right here, next to her.

Watching this enchanting woman spoon-feed his brother, James came to his senses. He straightened his shoulders.

Just walk away. Leave her for someone who'll stay in Tucson. Besides, I'm damaged goods.

"I'll ask again, Mister Colton. Are you in the army?" Morningstar touched James' arm.

James jerked his head up, held the mesmerizing woman's gaze.

She looks familiar, like someone I know. But who? Where?

Andy jumped in. "We both are, Miss Martelli, me and James. But not Trace. We've been in nine months now. Seen plenty of action, too."

"So you've mentioned." Morningstar rested the spoon in the empty bowl. "My pa will still be happy to examine you."

"I'm better now, ma'am." Andy touched his side and nodded.

The woman stood, her long fingers placing the bowl on the bedside table. James found his feet also, then helped her pull up the light blanket and tuck it under Trace's chin.

His older brother's eyes closing, James leaned in close to his ear. "I'll be back after a while, Trace. Get some rest now. You'll be fine." His voice dropped to a whisper. "We'll both be fine."

Once in the outer office, Andy turned to Morningstar. "I know we'll never be able to repay your kindness and help with our brother. So... may I take you to dinner tonight?"

James glared at Andy, then stared at the young woman. How could his brother ask that?

Andy was much too young for her.

Morningstar flashed a half smile at the youngest Colton.

"Thank you for your kind offer, Andy. But, there's no need. Your brother's recovery is all the thanks I want." She extended a hand to James. "I'll see you soon, Mr. Colton."

"Please call me James, Miss Martelli."

Her grin blossomed into a dazzling smile. Morningstar shook his hand. "Your brother kept mumbling your name, and I thought it was *his*. Glad we finally got it straightened out." She glanced at Andy. "See you soon."

The Colton brothers stepped into the street. After walking half a block, Andy grabbed James' arm. The brothers skidded to a quick stop. "What the hell was that?"

James faced him. "What?"

"That. That flirting you did. I saw her first."

James huffed. "Look. I'm not going to fight my brother over any girl. Even if she was interested in either of us, *which she's not*, we're

195

in the army remember? We'll be leaving in a day or two, never be back." He jerked his arm out of Andy's grip. "Just drop it."

Andy marched in time with his brother. Arriving at their horses, James untied the reins, then placed a foot in the stirrup. Andy grabbed his arm again.

James glared. "I said 'drop it'."

"Wait." Andy hung his head. "I'm sorry. Don't know what got into me. Trace wouldn't like me fighting with you. Especially over a girl." He raised his eyes to meet James'. "If you wanna ask her out, go ahead. Nobody'll come between us. Right?"

James studied his brother. Andy'd done a lot of growing in the past year. Most of it good. He nodded and squeezed his brother's shoulder. "Right. We're family." James swung up into his saddle. "As beautiful as she is, she's probably seeing someone anyway."

CHAPTER THIRTY-ONE

"Son, it's been a real pleasure watching you return to life." Doctor Martelli stood with the Colton brothers in the outer office. He handed Trace a bottle of brown liquid. "A spoonful twice a day and in no time you'll outrun these brothers of yours."

Memories of hundreds of foot races from school to home flooded James' thoughts. How often had he let Luke and Andy win?

"That's gotta be powerful medicine, Doc!" Andy gripped James' shoulder and shook it. "Trace always tries, but James here is still faster. Always has been, probably always will be."

Trace elbowed Andy. "That's 'cause I always let you two win. That's what big brothers do, right?"

So, his secret was revealed! James caught the playfulness in his brother's eyes and patted Trace's back.

Serious now, Trace turned to Martelli and shook hands. "Hope the money's enough to cover my stay. I'll never be able to pay what I really owe."

Doctor Martelli waggled a friendly finger. "Just take care, and stay away from those Confederates, young man."

James pumped the doctor's hand. "I'll make sure he does, sir."

"And thanks for looking at this bullet wound." Andy patted his side. "Feels fine now."

With a firm grip on his older brother's arm just in case Trace's knees decided to buckle, James waited for Trace to receive final instructions for a quick, full recovery. Trace had been given excellent care, James reflected, especially from lovely Morningstar. And during the past few days, Captain Greene had allowed the brothers plenty of time to get reacquainted. James would always be in debt to Martelli and Greene.

But right now, James couldn't keep his eyes off the woman

standing near enough to touch. There was something captivating about her. A final glance at Morningstar, then he turned his attention to the doctor.

"Thank you also, sir. Thank you for giving us our brother." As James took a deep breath, a tickle grew in his stomach. "Sir? May I take your daughter to dinner tonight? Kind of a 'thank you'?"

Doctor Martelli glanced over at his daughter, then at James. "You'll have to ask her, but it's all right with me."

"Would you? I'd be honored to escort you to a steak dinner." Morningstar produced a heart-stopping smile.

* * *

James held the door as Morningstar glided through. The aroma of cooking steaks and potatoes wafted through the restaurant and swirled around James' nose. He pulled in more air. Hunger pains and butterflies collided.

Once seated, they struggled for conversation. Neither could find the proper first-date topic. All ideas seemed either too forward, too political, or downright boring.

After a glass of wine, both relaxed enough to enjoy the evening. James stared into glistening black eyes and spotted a fire inside this beauty. Intrigue pushed its way through the butterflies. James spoke.

"I know I've said this often the last few days, but thank you again for helping Trace. You and your pa saved his life. We'll always be grateful, Miss Martelli."

"You're welcome. And, please call me Morningstar." She played with a woven silver chain around her neck, the turquoise pendant swinging like a clock's pendulum.

"All right, *Morningstar*. It's a beautiful and unusual name. How'd you get it?" Morningstar stared at the necklace. "My mother was White Mountain Apache, my father a prospector."

Apache?

"My father was killed when the Apaches found out my mother was expecting me. She somehow managed to get into town right before I was born."

James forced down memories and swallowed hard. He clenched his shaking hands.

Must've been hard on her.

"I'm sorry."

"Don't be. There's a happy ending to the story." She reached across the table and touched James' arm. "Matter of fact, I was born in the room your brother was in. My mother named me Tahtatzinupi. That's Apache for Morning Star. It's the first thing she saw when I was born. Apache custom."

He reached for his wineglass.

A drink. I need a drink.

"She only lived a few days." Morningstar lowered her voice. "The doctor and his wife adopted me."

James forced words. "More wine?" He poured himself a full glass and downed it in one long swallow.

Morningstar stopped playing with her necklace. "I've had a wonderful life. As far as I'm concerned, they *are* my parents and I'm blessed they raised me."

His chest and stomach twisting, part of James wanted to curse this woman, her Indian ancestry... ever meeting her. The other part couldn't ignore that this half-Apache woman across from him was just that—a woman. A beautiful one.

Damn Indians. Old injuries shot pain through his body. He gripped the empty glass and reached for the bottle. How could he now even consider liking her? On the other hand, hadn't he been the one a few months ago expounding on the virtues of Indians?

Hell, I even married one.

He poured a third glass.

Only for three days, but married is—

"...your only brothers?" Morningstar's voice cut into his thoughts. "James, are you all right?"

"What?" James refocused on the woman leaning close and noticed a loose strand of ebony hair fall over one eye. Cold chills raced up and down his spine.

Dark Cloud. That's who she looks like—my murdered wife.

"I was asking about your family, but you've turned quite pale." She frowned and leaned closer. "James, you're shaking. Are you all right?"

He slid his hands under the table and cursed this weakness. Morningstar's eyes probed his face. He knew they were taking in his scars, his past. What else did she see? What did she think?

James made up his mind right then. Time to get over the past, time to push it to one side, just like Andy and everyone else said. Time to move ahead. He dragged his gaze from the tablecloth up to her worried face. Her eyes showed true concern.

"I'm fine," James said. "Just been a while..." He let himself smell her femininity, let his eyes admire her smooth skin. "Now, what were you saying?"

James Colton and Morningstar Martelli spent two hours lingering over steak and dessert. A quick glance at his pocket watch showed that the time had sailed by. The doctor had made it clear his daughter was to be back early, and James had promised she would be safely returned by ten. He had fifteen more minutes with this woman, and then he'd have to say good night. He snapped shut the cover of his grandfather's gold watch.

Twinkling silver studs dotted the clear, late-spring night sky as they strolled shoulder to shoulder down the dim street. With his demons gone for the moment, James sighed at the peaceful world. A full stomach and a beautiful woman.

"James, I've had a lovely evening. Thank you."

Realizing they'd arrived at the doctor's house, James frowned, knowing their time together was over. She stepped up onto the porch. Eagles soaring on wind currents didn't begin to compare to her gracefulness.

He leaped the steps, landing within inches of Morningstar. "I had a great time, too." Hesitating, he mustered up courage then took her soft hands in his. "May I see you again?"

She nodded.

"Andy and I have to ride over to another mining camp tomorrow, but as soon as I get back, may I come over? That is, if it's not too late and all right with your pa." James glanced over his shoulder at the curtained window, the lamp glowing through.

Morningstar smiled. "I'm sure it's all right with him." Her eyes sparkled. "You're a true gentleman, aren't you?"

James ducked his head, warmth rushing to his cheeks. He wrapped his arms around her and pulled her close. A hint of lilac danced in his nose. He closed his eyes and breathed in her freshly-washed hair. Morningstar sighed. His hand reached up and cradled the back of her head, and his fingers entwined in her long hair. Memories flashed.

Limp head wobbling.
Gushing red liquid.
Terrifying screams.

His hand jerked out of her hair. A cacophony of memories screeched through his mind.

Not again. Leave me alone!

He gripped Morningstar's shoulders and held her at arms' length. His eyes locked on hers.

"James, what's wrong?"

Dark Cloud... Lila... The rancher woman. Face after face melded together. Screams. Moans. Knifes slicing...

James pushed Morningstar back, then leaped off the porch. He bolted down the dark street, never glancing behind him, never glancing right or left. He prayed he'd run until his heart burst.

His legs refusing any further movement, his lungs wheezing for air, he reached the last building in town. His forehead pressed against the side of the adobe stable, his fists beat the walls. Numb, he slid to the ground. He pulled his body in tight, his quivering chin resting on his knees. Tears stung his eyes.

CHAPTER THIRTY-TWO

Trace pushed the tent flap aside and stepped into the bright morning sunlight. He stretched. Peering around at the sea of white tents, he nodded, knowing the Union Army was at long last pushing the Confederates out of the territory. The Rebs were on the run. The Apaches had a lot to do with Union victory. Cochise and Mangas Colorado had succeeded in killing a few Rebel soldiers. But, coupled with lack of funding and poor knowledge of the West, the Confederacy had no clue what to do with the Arizona Territory.

After another stretch, gentler this time, Trace spotted Andy shoveling stew into his face. He joined his brother at the campfire. Andy glanced up and offered his bowl to Trace. "Want some? Made it myself."

Trace shook his head. "Smells good, but thanks, no. My stomach's still not quite right."

"Take your medicine?" Andy's words were muffled with stew.

"Yes, Ma, I did." Trace picked up a tin cup and poured steaming coffee to the rim. Standing with his backside to the fire, he surveyed the few men preparing for a day full of bayonet practice.

"Where's that ol' brother of yours? Didn't he come home last night?" Trace blew on the hot liquid.

Andy glanced around, then shrugged.

"Figured he was already up. Doesn't sleep much."

Soldiers emerged from their canvas cocoons to greet another glorious Arizona morning. Trace pointed his cup behind him. "His bedroll's still made up. I don't think he came back."

"Well, that son of a gun. Good for him. Must've had one helluva night!" Andy stared up into his brother's eyes. "He's fine. Just sewing his oats. That was the first date he's had since... well, you know."

Trace nodded. "Since before he almost married Lila." He

sipped the hot coffee. "Sure was nervous last night."

"Yeah. Washed his face I bet ten times." Andy chuckled over another mouthful of stew. "You know, first day I saw her, I asked her out. But then I decided she's too old. So, I let James ask her."

Trace buried his smile in his coffee cup.

Tin cups in hand, Reynolds and Fountain joined the brothers. Reynolds held out an empty cup and cocked his head toward Al. "*Somebody* forgot to buy coffee in town yesterday. Can you spare a drop for needy friends?"

Andy nodded toward the pot. "'Course. Help yourself any time." He took another bite of stew. "Either of you seen James this morning?"

Reynolds poured the steaming liquid. "Sure. Just rode in. He's over at the remuda."

Andy waved his spoon at Trace. "See? What'd I tell you? Went for an early morning ride."

"Uh huh." Trace turned his gaze toward the corral, then without waiting for company, strode across the camp. He wound around tents and sleepy soldiers.

He spotted James currying a horse, the brush sweeping fast and furious over the same spot. Trace stood next to him. "Gonna wear a hole in your horse." He pushed the tin cup under James' nose. "Coffee?"

Face close to the horse, James shook his head.

"Where were you?" Trace stepped around his brother and planted himself against the horse's side.

"Town." James turned his back to Trace. More brushing.

"All night?"

James nodded. The brush scraped the neck.

With his world focused on his brother, Trace planted a hand on James' shoulder.

James froze. Breaths spurted through his nose like an enraged bull. His knuckles gripping the brush turned white.

Trace leaned in as close as he dared. "What happened?"

James hurled the brush across the desert. He stared into the sunrise-laden sky.

"Dammit!" James cursed. He whipped around and trained his eyes on Trace's. "She's Apache. A damn Apache."

"What?"

"Morningstar's half Apache. The Martelli's adopted her."

"How—?"

"But, I've thought it over." James bit his lower lip. "You and Andy are right. It's time to get over the past. I wanna see her again."

"What about—?"

"They won't leave me alone." His shaking hand raked his hair. "Those Apaches. That rancher woman. Dark Cloud. Even Lila. Dammit, Trace, they're everywhere." He squeezed his eyes tight and spoke through clenched teeth. "Thought I was better. Thought I'd beat One Wing."

Trace lowered his voice. "You *did* beat him. He's dead. It's gonna be all right."

But Trace knew he was lying to himself, too. Clutching James' shoulders, Trace shook them. "Look at me. *Look at me.*"

Half a minute passed before his brother's eyes met his.

"James, we'll get through this. You and me. Just like before. It'll be all right."

"No, it'll never be all right." James tugged on Trace's shirtsleeves. "All I tried to do was hug her. That's all. Nothing else." His voice shook. "But there was that woman, her hair wrapped around my hands... You remember... God, I heard screams..."

Memories bombarded every corner of Trace's mind.

Most of those screams were yours, James.

James hung onto Trace's shirtfront and buried his face in the shoulder.

Knowing exactly what his brother was going through, Trace wrapped his arms around him. Squeezing his own eyes tight, he heard his trembling brother choke on rising sobs.

* * *

Within an hour, James and Andy stood in front of Captain Greene. James didn't have to tell the commander what had happened; somehow he seemed to know. He waited for what he hoped would be new orders.

"James, Andy." Greene's eyes swung from brother to brother. "Like I said yesterday, another mining camp was attacked a couple days ago. A few miners escaped, but they weren't sure who the Indian leaders were. I'm guessing it's Cochise, but I need confirmation."

James shook his head. "Wish you'd find somebody else. I can't do it, sir."

Greene nodded. "Yes, you can. Sometimes facing your greatest fear is the only way of conquering it." He paused, glanced at Andy, then back at James. "Just keep your eyes open and be careful. I expect a full report tonight."

James watched his feet carry him back to his camp, to the safety of his tent. Pushing the flap aside, he entered the sanctuary alone and sat on his bedroll. Head in hands, he stared at the ground. How could Greene ask him to do that again? But, maybe the captain was right. What's the worst that could happen? Being captured again. Worse than that?

Andy captured.

James pinched the bridge of his nose. Maybe he would just ride out of camp and never come back. Desert the damn army. Desert everyone. Hell, desert life. Or maybe if he rode far enough, the memories would stay behind, unable to follow. No, he'd been all the way across the desert and back and he still fought the visions, the horrors.

All right, only way to get rid of this nightmare is to get rid of me.

Suddenly, he knew what to do.

If I'm dead, those Apaches will have to haunt someone else.

Better now than later.

Like the comfort of a warm blanket on a freezing cold night, James reveled in the solution. It was so simple. So... easy.

Tugging the revolver out of his holster, James studied the weapon and checked the chambers. Loaded, ready to go. When he pulled the trigger, everyone would come running. Trace or Andy would be first on the scene. Trace would know why, but the rest could only guess. They would never understand.

Using his sleeve, he rubbed the barrel until it gleamed. His revolver turned in his hand. Finally—a way out. He pressed the gun to the center of his chest. At this distance, he couldn't miss. He'd be dead before he fell over.

He fingered the hard, cold metal in his hand, the round barrel pressing on his breastbone. He nodded at the permanence of what he was about to do. Visions of beautiful Morningstar paraded through his head, the words of Captain Greene assaulted his ears.

Don't want you to end like Elizabeth.

Too late.

205

Too late for Elizabeth and too late for me.

A deep breath, finger on the trigger. Guilt for not saying goodbye to his brothers raced through his mind.

Too late.

With his clammy hand gripping the revolver, and his eyes still closed, James heard his heart beat for the last time.

"What the hell you doing?"

James looked up just as Andy launched his body at him and grabbed the gun. The brothers fell back against the ground.

"Trace!" Andy yelled as he perched on top of James and tossed the revolver against the opposite canvas wall. "Trace!" He pinned James' hands over his head. "Trace!"

The oldest Colton brother ducked into the tent. "What the hell—?"

"Tried to kill himself. I got here just in time... Gun's over there." Andy nodded toward the corner of the tent.

Trace glanced where Andy indicated and knelt by his brothers.

"Let him up, Andy."

James took deep breaths as Andy lifted his weight from his chest. Sitting up, James stared at his lap.

Why can't they just leave me alone? Let me end it.

"Can't take any more. Can't fight. It's over." James' words came out mumbled.

Trace nodded to Andy. "Let's get him on his feet, get coffee down him, and he'll feel better." He pulled hard. "Let's go, James."

Bright morning sun blinded the men as they stepped outside. Reynolds held the tent flap while Fountain poured black coffee and handed a cup to James. The men sat on blankets around the campfire and made small talk while James just stared into the flames and sipped the tasteless liquid.

James took little note when Andy stood and disappeared from the circle of friends. Orange spires danced in time to the rhythm of James' still-beating heart. The heat from the fire and coffee burned inside and out. His skin, entire body, smoldered.

A deep voice behind him broke the silence. "James?"

James peered up and around. There stood Captain Greene and Andy. James pushed his tired body to its feet and faced his commander.

"Andy told me what happened." Greene glanced at Trace,

then at James. "I'm sorry. But, I stand by my orders. You need to get going—now."

Greene raised his arm to salute, but instead patted James on the shoulder. He spun a quick about face and marched away.

James' shoulders slumped. He took a final sip from his cup and tossed out the rest. He watched the desert sand suck the life out of the coffee.

CHAPTER THIRTY-THREE

Trace knew what needed to be done. Confide in Martelli. Maybe the doctor knew how to help James. Hell, how to help both of them. His own demons were coming often and hard now.

After waving good-bye to his brothers, he saddled while reviewing the information the doctor would need. But would he believe him? The story sounded more like fantasy than reality. Would the doc at least listen? Somebody had to have the answer, the cure. Trace knew it was only a short time now before James would succeed in ending the nightmare—permanently.

Trace swung up into the saddle. If it hadn't been for Teresa, his wife—his savior—he probably wouldn't be far behind James.

During the ride into town, Trace sorted through the stories he'd have to tell Doctor Martelli. James would be angry if Morningstar learned of his past, but even so, Trace knew this was the right thing to do.

Tying his horse to the hitching rail, Trace glanced up and down Congress Street, then frowned at the lack of people going about daily business. Where was everyone? All run out by the Confederates? Whatever the reason, he had more important concerns right now. Those other questions would have to wait.

Doctor Martelli looked up from his paperwork as Trace pushed open the door. Extending his hand, the doctor smiled. "Good to see you again, son. Feeling better?"

"Yes, sir, I sure am." Trace returned the handshake. "Thank you again for everything." His heart pounded in his tightening chest. Small talk didn't cover his... his... what? Remorse? Anxiety? Panic? Guilt? All of them melded into a knot of confusion.

"Sit down, Trace." Martelli pointed to a nearby chair. "I'm assuming this isn't just a social visit. What can I do for you?" Trace twirled his hat in his hand. "You're right, Doc. It's not. Wish it was, though." He paused. "My brother and I need help." The lump in his throat made speaking difficult. "Don't know where else to go. It's a matter of life and death."

"Sit down. I'll get you some coffee."

Trace sat, then started off one word at a time. Within a minute however, his story picked up speed. He related their capture and subsequent torture by the Apaches. He spoke of the nightmares and visions both he and James still experienced. Trace also explained to Morningstar, who sat in during most of the recitation, why James had run off the previous evening. He avoided graphic descriptions of how he and his brother scalped the rancher woman. She didn't need to know that part.

And he left out James' murdered Indian wife. Trace still had doubts that it was true, but his brother believed it. When it all came down to it, that was what really mattered. Maybe some day he'd know for sure.

His hand massaged his forehead. "It's been a lot harder on James, this trying to figure it all out. But, Doc..." Trace's gaze leveled on Martelli's face. "James *will* kill himself if I don't do something—now."

The doctor ran his long fingers through his gray-streaked hair. As if fighting off his own memories, he wagged his head and gazed inside the coffee cup.

Morningstar looked over at Trace and caught his eye. "Thank you for telling me. Poor James. I wondered about that nasty scar on his cheek."

"Apache whip."

Should've been me. I should've stayed behind to take that whip. James wouldn't...

Trace's gaze bore into the past, then jerked back to Morningstar. "He's got a lot more scars. Inside and out." Trace sipped his coffee and realized it was stone cold.

Doctor Martelli stood, refilled his own cup then poured more into Trace's. Turning his back on Trace, Martelli stared out the window and watched the few people pass.

"Time was lots of people lived here," the doctor said. "I remember just a few months ago you could hardly walk down the street without bumping into someone. Confederates took care of the crowd."

"Sir?" Trace set his cup on the desk, then stood next to the physician.

"Damn soldiers ran all the good people out of town. They declared martial law and shut down the saloons, our dry goods stores, and took over the territory. Just about ruined Tucson."

Figuring Doctor Martelli was forming a plan for his brother, Trace nodded and spoke.

"I remember when we were driving for Butterfield, before... it shut down. Tucson here was our turnaround point for most of the runs. Spent quite a few good days here. Had some wild times."

Rowdy nights his brother and their stage driving friends, Clay and Sunny, spent in town sprung to mind. They didn't get together very often, but when they did, all four partied until sun up. Drinking and singing in the saloon was their favorite pastime.

This time pleasant memories made him smile. Trace wished he and James could again feel that kind of exhilaration, that sense of freedom and innocence. Smile evaporating, he realized that he and his brother would never be free, never be innocent again.

Enough. Enough feeling sorry for myself. I gotta get James put back together and then I'll worry about me.

Doctor Martelli turned. "How about you bring him in here tomorrow? He and I'll have a long chat. I've also got some new medicine I can try." He stroked his chin. "Supposed to be a pain killer—just might do the trick."

"Gotta be special to kill his kind of pain." The knot in Trace's stomach tightened. Could the doctor just snap his fingers, work a medical miracle or something and fix his brother? If Martelli couldn't help, there was no hope for James.

Morningstar touched Trace's arm, waited for him to face her. "Trace, let me help."

Trace forced air into his lungs where a ton of boulders pressed on his chest. "Don't know what you could do." He shrugged. "But something's gotta help."

"What does your wife do for you?" Morningstar fixed her dark eyes on Trace's. "She gives you love and understanding. A lot of patience, right?"

Trace nodded.

"Right." Morningstar shot a coy grin at Trace. "I'm fond of your brother." She looked over at her father. "With a lot of patience and understanding, I think I can help James more than medicine can."

Wagging his head, Trace spoke into his chest. "He's been hurt so bad by Lila, I don't think you'll be able to get through."

Morningstar patted Trace's arm. A grin lifted her eyebrows. "Oh, I'll get through. Trust me."

CHAPTER THIRTY-FOUR

This mining camp resembled the last one. Garments hung from trees, dead animals lay beneath branches, the stench of death permeated the air. James again had no words for Andy. He'd already told him to be careful a million times. A million and one wouldn't help.

A noise from behind. Ponies coming up the trail. Before James could point to some boulders, Andy scrambled behind one. James ducked behind another one, not far from Andy.

James signaled for Andy to stay low, and prayed the Apache scouting party hadn't spotted them. He listened hard. Quiet steps of the unshod Indian pintos. A bird cawing. His pounding heart.

Six Indians rode through the scattered remains of the mining camp, then slid off their horses. Two red streaks of paint scarred each man's cheeks; a blue line divided their noses. James remembered the markings meant they would kill whatever crossed their path. He swallowed. They were out for blood. Close call. Those warriors had ridden into camp only minutes after them.

James cast a quick glance to his right. There was Andy, still crouched behind that boulder, wedging himself in between a rock and a scrub oak. He checked his rifle, sighting it on an Apache.

James waved in small gestures to get Andy's attention, then shook his head. Andy lowered his rifle, then put fingers to his lips. James breathed out and squeezed his eyes shut.

"Dancing Hawk, *bunito!*" A strong Apache voice called to another.

James' eyes flew open. His mastery of the Chiricahua Apache dialect was rusty but still intact. He'd understood the command. With stealth-like movements learned from his days with Cochise, James scooted around to get a clearer view. Not twenty yards in front of him, two Apaches squatted in the sand examining fresh horse dung.

One of the Indians held his hand over the pile. He glanced up at the other and nodded. Standing, both warriors swung their gaze around the area.

James eyed Andy, whose tanned face drained to a pasty white. He gripped the Hawken rifle. Watching his brother squirm behind the rock, James repositioned himself for a better shot.

The Apaches would find them. It was only a matter of time before they'd have to fight. The Indians could follow footprints even at night. James would have a minute, possibly less, to make a plan.

Getting Andy's attention, James pointed at him and then pointed toward their horses. Holding pretend reins in hand, James again raised one finger at Andy. He touched his chest and then raised an invisible gun, aiming it at the Indians. It was the best plan. Praying his brother wouldn't argue, he knew Andy's chance of escaping was pretty solid. Andy had ridden horses almost since birth and could stay on through the most formidable conditions. Yeah, he'd be fine.

But Andy shook his head. He held up two fingers, touched his chest, then pointed at the horses.

James frowned. Hardheaded kid. Why didn't he take the chance to escape? There was no way both of them could get away. Before James could argue, his attention snapped to the rest of the scouting party joining the two standing near the droppings.

Ripped white canvas tents littered the desert; pans and pickaxes lay helter skelter like toothpicks tossed on a sandy floor. The Indians kicked at overturned boxes and crates. This had been a small camp, James remembered Greene telling him. No more than fifty prospectors had lived here. Thankfully, no women were here who had come to civilize the men and turn it into a town.

James studied the rocks and the one boulder behind him. Several yards to the west their horses, tied to mesquite bushes, stood hidden. If all went well, they'd stay that way, but one whinny, one whicker, and the game would be up. All right. As soon as the warriors moved away, he and Andy would make a run for the horses. He prayed theirs were faster than the Apaches' pintos.

But they weren't. No use wasting a prayer. The pinto he'd ridden while a captive last year was fast and powerful. Their old Army horses, especially with saddles on, could never outrun the pintos.

"Uah tehei - iquite!"

They know we're here! James fought sheer panic.

"Tabebo? Silaada?"

White man or soldier?

Pointing southwest, one Indian gestured at the unmistakable horse tracks in the sand. "Silaada, Tunayoneuh."

Two Bears! James recognized the name and then the scowling face of one of the meanest Apaches in Cochise's camp. Many times he had been the one to torment James, taking every opportunity to abuse him, especially when One Wing wasn't around. Two Bears had been the one who surprised James with a kidney punch so severe his legs remained paralyzed for hours. And it was this Indian who once beat Trace so badly it took the good part of a day for his brother to regain consciousness.

Forcing out air, James blinked into the present. If he could kill just one of the Indians, he would aim for Two Bears. His gun grew warm in hand. He caressed it. Then it hit him. Suicide was foolish, stupid. What had he been thinking? Who was the real enemy? It certainly wasn't himself. A wave of desire washed over him. He wanted to stay alive, see Morningstar again. Live forever.

He vowed to do just that.

Catching Andy's attention, James pointed to both of them then at the Indian pintos. Andy nodded. One by one, the Apaches moved up the wide canyon away from them. James took a deep breath and nodded.

The brothers eased from behind their boulders and crept toward the six Indian pintos.

Please, God, keep the horses quiet.

Andy swung up on his mount seconds before James. Grabbing hold of the white mane with one hand, gripping his Hawken rifle with the other, Andy kicked the pinto and sprinted away from the camp. James swung up on a black and white horse, grabbed the rope reins, and spurred. Knees gripping the pinto's sides, he raced for his life.

Seconds later, the remaining four pintos and two Army horses carrying enraged Apache warriors galloped no more than a hundred yards behind. Most had lances poised over their heads. One clutched a shotgun.

Ramming his spurs into his mount's side, James caught up to Andy. The brothers leaned over the horses' necks. Cactus and sagebrush whipped by.

"Death to the white man!" The scream behind James didn't need translation.

"Kill... kill..."

James clamped his knees against the horse's sides.

"Soldiers die!"

James held onto his pinto's mane and prayed he and Andy had chosen the fastest.

Half an hour flew by as the Colton boys dodged warriors who couldn't seem to close the gap. Even though the Army camp was still hours away, James began to think they would make it.

Without warning, James' horse stumbled, flinging him headlong into the dirt. James rolled twice, then crashed into a sharp boulder. He shook his head, clearing the spinning sky, clouds, and rocks.

James scrambled backwards, his flailing arms and legs useless to make any true speed. Andy mumbled encouragement, leaned way over in his saddle and extended his arm. James reached up and yanked. Andy slid from the horse and landed on top of James. Both scrambled to their feet and bolted for cover. They wedged themselves in between boulders.

On his knees now, James grabbed his brother's arm and shirtfront, then jerked him toward the nearby horse. "Go on! Ride! Get outta here!"

"No!" Andy wrenched his body from James' grip. "Ain't leaving you."

James searched the ground. "My gun. Lost it when I fell."

Andy pointed. "There."

The weapon lay barrel-first in the sand several feet away. Andy pushed off from the rocks, sprinted to the gun, and grabbed it, but before he could run back, the Apaches raced into view. Bullets kicked up dirt. Andy ran for a close boulder.

James shouldered Andy's rifle, aimed dead center for Two Bears' heart. He heard the report, felt the recoil before he realized he'd pulled the trigger.

Two Bears swung his horse toward him, then closed in at a dead run. Less than thirty yards away now, James studied the Indian's eyes. Cold, raw hatred radiated from them. Knowing the Apache recognized him, James again cocked the rifle and fired. This time, Two Bears screamed, sailing backwards off his horse. The Indian thudded hard.

Lying under a mesquite bush, Andy fired his brother's gun. A horse whinnied and pitched sideways, its rider tossed off. Andy took aim again and dropped another Indian.

James swung his gaze from his brother to the Apache crouching behind his dying horse. The man leaned over the quivering animal, then pointed a shotgun at Andy. James stood, sighted his rifle, and squeezed the trigger. The Indian flew backwards.

Before James could take aim at the two remaining Apaches, the Indians shouted and waved their arms at the pintos, scattering all of them, including both Army mounts. The Apaches reined their horses around and kicked them into a raging gallop.

Andy aimed and fired. A fifth Indian grabbed at his back then pitched off his horse. The last Apache continued running and disappeared behind a boulder. James let out his breath and ran a shaking hand across his mouth.

Andy rolled to a sitting position, removed his hat, and then scraped back a hank of hair plastered over one eye. Hat back in place, he spoke under heaving shoulders.

"Damn, that was close."

Crouched on one knee next to his flushed brother, James kept his eyes on the retreating dust cloud.

Andy's voice was strong. "Think he's coming back?"

A nod. " I'd count on it."

"With more friends?"

"Yeah."

Andy turned to James. "We got a problem then."

CHAPTER THIRTY-FIVE

Trace paced from his tent to Captain Greene's white canvas office and back. The camp had been dark since the fourth trip. This was the ninth. Routine growing tiresome, he veered toward Fountain and Reynold's campsite. Fountain perched on a rock near the fire and cleaned his Remington handgun. In desperate need of other conversation to take his mind off his overdue brothers, Trace squatted next to him.

"Nice piece. Mind if I look at it?" Trace handled the pistol, tilting it toward the flickering fire. The light danced off the barrel.

Fountain nodded toward the south. "Had it realigned down in Mexico. Got a good balance now, I think. Fits me just right."

"It's a beauty, that's for sure. Thanks." Trace returned the single action revolver, then searched for another topic. Instead, he stared up into the star-filled sky and prayed he wouldn't have to write home telling Ma that two of her sons died on a beautiful day in early May.

Hooves. A couple of horses trotting into camp. Trace twisted around, then jumped to his feet. Had to be his brothers. He bolted toward the remuda. Then his heart sank. Their dark silhouettes were heavier than James and Andy.

The soldiers swayed in their saddles, then slid off their horses.

Trace walked over to them as they tied the reins to the rope lines. "Howdy."

The men peered into his face.

"I'm Trace Colton, Andy and James' brother."

"Howdy." One of the men extended a hand, but missed Trace's by inches.

The smell of liquor assaulted Trace's nose. He jerked his thumb over his shoulder. "Just come from town?"

Two heads bobbed up and down. Still bobbing, the men staggered back to their horses. The taller of the two leaned against his saddle and fumbled with the cinch.

Trace searched each face. "Did you happen to see my brothers around there? Thought maybe they'd dropped by a saloon, had a drink or two."

Silence.

A lump grew in Trace's stomach.

The second soldier took a breath, then shook his head. "Nah. Ain't seen nary a one of 'em. Did you, Matthews?"

Matthews dropped his saddle. "Don't recollect their faces in the saloon. They rode out this morning lookin' over that minin' camp the Apaches raided, didn't they?"

Trace nodded. "Yeah."

"Ain't back yet?"

"No."

Matthews grabbed a stirrup and dragged the saddle toward the row of leather goods lined up nearby. "Kinda late, ain't it?"

"Yeah."

The first soldier snapped his fingers. "I know what's happened to 'em."

"What?" Trace and Matthews leaned in close.

"Them two met up with a couple Indian women, got themselves some *pulque*, and—"

"Hell, let's go join 'em!" Matthews adjusted his shirt.

"I don't think so," Trace said as he held up a hand. Any hope, remote as it was, escaped through Trace's chest.

"Yeah, can't go, Matthews."

"Why?"

"Hell, I just unsaddled my damn horse. I ain't about to undo what I just undid." The soldier plunked the saddle down with the rest of the harnesses, straps, and various military saddles. He glanced at Matthews, then Trace. "I'm hittin' the sack."

Matthews shrugged at Trace. "Me, too. Sorry." He patted Trace on the shoulder. "Guess you'll have to go alone." Both soldiers stumbled into darkness.

Trace shuffled back to his lonely, cold camp, the lump mushrooming into a full-fledged knot in his guts. Something was wrong. Were they dead? Or worse, captured by the Apache? He tried to push aside panic, but it refused to let up.

Pouring himself half a cup of coffee, Trace thudded to a rock near the campfire's dying flames. He sipped the lukewarm liquid, thoughts lost in what-ifs. Movement to his right caught his eye. Fountain and Reynolds stood beside him.

Reynolds sat down. "They're fine, Trace. Don't worry."

Fountain held a stick in the fire, the flames catching the peeling bark and igniting. Sharp spires of orange-gold sprung to life along the end of the wood. Holding it in front of his face, he studied the crackling twig. Smoke wafted under Trace's nose. He sneezed. Were his eyes watery from the smoke?

Four minutes of silence melted into five. Fountain stabbed the remainder of the stick in the fire, then stood and spoke.

"We'll leave at first light."

* * *

A nudge on his shoulder. Trace's eyes popped open. A quick rub of the eyes, then he sat up. He ran his hand through his tangled hair. The fire was now gray ash, and the air cool. The sun threw rose shadows on the awakening world.

"Horses're saddled, Trace. Reynolds has coffee and biscuits over at the remuda." Fountain helped Trace to his feet.

Stretching, Trace's sore body reminded him again that sleeping on the hard ground takes its toll on bones. He ached in places that hadn't hurt since he'd been Cochise's prisoner. Within ten minutes, the three men gigged their horses toward the raided mining camp along the route James and Andy had been instructed to take.

Captain Greene, agreeing to this rescue mission, had assured Trace he would meet up with his missing brothers on the trail. *Don't worry, they're fine.* The words rang over and over. Trace reflected on the pinched look on the commander's face. Words didn't match the face. Did Greene know something he wasn't sharing?

Miles and hours dragged by. Tired beyond reason, Trace reined up, then swung out of the saddle. Reynolds' and Fountain's feet also hit the ground. The three men stretched. Sharing a canteen, they searched the area for any sign of the Colton brothers.

"You haven't said two words since we left." Fountain remarked as he handed the canteen to Trace. "They're big boys. They can take care of themselves. Don't worry."

"You keep saying that." Trace held the canteen to his lips,

but instead of drinking, he plugged it and shoved the container back into Fountain's chest. "Everyone keeps saying that! Don't worry? Don't worry? What if those were your brothers? Dammit it, Fountain, you know what James went—"

"Whoa." Fountain took a step back.

Trace reeled in his rage and shook his head. "I'm sorry. Didn't mean to snap at you. It's just that—"

"Understood." Fountain held up a hand. "Look. It's a long way to that raided camp. I'm sure we'll run into them sooner or later."

Trace's gaze shifted from his friend's face to the undergrowth in front of them. "Maybe you're right. Let's hope for sooner." He grabbed his horse's reins and threw himself into the saddle.

Close to evening, the three men rounded a sharp bend in the canyon. Trace, with Fountain and Reynolds close behind, yanked his horse to a skidding stop.

Before them lay a lifeless pinto.

Trace leapt from his horse and sprinted to the pinto. He ran a hand over the stiff animal's rump, then straightened up, eyes closed.

"God. No. Please, God, no."

Fountain joined Trace at the dead horse. "What's wrong?"

Numb, Trace opened his eyes, his stare shifting from Fountain to Reynolds. Mouth open, he shook his head.

"You're awful pale, Trace. What?" Reynolds asked, swiping his hand along the pinto's chest.

"Cochise." Trace pointed. "That red hand print. Cochise's mark. Horse belongs to his tribe."

Memories. Hopelessness. Rawhide binding his wrists and ankles. James begging for his torture to stop.

Fountain cocked his head at Trace. "You're not looking too good. Come sit down."

Drums beat. Apaches chanted. One Wing forced Trace to watch James kneel in front of the tribe while that knife pierced... Memories swam.

"Don't hurt him," Trace mumbled.

"I won't."

Trace's strong grip crushed the front of One Wing's shirt.

"I'll do what you want. Don't hurt him."

"Trace?"

A hand shook him. Someone pried his fingers from the shirt.

"Trace?"

One Wing's face melted into Albert Fountain's. Trace fought to match face with name. "Fountain?"

"Welcome back. Best sit down."

Trace's shaking hand raked through his hair. He pulled in air, then pulled in the present. "Sit down? Dammit to hell, Fountain!" Panic surfaced again. "My brothers are out here somewhere, maybe captured, and you say 'sit down'?"

"I understand—"

"You don't understand nothin'. Neither of you!" Trace glared at his two surprised companions. "Gotta find them."

Why did he have to explain?

"James was tortured 'til I knew he'd die," Trace continued. "Sometimes I prayed he would."

Fountain and Reynolds exchanged glances.

Trace's stare rested on Fountain's dark eyes. "It's a thought damn hard to live with. But, if my brother's captured again, he won't survive. He can't do it."

Fountain stepped in close to Trace, then held out a hand. "Take it easy, Trace. James is strong now."

Trace exploded. "Christ, Fountain. He tried to kill himself just yesterday morning! He's not strong any more."

Marching from boulder to mesquite bush to yucca, Trace muttered more to himself than the two men. "Probably tried it again. Probably killed Andy, too." He froze and stared into the sky. "God. Andy."

Trace swung his eyes to Fountain. "That's what happened. Cochise captured him and James, so James killed Andy. Then himself. He would do that." Sobs rose in his throat. "James would do that to keep Andy from—"

"Get a hold of yourself," Reynolds said as he eased toward Trace. "There's no way to know what's happened. Could be they're just up around the bend there eating supper."

Fountain nodded to Reynolds, who stepped to the other side of Trace. "They're probably sitting there telling stories about you as a kid."

"Or making them up." Reynolds clutched Trace's arm at the same time Fountain did. "Sit over here."

Shaking loose of the hold, Trace whipped his gun out of its holster, spun around and wagged it from man to man. Fountain moved forward, and in that instant Trace pulled the trigger. The bullet pinged into dirt near Fountain's leg.

Fountain leaped to the side. "Jesus, Trace! What the hell you doin'?" His gun cleared leather.

Reynolds spread his arms wide. "There's no need for gunplay. Nerves are just a bit tight is all." He nodded at Trace. "Put it down."

"Cochise'll make James' life a living hell again. Only worse this time." Trace buried more words.

Fountain holstered his weapon and eased forward just as Reynolds dove for Trace's legs. Both men hit the ground and rolled. They somersaulted down a shallow ravine.

Landing on top of Reynolds, Trace moved in rhythm to the man under him. Reynolds bucked and twisted, but was no match for Trace's uncontrollable anger. Trace bore down with a strength dredged up from pure frustration. Fist shoulder high, he pounded Reynolds' face. Again. A boot to his head knocked him off Reynolds.

Trace rolled up onto his knees. He struggled to bring blurs together. He turned to Fountain for understanding, but found none. Reynolds lay on the ground cradling his face, lumps on his cheek glowing bright red.

Events became clear.

"Good God, Reynolds. You all right?" Trace asked as he crawled over to Reynolds and examined the split lip and bruised face.

"I'm sorry." Trace stood, squared his shoulders, and then rushed to the canteen hanging on the saddle. He yanked it off, but he took a second to peer into the seamless sky. Would the sky give him answers? He knew better.

Please let Reynolds be all right. And James and Andy.

Hating himself, but knowing he had to face Reynolds and Fountain soon, Trace pulled in a second deep breath and walked back toward the assaulted man, now on his feet. He held out the canteen.

"I'm really sorry—"

"Don't come near either of us again." Reynolds met him halfway and jabbed an angry finger in Trace's chest. "Leave me alone." His eyes flared. "Got it?"

Trace nodded. What did he expect? Why didn't Reynolds lay him out right there? Sure had the right to do it.

Hatred stared back from the cold blue eyes.

Trace stammered. "I didn't mean it. You both just surprised me at the wrong time."

"Yeah? When's the *right* time?" Reynolds glared at Trace and lowered his voice. "In my book, both you Coltons are crazy." Veins stood out on his forehead. "*Both* of you."

"I'm truly sorry—"

"Not good enough." Reynolds spoke through clenched teeth. "Ever touch either of us again, Trace Colton, I'll take you down. Understand?"

Trace nodded.

CHAPTER THIRTY-SIX

The Doctor's door flew open.

"Doctor Martelli!" An out-of-breath man rushed into the doctor's office and called out again. "Doc? You here?"

Martelli stepped into the waiting room. He wiped his hands on a white towel. "Yes. What's wrong?"

"Me and the wife come across two men lyin' in the desert. Near dead. I give 'em water and tossed 'em in the back of my wagon." The rancher windmilled his arm toward the door. "They're right out front."

Doctor Martelli, the rancher, and his wife peered over the side of the wagon. Tucked between sacks of grain and three crates, lay two unconscious Union soldiers.

"Ma'am." Martelli spoke to the rancher's wife. "Fetch my daughter in the office, please." He climbed into the wagon, then pushed up Andy's eyelids. Nothing but a vacant stare. Martelli cradled the sunburned face, examining both sides. He spoke over his shoulder.

"Where'd you find them?"

The rancher scrambled into the wagon. He pointed northeast.

"Up by Tent Rocks, 'bout twenty miles from here. We were takin' a different road than usual and suddenly there they was."

"Lying on the road?" Martelli placed his hand on James' neck.

"Not 'exactly." The man paused. "I walked a little ways into the desert, you know, to answer a call of nature."

Martelli glanced at the rancher.

"Well, anyways, there they was. Both of 'em, curled up under mesquite bushes, tryin' to get out of the sun I'm guessin'."

As his daughter joined him at the wagon, the doctor looked

up. "Both unconscious?"

"Nope. This younger lookin' one could take a couple sips, mumbled somethin' 'bout Cochise and a trace of somethin' or other before he passed out."

Morningstar reached over the wagon's side, brushed back a hank of hair hanging over James' eyes. "It wasn't a trace of something, sir. Trace is their older brother. This is James Colton and his brother, Andy. They've been missing over a week."

"Let's get them inside, cooled down, and then notify the commander at the camp. I know Trace is worried sick." Doctor Martelli glanced at the rancher's wife. "Been in twice looking for them." He and the rancher tugged Andy out the back of the wagon bed while the woman held the office door open.

Once both Andy and James were settled and wrapped in cool, wet towels, Doctor Martelli offered his hand to the rancher and his wife. "Thank you both for bringing them in. You saved their lives. I'm sure they'll want to thank you personally when they recover."

Smiling, the rancher returned the handshake. "Just knowin' they'll live is thanks enough. Take care, Doc." He and his wife turned, then walked through the door before Martelli could ask names.

* * *

Doctor Martelli waved at Captain Greene standing in the doorway. "Come in. Glad you're here. Good news." He stood wiping his hands on a towel and cocked his head toward the Coltons. "Your men'll recover. Be fine in a few days."

"Excellent news. They conscious?"

Martelli studied the commander, noticed the mouth set in a tight line.

"Not yet. They're suffering from sunstroke and heat exhaustion. Awful hot for this time of year."

Greene pulled up a chair next to James and perched on the seat's edge. He stared at the young soldier covered in wet towels, then let out a stream of air.

"James Colton, you're a cursed man. How in the hell can I help you?"

Morningstar set a bowl of water on a table between the two beds. "Does Trace know his brothers have been found, Captain?" She wet a towel and, sitting on the edge of Andy's bed, patted

225

the dollar-sized blister, taking extra care to add moisture to his peeling lips.

Greene shook his head. "Rode out early today as usual. Probably won't be back 'til after dark just like the last several days."

Doctor Martelli stood next to the Captain. "You say James is a cursed man? You're right. Have you seen what Cochise did to him?"

Greene shook his head and looked up at the doctor, then back at the unconscious man. Martelli lifted up a damp towel around James' bare chest. Deep pink streaks of inch-wide scars covered his skin and long lash marks ran from his side ending in the middle of his chest. Several stripes encircled his arms.

The Captain winced.

"Good Lord in Heaven. I knew it was bad, but I had no idea." Greene inspected the marks and ran his finger over an especially jagged one on James' upper arm.

"When we peeled his clothes off, we discovered he'd been whipped head to toe."

Martelli dropped his voice to a whisper and pulled back the covers, exposing a scarred leg.

"They're not all from whips. Knives left their marks, too." He replaced the sheet over James' legs. "No way this boy should've survived."

* * *

"James gonna be all right?" Andy asked. He flopped a limp arm toward the bed on his right and squinted against the oil lamp's glare.

"Shhh. Don't try to talk." Morningstar supported Andy's head as she held a glass to his lips.

Cool liquid soothed his raw throat. He lay back against two pillows. Andy touched his swollen mouth, then patted a blister near his left eye. Wincing, he looked over at his unconscious brother, whose was face almost unrecognizable with welts and blisters. "All right?"

Morningstar nodded and placed a cool, wet cloth on Andy's forehead. "He'll be fine." Turning her attention to James, she spoke more to him than to Andy. "He's been through an awful lot. With patience and understanding, he'll recover."

Morningstar tucked the sheet under Andy's chin, then stood. "You both were lucky. My Pa says another few hours you wouldn't have survived." A smile lit up her face. "Glad that rancher found you when he did."

"What kinda trouble you in now, little brother?" Trace stepped into the room, the lamp's golden glow throwing warmth over the men. He looked at Andy, then at James.

"Hey, brother." Andy attempted a grin.

Trace eased onto the bed and embraced the youngest of the Colton clan. "You scared the hell outta me."

"Sorry." Andy pushed back from Trace's hug, embarrassed by the sentiment in front of Morningstar. "We knew you'd be worried."

Nodding, Trace ruffled Andy's hair, then moved over to sit on James' bed. He gripped James' shoulder, his voice dropping to a whisper. "Thank God." He glanced over his shoulder at Andy. "When Greene told me you'd been found—alive—I was afraid to believe him."

"My Pa says both of your brothers will be fine." Morningstar nodded. "In a couple days they'll be back to giving you trouble again."

Trace turned around to Andy. "Andrew Jackson Colton." Gruff words escaped his lips. "Ever do anything like this again, I'm telling your Ma. She'll be mighty angry. She doesn't take kindly to her boys taking off like that."

"I'm sorry. We were running from Apaches. Took us a couple days to lose them. Then we lost us." Andy's words faded into memories.

Trace eased down to Andy's bed and offered him water.

Andy spoke over the cup's rim. "James said they're from Cochise's camp. The leader was Two Bears. James knew you'd remember him."

Silence.

Andy tapped his brother's leg. "Trace? You all right?"

"Yeah, just remembering." Trace's hands balled into a fist. "Bad hombre. Him and One Wing. Pure evil."

"Two Bears's dead. James shot him." Andy's trembling finger stroked a sore blister near his mouth after handing the cup back to Trace.

"Good." Trace's mouth opened and closed a couple more times

227

before swinging his gaze back to Andy. "You're not looking right. Those purple blotches are turning gray. Best sleep now. I'll be here when you wake up." He grasped Andy's hand.

Half of Andy felt like a little kid, the grip of his brother's hand comforting. The other half wanted to pull away. To be a man. More thoughts collided.

Trace needs to hold on as much as I do.

Andy squeezed back.

Morningstar placed a hand on Trace's shoulder. "They'll be all right. You need some sleep, too. It's late."

Trace shook his head. "No. I'm staying right where I am. I'll just sit here 'til they're both awake." He released Andy's hand and tucked his brother's arm under the sheet.

Despite the welts and blisters, Andy smiled.

Morningstar pointed. "There's an empty room right next door with a soft bed. I'll sit up with your brothers, and if anything changes, I'll wake you."

"Trace?" Andy fought the curtain draping over his eyelids. "Me and James. We'll stay here." He closed his eyes. "You go get some sleep."

"All right. I am tired."

The side of Andy's bed dipped, then sprung up into place when Trace stood. Footsteps stopped at the door. "Which way, Miss Martelli?"

* * *

"That cactus poultice on your blisters has certainly helped, Andy. They're shrinking nicely." Doctor Martelli perched on the edge of a chair, nodded to Trace at his elbow, then continued examining Andy's face. He pressed the stethoscope against his chest. A cock of the head. A nod. He draped the stethoscope around his neck then patted Andy's knee.

"You're still a little weak but ready to go back to camp," the doctor said. "Three days of lying around here probably felt more like three weeks, didn't it?"

Andy buttoned his shirt. "Yes, sir. First day was fine, but after that I was wanting to get up and do something. Room kept spinning, though."

Doctor Martelli handed Andy a small jar. "Keep this salve on those lesions and you might not have any scarring. Should heal up in a week or so."

"Thanks." Andy removed the lid and peered inside. He wrinkled his nose, then nodded.

Trace gripped his brother's arm, guiding him to his feet. Doctor Martelli scooted his chair over to James' bed, then pressed the stethoscope against his chest.

"James," Martelli said. "I'm afraid you're not quite ready for duty, yet. That's what I told Captain Greene this morning when he was in." The doctor examined James' face, then rubbed salve on a shrinking blister. "Tomorrow, I think you'll be up and around, son."

James glanced over at his brothers. "Tomorrow."

Trace leaned over James and smoothed the sheet covering his chest. "I'll ride back to camp with Andy, get him settled, then you and me'll have supper together." Speaking over a knot in his throat, he patted his brother on the head. "Get some beauty sleep. You need it."

"Thanks. But there's no hope for you, big brother." One corner of James' mouth angled up as his eyes closed.

Stopping in the outer office, Trace studied Andy. The purple blotches on his face were fading. Maybe this doctor *was* a miracle worker. He jerked a thumb over his shoulder. "Wait by the horses, please, Andy. I need to talk to the doctor."

Eyes narrowing, Andy took a breath, opened his mouth, but only nodded. He waved as he closed the door.

Trace leveled his gaze on the doctor. "What do you honestly think? How is James?"

Martelli wagged his head. "Apparently he made Andy eat most of the game they shot. Wouldn't take much himself." He shrugged. "Didn't want to alert the Indians as to their location, so they didn't dare shoot until they figured they were out of range. When they ran out of bullets, they ran out of food."

"But James knows desert survival. Learned it from the Apaches."

"That's probably why he's alive today. Thanks to them." Martelli clasped his hands behind his back, stared out the window. "But spending all those nights running, days hiding, they didn't find much food or water."

Martelli turned around and faced Trace. "Your brother's a sick boy. He's awfully weak. I'm not sure he could survive another round like this. Any way to get him out of the army?"

Trace ran his hand across his mouth and shook his head.

"I don't think so. We'd have to get a special order from the judge and right now, no one knows where he is. Since the Confederates took over, law in Mesilla's been a bit one sided."

Martelli's eyebrows arched over his brown-green eyes. "If your brother could just rest for a few weeks, none of this walking through the desert chasing Indians and Rebs, I think he'd heal pretty well."

"If he's not in the army," Trace spoke to the floor, "he's in prison."

A pat on the shoulder, then Martelli nudged Trace toward the door. "Then army he stays. I'll talk to Captain Greene again."

"Thanks, Doc." Trace closed the door behind him.

* * *

Morningstar placed a water glass on the bedside table. Her gentle grip around James' wrist cooled his skin. He listened to her count the rhythms of his pulse. Closing his eyes, he focused on her touch.

Time ticked by. The touch gone, he peeked under half-open eyelids. Surprised she remained within reach, he attempted a grin, the effort hurting his mouth. At least he could talk now without the blisters interfering.

"You're still here. You don't hate me?"

"Now why would I hate you, Mister Colton?" Morningstar wiped his face with a warm, wet cloth.

"For standing you up. Missing our second date."

"James Colton." Morningstar sat back and flashed a smile. "That's not what was on my mind. I was worried about you."

"I'm sorry."

Morningstar lowered her voice and eyes. "Me, too."

Silence forced itself between them until James gathered the rest of his courage. He pulled the sheet up tighter. "I'm sorry for everything."

"Everything?"

"Running off that night... my past. Especially sorry for these scars." James avoided her quizzical gaze. "You've seen them, right?"

She tilted her head. "Don't apologize for those marks. If anything, I admire you for your bravery, for the fact that you endured. And survived that kind of punishment."

"They don't bother you?"

"Honestly?" Morningstar paused. "When I first saw them, they did. There's so many. But now I think of them as your badges of courage. They're certainly nothing to be ashamed of." She smiled at James lying in front of her. "You should be proud of yourself."

He reached up and took both her shoulders in his trembling hands. James pulled her toward him. The kiss was gentle, yet passionate.

* * *

"You've got a silly look on your face, little brother." Trace glanced over at James riding at a slow trot next to him. "What's going on in that head of yours?"

James pulled his horse to a stop, then turned in his saddle. Could life get any better?

"I kissed her."

"What?" Trace reined up.

James ducked his head. "Not just once, several times. Morningstar's wonderful."

"See any... ghosts?"

"They left me alone. Never saw Lila or those women." The world that was once dark and ugly turned bright and beautiful. "Think I'm in love."

Trace leaned over and smacked his brother on the shoulder. "That's the best news I've heard in years. I'm happy for you."

Now serious, James lowered his voice. "Hope they stay away. Don't want my past haunting me any more. They've owned me too long. I gotta move on."

Trace stared up at the cloud-dotted sky. "We both do."

Continuing their ride back to camp, the brothers shared intimate stories of the past year, knowing that they were the only ones who truly understood what each was going through.

Camp in sight, James pulled up and turned to his brother. "Thanks for coming to get me again. Seems you're always rescuing me. But I know you miss Teresa and she's probably missing you a lot, too. Isn't that baby due soon?"

"Couple more months. Yeah, I sure do miss her." Trace patted his pocket. "Got three letters just this week." His words turned serious. "Truth is, *I* need to be rescued this time. I've worked so

231

hard this past year covering up what happened, but it's surfaced anyway. I'm having trouble getting past it."

James knew exactly how his brother felt. "Not easy, is it?"

Trace shook his head.

His gaze releasing his brother, James glanced around the expansive desert and up into the endless blue. Crows gliding on the warm wind currents circled and swooped. He filled his lungs with sweet, fresh air.

"Enough talk for now," James said. "I've been gone more'n twelve days. Time to see how they got along without me."

CHAPTER THIRTY-SEVEN

Andy elbowed his oldest brother. "Smells pretty, don't he?"

Trace made a show of pulling in a lungful of air. "Sure does. Leastways smells a might better than those horses he's been tending all week."

James smoothed his straight brown hair, ran his hand over his freshly-shaven face, inspected his chin and cheeks in the small mirror reflecting the setting sun, and pretended to ignore his brothers.

"What d'you suppose the big occasion is, Trace?" Andy spoke in a stage whisper as his eyes roamed over the sea of tents. Other soldiers held pokers of quail or rabbit over evening fires, and soft conversations wafted across the encampment. "Nobody else's getting all duded up. Suppose our brother's going to church?"

Trace shrugged, moved in close to James for further inspection. "Let's see. Clean clothes, combed hair, bath even. But it ain't Sunday." He wagged his head and shot a glance at Andy. "Must be something special. Third time he's ran that comb through the same spot."

Andy stood on the other side of James. "I know! It's his birthday and he's taking us to supper in town."

Trace snapped his fingers. "That's it. Plumb forgot." He grabbed James by the arm and spun him around. "We'll be ready in two minutes. Don't leave without us. Hurry up, Andy."

"Just hold on, you two." James grabbed Trace's arm before he reached the tent, two steps away. "You know it's not my birthday and no, you can't tag along. Either of you." A deep breath, he stood straight, smoothed his shirt, and presented himself to his family. "How do I look?"

Andy moved in closer, peered at James' face, then patted his cheek. "Smooth as a baby's bottom."

"Kinda looks like one, too." Trace punched Andy's arm.

James fought a grin. "Dammit. I'm serious."

"Look fine, James." Trace nodded. Still grinning, he flicked a dust speck off his brother's shoulder. "There."

James took another look in the mirror. That scar still ran deep pink across his cheek, but he chose to ignore it. He squared his jaw.

After a final swipe over his face with a towel, James stared at Andy but launched the towel at Trace's face. It landed on his shoulder. The three brothers laughed.

Andy hung his arm around James' shoulder. "Who is it tonight?"

The corners of Trace's mouth spiked upward, matching his eyebrows. "Don't know, Andy. There's been so many lately."

Andy stared into the dimming evening desert and pointed to an invisible row of women lined up waiting to be selected. "Lizzy over there? She's pretty, James." He hugged James' shoulders tighter. "Or how about that big bosomed gal in the white dress standing beside her?"

"No, I know." Trace pointed also. "The one over at the end. Look at that bright red hair, big green eyes, and... those lips! Oh, what they could do to you!"

James felt his cheeks burn. He pulled out of Andy's grip and faced his brothers. "Knock it off. You know damn well who I'm going to see." He studied his grinning brothers, their eyes shining. "You're just jealous, that's all. Jealous 'cause Morningstar chose me."

"We are. But Ma always said you're the prettiest." Andy ducked as James splashed soapy basin water at him.

A deep breath, then James let out the air. He re-tucked his shirt. "Guess I'm ready."

"Special night?" Trace dropped his voice and glanced at Andy. "Come on, James, you can tell us. We're your brothers."

James knew they wished him only happiness, but he also knew they weren't about to let him leave until he explained. Were those butterflies in his stomach?

"It's been a month since I've been courting Morningstar," James explained. "Kind of an anniversary for us. Just want tonight to be special."

Trace stepped in close and gripped James' arm. "Nervous about making love?"

James shook his head. "It's not like that at all. She's a respectable woman." His gaze took in Trace's narrowed eyes, the serious look on his face. "Not like those doxies... those women, in Mesilla."

"What is it then?"

Andy leaned closer.

James' stomach turned sour. A glance around. Only his brothers were close enough to hear. He sure as hell didn't want anyone else in camp knowing.

"Don't know if I'll *ever* be able to love her. You know, like I'm supposed to?" James hung his head, kicked at the dirt under his feet. "The Apaches took everything from me... even that. All those women in Mesilla? Well, they were safe from me." He glared at a nearby boulder.

Trace swung an arm around his brother's shoulders. "When the time's right, you'll be fine. Don't rush. Trust me."

A strained silence swirled around all three brothers.

Trace hugged James, then pushed him away. "Better go. Don't wanna miss your big date."

Andy jerked a finger over his shoulder. "There's a whole patch of wild flowers on the way to town. Out in that meadow. Bet she'd like some."

Hope pushed back into James' chest. "Thanks." Scooping up his hat and adjusting it on his head, he turned his back on his brothers. "Don't wait up. I'll be home late."

"Or when her pa throws you out of his house. Watch out little brother." Trace chuckled. "He knows how to use knives."

James glanced over his shoulder, then waved as he walked toward the remuda.

* * *

Something kicked his foot. Mumbled words. Another kick. James forced his eyes open. He rubbed his face, then stretched and yawned. A hand shook his shoulder.

"Wake up. Rise and shine, Romeo." Andy's voice bounced off the canvas. "Captain Greene wants everyone on the double."

"Huh?"

"You heard me." Andy pulled on James' leg.

"I'm up, I'm up. What's the hurry?"

"As a famous older brother once told me, 'You're in the army.

235

Can't sleep 'til noon'." Andy pushed James to a sitting position, then threaded his brother's arm through a shirtsleeve.

James ran his fingers through his hair while Andy fastened the top button on his shirt. Enjoying the game, James yawned and stretched again. He frowned when his brother stopped with the second button.

"You're not done."

"Oh, yes I am." Andy replied as he tossed wadded up britches in James' face. "You're old enough to dress yourself. Besides, already told you—I ain't your nursemaid." He straightened up extending a hand. "Hurry. We gotta go."

Hunched over in the middle of the tent, James fastened his pants then pointed to his socked feet. "Boots?"

Andy glanced around the small tent, located one jammed in the corner and affected a British accent as he picked it up. "So sorry, your majesty. Did you need this?"

James nodded.

Andy pitched the boot at his brother's head, but caught him square in the chest instead. Laughing, Andy ducked through the tent opening. James threw his boot at Andy.

Tent flaps thrown aside, James rushed into the warm May morning ready to tackle Andy. Instead of his brother, James crashed into Fountain, who was standing with a boot in hand.

Fountain waved it in James' face. "This the way to treat a friend?"

Andy peeked around Fountain's side and pointed. "You kinda hit him in the back," Andy said to James. "Good shot, though."

James fought a grin. "Sorry 'bout that, but my servant missed my foot."

"You're lucky you missed my head." Fountain shoved the boot into James' chest. "Greene wants us right away."

James sat on a rock near his tent and tugged on one boot while Andy handed him the other one. "What's going on?"

Fountain raised his shoulders and took a deep breath. He paused.

"Ah, hell, James, might as well know now," Fountain said. "We're moving out tomorrow."

James' chest tightened. "Dammit. Why?"

He tasted Morningstar's most recent kiss.

"Appears Baylor and his boys have left Mesilla and we need

to make sure that pretty little town stays peaceful." Fountain gripped James' arm. "There's something else."

"What?"

"Greene wants to talk to you personally after he addresses the company. Be ready."

"Now what'd I do?" James glared into the morning, then noticed Trace walking toward him.

Albert Fountain shrugged. "Don't know. The captain doesn't tell me everything." He turned his back and marched off.

Trace joined his brothers near the campfire. "You're awfully pale, James. Too much celebrating last night?"

Andy spoke for James, who stared into the cloudless sky.

"Greene says we're leaving."

"Uh oh."

"And he wants to see James personally."

CHAPTER THIRTY-EIGHT

The knob warmed in his hand. Hot. James wiped his sweaty hand on his thigh, then gripped the knob again. This time he turned it. He swung the door inwards and eased into the doctor's office. Numb, he cast his eyes around the waiting room.

Empty.

Heart hammering, he forced air out and smoothed his shirt. Again, he swept the room for Morningstar, the woman who made him smile again. The woman who now meant everything to him. The woman who had saved him from certain destruction.

He pulled his hat off his sweaty head, ran his stiff fingers through his shoulder-length hair, and perched on the edge of a hard, wooden chair. Would she smell the liquor on his breath? He'd tried to quit, or at least cut back. But now... well... now he needed it.

His thoughts turned to the past month. On one hand he could count the Indians and demons who had chased him in those four weeks. Never before had they retreated to the far corners of his mind like now. Maybe he was truly healing and maybe, just maybe, some day he'd never see the terrors from his past. No, he knew better. They'd never completely go away, but now at least there was hope they'd fade into the background.

Lost in thought, he cradled his head in his hands.

"This is an unexpected pleasure, Mr. Colton."

James jumped, then bolted to his feet.

"Morningstar. Didn't see you come in."

He dropped his hat and grinned at the beauty leaning close to him. The aroma of soap, her freshly-washed skin, only served to remind him how much he'd miss her smell, her face, her touch.

"James, you're awfully pale. Are you sick?" She held her hand against his forehead.

Her touch—so gentle. Enough to catch his breath. A tickle rose in his throat. Or was that the whiskey? He took her hand in his and spoke.

"Can you get away for a few minutes? We need to talk."

Worry lines inched over her forehead. "I'll tell Pa."

A couple of steps toward the back rooms, she then stopped and turned to James.

Their eyes met.

His heart crumbled.

* * *

Arm in arm, they strolled down the boardwalk, silence wedging itself between them. A complete sentence wouldn't come to James no matter how many ways he reformed the same group of words in his mind.

They stopped in front of the restaurant. James held the door while Morningstar stepped inside.

"Thought I'd buy you dinner," James said, "but it's too early. How about some lemonade?" He pulled out a chair and motioned to the waitress for two glasses. What he really wanted right now wasn't lemonade. He wanted something a whole lot stronger. Whiskey would ease his pain. Or would it?

He caressed both of her hands with his trembling ones. Eyes closed, he chewed on his lower lip. Uncounted seconds ticked by. He opened his eyes when he heard two glasses sliding across the table.

"Whatever it is, James, it can't be all that bad." Morningstar patted his hand. "Did someone die?"

Die? Yeah, I did, but you brought me back. Back from a black world of certain death.

And now... and now?

He stared at the woman who had changed his life.

How can I face my demons without you?

The knot in his throat plunged to his stomach. He swallowed his lemonade, draining the entire glass.

Morningstar leaned against his shoulder. "Whatever it is, James, you can tell me."

James choked out the words. "I'm leaving tomorrow."

Tears brimming, Morningstar studied the inside of her glass and spoke softly.

"We both knew this day would come. You being in the army and all." Her eyes trailed up to his. "Just hoped it wouldn't come this soon."

James squeezed her hand. "You mean everything to me." He searched her ebony eyes and dropped his voice to a whisper. "Think I love you."

Tears trickled down her cheeks. Morningstar rested her head on his shoulder. "I think I love you, too."

Arm wrapped around her, James drew her as close as he could. "I won't ask you to wait."

"But I will. I'll wait forever."

"No. Don't."

He couldn't shake his head fast enough. No need for her to waste her life. Wasting *his* was enough. Unsure whether to tell her the rest or just ride away, he took a breath and chose to explain.

"Morningstar, there's something else... You need to understand. I might not ever be back. Captain Greene says we'll be heading through Apache Pass."

Confusion clouded her face as she clutched his hand. "Isn't that where you were... where they... *held* you for those months?"

James studied their entwined fingers. "Near there."

He raised his head but couldn't meet her gaze. "Washington wants me to negotiate with Cochise," James continued. "Try to get him to stop killing and move his people onto a reservation."

"But Trace and the army tried that before."

"I know."

"It didn't work." Morningstar twisted her mouth into a frown. "So, that means..."

"Uh huh." James spun his empty glass with his other hand. "Suicide. The Captain's thinking is that Cochise knows me and respects me. Whatever that means."

"He didn't kill you when he had the chance." Morningstar swiped at a tear dripping off her chin.

"I suppose. Anyway, they want me to talk to Cochise, get him to see things the Army's way."

Morningstar's hands trembled and her bottom lip quivered. "But that's crazy. Cochise's declared all out war."

James hung his head.

"Can't Trace do it?"

"And let *him* get killed?" James shook his head. He stared at the young woman leaning into him and breathed a hint of lilac. "Never. I don't want him dead. But truth is, between the Rebs and Indians, all of us might die. It's war."

Morningstar sniffed and grasped her silver necklace.

James turned one hand palm up. "Look, he's a civilian. Greene can't ask him or even let him if he offers."

"How does Trace feel about this?" Morningstar swallowed half of her lemonade.

"Haven't told him, yet." James ran his finger along a scratch in the table. "How can I tell my brother I have to go back into that hell?"

His agonized words hung in silence.

James tightened his grip on her hand, then afraid of squeezing too hard, relaxed. His gaze met hers. "I'm much stronger now than I was before I met you, but I don't think it's enough. I made it out once, but... I couldn't do it again."

"You can run away. Leave the army behind. You can go to Mexico. They'll never find you."

James thudded back against his chair. He shook his head. "No. I don't run. I've tried it before. It doesn't work." Fighting, drinking, attempted suicides—the memories—pushed into his mind. He shoved them to one side.

Morningstar's hand slid up his arm. She stroked the back of his neck. "But, I want you safe, alive."

"I want that, too. But, I won't run."

James took a deep breath, removed her hand then kissed it. He pushed his chair away from the table.

"We better get going," he said. "Your Pa's needing your help and I got a thousand things to do."

Hand in hand, they strolled down the street, each lost in thoughts, pain. Stopping in front of the office, James gazed into her face, her dark eyes red around the edges.

"Guess this is it."

"Will I see you tonight?" Morningstar's lips inched upward.

"No. Can't say goodbye twice."

It was more than that James knew. He'd want to make love with her tonight. And if he couldn't... He couldn't face that disappointment. Not yet. No, better say good-bye this way, never knowing what might have been.

Morningstar slipped her sliver-chained necklace over her

head and cradled the turquoise pendant in her hand. "This was a present from my father on my eighteenth birthday. The stone symbolizes strength and courage." She placed it in his hand. Folding his fingers around it, she stared up into his eyes. "Take this. Keep me in your heart. You'll always be in mine."

He drew her into a tight embrace.

"Forever. I'll keep it forever." His face in her hair brought only heartache. "I'll never be able to thank you properly, tell you everything I've wanted to."

"Just come back to me, James Colton. Just come back."

CHAPTER THIRTY-NINE

By the time the first rays of the sun hit James' eyes, he and the entire Union company, now calling themselves Carleton's California Column, had marched well past the sleeping village of Tucson. James breathed a sigh of relief when they skirted the town. If he'd seen Morningstar, he knew there would have been no way he could have moved on. Probably would have deserted right then and there.

As he trudged next to Andy, little puffs of dust escaped from under each footfall. James eyed his brother. He'd changed this past year. His shoulders spread wider now and he'd added weight, all muscle. Ma would be proud of her youngest son, all grown up. Would she be equally proud of him? His letters home hinted at his problems, but he'd never had the courage to come right out and tell her about his captivity or the ensuing nightmares. He didn't want her worrying about something she couldn't help. More and more he wrote about Morningstar.

Thoughts turned to his older brother. Trace had been gone from Teresa more than two months. Here it was already June and their baby was due soon. Why hadn't he left his brothers and gone back to his wife? Was something wrong he hadn't mentioned? Maybe Trace wasn't as healed as he thought he'd be. James looked at Trace, reins in hand, walking alongside Andy.

Trace always seems so sure of himself. Always has the answers. Will he have the answer about Cochise?

* * *

Long days of trudging through the heat-stained desert brought the foot-weary soldiers closer to Mesilla. James recognized the landscape less than two hundred miles west of Mesilla, with the looming Little Dragoon Mountains, the wide-stretching valley ahead of them. Over a year of driving for Butterfield Stage with

Trace allowed him the opportunity to study the country. Although harsh, it certainly was spectacular—the purples in the rising sun, the orange-red of the mountains. The green pointed shafts and white flowers of the yucca plant reminded James of Morningstar's favorite scarf, the one she wore to the last dinner they shared. Emotions caught in his chest.

His thoughts turning to his family, James watched Trace, who was still leading his horse. Their stage driving days popped into his mind. He missed them. More than he liked to admit. Those days and miles had been enjoyable, except for the dust and raiding Apaches. Icy jolts shot up and down his spine. Apaches. Maybe they were watching right now, watching and waiting for him to make the same mistake as last year. The mistake of not being vigilant enough.

Walking in time next to Andy and Trace, James watched his brothers' faces, searching for any indication that they knew what lay ahead. James knew what lay ahead for him—Hell. He and Greene were the only ones who knew. Vowing to keep it that way, James noticed his brothers' eyes sweep the desert, always alert for movement. Trace's mouth was tight with worry. Although Trace tried to hide it, James knew that his brother's thoughts were on Cochise. Just like his.

James clenched his teeth and chided himself for again imagining trouble. He surveyed the plodding soldiers. His brothers, Fountain, and Reynolds led the reluctant procession on foot while Carleton and Greene rode ahead. A point man was just a dot on the horizon. Turning around and glancing behind him, James spotted the four supply wagons bringing up the rear, eating everyone's dust. He shook his head. Now, *that's* a thankless job.

Even though they weren't following the stage road, which no longer saw many travelers, the soldiers skirted the area, staying less than a mile from it. James thought back to the days when Cochise allowed thousands of people to use the road, allowed the stages to rumble through with no problems. Would that Apache leader ever relinquish his stranglehold on southern Arizona?

By noon, when the relentless summer sun was scorching the earth, Captain Greene gave the nod to halt and rest until after sunset. James and his brothers discovered a rocky outcropping and scrambled into the welcomed shade. After a quick meal of cold venison and dried biscuit, the brothers closed their eyes and fell asleep.

* * *

Something tapped his foot. Fingers snapped.

"Colton."

James jerked awake. It was Captain Greene.

James rubbed his eyes and ran a hand through his hair. He gave a quick nod to his captain, then a glance at his sleeping brothers. Careful not to awaken them, he crawled over Andy and stood in the bright sunshine. He stretched.

"Come with me." Greene crooked two fingers toward the canvas shelter erected for the officers.

On his way over, James watched General Carleton smoke his cheroot cigar and sip a glass of wine. Wine? Out here? Where was it stored? Better question, why he would have wine in a situation like this? James stared at the general.

Greene nodded to the senior officer.

"General Carleton, this is the young man I was telling you about, James Colton." Captain Greene pointed to a blanket on the ground. "Please sit, James. At ease."

"Thank you, sir."

James sat cross-legged on the red and black striped Indian blanket. Last time he'd seen a blanket like this was in Cochise's wickiup underneath the feared Apache leader's rear end.

Carleton stared at James, blew smoke toward him, then turned to Greene. "He's younger than I thought, Homer. Way you talked, I figured him at least thirty." He cocked his head and ran his gaze up and down James. "How old are you, son?"

"Twenty-one last September, sir."

"And you were captured by Cochise a year ago?"

James forced back horrendous images and nodded. "My brother and I were held a little over two months." He paused, swallowed hard, pointed south. "Not too far from here."

"And you know Cochise?" Carleton drained his wineglass.

James again nodded, the knot in his throat pounding with the beating of his heart.

"Not many white men live to say that." Carleton leaned forward handing the empty glass to Greene.

James squeezed his eyes shut. Images he had spent months erasing now thundered across his mind. He watched not only Cochise and One Wing, but soldiers, close in around him. Cornered,

245

knowing escape was impossible and death was imminent, James scooted back, buried his face in his hands.

Strong hands bound one arm behind him. "Calm down, James. You're safe." Greene said, the grip tightening.

Memories fading, James opened his eyes and stared up at Greene. James pulled in air and squared his shoulders. Greene released his hold. James met Carleton's piercing stare. He rubbed his eyes as the captain sat down beside Carleton. James shook his head.

"Captain, General Carleton, I'm not the one you want negotiating with Cochise. I can't do it."

"Yes, son, you can." Greene nodded. "You're the best man for the job."

"I agree." Carleton took a long drag on his cigar. "You said Cochise knows you."

"Yes, sir, he does. It's true he saved my life a few times, even called me brave once." James ran a trembling hand across his face, the stubbled cheeks like sandpaper. "But, I've got to be honest with you." His gaze swung from Carleton to Greene. "Once I go in, I won't be coming out. I'm sure Cochise won't let me live this time, but even if he does, all the demons I've been hiding from will come back."

Greene leaned forward. "James—"

"Either way, you're sentencing me to a sure death."

"You're a better man than you think you are. You'll survive. Just like before." Greene handed a canteen to James. "I've seen your scars."

Mouth open, James cocked his head. "You have?"

"At the doc's in Tucson after that rancher brought you in." Greene turned to Carleton. "Head to toe, General. Cochise and his war chief were brutal."

Carleton exhaled more blue smoke and watched it hang in the still summer air. He traced a line on his cheek that mirrored the scar on James' cheek and dropped his voice. "Damn savages. Kill 'em all."

"Sir?"

"You're the right man for the job, Private Colton. Can't imagine anyone else who Ol' Cochise would listen to more than you. You know, with your history and all." He pointed his cigar at James. "You'll be doing the Army and the United States a great service."

James glared at Carleton. "Be sure to let my ma know what a 'great service' I performed when you tell her I was killed by Cochise, General." He leaned in, his voice cold. "You'll tell her to be proud of me, right? You'll tell her that her second son died for no reason, right? That he gave his life for *nothing*." Bile rose to his throat, and his stomach knotted and twisted. On his feet now, James tossed the canteen on the ground. "Cochise won't give up! This's ridiculous!"

Captain Greene stood and clutched James' arm. "I know it's not what either of us envisioned, but you have no choice. Gotta face a few facts." He held up a finger. "One, you were sentenced to the army because you stabbed someone."

James narrowed his eyes.

"Two, because you're in the army," the captain held up two fingers, "you can't disobey orders."

James balled his fists and clenched his teeth.

"Three," Greene released James' arm, "if you do refuse, you'll go to prison for a long, long time."

"And four, Captain." James swung his vision from Greene to Carleton. "When I go into Cochise's camp, I'll die." He spun around, kicked at the canteen, then started to step away. Greene grabbed his arm.

"That's insubordination, Private." Carleton pointed his cigar at James. "You can be court-martialed and hanged for that outburst."

"Fine. Better 'n being tortured again."

Greene held up a hand, the other one still clutching James' arm. "Calm down, Private. No one wants you tortured or dead. We'll keep an eye on you. Any sign of trouble, we'll come in."

"Right." James glared at Greene until he released his arm, and then marched across the camp of exhausted soldiers. He paused in front of the overhang where his brothers lay sound asleep. He snagged a canteen, wishing it was his whiskey flask, and stalked away. He walked a while before finding a large boulder to lean against, a sliver of shade to rest his trembling body.

How in the hell can they ask that of me? Greene knows the price I'm paying. Thought he was my friend, that he understood.

Bitterness roared up and down James' entire body, every muscle stiffened. First imprisoned by Cochise, now imprisoned by his own country. Life was coming back together. There was even a beautiful woman who loved him despite his past and his scars. Now it was gone. And for what? Cochise wasn't about to take his people to a reservation. He was too independent for that.

Why couldn't the damn army figure it out? Just leave things be.

And Cochise, inflamed by the death of his brother, would continue to kill everyone who crossed his path. James understood, and he couldn't blame Cochise for being angry. Killing everyone in southern Arizona wasn't the answer, wouldn't bring his family back. But still, James knew a rage that deep.

* * *

An angel, her tender arms wrapped around him, kissed his cheek. Her soft lips caressed his. A hint of lilac wafted around his nose. He pulled in more sweet air. Her warm body snuggled against his. Seductive fingers cascaded across his chest—a chest without scars. He stroked her silky back. A kiss—deeper now.

Something gripped his ankle and shook it. A voice assaulted his dreams.

"James. Wake up."

Eyes flying open, James bolted upright, and stared into the worried face of his older brother.

"Why'd you wander clean over here? I was afraid that Indians..." Trace's eyes flicked to the scar on James' cheek. He held out a canteen. "Water?"

Reluctant to leave his dream, James nevertheless nodded and unplugged the cork. He shoved reality back into his thoughts. Gulping the cool liquid, he wiped a dribble off his chin, then shook his head to clear lingering visions of Morningstar.

"Got something to tell you—"

"Need to tell you—"

Once again they spoke as one. The Colton brothers grinned.

James pointed to Trace. "You go first. You're oldest."

Trace took a deep breath. "All right." He glanced behind him where the soldiers were busy packing. "As you know, I've been gone from Teresa too long. Time for me to get home."

"Wondered when you'd figure it out."

Trace stared into James' eyes. "There was just so much to deal with, to put in place. Think most of the problems are gone now. The images, memories are still there, but I feel like *I'm* in charge, not them."

"Good." James nodded. "I know it's damn hard."

"Anyway, soon as we get through Apache Pass, I'm taking off. Back to Mesilla. I miss Teresa so much my heart feels like it's gonna break. I gotta go. But, we'll all get together when you get back." Trace held his brother's shoulder. "You're doing so much better than last summer, I can't wait to tell the judge how you've changed. He'll be real pleased."

Trace stood, then pulled James to his feet. "What'd you want to tell me?"

I'll be dead in twenty-four hours. Cochise is gonna finish what he started last year. All the happiness you're feeling right now will be gone. Gone. Just like me.

"James? You all right?" Trace grabbed his brother's arm. "You're looking funny."

A deep breath, James struggled to talk around the knot in his throat. A glimmer of hope wedged into his mind. Maybe there was a chance. "If... *when* we get through Apache Pass, I'm gonna get a message to Morningstar. I've made up my mind. I'm gonna ask her to marry me."

James found himself in one of Trace's famous bear hugs. Trace released him.

"Wondered when you'd figure it out. She's a great girl," Trace said.

"Think she'll say yes?"

"Don't know why not. You're a helluva man. And..." Trace lowered his voice, "...you've got three incredibly handsome, charming brothers, two at her beck and call. What more could she want?"

A man who's alive? A man who isn't chased by imaginary demons? A man who—

"With a woman like Morningstar, you won't have any problems with... well, you know, what we talked about." Trace's eyes tracked something in the sky, then rested on James. "Look at Teresa and me. I had the same problem you do now."

"You did?"

Trace hung his head and nodded.

"But now it's better?"

Trace raised his eyebrows. "We're having a baby, aren't we?"

"Damn right." James smacked Trace on the arm, knocking his brother off balance. More hope grew in James' heart. He listened

249

to officer commands and the grumblings of tired soldiers. Time to go. The setting sun scattered brilliant streaks of purple-gold across the desert hills.

Reality pushed aside hope. James clutched his brother's arm. "Trace?"

"Yeah?"

"If something happens to me… if I don't get—"

"What's going on?"

"Just listen."

Trace nodded.

"Will you send a message to Morningstar? Tell her I loved her and wished it could've worked out for us. Will you tell her for me?"

"You hiding something?"

"Promise you'll tell her."

"On Grandpa's grave, James. Now, what's going on?"

James studied Trace and knew he could never tell his brave brother what Carleton had ordered. What the Army demanded. If he told Trace and went despite the objections, Trace would never recover from the guilt, the new demons swirling in his head. James hoped his calm voice would do the trick.

"Tell me." A hint of anger and heightened concern laced Trace's words.

James shrugged.

"Nothing. It's… just that I get jumpy going through there." James patted Trace on the shoulder. "Once we get through, I'll be fine." He turned his back on Trace, knowing that he'd never perfected his poker face and that his brother would find out. Was there really a chance he would survive and marry Morningstar? Could he hold on to that hope?

His shoulders straightened as he realized that's exactly what he'd done with Lila. He'd held on to hope—and made it through.

Trace planted his arm around James' shoulders and nudged him toward camp. "Better get a move on, little brother. Sooner we get through Apache Pass, the sooner we can get on with our lives."

CHAPTER FORTY

Grayed shadows played with James' imagination as he and the rest of the army trudged through the sand, around thorny barrel cactus, and across sagebrush-filled arroyos. Twice he'd jumped, whipping out his revolver only to spot a startled jackrabbit leaping out of harm's way.

By the time false dawn caught the army, Captain Greene marched back and stopped James. "A word with you, Colton."

James waved Andy, Trace, and Fountain on. "Catch up with you in a minute." He turned to his commander. "Tell me Carleton's changed his mind. Tell me."

Greene's eyes darted over James' shoulder. A shake of the head. "Our two Indian scouts just came in. Cochise waits south of here in a place called 'Devil's Gulch'. Know the area?"

James nodded.

"Now's as good a time as any. Did you tell Trace or Andy?"

James shook his head.

"You want me to?"

James held Greene's arm. "No."

You can always run to Mexico.

Morningstar's pleading voice. She might be wiser than the entire Union Army.

Captain Greene turned to James and saluted. "Good luck, soldier."

James returned the salute, then turned his back on his commander. As he walked into the desert, he straightened his shoulders and again vowed that he wasn't a deserter, a man who ran. He'd spent the last year running, and it didn't do any good. No, he would face this as best he could. Face it with strength and determination, dignity, all the fortitude he could muster.

Morningstar would be proud of him. He'd meet his enemy, his death, however needless, with pride and courage.

James stared at the receding parade of men, his brothers out in front. The supply wagons rolled past while he walked away, walking toward certain death. His conscience reared its head. He should tell his brothers that he's going. Then again, they'd find out soon enough when he didn't come back that he'd died.

And for what?

So that Carleton could be a big man, get another promotion. Or, just maybe, on the other hand, Cochise would stop his killing? Maybe Cochise had seen the futility of holding on and would take his people to a reservation. James held on to hope.

Alone now, lost deep in thought, James put one foot in front of another. He surveyed the vast Sonoran Desert. A grouping of rocks he recognized from a year ago. Somewhere close by was a spring. Deer and all the desert creatures drank there. He had, too, a few times.

A drink. I could use a drink right now.

James patted his pocket for the flask. Gone.

Just like everything else.

A faint dust cloud to the north pinpointed the army.

I must've walked close to a mile south since speaking with Carleton. South toward my demons.

Moccasined feet scraped the sand behind him. Someone jumped on James' back. Strong arms grabbed him around the chest. Both men wrestled to the ground.

With his ribs on fire, James struggled to his feet. A quick look at that Apache revealed what James already knew—one of Cochise's warriors. The Indian jumped to his feet wrapping strong arms around James again. James wiggled, determined to get loose of the Indian's hold.

James reached skyward, then slithered out of the clutch. He clenched his fist and turned just as a different Indian, face striped with red and blue, planted a knee in James' stomach.

Doubled over, James swung his fist upward and caught the red and white painted warrior on the chin. Apache war whoops, moccasins in sand, victory trills surrounded him. James straightened up in time to see several other Apache swarm around him.

Trapped. Again.

Someone behind him encased him with muscled, tanned arms. James squirmed, wriggling like a worm impaled on the end of a barbed hook. The paint-streaked Indian straightened up, his face inches from James. Those dark eyes bore a hole clear through James. That Apache raised his arm shoulder-high, then formed a fist. James took it square in the middle of his face. Blood spurted. Images swirled into grays and blacks.

Dirt in his mouth. James spit out sand, his split lip throbbing. Someone's knee planted in his back ground his chest and shoulders against small rocks.

Kill or be killed.

James jerked and twisted. The Apache mashed down with strength reminiscent of Cochise.

Someone wrenched his arms behind him, then wrapped rawhide strips around his wrists. The bindings dug into his scarred flesh. It burned. Tears of frustration blurred his vision. Too familiar. Too damn familiar.

An Apache grunt. Strong hands yanked James to his feet. He met the gaze of the enemy. In front of him stood a young Apache, a man he recognized as a child last year, a child who waited on the edges of the tribal campfire. Waited to be included with the adults. Now he'd grown into a man, a man with something to prove.

The other Apache gripped James' arm and tugged him forward. For the first few steps James stumbled, but he knew if he moved wrong these two buck warriors would slice his throat from side to side without thinking twice. They'd learned from One Wing and his violent friend, Two Bears, how to torture an enemy and play with him before he died. One of these young warriors, James remembered, had held him down while the other crushed his little finger between two rocks.

James filled his lungs, stared at a yucca, and brought his life back into focus. He watched his feet carry him closer to Cochise, closer to a life he'd fought to forget.

The blinding sunrise attacked the entire desert. Even the rocks glowed. Another beautiful June morning.

Last one I'll ever see.

He stumbled on through the desert.

A violent jerk on his arm brought him to an abrupt halt. James looked up into the hard gaze of Cochise. Out of the corner of his eye, he spotted at least twenty warriors gathered around their leader. Several he recognized from his captivity last year.

His eyes swept further. To the right of Cochise stood Standing

253

Pony. Good Lord! Standing Pony, brother of his tormentor, the man he'd killed last year. James' chest hurt. He tried to swallow, but his mouth had turned sand dry. If only out of retaliation, Standing Pony would kill him. James stared into the coal-black eyes piercing his own.

The warriors glared at their prisoner with an intensity that brought tiny bumps to James' skin.

I won't die without a fight.

Cochise's eyes, no more than a foot in front of his, scanned him from toe to head. James squirmed under the scrutiny. Without speaking, Cochise grabbed James' shirtfront, then ripped the material, exposing his chest.

James lifted his chin, determined to show no fear.

Rough hands slid over the bumps and raised lines. Cochise snorted. James twisted to wrench free of the strong grip on his arms. The Apache chief grabbed James around his throat, thrusting his head up and back. James choked and stared up into coal-black eyes, then closed his own, knowing that whatever short life he had left would be shrouded in pain. He felt his body lifted off the ground. Cochise's strength was still hard to believe.

He couldn't swallow, couldn't breathe. His hands tingled.

Cochise tightened his hold.

James' world turned numb.

Cochise lowered James, then loosened his grip, allowing James to gulp in air. James pried open his eyes.

Pointing to James' scars, Cochise puffed out his chest and turned to his braves.

"Marks of shame," Cochise said. "He has no honor, only the brand of Apache victory!"

Indians whooped and hollered, their cries echoing against the boulders.

"Death to the white man!"

"Our land, our people, forever free!"

James shook so hard his teeth chattered. Once the shouts and taunts died down, Cochise turned his eyes on James. "You bring army men, James Colton. You know you will die first, then the others."

"I didn't come here to die, Cochise." James' throat burned as he spoke. "I came here to ask for your help."

The feared Apache leader stared at him. Then he waved his

hand at a young brave.

"Water," Cochise ordered.

Strong hands pushed James down to a round rock. He sat with sharp lances poking his bare back. He knew not to make any sudden, unnecessary moves.

Cochise squatted on a rock in front of him. "I am surprised you live." He pointed to the scars. "Much fire was in your body. One Wing would be disappointed. His torture was enough to take your life. Many times."

"I am strong now, Cochise."

Was he lying? No, this past year he'd regained most of his strength and sanity. He drank from the offered water pouch.

"Strong enough for more torture?" Cochise tilted his head. "Even now, at night sometimes, I hear your cries."

James straightened his shoulders. "I don't remember crying." He prayed his bravado was in place. "That must have been another captive."

Something close to a chuckle shook Cochise's shoulders.

"Some things about you have not changed, James Colton." Cochise poked a long finger into James' chest. "I know you still dream at night, still flinch at the sight of a whip. Still cry out at times... I know."

Yeah, James did. But how did Cochise know? James nodded. "Some things about *you* have not changed, Cochise."

The leader's lips spiked upward, then returned to their tight line.

"Why are you here?"

The lance tip poked further into James' back. James ran his tongue over his split lip and considered exactly how to say what he had to say. He decided on honesty.

"I'm in the army now. We're fighting the Confederates, other army men. Not you. Not the Apache."

Cochise's eyes burned into James. "But we are fighting *you*."

"There's no need."

Silence. What was Cochise thinking? As usual, it was impossible to tell. James knew to continue the truth. "My army sent me to talk to you."

"And why did your chief not come himself?" Cochise stood, glanced into the desert. "Is he a coward?"

James stared up into the towering Apache, then willed his

rubbery legs to take his weight. He stood also.

"No, he is not a coward. I told him you know me and may listen to me. I told him you are an honorable warrior, a decent man and a true leader who will do what's right for his people. A man I respect."

Cochise raised his eyebrows. "What is it they want?"

"The army men want you to save the lives of your women, children... your warriors... move to a reservation. They also ask you to stop killing. Let innocent people pass on your land. The way it was before—"

"Before what?" Cochise's cold words drilled into James' heart.

"Before your brother was killed. Before many people were slaughtered by your warriors."

Images of the rancher and his family fleeing for their lives bombarded James' mind. He once again heard their desperate screams, smelled the stench of burning buildings and flesh, felt the dead woman's head flop in his hands.

Hair once again entwined around his fingers, the other hand grasping a hunting knife, James watched his hand slice the woman's scalp. Blood streamed down her face.

He jerked against iron grips. James screamed curses at his captivity, at the loss of life, at the demons possessing him.

Last thing James saw was the moccasined foot hurtling toward his head. Apache dark took him down.

CHAPTER FORTY-ONE

Antagonizing beams of light pierced James' eyelids. Moaning, he rocked side to side, eyes fluttering open and shut. With a tug against the tight bindings securing his arms, he thrashed like a roped calf on its way to slaughter.

Reality came into focus. Ankles bound, wrists still tied behind him, shirt around his elbows, James wriggled. As he lay on the sandy desert, a sharp rock poked his side. Brown and greens melted together as he became aware of the Arizona summer sun cooking his body.

A wide, bronzed face appeared in front of his. The eyes narrowed with hatred. Hot breath struck his face.

"It's time, James Colton."

The Apache untied the ankle hobbles.

Head throbbing, James found his knees then stood. The tight bindings around his wrists seemed to shrink with each pull. His hands were numb.

Tugged around to the opposite side of the boulder, James froze. In front of him lay four bodies, each bound hand and foot.

Struggling to pull loose from the tight grip, James stared at his unconscious brother.

"Oh, God, Trace. No."

James' gaze wrenched to the others. He spotted Andy and the rhythmic breathing of someone still very much alive. Fountain and Reynolds, also bound, also unconscious, but also breathing. Andy, along with Reynolds, had dried blood caked on their faces.

Cochise stood beside James.

"They live." Cochise's words were quiet but definitive. "We parley before you die. Before they die."

James faced his captor. "There's no need for anyone to die, Cochise." He peered over his shoulder at his family and friends. "I didn't come to bring death to your people—or mine. I came to offer peace."

Cochise sat on a small boulder and motioned for James to kneel. Two Apaches shoved him to his knees. Cochise nodded.

"Speak, Colton."

James gazed up at the leader and found words. "Cochise, one time you called me brave, a warrior. Do you still believe that?"

Cochise again nodded.

"Then believe what I tell you." James took a deep breath. "The Army fights you only to protect the settlers and miners who want the same thing you do."

"Which is?"

"A place to raise their families. The miners search for metal from the earth so they can buy food and clothes for their children. No one wants to take this away from you. They simply want to share it."

Beads of sweat rolled down James' back.

Cochise stood, gazed across the expanse of desert. "This is our land. We do not 'share'." He turned back to James. "Much blood has been shed by my people. The price is high, but we will all fight to the death to keep what is ours."

"Listen to me, Cochise. No more blood needs to be spilled, by Apache or white man. Order your braves to stop this killing. Take your people to a safe place, a place to hunt, to fish... where no white men will interfere again. No one will have to die needlessly. Your women and children will live and grow old."

Lines bunched across the leader's forehead as he gazed into the sky.

Please God, make him be reasonable. Too many people have died.

While Cochise sat thinking, James glanced around at the warriors. Other Apaches gathered near by. James twisted his hands, trying to get the feeling back, but the rawhide strips dug deeper into his wrists. His face throbbed.

James' roaming gaze stopped at Running Wolf, an Apache who once dropped a gray scorpion on his bare chest. An Apache, who along with two others, cackled and jeered while that insect's stinger plunged into his skin. Over and over. James swallowed, despite his dry mouth. He remembered the days spent throwing up. The sickness. The shaking—

"James Colton." Cochise shook his head. "I have decided. I will not take my people to a reservation, to be held captive as you were. As you *are*."

James couldn't make himself argue. He'd never accept the conditions if he were Cochise. What had the army been thinking?

Maybe he'll spare Trace and Andy. I'll offer my life for theirs. No, he'll kill all of us. No reason to let any of us live.

Cochise slid off the rock and towered over James. "Stand."

A strong bronzed hand pulled James to his feet. He stood as tall as possible.

The Chiricahua leader leaned closer. "You *are* a brave man. Brave to return to my camp, knowing you will die. Brave to do what you are asked by the army men." Cochise stared over James' shoulder. "But foolish."

"Sir?"

"Foolish to bring these men with you. They and the rest of the army men will die."

"No one has to die." James turned to his family. Four pairs of eyes blinked at him. Maybe one of them could help talk sense into Cochise.

Hand motioning toward the four bound men, Cochise dropped his baritone voice. "Your brother, Trace, is well?"

A nod. James gathered his courage and stared up into Cochise's face. "Yes, he is strong. He now has a woman and will be a father soon. Please, Cochise, let him live and return to his wife and child."

"I hope he has sons. Every man should have sons." Cochise cocked his head toward a painted warrior on his left. "This is my son, Natchetze. He is brave like you, like your brother." He pointed. "Who are the other men, the one who looks like you?"

Stomach knotting, James weighed whether he should tell Cochise that one of the men was another brother or hide the fact. Would he save Andy's life by lying? Not hardly. The Indian had an uncanny knack for detecting a lie.

"Two of the men are soldiers, my friends. They both have fought for me. The one who looks like Trace and me is our little brother, Andy."

"Little brother? He's not so little, James—he's big."

A grin lifted one corner of James' mouth. "Not little like smaller, Cochise. Little as in younger. Four years stand between us. Another brother was born before him. Andy's the baby of the family."

"You wish to save his life?"

"Of course." Eyes darting from brother to brother, James nodded. "I'll do anything. We mean you no harm, Cochise." James prayed his words sounded as convincing to the Apache as they did to him. "Let the army go through the pass in peace."

Fountain spoke up. "Listen to him, Cochise. I also speak for the Army. We mean you no harm."

Cochise barked orders. A paint-streaked Apache rushed to Fountain and tied a piece of cloth around his mouth.

Cochise's eyes narrowed on James. "You speak. Not him." The words sailed across the desert. "Now, I will give you the chance to save lives. Everyone's lives." He spoke over his shoulder. "Standing Pony."

The decorated warrior stepped beside Cochise. The brave's leathery face was framed by the black hair tied down with a red band. Those muscled arms, that scar running across his chest stood out from the other Apaches. He was bigger, meaner, more cruel than the other Indians, except for Two Bears. James fought down panic.

Drilling his finger into James' chest, Standing Pony continued the insults. "These marks. They show that you have been crushed, that you are a coward."

"You're wrong." Morningstar's words echoed in James' ears. "I wear them with pride. I survived. Men like you who tortured my brother and me to make you feel strong. My scars remind me of my strength, my determination to live. They remind me…" James knew to stop but something compelled him to continue, "…that I am a White Warrior."

Chancing a quick peek at Cochise, James noted a semblance of a grin cross the man's face, a slight nod of the head.

Standing Pony lunged at James and knocked him to the ground. James hit the dirt on his hands and back, rolled to his side then struggled to his feet.

"Enough." Cochise held up his hand. Motioning to James, he spun his hand in a circle.

Turning his back to Cochise, James steeled himself for what he thought would be a knife in the ribs, across his throat or impaled in his guts. He steeled himself for death. Instead, he felt strong hands untie the rawhide bindings around his wrists.

Facing back around, James tugged his shirt up over his shoulders, rubbed his wrists, felt the blood return to his hands.

"I'm free?"

Cochise shook his head. "Do you have woman, child, James Colton?" Cochise's voice reverberated in rich, warm tones.

James looked away. "Not any more."

No Lila. No Morningstar.

Cochise motioned for Standing Pony to step closer. Eyes riveted on James, the Apache leader nodded. "Now you will have a chance to save your life and the lives of these men here." Cochise swept his hand toward the four bound men. "And the lives of army men."

James stood straighter, glanced at Trace, then returned his attention to Cochise. "Whatever it takes."

"It is settled." Cochise stepped back. "You will fight Standing Pony. To the death."

Standing Pony glared at James and turned to Cochise.

"You would have me fight such an old woman?" Standing Pony asked. "Give me someone who will fight back, someone worthy." He pointed to Trace. "Give me him."

Cochise glared. "James Colton is worthy. You will fight him."

Trace, Andy, Fountain, Reynolds. Each face turned to James. Fear paraded across all four.

Cochise continued. "If you win, James, you and these men, the army, will walk away alive, free. If you lose, your 'little' brother will die next. Trace will watch his friends' and brother's throats slashed before he feels the knife himself."

"And if I don't fight Standing Pony?" James again looked at Trace and noticed the color draining from his tanned face.

An Apache warrior sporting red and blue stripes across his chest grabbed Andy's head, jerked it back and planted a hunting knife at his throat. James spotted a red trickle down his brother's neck.

Cochise's voice rang icy. "Then the 'baby of the family' dies now."

"No, James, don't. I'll be—" Andy gasped as the warrior pushed the knife further into his throat.

"I'll fight."

James ripped off his shirt.

Cochise planted a hand on James' and Standing Pony's shoulders.

"There is only one rule," Cochise said. "No guns. Guns have no honor. You may use knives, sticks, rocks, anything else to win."

He stepped back and sauntered a few feet away, perched on a rock, then nodded toward the men.

James' vision narrowed to include only Standing Pony, the man whose death meant life for others. Muscles tensed, he struck out at the Apache. He punched only air.

Standing Pony stepped aside, kicked out and caught James in the stomach.

Doubled over, struggling to breathe, James noticed the Indian pull a knife out of a sheath tied around his calf. He straightened up just in time to feel its razor-sharp blade slice his upper arm.

He grabbed at the pain. Sticky liquid oozed between James' fingers. Rage taking over, James head-butted his assailant and both men thudded to the ground. James recovered first. Straddling the Indian, he gripped Standing Pony's knife hand. Both men wrestled for control of the weapon. The blade swayed back and forth over Standing Pony's face. The Indian bucked. The knife slashed across James' chest.

Fire raced across his chest.

I'll take you down, Indian. This White Warrior's gonna win.

James slammed Standing Pony against a rock. The weapon flew toward Reynolds, too far away for the Apache to reach.

Standing Pony bucked again, thrusting James up and over. Slamming against the ground on his back, James struggled to breathe. He shook his head, hoping to clear the spinning sky.

Before he could fill his lungs, James turned his head while Standing Pony clambered to his feet. Moccasins slammed into James' ribs. Rolling to his left, he pushed his body to his knees. His attacker smashed a rock into his lower back.

James hit the sand.

"The knife, James, the knife!"

James glanced at Reynolds just as an Apache struck his friend silent. Reynolds slumped. James focused on the knife planted handle first in the sand ten feet away. The blade glinted in the mid-afternoon sun.

Crawling toward it, months melted. James again fought his old enemy. "No!" He screamed at the Indian rushing him, at the Indians surrounding him, at the Indians rampaging through his memory. "No! Not again!"

Arm outstretched, James grasped for the knife. Standing Pony's foot stomped down on his hand. The blade sliced into James' palm. His fingers burned. Using his other hand, James grabbed the Indian's leg and sunk his teeth into the muscled calf. A low Apache cry. James inched closer, then gripped the knife.

Ignoring the fire in the palm of his hand, James scrambled to his feet. He jabbed the knife toward the enraged Indian. It slid from his bloody grip, but he worked to keep the knife in his fist. He thrust it again and again toward Standing Pony.

Circling each other like rabid dogs, the two enemies locked eyes. Hatred flowed from Standing Pony's icy-black stare. James watched the man calculate every move, reserving his energy for the final thrust.

Give it up Standing Pony. It's gonna be my victory.

Standing Pony dove for James' legs, taking him down at the knees. James fell on top of the Indian, who then stood. Draped over the Apache's shoulder, like a sack of grain, James saw the ground swirl around him. James raised his hand, surprised he still held the knife. Using strength dredged up from sheer survival instinct, James plunged the blade deep into the Indian's hip. The metal lodged against bone. The Apache sucked air, then collapsed to the ground.

James rode him down. He rolled off, then sat on Standing Pony. He held the bloody knife to the Indian's throat.

The man under James glared back, but James knew he'd won.

Eyes locked on the Apache's, James pushed the knife tip into flesh and watched blood ooze up. James nodded. He raised his eyes to Cochise.

The mighty Apache leader stood, approached, and looked down at James. A firm grip on James' arm lifted him to his feet.

Sky, rocks, and Apaches blended together. Blues and browns swirled. James concentrated. The images stopped dancing long enough for him to focus on Cochise.

"You did not kill Standing Pony." Cochise nodded toward his warrior. "Why?"

James' chest wound burned as he straightened his back. He stood as upright as possible and wiped the sweat from his eyes. Gripping his bleeding arm, he attempted to hide a grimace.

Surveying the warriors, James said:. "There has been too much blood shed already, too much death."

"I said 'to the death', James Colton."

"I know you did." James held out his hand, blood dripping, staining the sand. "But Standing Pony's death will serve no purpose other than to cause more bad feelings between the Apache and the White man. I don't wish him dead, Cochise."

James' words echoed against the boulders; his heart pounded in his chest. Standing Pony lay on the ground.

Wiping his hand on his pants, James offered it to the defeated warrior. Hesitant at first, the Indian extended his own hand, allowing James to help him to his feet. Both men stood side by side in front of Cochise.

"May I take my brothers and friends and return to my leader?" James dared to hope it was over.

Silent seconds spread into a minute as Cochise stared at the two men in front of him. What was he thinking? Would he go back on his word? No, James knew better. Cochise was an honorable man and would keep his promise.

Cochise nodded. "You are free to go, James Colton."

"Will you reconsider taking your people to a reservation?"

"Nobody wants peace more than I do. I have killed ten white men for every Indian I have lost, but still the white men are no less, and my tribe grows smaller. But my Apache brothers will continue to fight."

Cochise paused, looked at his warriors, then looked back at James. "Tell your leader you fought well, but taking my people to a reservation is not the answer." He paused. "I will allow the army men to continue without attacking them. They have safe passage through the mountains and into Mesilla. But, heed these words. My warriors and I will continue to fight for what is ours. Your fight may be over, James Colton, but ours is not."

Courage and determination drew across Cochise's face. James noted perhaps a bit of sadness there. Extending his wounded hand, James gripped the leader's hand. Rough skin, muscles of a firm handshake. "I wish you only peace, Cochise."

One corner of the leader's mouth inched upward.

Releasing Cochise's hand, James stepped toward Trace. "I'll untie my friends and be on our way."

"No." Cochise grabbed James' arm.

Ice stung every nerve in James' body. He swung around to meet Cochise's stare.

"*I* will release them. They are my prisoners." Cochise marched over to Andy and nodded to the Indian whose knife was still at Andy's throat. Cochise untied the ankle ropes while the other Apache released Andy's hands.

Helping Andy to his feet, Cochise kept a firm grip on his arm. His eyes roved up and down Andy. "I hope you are as brave as James, 'little' brother."

Within minutes, the five men stood in the middle of the circle of warriors. James picked up his wadded shirt. He swayed.

Feeling Trace's and Fountain's strong hands grab each arm, James nodded to Cochise, then stepped toward freedom.

"Cochise! Cochise!" An Apache James didn't recognize raced into the group. The Indian slid to a stop in front of the leader and pointed. "Cochise, army men killed two of our braves."

"What? Speak."

The warrior spit out words. "We were watching them pass, as you ordered."

Cochise's face hardened, the eyes glowing with a hatred and passion James had never seen before.

"A few of the soldiers spotted us and fired. We killed three of them before the soldiers could take cover." He pointed over his shoulder. "They ride toward us, Cochise."

"Then we ride toward them." Cochise thrust his arm at the sky. "We fight!"

Angry Apaches whooped and hollered.

Trace swore. But James knew what had to be done. "Cochise, let me help."

Cochise glared at James, his angry words shooting rapid-fire. "You brought army men."

"No, I didn't... I didn't, Cochise. You know I won't lie." James watched the cactus-covered hills, the boulders, his friends melt into a blur of brown. "Let me try to stop them."

"You can't, James. You're hurt." Trace tightened his grip on James' arm. "Let me, Cochise. You know me. I will parley." He glanced at James. "My brother is wounded, lost too much blood."

Wrenching away from the hands holding him, James stepped forward.

"I'll go. I have to do this. I can't promise, Cochise, but give me time to talk to my leader. One hour. Just wait one hour. Please."

Before anyone could argue, James scooted between two warriors and disappeared around a clump of bushes.

* * *

Rifle volley and gunshots punctured the serenity of the desert, the surrounding hills, and the valleys. James rested behind a large rock, squatted down and sucked in air. The run had taken much longer than he'd wanted. He'd been forced to stop several times until his world quit spinning.

His shirt was now a bloody rag; his left arm was on fire and his right hand was numb. He brought his hand up to his face, his fingers refusing to close in on each other. Before the three-inch gash across his fingers swelled with blood, he spotted a white line at the bottom of the cut. Bone.

He pushed off from the rock and listened for the direction of combat.

Stumbling from mesquite bushes to yuccas to rocks, James skirted the Apaches and came up behind the army. Hands out at his sides, James called to a private near the back of the skirmish.

"O'Donnell! It's me, Colton." James waited for the private to spin around and point the Sharps rifle.

The private eased closer, weapon still aimed dead center of James' chest. "James? You're a mess." O'Donnell blinked twice and furrowed his forehead. "What're you doing here?"

"No time." James pulled in air. "Where's Greene?"

Mouth open, O'Donnell lowered his .44 rifle. "What happened to you?"

"Where's Greene?"

O'Donnell pointed to his left.

Without further words, James staggered on.

Spotting Captain Greene hunkered down behind a rock, James dodged cactus and soldiers to reach him. Greene arched his eyebrows as James crouched next to him.

"James Colton! Figured you for dead, son."

"Call off the troops. Right now. Cochise'll let us through... call off—" James gasped for air, clutched his chest and doubled over.

"What? How do you know this?" Greene grabbed James' arm, steadying him. He barked orders to a nearby soldier. "Get me Carleton and the medic. On the double."

Untying the bandana from his neck, Greene gripped James' right hand, then wound the material around the gash.

A glance over his shoulder. Words were hard for James to

spit out. "I've been in Cochise's camp. Won't go to a reservation... I beat Standing Pony. Cochise'll give us safe passage..." He jerked his pointed finger at the army. "We gotta quit shooting."

"I don't trust that heathen Indian. How do I know he won't kill us all soon as we're in plain sight?"

"Gave his word. Trust him." James jabbed his chest with the same pointed finger. "Hell, Captain. Trust *me*. For once, trust *me*."

Carleton scrambled over a rise and kneeled behind Greene. James realized his biggest challenge would be to get these two Army leaders to agree to Cochise's terms. They would be harder to convince than that 'heathen' Indian.

Greene yelled over gunfire. "Colton's been with Cochise. Says he'll guarantee us safe passage if we stop fighting now."

"You were in Cochise's camp? And he let you live? Hard to believe." Carleton spoke in James' ear.

James turned to Carleton. "Well, believe this. I went in there and did what you and your so called officers *wouldn't* do. What you *couldn't* do. Yeah, that was me, James Colton, who went into Cochise's camp—again. And survived. Again."

"But—"

James formed a fist with his good hand. "You... *you* General. Get off your ass and order your men to stop shooting." He drew in breath. "Pay attention to me, dammit. Cochise doesn't lie. He'll kill everyone. Listen to me, dammit. Call off the shooting! Call off the shooting!"

Carleton tapped Greene on the shoulder, nodded, and spoke. "Order the men to stop shooting."

CHAPTER FORTY-TWO

James sat in the familiar courtroom in Mesilla. To his right, Trace sat studying the judge perched behind the desk. General Carleton and Captain Greene sat at the table beside them. To his left, his lawyer thumbed through sheaves of paper, the slight rustle disturbing the silence of the tomb-like courtroom.

A flicker of movement caught James' attention. Judge Falls removed his gold-framed spectacles before he spoke.

"James Colton, approach the bench."

James pushed his body to its feet and adjusted the sling supporting his arm. Now standing in front of the high desk, James knew Trace was at his elbow and that Andy, Fountain, and Reynolds were seated in the first row behind him. Would things at long last turn around for him? Could he ever start making plans for his future? At least he'd finally stopped drinking to excess. That in itself was a major victory.

Judge Falls pointed his glasses at James. "James Colton. You've been in this courtroom and before me too many times. I pray this is the last I'll see of you. Ever."

A deep breath. James nodded. "Yes, sir."

Falls chewed on the glasses' earpiece. "Your commanding officers have requested that you be honorably discharged from the services of the Union Army. That your sentence be commuted and whatever time left served here in Mesilla."

Another nod.

Judge Falls leaned over the desk, then stared down at James. "I've given this matter a great deal of thought and consideration. I've spoken with many people in regards to this situation." He pointed his glasses at Carleton. "According to their reports, apparently you saved an entire army company from slaughter and many Apaches from death."

Allowing the tension to build, Judge Falls put on his glasses, then shuffled some papers. He looked over the top of his spectacles now perched on the end of his nose.

"Therefore, Mr. Colton, I order that as of right now, you are officially released from the Union army and will serve the remainder of your sentence here in Mesilla in whatever capacity your wounds may allow." He paused. "I am granting you an honorable discharge."

Could life get much better? Free at last! He couldn't do anything but grin. Recovered, James reached up with his bandaged right hand and shook with the judge. "Thank you, sir. Thank you." Trace slapped his brother on the back as he reached up and shook also.

Judge Falls pointed to one man in the front row. "Andrew Colton."

James and Trace spun around as their youngest brother brought himself to his feet.

Falls' words were stern. "Approach the bench."

James' brother stepped beside him. He could feel Andy shaking, heard his rapid breathing.

"Andrew Jackson Colton?" Judge Falls' gruff voice echoed off the silent walls.

"Yes, sir?"

"How old are you, son?" Falls frowned into Andy's face.

"Seventeen, sir."

"When you joined the army?"

"Sixteen, sir."

"Um uh." Judge Falls' gaze started at Andy, swung over at James, then ended on Captain Greene. Falls leaned over the bench, and his gaze returned to Andy.

"Son, what you did was admirable," Falls said. "You spent a year of your life serving your country, fighting for what you believed in."

"Sir?" Andy's words were laced with confusion. "I signed up with my brother, to help him recover from Cochise's treatment, to keep him safe. Defending my country was not the reason I joined. Although I'm glad I did."

A chuckle grew from Falls. "Another honest, straight-forward Colton, I see. Son, what I'm telling you is that you were too young to legally join the army. Captain Greene knew that at the time, but seeing as how we needed every able-bodied man the Union Army could get, he let you enlist."

"Sir?"

269

"You heard me, Mister Colton. Therefore, you are also granted an honorable discharge and are hereby a civilian." Judge Falls smiled. "Welcome to the world, Andy." He extended his hand.

Fountain and Reynolds joined their friends in front of the courtroom, shook hands with Judge Falls. With his arm planted around James' shoulder, Trace pushed him toward freedom.

"One minute, Mister Colton." General Carlton held up his hand as he stood. "Wait there."

James looked from man to man as Captain Green and Carleton walked up. He noted the serious look on both men's faces. Now what? The judge had just declared him a civilian. What could they possibly want now?

General Carleton pointed to a spot in front of the judge's bench. "James, over here."

James stopped at the end of the pointed finger.

"James Colton." The General planted a big hand on James' shoulder. "I've seen many brave men in my years in the army. Yes, sir, many brave men. But I've not seen one act like you did—lay your life on the line, not once, but five times, to save many other lives."

James glanced at Trace and Andy, who both stared at Carleton. "Sir?" James said.

The General ticked off on his fingers. "Saving Fountain and your brother over at Fort Yuma, Reynolds from the snake, your brother from the Reb at Picacho Pass, Standing Pony, and..." Carleton smiled, "Company D of the Union Army."

Speechless, James could do nothing but stare at General Carleton.

"Didn't think we noticed, James? You're a helluva man, son."

Extracting an object from his pocket, the General stepped within inches of James. "Therefore, for gallantry in action and heroic effort above and beyond the call of duty, I hereby am pleased to award you Mesilla's first Medal of Honor."

General Carleton pinned a bronze star suspended by red, white, and blue ribbons on James' shirt.

Taking two steps back, General James H. Carleton and Captain Homer Greene saluted the hero. James returned the salute.

* * *

James slammed the door behind him and waved a letter with his bandaged hand. Sheriff Trace Colton looked up from his desk, papers hiding the entire wooden top.

"I got it, Trace. I got it. A letter from Morningstar. Came in this afternoon's mail train."

James flashed his wide smile as he ripped open the envelope, the white sheath floating to the floor. While he scanned the handwriting, James mouthed the words and stood trembling in front of his brother.

"Well, what does she say? Out with it." Trace came from behind the desk and stood next to him.

James glanced at Trace, down at the letter, and then back over at his brother.

"She said yes! She'll be here in two weeks. Her Ma and Pa, too."

Trace hugged him. "Congratulations. It's been a long time coming. See? Didn't I tell you it was worth the wait?"

James nodded, reread the letter, then handed it to his brother. "Wait 'til Andy hears this. Wait 'til Ma hears about this. Wait 'til—"

"She gets here, little brother." Trace returned the note to James and grinned. "Teresa's gonna be as happy as I am. We're gonna have a helluva wedding, James. A helluva wedding." He patted his brother on the back and shook his still-bandaged hand.

"Let's go tell Teresa right now." James cocked his head toward the door. "I wanna go see my little niece anyway. Haven't seen her since yesterday, and I'll bet she's already grown up. Probably walking and talking by now."

Trace grabbed his hat from the hook, then planted it on his head.

"Faith's only four weeks old," Trace said. "Give her time. She won't be walking until next week." He shoved James out the door. "Let's get Andy over at the livery stable first."

The six-block trek to Trace's house flew by as the three brothers made plans for the upcoming events. James clutched his still-healing arm and chatted about the future. Nothing could go wrong, he knew. There was nothing that could keep him from such happiness. Nothing.

Pushing open the door, Trace stepped in. He stopped. James and Andy plowed into him. James maneuvered around his brother and stood in the small living room. He froze.

There sat Teresa cuddling the baby in a wooden rocking chair with Lila Belle Simmons Fuente resting in the other chair. Lila's six-month-old son slept in her arms.

271

Mouth opening and closing, James gaped at the two women. He focused on Lila. Andy squeezed between his brothers, approached Lila, and held out a hand.

"I'm Andy, the youngest brother."

"Lila Belle Fuente. Pleased to finally get to meet you."

Trace found his feet, stepped beside Andy, then frowned at Lila. "What're you doing here?"

"Trace Colton." Teresa stood. "Mind your manners. You and Andy, in the kitchen. Now." She marched into the adjoining room, both brothers on her heels.

Alone now, James shook his head, bringing his world into focus. He took two halting steps toward Lila.

"Mrs. Fuente. What a surprise to see you here."

Lila stood, tears forming in her eyes, one drop sliding down her cheek.

"James, I didn't know where else to turn."

Staring into mesmerizing blue eyes, his heart thawed. "What's wrong?"

"I know you hate me and have every reason in the world to." Another tear rolled down her pale cheek. "But, James..." She looked away. "Alberto's dead. He died a few weeks ago."

"What?" James held the trembling woman by both shoulders. He glanced down at the yawning child.

Lila hung her head, then raised her eyes to his. "When you stabbed him, James, he never fully recovered." A tear hung at the corner of her mouth. "You killed him."

Sobs broke the stillness of the room.

Surprised beyond words, James turned his back on his first love. The woman he had cherished more than life itself. The woman who nearly destroyed him. He found his voice.

"Killed him?" James shook his head. "No, I stabbed him. He deserved it. Shouldn't have pushed me like he did." Memories of that fateful afternoon swirled in front of his eyes.

"He didn't deserve to die!" Lila's southern accented words echoed in the small living room.

"What do you want me to do?" James balled his fist. "Bring him back? Feel guilty for hurting him?" He whipped around to face her.

Tears streamed down Lila's face while her baby wiggled.

James cringed as the words poured out. "I got enough guilt to last a lifetime. Hundreds of lifetimes. I can't take back what I did.

I can't take back any of it. But I've paid for everything I've done—in more ways than you'd ever imagine. Oh, God, I paid for it."

"I thought—"

"But I'm through with it." James spoke through months of pent-up anger. "The guilt, the pain, the anguish. I'm through."

Lila blinked tears. "I thought you would—"

"Would what? Take you back? Marry you?" James fought to keep his voice low. "No way in hell, Lila. No way in hell." He held up Morningstar's letter. "I've found someone who'll stand by me. *Wait* for me. Who loves me for *me*. Even with the demons and scars, she loves me."

"I need a husband." She coddled her child. "A father." Lila's pleading words soaked into the walls.

"Won't be me."

"But you owe me." Lila's mouth set a tight line.

James stepped back.

"Owe you? Owe you! Dammit, Lila. I don't owe you anything. You gotta understand. I'm done with you. Our past is just that—passed."

James took more deep breaths, his emotions now under control. He held her shoulders and gazed into her eyes.

"We loved each other once," James said. "But that was a long time ago. I'm not the same man, and you're not the same woman. Too much has happened. We've both changed." His breathing was long, slow. "I've let you go."

"James, I—"

"I don't love you any more." He stared at Lila. "I'm in love with someone else." James swallowed. "I'm going to marry *her*."

Tears dripped off Lila's chin. She reached up and ran her trembling finger over the scar on his cheek. Her finger traced the pink line then brushed over his lips.

James closed his eyes at the familiar touch. What once had been pure joy now brought only sorrow. Her warm breath on his face. Her lips caressing his cheek.

"I'm sorry."

Were those her words or his? James couldn't be sure, but he chose to remain suspended in time.

Silence.

His eyes opened in time to watch her walk out the door. Out of his life.

About the Author

"I don't believe in reincarnation," says author **Melody Groves**, "but tendrils of the Old West keep me tied to stories yet untold. As long as I can remember, I've lived in the Old West, walked the plank streets, listened to the clip clop of horses trotting out of town, the occasional gunfire of cowboys whoopin' it up, or a sheriff going toe to toe with an outlaw."

For years, she denied this connection, but the people, the stories, the tendrils kept pulling. She lives, she says, not only in the real West, but also in the Old West. Groves is a member of New Mexico Gunfighters, a group of Old West re-enactors who perform skits and shoot outs in Albuquerque's Old Town every Sunday. Therefore, she knows what it's like to face down a sheriff or to stand with her "gang" and harass the "law." Her .22 Ruger single-action six has been busy—shooting hundreds of times—almost as often as she's "robbed" the bank! A performance highlight came in the form of performing as Morgan Earp at the famous shoot-out in Tombstone's OK Corral. As a writer, she uses those experiences to enhance her western fiction stories.

Groves grew up in Las Cruces, New Mexico, in the far southern part of the state, and rode horses and explored the desert. Heading for a jaunt in rodeo as a barrel racer, her life sidetracked when she moved to Subic Bay Naval Base, Philippines. As a teenager during the Viet Nam War, and only 800 miles from there, her life experiences were drastically different from her friends' back in the States, her barrel racing career extinguished.

She returned to attend college at New Mexico State University, earning a bachelor's in education. After moving to Albuquerque, she worked for the public schools and earned a master's degree in education. While sitting with students in front of her, Groves says, her mind raced with shootouts, dastardly outlaws, and women and men who wanted to tame the West. "Finally," she says, "I allowed the tendrils to take hold, the stories to unfold, and my pen to take flight." She quit teaching and now writes full time, magazines, screen plays as well as books.

A contributor to *True West, New Mexico Magazine, KetchPen*, and *albuquerqueARTS*, **Melody Groves** is the publicity chairman for Western Writers of America, the public relations chairman of SouthWest Writers, vice-president of New Mexico Gunfighters Association, and a member of the New Mexico Rodeo Association.

Groves' first non-fiction book, ***Ropes, Reins and Rawhide: All About Rodeo,*** explains the ins and outs of rodeo. It is designed as a "how to watch rodeo" book, complete with 93 photos.

Arizona War is one of the stories in her Colton Brothers Saga, to be published by La Frontera Publishing.

Ordering Information

For information on how to purchase copies of Melody Groves's *Arizona War, A Colton Brothers Saga*, or for our bulk-purchase discount schedule, call (307) 778-4752 or send an email to: company@lafronterapublishing.com

⊔ꟼ

About La Frontera Publishing

La frontera is Spanish for "the frontier." Here at La Frontera Publishing, our mission is to be a frontier for new stories and new ideas about the American West.

La Frontera Publishing believes:
- There are more histories to discover
- There are more tales to tell
- There are more stories to write

Visit our Web site for news about upcoming historic fiction or nonfiction books about the American West. We hope you'll join us here — on *la frontera*.

La Frontera Publishing
Bringing You The West In Books ®
2710 Thomes Ave, Suite 181
Cheyenne, WY 82001
(307) 778-4752
www.lafronterapublishing.com

OldWestNewWest.Com

It's the monthly Internet magazine for people who want to explore the heritage of the Old West in today's New West.

With each issue, **OldWestNewWest.Com** brings you new adventures and historical places:

- Western Festivals
- Rodeos
- American Indian Celebrations
- Western Museums
- National and State Parks
- Dude Ranches
- Cowboy Poetry Gatherings
- Western Personalities
- News and Updates About the West

Visit **OldWestNewWest.Com** to find the fun places to go, and the Wild West things to see. Uncover the West that's waiting for you!

www.oldwestnewwest.com

La Frontera Publishing's eZine about
the Old West and the New West